## Amazon Reviews for Steve Roach's Stories:

*I find that many books merge into one another in my mind and after a year or so I can't remember what it was about, or even what I found so special about it. With Steve Roach you know you'll never read another story like his. His work has a way of fixing itself in your mind forever. These stories are often not a comfortable read but if you want your ideas stretched and challenged, have a go.*

**Ignite, Amazon Review and Vine Voice.**

*This is a gem floating among the flotsam of self published stories on Amazon. The author grabs the attention of the reader early with a dark yarn told over a cold brew in worn down pub by the sea. What better place to hear a frightening tale of the black depths? Overtones of Poe can be felt throughout and the story didn't falter once as the horror continued to build.*

**Amazon.com review of The Whaler**

*I found the historical period to be accurately depicted, the gloomy coastal and shipboard settings to all ring true, and the central characters to have some genuine depth. With convincing scenery put quickly and efficiently in place and competent actors on the stage, the author proceeded to roll out a period American horror tale that kept me awake later than I had originally intended. I found myself needing to read just one more page until the entire story was satisfyingly done. That, in my opinion, is the sign of a well-made tale.*

**Amazon.com review of The Whaler**

*It's a well told tale and the descriptions of the hardships of life aboard a whaling ship, especially during the butchering, flensing and rendering stages are graphic and believable. I live near a town with a museum largely dedicated to the old whaling fleets and I've seen some of the tools used. Steve Roach knows of what he speaks.*

**Amazon UK review of The Whaler**

*I quite enjoyed this short story and despite it's bleak content felt it was well written and thought provoking. The blurb hinted at the dark turn the story takes yet I was still shocked by the finale. I felt there were various layers of hidden narratives; the cruelty of children, loyalty of a beloved pet and almost a Karmic climax.*

**Amazon UK review of A Dog's Life**

*I enjoyed this, it was a nice little read on a warm evening and I can honestly say I loved it, well written, poignant and engrossing, I just wish it had been longer, if I hadn't read it one sitting it would have been one of those books I would have laid awake at night thinking about and read some more as soon as I woke up next morning.*
**Amazon UK review of A Dog's Life**

*This is, without a doubt, the darkest and most disturbing book I've ever read....and I've read many. I will spend the rest of my life trying to forget it and wishing I'd never purchased it. I worry about the author.*
**Amazon.com review of A Dog's Life**

*The growing relationship between the man and the spider is a delight as we watch it unfold. Steve Roach has a dark side to his humour though. Things go downhill! This is a short story but as there's a small cast there is time for character development and the plot has a slight inevitability although I didn't see the final page coming. The author's writing style is skilful and accessible without being in any way simple. Short but sweet, this one, and well worth a read.*
**Amazon UK review of The Farda**

*If you have arachnophobia, then this story will probably make you very wary of reaching into a pile of bananas and keep you scanning the uppermost corners of your house. I really liked the connection and parallels between human and spider. It is also an example of how humans are more likely to act upon base instinct than they are aware of and how we imagine ourselves to be superior to all live forms. I enjoyed the read.*
**Amazon UK review of The Farda**

*Describing the ugliness that can happen in life is a delicate business, something that is handled sensitively in this unusual tale. It draws you in in a menacing way, and within its obvious desire to shock it also carefully balances a very human story throughout. Raw and thought provoking, I found it to be well written and an enjoyable read, which surprised me given the nature of its subject matter.*
**Amazon UK review for Bébé**

*This is a dark tale about a child born from a sexual assault that handles the subject in an honest manner. As a previous reviewer quite rightly said it is raw and thought provoking in a way that is both careful & sensitive. That being said, this book is not really for the faint-hearted or sensitive reader.*
**Amazon UK review for Bébé**

*This can't be called an enjoyable book; it's horrifying and fascinating though. Steve Roach often pushes at the boundaries of destructive relationships. It makes for the sort of book from which you can't look away - like a road accident. As I said, it's wrong to say it's enjoyable, showing as it does, scenes of abuse. It's a hard book to put down though!*
**Amazon UK review for Bébé**

*This, although ostensibly a story about fraternal hatred (it's much more than simple sibling rivalry!) seems rather deeper than its surface story. Twins who fought even in the womb and who spent their childhood fighting to the extent they were regulars at A&E finally seem to settle to ignoring one another. However, a love feud results directly in the death of one and indirectly the death of the other. We have all heard the term, 'Death is not the end,' and that's so true here. The depth of their mutual hatred is such that they still try to find ways to annihilate each other. The story, through some interesting descriptive prose, takes us much further, deeper, than you would imagine. Can hatred ever die? They say love never dies and hatred is just the other side of the coin. This is another intriguing idea from a man who can really come up with a good story line. The writing style is clear and unfussy but Steve Roach can use language well and pull the reader into a darned good tale.*
**Amazon UK review for Twins**

*This very short book made me laugh. Oh it shouldn't have but it did. Maybe I'm demented or I've been reading too many horror stories. This is a sick way to look at Santa. I took a star off because it's Christmas and I felt guilty.*
**Amazon UK review for XXXMAS (contains Glitter)**

*Another corker from Steve Roach. Amazing, thought provoking, scary stuff. Timeless – tackles our basic human insecurities.*
**Amazon UK Review for All That Will Be Lost**

# Glittering Treats

**Selected Stories 2011-2021**

# Glittering Treats

**Selected Stories 2011-2021**

# CONTENTS

## RESONANCE



## TINY WONDERS



## THE HUNT

# RESONANCE

# TERRORZOID ATTACK!

I have a lunchtime appointment scheduled with my agent. Three years ago, I'd have paid good money for an opportunity like that. Now, the idea just leaves me feeling drained. What is it going to be this time? What sage advice is he going to ruin my day with?

And, more importantly, is the bastard going to slope off early and leave me with the bill again?

If our relationship was anything other than writer-agent I'd probably like him. But you can't really enjoy a friendship when the other person has such a powerful hold over you. In the early days, I found him on the strength of a travel book I'd written (I've since grown to hate that book). He loved it and signed me up. Ever since, he's been trying to get me to rewrite slightly different versions of that same book.

He hates the idea of my writing fiction, which is what I want to do. I wonder if this is the day he's finally going to tell me he's had enough, that he no longer wants to represent me. I'll be back in the wilderness. One can only hope, I suppose.

I dress in the only suit I own and head out, catching a bus along the Old Kent Road towards the city. I get the one available seat, next to a man dressed all in black – black, knee-length trench-coat, shades and a black fedora hat. He turns his head and stares at me for a moment. Jesus. I feign disinterest as he takes something out of his pocket and holds it up for me to look at.

"Do you recognise the man in this picture?" he asks.

I turn to see a photograph of a man I've never seen before.

"Sorry," I say. "Can't help you there."

"Are you sure?" he asks. He sounds so sad. I offer a tight smile and shake my head. He pockets the photograph and turns away.

That was all a bit weird.

We're not five minutes along before there's a terrific bang from somewhere outside and bits of metal start raining down from the sky, some of them in flames. Everyone inside the bus tries to get a good look through the windows, and we all jump again as something huge smashes down into the road and explodes about fifty metres or so behind us. Somebody at the back shouts that's it's a helicopter. The traffic keeps moving, faster now, and we're all in a panic, wondering what the hell is happening. There are frightened cries and mentions of terrorism.

It's not long before the bus reaches my stop and I have to shout at the driver to pull over – the bloody idiot just wants to keep driving. I get off and look around – traffic is moving quickly, and I spot a car with a piece of smouldering wreckage on its roof. Some people are running on the other side of the road, towards the city. In the distance, a thin trail of smoke reaches into the sky. My eye is caught by a formation of huge aircraft high above, triangular and of a sort I've never seen before.

I head for the Elephant and Castle and catch a tube. Underground, everything seems normal. A quick switch at Oxford Circus sees me at Shepherd's Bush for just after 11. I emerge onto a street wreathed in smoke, with hordes of people screaming in panic. Looking around, I see buildings on fire and a tangle of crumpled metal as crashed cars block the road. Somebody is lying in the gutter, a trickle of blood running from their head.

Something serious is happening, that's for sure. I think we must be under some sort of attack. Is it the Russians? The Chinese? Aren't we all friends now, aren't we past all of that Cold War stuff? Whoever it is, they seem pretty intent on causing a bit of mayhem. Perhaps the safest thing would be to head back down into the underground system and make my way back home. A sudden, muffled explosion from somewhere deep beneath my feet gives me enough cause to abort the idea and keep going.

The restaurant isn't far from here, so I decide I might as well carry on. The last bit of the journey is a nightmare. People are running around screaming. There are gunshots. Explosions. The pavement beneath me shakes with the rumble of further explosions, deep underground. And then I see them – enormous metal things clambering up the sides of distant skyscrapers. They look like gigantic, robotic ant-like creatures and as I watch, open mouthed with fear, one of them turns its head and beams a red laser of destruction from its eyes. In the distance, buildings explode.

I run, joining the flow of people heading away from the more immediate carnage.

Through the smoke, the flames and the panic that has descended over London, I become aware of people running the other way, towards the conflict. They are dressed in black combat uniforms and gasmasks, carrying semi-automatic rifles. This must be some sort of military response.

The streets have become a battleground.

The restaurant has a number of people pressed up against the window, taking in the spectacle of our city being destroyed. I barge through the door and spot Allen sitting in the corner, drinking a glass of red wine, seemingly oblivious to everything happening around him.

"Ah!" he says upon seeing me. "Sit yourself down!" He gestures to the wooden chair on the opposite side of his small table. "I hope you don't mind, I started without you," he says, raising a half-empty glass.

In the comparative safety of the restaurant interior, I realise that I'm breathing heavily and force myself to calm down. I wipe sweat from my forehead with the sleeve of my jacket.

"Have you seen what's going on outside?" I ask him, incredulous that he isn't at least curious enough to be pressed against the window with the others.

"The usual carnage, I expect," he says, reaching for the bottle and topping his glass to the brim. He pours a large measure into a second glass and nods at me to take it.

"It's utterly insane out there."

"Isn't it always? Sit yourself down and tell me what you've been up to lately."

"Don't you think we should get out of here?"

"Not at all! I'm starving. Sit, sit! You're making me nervous hovering like that."

I sit down and take a large glug of wine. An explosion outside makes me turn my head just in time to see the head of a giant robotic ant roll down the street, aflame.

"Well?" he asks, ignoring the commotion. "Spit it out, man. I need an update! How's the short story thing?"

My mind is reeling but I force it back to more practical concerns. A few months ago, he'd advised me to compose a short story to enter into a number of literary competitions as a way of kickstarting my fiction 'career'.

"I've almost finished it," I say.

"It's not the one with the all the flies...?"

"Yeah."

"Jesus. I hate that one. I don't know why you persist with such an abstract idea but I suppose it's better if you get it out of your system. At least tell me you've got a better title for it."

"I'm sticking with *'Musca Domestica'*."

"That's a terrible title. Who the hell is going to want to read something with that as a title?"

"An entomologist?"

"What the fuck are you talking about? Change the title! Story titles have got to be dynamic! Exciting! If you don't come up with a magnificent title, people won't read any further." He clicks his teeth and shakes his head, disgusted. "What about the novel? Much progress?"

There used to be a time when I wrote exactly what I wanted to with no thought to current trends and market expectations. I was a lot happier back then, but very poor. Working with Allen had at least meant I could quit full time work and get something with less hours to free up extra time to write. He'd managed to get me some overseas sales and a semi-regular gig contributing to a travel magazine, but he was still waiting for the mother lode. The Big One. And I was constantly disappointing him. Quitting that job was a big mistake, in retrospect, but I never mention it. These days, I seem to spend my time procrastinating, typing up half a page and then deleting it as I imagine Allen's face reading it. He'd advised me to scrap most of what I personally thought were my best ideas and come up with something a bit 'pacier'.

"It's going well," I lie. "Should have something for you in a couple of months."

He raises his eyebrows and looks as though he doesn't believe me.

"So give me some details."

"It's still a bit vague."

"I can't pitch 'vague', you know that. You *are* still working on the serial killer novel, aren't you?"

I look down at the table.

"Jesus!" he exclaims, taking another glug of wine.

"I can't write that shit!" I tell him, slapping my hand down onto the table to punctuate my stance. "Every fucker's writing serial killer novels. Detective Blah-blah-blah investigates a series of separate murders before realising that it's the work of a single killer. Once he gets too close, the killer turns his attention to the detective. *Yadda yadda yadda.* That kind of thing bores me shitless! You can't find anything other than that sort of crap these days."

"That's because it sells! Do you want a career as a fiction writer or not?"

"Of course I do."

"Then you'd better start listening to me. What *are* you working on?"

"You won't like it."

"Just tell me."
"Another short story, for now. It's a character piece."
"You mean there's no plot?"
"Not at all. A couple of people meet up for drinks and a meal, and the reader gets to learn things about them by the way the characters interact. It's a sort of study, but don't ask me about what. I'm only halfway through and it's slowly coming together."
"So there is no plot."
"The plot's all in their heads."
"Jesus."
"All right, maybe the meal doesn't turn up, maybe there's some sort of problem with the food."
"You call that a plot?"
"It's an obstacle that has to be overcome. Plots aren't always about exploding helicopters and people getting shot!"
"You bloody writers."
"What's that supposed to mean?"
"It means you're giving me heartburn. Write something else."
"Shouldn't you read it before having an opinion?"
"I don't bloody need to! Who in their right mind would read a story about a couple of people having dinner?" He knocks back the rest of his wine and refills his glass. "Please tell me you've got something else on the back-burner, for God's sake."
He really has no idea how much pain his words bring me. Sometimes it's like sitting with a man who spits needles in my face.
"There is something but I wasn't going to tell you."
"Go on," he groans.
"That's exactly why I didn't want to mention it! All you ever..... Aren't you supposed to be offering me encouragement?"
"I'm not your fucking mother. Out with it."
"It's a bunch of short stories."
He looks distinctly underwhelmed. He looks at me for a few seconds and lets out a long sigh.
"What's all this pissing about with short stories? You told me you were interested in writing fiction and I went along with the idea. I asked for a novel. A *novel*."
"It sort of *is* a novel. The stories are connected to each other. Well, most of them are. There are different types of short story – the sting in the tale, the sketch, the character piece and so on. Things that happen in

some stories will directly affect the outcome of others, give them an extra punch-line, so to speak."

"But it's ultimately just a bunch of short stories."

"Yes and no. It's a concept piece. I think it's pretty clever. It took me fucking ages to work out all the connections."

"Wasn't your last book a 'concept' book? The travel thing in the campervan where you chop off your girlfriend's leg and your dog kills a load of old people?"

"Yeah. And?"

"And the public really went for that mash-up concept! How many copies did you sell? Six?"

"More than that."

"How many?"

"Eight."

He sits there and looks at me in silence. Outside, a car hits the side of a building, explodes, and crashes back to the ground. An enormous metal ant picks fleeing people between its mandibles and chops them in half. Blood splatters on the restaurant window.

"Let me get this straight," he says at last. "You've ignored my advice to write a serial killer novel and have come up with a bunch of interconnected shorts. You already know that short story collections rarely sell by the truckload – even Stephen King struggles to sell short story collections – and you're doing it anyway?"

"That's right."

He stares at me, frowning. He's so negative.

"People don't want that sort of shit," he says.

"I disagree."

"People are sheep. They don't want 'clever'. I can't see you selling any more than the last one."

"Well, it's not about the sales."

"Of course it is. Take my advice. If you can't, at least jazz the stories up a bit. Don't make them all boring character pieces."

"Jazz up how?"

"Plenty of killings! Lots of death! Explosions! Aliens! Gigantic robots! Anything but 'clever'."

A waiter walks past and Allen summons him over.

"We're about ready to order," he says.

The waiter looks at him with a grave expression.

"I'm sorry, Sir, but it looks like our chef hasn't made it in today. I'm afraid there won't be any food."

"No food?" asks Allen, dumbfounded.

"It is pretty manic out there," I say.

"That's no good to me. I'm fucking starving. Can't *you* knock something up?" he asks the waiter.

"I'm afraid not."

"Oh well, better bring us another bottle of red then."

The waiter gives a curt nod and continues to where he was going before Allen called him over. Almost immediately, he's back, opening a second bottle. He leaves it on the table and walks away.

"Bloody waiters," says Allen, sniffing haughtily. "I'll have to get a kebab on the way home." He drains his glass and starts the second bottle. Christ, this man can drink. He looks at me and it's easy to see what he's thinking. He seems about ready to tell me he can no longer represent me. Well, for all I care, he can do what he wants.

He surprises me by softening his expression and telling me how much he admires my work. For the next hour, during which there are intermittent gunshots and explosions in the street outside the restaurant, he tells me how much he liked my original travel book, and how he can see such promise in me, if I'd only listen. He's flattering me, and it's all bullshit, but I sit there and listen and enjoy the praise. Other than this, nobody has praised my writing for what seems like years. He keeps pushing at me to write something "a bit more exciting!"

Eventually, he draws to a close and sinks the last of the wine in his glass.

"Listen," he says, "I have another appointment at one. Just think about what I've said."

As he gets up to leave, the restaurant window implodes and the other customers fall back, screaming, glass embedded in their faces. Outside, a tank crunches its way over cars and dead bodies and briefly pauses to fire some heavy artillery shells at a distant target. Almost immediately, the tank is crushed as a gigantic robot ant drops down onto it. The ant starts ripping the tank to pieces, tearing off great chunks of armour plating with its mandibles.

Allen shakes my hand.

"Be a good chap and settle the bill, will you?" he asks, grabbing his coat and shuffling off towards the door before I can protest. I *knew* the bastard would try and drop the bill on me. He crosses the restaurant, opens the front door and steps into the street.

He is briefly turned to shadow in the flash of a distant atomic bomb explosion. The street freezes in a scene of total whiteout and I turn away, momentarily blinded. With watery eyes, I blink furiously to get my vision back. After a second or two of complete, utter silence, there's a roar as everything in the street is picked up and propelled by the shockwave from the blast. What's left of the restaurant window is ripped from the woodwork. Chairs and tables are flung over and people start screaming again.

There's a full scale war occurring right across the city, but my primary concern is the bill I've been lumbered with. I hope he enjoyed the booze because it looks like I won't be eating for the rest of the week.

Finishing off the last dregs of wine, I mull over his words. Were it up to him, I'd churn out the serial killer book-of-the-week, a brief white flash of fodder for readers with zero interest in originality. At some point, a tv movie-of-the-day, buried on some obscure channel. There's money in that, and he's right, but should I really sell my soul?

Aliens, explosions and giant robot killing machines? I would never lower myself to producing such ridiculous rubbish. I might have no money and no readers but I still have my pride.

I finish off the wine and stand. Now I just have to find my way home, through the fiery aftermath of a city destroyed by a nuclear explosion.

I'm a little bit pissed, too.

# THE LOTTERY

Charlie and Dave unpacked their toolbags from the back of the van, rang the doorbell and waited. It was just after 8am on a cold spring day, and their breath emerged in plumes before dissipating above their heads. Presently, the door was opened by a young woman in a beige leisure suit.

"Morning, Mrs Knapp!" they chimed.

They knew she wasn't really Mrs Knapp, having only recently moved into the mansion (after leaving her husband, it was rumoured) but they had to call her something and she seemed to like it.

"Good morning, boys," she said, stepping aside to let them in.

Not five minutes earlier, as they were just about to turn into the gated driveway that wandered through an avenue of impressive oak trees leading up to the house, Charlie had commented to Dave that he would like some time alone with Mrs Knapp for the purpose of some really quite disgusting physical activities. Joining in the convivial banter, Dave had commented on the rather bouncy nature of Mrs Knapp's breasts, and together they had wondered if she'd had any work done on them.

Such talk had naturally concluded at the sight of the Knapp house, an imposing country mansion that swept into view after the last of the oaks, and always, without fail, reduced them to a kind of reverential silence.

They were led through an open reception, past the vast lounge and dining room to the kitchen area, where they turned right and went through a short corridor lined with wood panelling. They had been here a number of times before, and it was always impressive. A set of stairs led to the huge conservatory, containing a gym, sauna, swimming pool and a table and chairs offering a sort of dining area. Enormous plate glass windows formed the roof and the far wall, affording a staggering view over the open countryside. The pool was empty and they walked over and gently laid their tool bags onto the tiles.

"John will be down in a minute," said Mrs Knapp. "Can I fetch you boys some tea?"

"That would be lovely, thank you," said Charlie.

She turned and walked away. Both men watched the wiggle, their heads full of thoughts that were never, ever going to come to fruition.

Presently, John Knapp jogged down the stairs and came over to shake their hands.

"Good to see you," he said, smiling. "Thanks for coming at such short notice."

"Not a problem," said Charlie. "You told me on the phone that there's a leak?"

"Yes, I think somewhere at the deep end. The area outside was like a swamp at one point."

"I see."

"So how are you both – everything good?"

"As well as can be expected, you know."

"Good! The wives OK?"

"Not bad," said Charlie. "Same as usual, you know."

"Still planning on going to the Isle of Wight again this year, Dave?"

Dave turned, brought out of some idle daydream, and nodded.

"Every year without fail, Mr Knapp."

"Excellent."

There was an awkward little silence. Charlie smiled and raised his eyebrows, hoping that Knapp would finish with the pleasantries so they could get on with the job.

"There is one other thing," said Knapp.

Charlie and Dave waited for him to continue. Knapp looked a little embarrassed, as if he didn't know how to begin. "The thing is," said Knapp, wringing his hands, "I've always found you two gentlemen to be very obliging with your prompt response times, and your work is always excellent. It's why I keep calling you back."

"Thanks very much, Mr Knapp," said Charlie. "We appreciate you saying so."

"I don't have that many friends. Poor friends, if you like. Does that sound patronising?"

"Go on," said Charlie.

"All the people I know are millionaires. Arseholes, the lot of them, if I'm being honest." Knapp paused, and offered the men a broken sort of smile. "You obviously know that I'm a very wealthy man. Why I played the lottery in the first place is beyond me. It's not as if I needed the money. Anyway, two weeks ago, I won the jackpot. Now, the money doesn't mean that much to me, but it made me think. Such an amount of money could literally be life changing for the right sort of recipient. A chance to retire early, and take some time out to enjoy life."

He reached into his back pocket and pulled out two cheques.

"I want you to accept this, each of you," said Knapp.

Both men remained silent, staring at Knapp in a sort of stupefied daze.

"There's only one condition. You must see out the work on the pool, whilst the cheques are clearing. Is that acceptable?"

"How much money are you giving us?" asked Dave, his voice barely a whisper.

Knapp handed over the cheques.

"Is this some sort of joke?" asked Charlie.

"Not at all."

"You're really giving me and Dave a million quid? *Each?*"

"I am, yes."

Charlie stood and stared at Knapp, smiling.

"Why?" asked Dave.

"Well, like I said.... The money isn't going to make that much of a difference to me. Or anybody I know. These days, the kind of friends I have pootle about in private jets, and a million pound is just a top up for the jet fuel fund. But to you – it means a lot more. I know neither of you are exactly youngsters, but this money might give you a chance to enjoy life before you're too old. I just want to do a bit of good. Bring a bit of happiness to someone. Am I making sense?"

"You are, but why *us*? Why not give the money to a charity or something – why not make a difference that way?"

"I'm afraid I'm rather cynical of charities. I happen to believe, rightly or wrongly, that a lot of charity money gets diverted away from where it's really needed. So, to answer your question, I'm giving it to you because you are two people I know whom this money could really make a difference. I'd like to think I knew you well enough to say that without you being offended."

There was a long pause as they considered Knapp's words.

"Where's the camera?" Charlie asked at last. "Come on, fair play – you had us for a moment, I'll give you that. A million pounds! Blimey, for a minute there I almost believed you."

"No, really," said Knapp. "I really *am* giving you the money. But you must finish the job first. I don't want to have to find another set of workmen, I have enough on my plate already."

At that moment, Mrs Knapp came down the steps carrying a tray loaded with tea and biscuits.

"Have you told them the good news?" she asked, smiling.

"I have!" said Knapp.

"Excellent."

There were four mugs of tea on the tray, and they each took one.
"To your health!" said Knapp. Everyone clinked mugs.
"Thank you," said Charlie.
"Yeah, thanks Mr Knapp," said Dave. "You too, Mrs Knapp," he added sheepishly.
"Excellent," said Knapp. "Now, I have to go away on business for a few days, so Brenda here will be looking after you if that's OK. Just shout up the stairs whenever you want a fresh mug of tea."
With a nod, Knapp excused himself and was followed back upstairs by Mrs Knapp.
Charlie and Dave stood and looked at each other.
"Do you think this is real?" asked Dave.
"I think so."
"I can't bloody believe it. We're going to be millionaires, Charlie!"
"I know. The missus is going to have a heart attack."
"I'm going to be pissed if this is some sort of joke."
"Let's just bank the cheques and see what happens. In the meantime, we've got work to do."
They spent the better part of the morning chiselling away tiles from the pool. It was delicate work, but even so there were ceramic casualties. Dave took a careful note of how many tiles they'd need to order.
"I hope we can get these in a close enough match," he said.
"I don't think it'll matter too much," said Charlie. "The whole lot'll be underwater anyway."
For the rest of the day, they went about their work, quieter than usual. There was a huge metaphorical elephant in the room, something huge that neither could bring themselves to discuss. By four o'clock, they still hadn't managed to find the leak, but that was the least of their concerns. They packed all of their tools away and Charlie swept up the mess. On the way out, they called goodbye to Mrs Knapp and left.

They drove straight to the bank.
Charlie handed his cheque to the cashier and waited for something to happen. For some reason, he felt like a fraud, as though he were somehow trying to rob the place. The thought of all that money made him feel shifty, as though any moment the Manager would come storming out of his office and demand to know where it came from.

The cashier, a middle-aged woman with spectacles paused and momentarily looked at him when she realised how much the amount was for, but said nothing. She handed him a receipt slip.

"How long will that take to clear?" he asked.

"Three working days."

"Does that include today?"

"No. It should be ready to withdraw by close of business on Thursday."

"Thank you," said Charlie, and walked away. He wondered if he'd be fined if the cheque bounced. Isn't that what banks did? He felt a flutter of panic in his guts. The last thing he needed was a bank fine, things were hard enough as they were. He decided not to tell his wife, Jean, anything about the money until the cheque had definitely cleared.

The next morning, Charlie pulled up outside Dave's house and waited for him to emerge. It had been this way every working day for the last seven years. Dave was the relative youngster at thirty eight years of age. Charlie, the company owner and employer of Dave, was in his late forties. They had met whilst on holiday with their respective partners in Spain, and had hit it off immediately. Ever since, they had all been as thick as thieves. When Dave had been made redundant, Charlie offered him a job and had him retrained. Dave now had the skills to build, plaster, plumb and carry out simple electrical work. He was a grafter, and had never missed a day.

In fact, this was the first day he'd even been late. Usually, he was outside waiting, standing in the garden finishing off a roll-up. Charlie was just about to bib the horn when Dave emerged. He looked awful, and sighed heavily as he climbed into the passenger side.

"You look rough!" said Charlie. "Are you sure you're up to it?"

"I'm fine. Had trouble sleeping, that's all."

"Thinking about the money?"

"I haven't thought about anything else! I couldn't eat my dinner, couldn't watch the telly, couldn't even take a leak without the thought of all that money filling my head. I dunno if I can take the pressure, Charlie. It's driving me mad."

They drove for a few minutes in silence, heading out of suburbia into the countryside, towards the Knapp house. Dave sat fidgeting, looking out of the window. Eventually, he turned to face Charlie.

"What are you going to do with it?" he asked. "What are you going to spend it on?"

"Bloody hell!" laughed Charlie, slapping his hand on the steering wheel. "I *knew* you were still thinking about the money!"

"Come on, seriously. What are you going to buy?"

"Nothing. Well, perhaps a house in Spain. Maybe pay off the mortgage here and flit between the two. Six months in the Spanish winter, six here in the summer. Yeah, maybe I'll do that. Invest the rest and live off the interest."

"Boring! Aren't you even going to buy a new van?"

"What's wrong with this van?"

"Nothing. Wouldn't you want a new one though? Just because you could?"

"Why would I want a new van? You don't seriously think I'm going to be doing this for much longer if that cheque clears?"

Dave looked stunned.

"You're going to wind up the business?" asked Dave, his eyes wide. "What about me?"

"What about you? You're a millionaire, you bloody idiot! "

"Yeah, but I thought we'd still carry on working together."

"What?! Don't talk wet, Dave, you'll have me crash the van in a minute. Why would we drag ourselves out of bed every morning to carry on doing this, when the only reason we're doing it in the first place is to earn enough money to retire?"

"Yeah, but I *like* my job. You might be old enough to think about retiring but I've got years left yet."

They carried on towards the Knapp house, but a slightly weird atmosphere had descended. Both men were deep in thought, silently contemplating their futures. Charlie couldn't quite believe what he'd just heard. Getting up and building walls, unblocking toilets and clearing out gutters – was this the only purpose Dave had in life? Yesterday he'd have applauded that sort of commitment to the company, but everything had changed now. On Friday, they could ride off into the sunset and live very comfortably for the rest of their lives.

Mrs Knapp opened the front door and gave them a "Good morning, boys!"

"Good morning, Mrs Knapp!" they said as one.

A few minutes later, they were back at the bottom of the deep end of the pool, gently peeling away strips of tiling. Mrs Knapp brought down a mug of hot tea for each of them and left it at the shallow end.

"Are you really going to pack it in?" asked Dave, unable to concentrate on the task at hand.

"Yes, Dave. I'm a millionaire. Of course I'm going to pack it in. Look, I know that this has come as a bit of a shock to you, but if you want to keep working you can team up with any number of maintenance firms out there."

"But I like working with you."

"Well, I appreciate that, but like I said, this is our last job. After this, I'm winding the business up."

Charlie kept chipping away at the tiles, conscious that Dave was simply kneeling there, deep in thought. Just as it was getting a little awkward, Dave said "OK. I get it. It's not a problem."

"Well, OK."

"So you're going to buy a house, pay off your mortgage and then bank the rest?"

"Yep."

"How much interest will there be on what you leave in the bank? Enough to retire on?"

"I think so. I haven't really worked it out yet. Let's say a decent villa costs three hundred grand, and I clear the remaining fifty on my house. That leaves six fifty which, at an interest rate of, say, four per cent gives.... Erm..."

"Twenty-six grand a year."

"No, it's more than that, Dave."

"No, four percent is twenty-six grand."

"Really? Bugger. That really isn't as much as I was hoping for. Take out the flights, the cost of living, the cleaning lady's wages, the-"

"Cleaning lady? *Ooh, get you.*"

"Gotta have a cleaning lady, Dave. Don't want to come back to either of the houses after six months and find them full of bloody spiders."

"Sounds like your plan is flawed, Charlie. How are you going to pay for all of that? You'll have to keep your end in the maintenance game anyway, by the sound of it."

Charlie turned away, irritated. As Dave continued chipping away at the pool tiles, Charlie knelt in silence for a while. Was that *really* all the interest he'd get? The idea of buying a villa had been a long term dream, and now that he had the money – *almost* had the money – a rudimentary totting up of the figures suddenly revealed that perhaps the dream was no more than that – a dream. Was it really so easy to see his plans wither and crumble? All his life, he never thought in a million years that he'd get his hands on a million pounds, and now that he had it suddenly didn't seem so much after all. How on earth would he ever have retired without the cheque from Knapp? Had his entire life been spent working towards an unattainable goal? And, even worse, was that goal still unattainable even though he would soon be loaded?

It was a depressing thought. He knelt there, working out the figures for himself. It was possible that maybe Dave had made a mistake. After a few minutes, he realised that he'd been correct after all. Bloody hell. Now what? Was it time to get a new dream? A more economical one?

Dave disturbed him from his dark thoughts.

"I'm going to buy myself a Jag," he said.

"How much does one of those cost?"

"I was thinking about sixty grand?"

Charlie sighed. After a moment's hesitation, Dave spoke again:

"And I've already ordered a new motorbike."

Charlie sighed again, exasperated. Bloody idiot, frittering away his money.

"Do you even know how to ride a motorbike?" he asked.

"I've always wanted to take a ride across the States, like Easy Rider. Travel Route 66 and all that."

"What, with the missus in a little sidecar, like Olive from 'On the Buses'?"

"She'd be on the back."

"Hasn't she got a dodgy hip?"

"Yeah....."

"How's she going to last, sitting on a bumpy motorbike for hours every day?"

"Don't be a dream stealer, Charlie. I don't see the point in leaving all that money in the bank. Life's too short."

"Let's talk about something else for a bit."

"Why are you so touchy?"

"Leave it, Dave. I'm not in the mood."

"Just saying."

"Bloody hell, Dave!" shouted Charlie, standing up and walking off.

Dave watched him go, stunned.

They finished at half four and drove home in silence. It had been a weird day, and things hadn't settled back to normal at the end of it. That night, Charlie had trouble sleeping, tossing and turning until his wife elbowed him in the ribs and told him to "Pack it in!" Charlie climbed out of bed, made himself a cup of tea and sat in the lounge, thinking. He was still there when dawn broke.

Charlie was in a foul mood. This was the first time he'd ever rowed with Dave, and he wondered how to fix things. Dave sulked, and the drive to the Knapp house was an uncomfortable one.

When they arrived, Mrs Knapp let them in and said that she'd be out for most of the day at a spa appointment, but her husband should be back in the early afternoon.

They headed down to the annexe and worked in silence.

After a while, Charlie stopped work and went for a mooch around the house. He'd seen bits of it before, on previous jobs, but had never been given free reign to simply roam around and take it all in at once. It was enormous, the sort of place only the *really* wealthy could afford. Every fitting was top of the range, built to the highest spec. It didn't seem right, somehow, that only two people lived here. Charlie counted four bedrooms, all with en-suite facilities. The kitchen was as big as the entire ground floor of his own house. They had a library room, lined with oak panelling and heavy, velvet curtains. There was a gym room, a cinema room, a utility room. Rooms that ordinary folk would never have.

Even with his million pounds, Charlie would never be able to afford any of this. Knapp was a multi-millionaire, and it showed. The more Charlie walked around, the angrier he got. He knew – he'd checked - that the lottery prize Knapp won was six million. Giving him and Dave a measly million quid each was worse than giving them nothing – it was just enough to show them their dreams were futile.

A joke.

Why hadn't the rotten bastard just given them the whole six million? He didn't need it, the dirty rich bastard!

He returned to the pool in a foul mood. Dave was waiting for him.

"I won't let you do it!" said Dave, standing.

"Do what?" Christ, what was he on about now?

"Take Jean to Spain."

"What?! What's that got to do with you?"

"Everything. We've been seeing each other."

Charlie felt like he'd been punched in the gut. For a moment, he thought that he might faint. Dave had never been much of a joker and this seemed like an unlikely gambit to start with. Seeing another man's wife was not a funny business. Why would he say such a stupid thing?

Dave stood there waiting, a strange gleam in his eyes. It slowly dawned on Charlie that he wasn't joking. He was bloody serious.

"You what, Dave?" said Charlie, taking a step forward.

"You heard. We've been seeing each other for a couple of years. Every Tuesday, when you think she's out playing bridge with an old college friend, we've been shacked up in the Premier Inn, fucking each other like monkeys. That's right, you heard me! She's not going anywhere with you, Charlie. She's been talking about leaving you for a while, but I kept talking her out of it. I just wanted things to stay as they were, and then all this money suddenly comes into the mix. I didn't buy a new motorbike to take Nancy across America, Charlie – it's Jean who'll be coming with me."

Charlie felt his blood coursing through his veins – boiling, liquid anger. A sort of red mist descended over him. He reached down and picked up a hammer.

He took another step towards Dave.

"No, Charlie!"

Knapp landed at Heathrow just before midday, collected his car from the car park and drove home. It had been a good trip, and the Displacement Machine had been ready to collect as promised.

Brenda wasn't in when he arrived home, so he placed his suitcase in the hallway and carried the machine down to the conservatory. He was aching to see how the pool repairs were shaping up. The work van wasn't outside, which gave him hope that the job had been simple and was now completed.

The conservatory was empty. At the deep end of the empty pool, he saw some scattered tools and what looked like a smear of blood. Along the side of the pool, in huge letters daubed in blue paint, he read: FUCK YOUR MONEY!

Knapp stood there, scratching his head, wondering just what it was that he must have done to upset his workmen so badly. He couldn't, for the life of him, think what it was.

That night, he set the machine up to show Brenda. It was supposed to be top secret but he couldn't stop himself – he still felt the need to impress her. They sat and talked over cups of *lapsang souchong* tea. Casting about for an object to displace, he happened to glance upwards and saw, bathed in the late afternoon sun, a large object falling through the sky directly towards them.

It was a man, dressed in a clown costume, hurtling their way at terminal velocity.

*Figgis.*

Brenda looked up and screamed.

Knapp raised the Displacement Pulse Dispenser and fired.

# DOWN IN NEW ORLEANS

Schwarzesloch listened to the words of the Finance Director on the speakerphone and looked around the office at his staff. Across the country - in California, Arizona, Texas, Florida, Massachussetts, New York and there, in Louisiana – almost twenty thousand people were listening to those same words. The voice of Bob Anderson, originating in a plush office in Phoenix, told the employees listening in to the teleconference that market forces were tearing the company in half.

The company needed to diversify, to channel new market synergies.

We need to repatriate core skills from the company resource, he told them.

We have to play *hardball*.

Schwarzesloch looked at the eighty staff under his care and knew that within three months most of them would no longer be there.

Afterwards, he sat with his staff and listened to their questions.

"What does 'repatriate core skills from the company resource' mean?"

"Does 'Redeployment' mean we'll get more money?"

Being a young department, the employees were little more than teenagers, and had no idea what 'hardball' was, let alone how to play it. Schwarzesloch remembered being asked to set up this department, remembered standing in this open plan office when there was just one desk. His desk. Every one of these eighty people now looking at him with blank expressions, Schwarzesloch had interviewed them personally. Between them, they had built the department from scratch.

Now the telecommunications industry had reached a crisis. A company that had been operating for over sixty years, with offices in eight countries across Europe, America and Asia, was now a lumbering dinosaur looking at a new Ice Age.

When Schwarzesloch first joined, almost eighteen years to the day, he'd travelled the world as an engineer, helping to upgrade the telephone systems of numerous countries. He worked his way up through the ranks, migrating into the training department to deliver courses to other engineers, and then back to America to set up a new training division from scratch.

He'd moved initially to Florida, met Valerie, and settled down. After three years he was promoted into Management. Seven years ago, just before they had Jenny, the company offered him a promotion in the New

Orleans office. They came and stayed in a hotel on expenses whilst they looked for a house, and the week they moved in was the same week that Valerie announced she was pregnant.

Everything he'd worked on was a success, or so it would seem to an outsider, but the secret was nothing more than a little bit of luck and a lot of hard work. Hard work will get a person within grasping distance of success and a dash of luck would do the rest. The path had been strewn with challenges, including crossing the blue collar – white collar divide, the endless bureaucracy and, not least, the casual racism he'd encountered across the decades. Once, he'd attended a Managers' conference in New York and had overheard one of the other managers joke how the janitor was getting ideas above his station. Fortunately, those days were mostly over. The world was slowly coming to terms with the fact that the colour of a person's skin did not matter, it was the person beneath that counted. And Schwarzesloch had slowly and patiently worked through all obstacles with a quiet determination, and his efforts had been recognised.

Anderson, the voice on the end of the teleconference lines, was one of a new breed of senior management, brought in from backgrounds as diverse as banking, sales and even the media, who knew nothing about telephones or telecommunications, but knew all there was to know about playing hardball, and focussing market synergies.

The Internet was their nemesis, as more people opted to use it for long distance calls than the traditional phone lines. Cheap webcams had flooded the market and wiped out the chance of selling the new videophones the company had poured cash and time into developing.

It meant cutbacks, and things like 'repatriating core skills from the company resource'. It meant change in the real world, the world of bricks and mortgages, flesh and bone. It meant people had to leave.

Home was a three-bedroomed, slightly run-down property in the Garden District, mostly paid for and a place of relative quietness amongst the sprawl of suburbia. Some mornings, when he felt like it, Schwarzesloch would take the car down to Lakeshore Drive, park up and head off for a jog, enjoying the cool breeze coming of Lake Pontchartrain. He loved the city and couldn't imagine moving on again, no matter what promotion was dangled in front of him. New Orleans was so vibrant, so *alive*, and it had found its way into their souls as though filling a space that had always been empty.

Val disliked the summer heat, that much was true, but she'd started painting again and had even found time to join a local theatre group, things that other cities hadn't inspired her to do. She had friends in the Garden District, and now that Jenny had settled into school often met them for morning tea. It was all very civilised. Her parents lived on the outskirts of Houston, just five hours away on the I-10. Every couple of months, they'd visit, not minding the drive and insisting that Schwarzesloch and Valerie were simply too busy to come to them instead.

Schwarzesloch knew his family had a good life, and often took the time to simply pause for a moment and reflect on how lucky they were.

Despite the encroaching dilapidation, the slow and inevitable disentegration destined for any building where wood was integral to the structure (particularly in the damp mugginess of the climate this far South), they had fallen in love with the house on first sight. It needed work, and proved to be something of a money-pit, but this wasn't just a house, it was a *home*, the hub of their existence.

The detached property stood on its own parcel of land. The street was wide, and not a thoroughfare for traffic. There were a lot of open green spaces where the neighbourhood kids gathered and played games. Unlike most of the rest of the country, if you believed the news reports, it felt like a safe neighbourhood, and everyone mostly knew everyone else.

Schwarzesloch parked the SUV in the street outside the house. He could smell the sweet perfumes of plants, gently sweating in the afternoon heat.

He walked into the lounge and flopped down into his armchair. Valerie came in from the kitchen and bent down to kiss the top of his head.

"Another bad day?" she said, more of a statement than a question.

"One of the worst. Another batch of redundancies coming up."

She came and sat down next to him, on the arm of the chair.

"You look tired," she said, her eyes wandering around the contours of his face.

"I feel tired. I've spent years building up my damn team and they're going to take most of them away from me again. What's the point of it all?"

Valerie was a wife who'd spent years watching Schwarzesloch toiling at his career. He was a man that brought work home with him, who often sat long into the evenings looking over reports and figuring out ways to improve service.

Such focus had come at a cost – he had no real friends that she knew of, he pursued no hobbies. Valerie and Jenny were all he had in the world.

She knew he wanted to be a director, one day, and had shared months of anguish as new people were often brought in over his head, appearing in their empty offices as if by magic.

"They're young," she said. "It's not the end of the world for them."

"They might be young, but losing your job is still a stressful thing. Some of them have houses already, and one or two have kids. A redundancy is the last thing they need."

Redundancy. He turned the word over in his mind. Such a horrible, clumsy word, and yet still sharp enough to be personal. He would have to tell some of them "You're being made redundant". No longer of any use. Everything you did on a daily basis, it's no longer wanted. Goodbye.

He was pulled from his thoughts by the clattering of feet in the hallway. Valerie got up from the arm of the chair.

"Here comes trouble!"

Jenny ran across the lounge to jump on him.

"Daddy!" she cried, treading all over him and causing him to wince when she planted a foot straight in his balls.

"Chicken for dinner," said Valerie, walking back into the kitchen. Jenny turned and sat in her father's lap, concentrating on the television. Schwarzesloch stroked Jenny's hair, his eyes riveted to her scalp, and tried not to think about the world his daughter would find herself growing up in.

A world where multi-national conglomerates extracted every last ounce of work from their employees, and then wrote the lot off in order to move manufacturing to Malaysia, or China, or somewhere equally cost-effective. Where the workforce could expect redundancy to hit them three, four, maybe five times in the course of an employed lifetime. Where the markets wanted only temporary workers, and technology changed business so rapidly that skills were outdated in a matter of weeks.

What hope was there for her? For anyone?

Three weeks later, Schwarzesloch was called into his manager's office, and knew that something serious was about to be discussed when Jackson told him to close the door behind him.

Schwarzesloch had visualised this conversation many times. In one version, he'd asked Jackson why his staff had to go, why the department couldn't use them for other tasks on-site.

He managed the staff who administrated the portfolio of in-house training courses offered to the rest of the workforce. They created the documentation, they administered the wait lists and organised the logistics. He knew that the classroom based courses were being reduced because Management had decided many teacher led courses could be replaced by online tutorials, something he himself didn't agree with. Maybe it was his age, maybe at forty-four he was too far gone to learn new ways of doing things, but Schwarzesloch felt that he learned best when a real person stood before him and explained things, and answered questions when asked.

In his visualised conversations, Jackson always ended up saying that the people had to go. Not once did he relent, not once did Schwarzesloch find an angle in which the redundancy of his staff was deferred. At the end of the day, he knew deep down that even Jackson was under orders, and held no real power.

He knew they would now discuss redeployment, and they both knew it was no more than a euphemism. There was nowhere for the people to go except for the street.

He was disgusted, angry at the entire process. It sullied his history with the company, and put a dark filter over previously happy memories.

"There's no easy way of saying this," began Jackson.

Schwarzesloch let him speak, knowing that this kind of thing had to be said. He expected Jackson would tell him how things always looked bleak at such times, but they would inevitably improve.

"You've accomplished a great deal," continued Jackson, his mind no doubt wandering to what he was having for dinner, or his upcoming game of golf with the Directors, "and it's a sad day that's come to pass. I'd hoped things could have stayed as they were for a little longer."

He listened as Jackson outlined a future for the company as he saw it (or rather recanted the vision senior management had instilled in him), and talked about all kinds of things that floated on the boundary of Schwarzesloch's understanding. Exponential growth in drift markets, cutbacks leading to a more streamlined business contingency, blah-blah-blah. Schwarzesloch let the words drift over him, uninspired even for contempt.

He became aware of the pitch of Jackson's voice changing, heading towards a summarising of their conversation. He tuned in again, and heard how opportunities would present themselves, and it was never too late to start again.

He thought 'Why is he telling me this?', and then came the bombshell:

"I'm sorry," said Jackson. "I'll do all I can to get you an excellent reference."

Schwarzesloch felt his stomach lurch, and played that sentence over in his mind to see if he'd heard correctly. Stunned, he looked at Jackson and blurted "What?"

"I thought you would have foreseen this," said Jackson. "It can't be a bolt from the blue, surely? We're scaling down training, and the future is online. We don't need a training department any more. I'm sorry."

A month later, Schwarzesloch sat on his couch, alone, and wondered why his life had turned out like it did. Eighteen years he'd given to that company, and when the mood suited them, they'd tossed him away like garbage, out of date and unwanted. It still hadn't sunk in, though he now doubted anybody would phone him up to say: "It's all been a terrible mistake."

He had spent his last working weeks in a daze. It had been his duty to break the news to all of his staff and help them come to terms with their loss. He felt useless, and against all his expectations had found himself uttering the same blithe company statements he'd despised, telling them in a stupor how future opportunities would present themselves, how it was essential for the company to cut back now to reap the rewards of better profits in the future.

Eighteen years of sharing the life of the company, to be cut off and left in a void, in utter, utter silence. Eighteen years of moving forwards, only to find himself thrown off the ride in a place he didn't recognise: unemployment.

Schwarzesloch found his situation incomprehensible. The idea was too abstract for him to grasp. He wasn't ready for an early retirement, he wasn't ready to slow down, even if he could afford to. Surely all that experience meant something? How could they just throw him away?

Valerie also found his predicament difficult to fathom, not least because he'd taken it so badly. With the redundancy payment, they were in no need for his regular income, and could easily weather retaining their current lifestyle for a number of years before their belts needed tightening. She joked that Schwarzesloch could make himself useful around the house, something he didn't find amusing. She showed him an iron, and offered to show him how to use it, but he looked at her as if she'd found his mother's dildo.

For a few weeks, Schwarzesloch roused himself to something

approaching optimism and spent some money on a new computer. He knew his way around a company laptop, and noted little difference with the PC. However, having spent the last years of his career managing people instead of systems, he found the preinstalled software baffling. He quickly realised that his skills were hopelessly out of date, and, to his utter contempt, found the online tutorials disorientating and badly devised.

He persevered enough to fumble his way around a word processor and even learned how to use the fax facility, and was soon sending CV's out to potential employers and agencies. The other telecomms companies were apologetic but uninterested, also in the throes of downsizing. Maybe when things picked up, they told him.

The agencies were initially helpful, persuading him to leave the sanctity of his house to register with them in person, one even as far away as Shreveport, but the promises of finding work proved empty, his efforts in retaining regular contact fruitless. He came to understand that the agencies wanted his CV to beef up the content of their databases, not necessarily to pass around the office in the earnest task of finding a job for him.

The novelty of setting himself up in the business of finding a job quickly wore off. He turned on the computer less and less, and grew despondent.

There were offers of work, though Schwarzesloch found himself angered at what the agencies put his way. There came a trickle of junior roles, employment opportunities that paid no heed to his skillset, almost as though the jobs being offered were random (and perhaps ones that had been turned down by countless others before him). He was disgusted to find himself being offered a position in a slaughterhouse office for $8 per hour, and an assistant greenkeeper's role at the Bayou Oaks. He imagined the humiliation of being seen by Jackson and the other directors, pausing at their tees to point and stare.

In the early days of his being home alone, Valerie backed away and let him stew in peace. At first, when she got up to take Jenny to school, Schwarzesloch would rouse himself and make breakfast for them all, but soon came into the habit of staying in bed for an extra half hour, which turned into an hour.

Valerie worked behind the counter of a store selling school uniforms and equipment, and enjoyed the lightweight ambiguity surrounding her own career. At three each day, she would leave to pick up Jenny from school, and would be home by four.

Most days, she found her husband sitting on the couch under a prevailing torpor. He'd look stunned to see her, as though amazed another day had passed. In the agony of trying to fill up his days, Schwarzesloch found them disappearing under their own weight, in a blur of intangible thoughts and bitter daydreams.

"You need to get another job," she told him, and he looked at her with anger flashing across his eyes. In years of marriage, she had never before seen that look. From that moment, she chose not to broach the subject again. She'd let him lick his wounds and hope some sense materialised.

One miserable day followed another. And then came one that was worse than the others. He sat on the couch and watched television as normal. Spread out on the coffee table in front of him was a half-empty bag of Brazil nuts and three mugs containing the dregs of coffee. The local paper, containing situations vacant, lay unread at his feet.

He heard the front door open as Valerie brought Jenny home, and waited for his daughter to run in and greet him. She rushed over, holding up a painting for him to look at.

"That's very good. Did you paint that?"

His daughter nodded, and climbed up onto the couch to join him. Valerie entered the room and looked around, unable to hide the flicker of disgust. Wordlessly, she picked up the empty mugs and took them into the kitchen, where she found a pile of washing up still bundled in the sink. Angry now, she went back into the lounge.

"How much longer is this going to go on?" She had finally reached the limit of her patience. For three months, she'd watched him slide into a black funk, become little more than a barely functioning human being, concentrating on living and breathing and little else. Where was the drive and vitality that once defined him, that attracted her to him in the first place? Somewhere, deep down in his psyche, the things that made her love him were locked away, imprisoned by his fear, and doubt, and though she understood his world had momentarily been turned upside down, she knew that he had to bite the bullet and get over it.

"Please, don't start," he said. "I've had a bad day."

"Every day's the same for you," she said, "How can today be worse than yesterday? I'm finding it hard to cope when you're like this, and so is Jenny."

"Leave her out of this."

"I can't. I'm the one that takes her to school, I'm the one that brings her home, I'm the one that's out there every single day whilst you sit here and watch tv and do nothing. She told me in the car on the way home that you'd promised to take her to the cinema, and she's still waiting."

"I thought she'd forgotten all about it! Jenny, do you want to go to the cinema?"

Jenny was silent, afraid of the dark edge in her parents' voices.

"She's upset," said Valerie, scooping her away from him. "I want some changes around here. I can't go on like this much longer. It's like a fucking morgue in here."

"Don't swear in front of the child!"

"*I'm* upset, damn it! Can't you see what's happening to us?"

She stormed into the kitchen. Schwarzesloch momentarily thought about going after her but couldn't find the energy to move. He felt so drained lately, so lethargic, that the thought of rejoining the grind of daily life left him terrified.

Five minutes passed, in which he heard soft crying sounds from the kitchen. Schwarzesloch abruptly decided he wanted to get away from that fucking couch, and the only place he could think of to get some peace and quiet was the bath. He forced himself to get up, a tremendous effort because the couch seemed to possess a kind of gravitational pull, and walked to the bathroom at the back of the house.

He was lying in the bath, enjoying the blankness in his mind as the hot water relaxed his body, when he heard the scream.

In all his life, he'd never heard a noise like it. A single, guttural screech that sounded like the end of the world. Instinctively, he leapt out of the bath, delaying himself only to grab a towel and secure it around his waist. Valerie was screaming his name now, utterly terrified, and his mind raced as he ran through the house, expecting to confront some kind of intruder.

In the lounge, Valerie was on her knees over their daughter, who lay on the floor in a choking fit. Already he could see her face had turned pale and her lips were tinged with blue.

"She's got something in her throat!" screamed Valerie. "Do something!"

Schwarzesloch reached out for his daughter, who was struggling frantically, fighting for breath. He held her down and prised open her mouth.

"I can't see anything!" he shouted, bending right over her to peer into her mouth. "I can't see anything!"

They were gripped by a rising tide of panic. Quickly, Schwarzesloch lifted his daughter and enveloped the tiny figure from behind, half-remembering the Heimlich manoeuvre from a first aid course he'd attended more that fifteen years ago. He grabbed his own wrist and pulled his arms into himself, squeezing just beneath his daughter's ribcage with a hard, jerking motion. She tried to fight against it, summoning one last defiance of her approaching death, and Schwarzesloch tried again. Still she choked, her little body caught in spasms, and Schwarzesloch felt his insides turn to ice.

"Phone an ambulance!" he shouted. Valerie stared at him in complete shock, and he shouted at her a second time. Her eyes filled with tears, she ran to the telephone and frantically dialled the emergency services.

Schwarzesloch was already doing the reckoning inside his head. If he couldn't move the blockage, Jenny would go unconscious, and it would be a race against time for the ambulance to arrive. If she was no longer breathing, it meant her brain was deprived of oxygen. How long would it take before she died? Ten minutes? Two? He had no idea. How long before she succumbed to irreversible brain damage?

"Oh, God!" he cried, complete despair taking hold of him. He placed Jenny back down onto the floor, and saw that she had already stopped breathing. Her eyes were glazed and half closed, and her face was covered in spittle and tears. Talking to her constantly, telling her to hold on and not to die, Schwarzesloch opened her mouth again, hoping that he would see the blockage. Maybe she'd swallowed her tongue, and he'd missed it first time around. He saw nothing wrong. Whatever had choked her was stuck down in her windpipe, out of view. He forced his fingers down her throat, desperately trying to locate the blockage.

*She's dying*, he thought, *and I'm helpless*. Valerie rushed back into the room, and cried out at the sight of her daughter laid out on the floor.

"How long?" screamed Schwarzesloch, wanting to believe that any second somebody would knock on their front door and save the child.

"I don't know!" she screamed, falling to her knees. She looked at Jenny, and reached out to touch her face. "Do something!"

Lifting up the child, now as lifeless as a rag doll, Schwarzesloch placed her into position and tried the Heimlich manoeuvre again. She folded almost in half as his arms loosened their grip, and slid limply to the floor.

"I don't know what to do," he said, tears sliding down his cheeks. He wondered if he should attempt a tracheotomy, though the thought of slicing open her throat revolted him. He didn't even know what to use, or how to go about it.

They waited, Schwarzesloch cradling his daughter's head in his lap, and watched helplessly as she died. Ten minutes later came a frantic knocking at the front door, and Valerie ran to answer it, momentarily believing that everything would turn out fine. The paramedic ran into the lounge and inspected the lifeless body. Then, standing with a calmness that told them everything they needed to know, the medic stared at the floor and said that he was sorry.

Jenny was buried eight days later, after an autopsy revealed she had died choking on a Brazil nut. They both recalled Schwarzesloch leaving a half empty packet of nuts on the coffee table that terrible day, and Jenny had taken one of them and had died because of it. Such an innocuous, easy mistake to make, and they had paid the ultimate price.

They would outlive their only child.

The funeral was held in driving rain, attended by perhaps twenty people. The sight of a wreath spelling 'JENNY', sent by the parents whose children attended the same school, overwhelmed Valerie, and she broke down in front of everybody, falling to her knees in the mud.

Schwarzesloch watched sombrely as her father picked her up and comforted her.

In the following weeks, Schwarzesloch sat at home and brooded in silence. He stopped eating, he started smoking again. He lost all interest in his appearance, and came to regard washing himself as unnecessary.

Valerie was coping in her own way, trying to be strong for the both of them. After only a few days off, she went back to work, sticking it out despite embarrassing herself by breaking down in front of complete strangers on a number of occasions. Her friends rallied round, meeting her for lunch, and she spent many evenings at their houses, sometimes sleeping over. After a few weeks, when she could stand his company no longer, she spent most of her time there, and headed out to Houston at the weekend.

Schwarzesloch, however, had nobody. He would sit at home and stare at a photograph of his dead daughter for hours. And then, one day, he went crazy. All of a sudden, he was quickly and violently overcome with grief. He dropped to his knees on the floor and shouted words that made no sense, the language of pain, of loss. He sobbed until he was exhausted, and lay on the floor with drool spilling from his mouth.

The darkness came for him, and he awoke feeling sick and empty and cold. His senses were ravaged and his eyes raw. He climbed to his feet, and stood swaying for a few moments, and was engulfed by a rage so extraordinarily powerful that he thought he would explode. He picked up the coffee table and hurled it against the wall. He kicked out at the television, sending it crashing to the floor, and this violence made him feel alive for the first time in months. He felt the blood pounding in his head, felt it coarsing through his veins.

There was no stopping him. He smashed up the lounge, and staggered into the kitchen. Here, he grabbed handfuls of crockery and flung them at the walls, sent them shattering into fifty pieces at a time. He picked up the microwave and threw it through the window into his back yard. He took food from the freezer and cast it to the floor, and jumped up and down on it like a madman, and when he'd done with this he upturned the freezer itself.

After months of living in air as thick as treacle, Schwarzesloch sucked in the oxygen until it burned his lungs. Now it was clean, and sharp, and as intoxicating as liquor. He seized the urge to keep moving, to keep destroying everything he'd spent years paying for.

He went deeper into the house and trashed the master bedroom, the bathroom and all of the accumulated junk stored in the spare bedroom. Only when he came to Jenny's room did he stop. The sight of her bed, loaded with her collection of stuffed toys, was like a slap across the face, a sudden jolt into reality.

He sat on the bed and picked up her things, one by one. He hugged her toys, he stared at a pair of her socks still scrunched up on the floor. He picked up the pillow and sniffed it, inhaling the smell of his child, a smell that would grow stale and vanish. He'd never again hear her voice, or look into her eyes. All he had were his memories, a few possessions and a bundle of photographs. He'd never see her grow up, never see her turn into a young woman.

He sat staring at the floor, and thought that his life was over.

That evening, Valerie came over. Schwarzesloch was sitting on the couch again, staring into space, and she gently pushed open the front door and called out his name. He heard her say "My God," to herself, heard her stepping over the fragments of debris as she slowly made her way towards him.

"What have you done?" she asked.

Schwarzesloch turned away and said nothing.

Valerie tip-toed her way through the wreckage and sat on the arm of the couch. She was dressed in a smart suit, and wore a little make up. She was trying her best to get on with her life.

"Why do this?" she asked him.

Slowly, Schwarzesloch looked at Valerie and saw a woman he hardly recognised. He saw a great distance between himself and his wife, a divide of enormous magnitude.

"I couldn't save her," he said.

"It was an *accident*! A terrible, tragic accident. We loved her, we'll always love her, but she's gone. There's not a second of the day I don't think about Jenny, and I know the pain will never go away. But we are alive, and things have to go on. You can't behave like this. I don't understand you any more. We should be helping each other through this."

Schwarzesloch turned and stared at her.

"How can you talk like that?" he asked, his voice flat and cold. "Our baby girl is gone."

She sighed, and her shoulders slumped. Sometimes, the fight just left her, and she too felt like she could just crawl into a hole and lie there, forever.

"I know," she said simply. She placed a hand on his arm.

"Don't," he said, pulling his arm away.

She was quiet for a few moments and then she stood. A new fortitude seemed to give strength to her bones and make her straighten up.

Schwarzesloch didn't know how to begin telling her that she was like a stranger now, a person for whom he no longer had feelings. She wouldn't understand that he felt completely dead inside, cold and as lifeless as a stone.

"I can't live like this anymore," she said. With one last look at her husband, she turned and walked out of the room.

The next few days were little more than a blur. Schwarzesloch walked to the local store and returned with two plastic bags, each containing four one-litre bottles of whiskey. He had never been a big drinker but considered this to be a good time to start. The days were interminably long, and he needed something, *anything*, to get through them. He needed the pain to be dulled.

He needed oblivion.

Amongst the wreckage of the kitchen, he laid out the bottles neatly on the counter. At the back of one of the cupboards, he found an intact shot glass and sat down. With warm air pouring into the kitchen through the smashed window, he unscrewed the cap on the first bottle and filled the glass. He already knew he didn't like the taste of whiskey, and knew that the key to making this work was to concentrate on throwing as much as he could bear down his throat. He lifted the glass to his mouth and grimaced at the smell, and then forced himself to drink.

It was harder than he thought. The liquid burned the back of his throat and he had to fight a gag reflex. Immediately after downing the contents, the burn lined his gullet and seemed to spread into his lungs. His face wrinkled in disgust, and he coughed, and then swallowed the sudden flood of spit that lined his mouth.

For a few minutes, he reconsidered this new road. But the vile taste diminished, and the burn settled down to a kind of warm glow in his chest, and he realised that he might just manage it after all. He filled the glass again, and drank. He had to be methodical. Fill the glass, drink the contents. Repeat until oblivion. Wake up. Fill the glass.......

With the help of an entire pack of cigarettes, he managed to down more than half a bottle. Instead of oblivion, he found that his thoughts were tending to focus on his misery. After a few hours, tears lined his face and he felt sick. He stood, and realised he was drunk, but not the kind of drunk he was looking for. Instead of clearing away his problems, the drink compounded them. Nothing had been resolved and he felt dreadful. He made his way to the toilet, spent twenty minutes hunched over it, dribbling bile down the pan, and then felt so ill that he had to go to bed.

Six hours later, he woke up. He felt even worse, but took some comfort in the fact that his plan had worked after all. Slowly getting out of bed, he wasted no time in going to the kitchen, swilling out the shot glass under the cold tap, and then sitting down at the table. He filled the glass with whiskey.

He had to keep going.

It was soon after this that he started to think about oblivion of a different kind.

It crossed his mind, on more than one occasion, that he should get in the SUV, drive south past Houma to the wetlands, and plough the car into the nearest swamp. There are roads in Louisiana where you could slide off the road and never be found again.

At least, that way, his problems would be over. There would be no resurfacing, feeling even worse than before. Things would conclude with a definite finality. No blurs, no grey, foggy days blundering around in distress. It would be done.

He idly thought the idea through. The consequences of anybody discovering what he'd done would probably rest with Valerie. No ex-work colleagues would miss him. The neighbours barely knew him, and probably would never even notice him missing. Whilst he was rotting away at the bottom of a bayou, the mortgage payments would continue to evaporate the bank account, and there was enough money in there for a couple of years. Life would go on, the world would go about its business, nobody would ever know he was no longer a part of it. Except, maybe, for Valerie. He hadn't seen her since that time she'd walked out, and there had been no contact. Would she, one day, change her view of things and drive over to see how he was coping? Did she have it in her to think that their marriage was ultimately salvageable?

He didn't know.

With nothing better to do, he drove down the I-90 and out past Houma one day, taking the SUV along roads of diminishing traffic. Here and there, dilapidated old buildings slumped in the Louisiana heat. People stood in their yards, watching him drive by. Everyone, and everything, looked tired and run down. Oak trees stood in empty fields, draped with Spanish moss. Cypress lurked in the swamps lining the road. Dead things were flattened out on the asphalt, some old, some fresh, husks and pancakes wrapped in matted, dirty fur.

Somewhere, he parked up and looked out the open window at the waters of a swamp. With a cold disassociation, as though surveying the scene through the eyes of someone else, Schwarzesloch idly wondered where the best point would be to launch the SUV from the road. He wondered what the swamp would taste like as he drowned, and whether his body would be eaten by crayfish.

For a long time, he sat in the car and turned things over in his mind. He could still hear Valerie's screams. He could still feel the weight of Jenny, dying in his arms, and the memory of her eyes glazing over as her final struggles subsided was as fresh and vibrant as if his mind had recorded it in high definition. He was disturbed from his morbid thoughts by the feel of warm tears siding down his cheeks. Alone, sitting in an automobile at the edge of a swamp, Schwarzesloch sobbed until his eyes were raw.

It was a further catharsis of the most painful emotions, an exorcism of more of the despair that had recently crushed him under its insufferable weight. Such pain would never go away, but the heaviest baggage seemed to leave him that day.

Unexpectedly, he felt a little lighter, a little cleaner.

Suddenly, the idea of driving into a swamp seemed marginally less attractive.

He couldn't fathom it, this lifting of misery. Despite all of the grief and the self-loathing he'd welcomed as friends these last few months, despite the constant soul-corroding burden of guilt, he felt as though his real penance hadn't even started. If anything, he noted with a dry masochism, the awful feelings he'd been living through should last forever.

It wasn't right that time was already starting to heal, that the most painful grief had suddenly dissipated.

He smoked, dangling one arm out of the car. He caught the blue, iridescent flash of a large dragonfly out over the water. Close by, a heron dropped clumsily from the sky and landed on solid ground with a brief rush of flapping wings and spindly legs. Once down, it looked around as though searching for any witnesses, and caught Schwarzesloch's eye before turning and marching awkwardly to hide behind a clump of rushes.

*So now what?* he thought. If he couldn't bring himself to drive into a swamp, what was he going to do with himself? He still didn't see the point in living but if he couldn't bring himself to finish things right there, it seemed that living was the only other option. Somehow, could he find a way to go on? Could he really pull himself together and get on with his life, knowing that he had brought about the death of his daughter and had destroyed his own family? How would it begin, this new life? Was this the beginning, the rejection of suicide? Would things somehow fall into place and, by putting one foot in front of the other one step at a time, would he slowly march onwards into some sort of old age? Could he really face that, alone?

He had answers to none of these questions.

He tossed the cigarette onto the road, gunned the engine and turned the car around.

Driving home, he realised that he had to do something. *Anything*. If he couldn't stay sunk enough to wallow, the only thing he could do was try to get back on track. Oblivion wasn't for him. He sensed the months of abandoning all hope had come to an end. He had to pick up the pieces, arrange them into some sort of order he could cope with, and carry on.

His daughter was dead in the ground, and it was his fault. That would never go away, that guilt would be with him forever, but he knew now that it wouldn't destroy him.

It was time to rebuild.

Heading back into the city, he noticed more traffic on the roads than usual, particularly heading the other way, out of town. Roof racks were loaded down with suitcases. He wasn't naïve enough to assume that so many people had suddenly decided to go on vacation, especially when he saw a couple of station wagons loaded down with items of furniture.

*Must be another storm coming,* he thought. *People panicking, like they always do, and fleeing the city.* Having spent so many years down in the southern States, he was aware that the coastline was battered on a frequent basis by big storms and hurricanes, and the damage was usually far less severe than anticipated. The media whipped everybody up into a frenzy and there was gridlock on the roads, often for nothing – these storms often blew themselves out before landfall.

Assuming this was just another storm, he could sit in the house and ride it out. No big deal. He stopped at the store to grab some supplies. He wanted a couple of bottles of fresh water, some fruit, a few ready-meals to act as a stop-gap until he'd cleared the decks for a larger shopping trip.

There were a lot of people in the store, the queue stretching almost to the door. Schwarzesloch grabbed a basket and noted, with dismay, that all of the bottled water was out and the rest of the stock was pretty much depleted. A long line of people stood with baskets filled with whatever they could get their hands on. There were a lot of serious faces.

He grabbed a carton of juice, some chocolate and the last jar of coffee. His thoughts were occupied with plans for the next couple of days. He'd go from room to room, fill the trash bags with all the things that were now broken, and put them out in the back yard until he had enough to arrange some sort of collection. He saw no reason that the house couldn't be back as it used to be, more or less. There'd be a few rips on the wallpaper, a few gouges that would need replastering, but nothing major. Considering the maelstrom of violence he'd embarked upon, it was surprising that so much of the structural damage to the house could be considered superficial. He'd need to arrange a new window fitting, but he thanked Christ he hadn't been so crazy that he'd taken a sledge hammer to the walls.

He waited patiently until it was his turn to be served. The elderly store owner smiled a greeting as Schwarzesloch dumped the basket onto the counter.

"Doing a fairly brisk trade today, Albi?" he asked.

"Something like that," replied the old man, his forehead beaded with sweat. "Lot of folks stocking up for the big one."

"I'm sure it'll be nothing more than a damp squib. You know how it is."

"Not this time. Reckon it's gonna hit us square on, cause a lotta damage. Ain't you been listening to the weather reports?"

Schwarzesloch thought about his tv set, all smashed up in the corner of the lounge. The new DAB radio set too, nothing more than broken plastic and circuit boards on the kitchen floor.

"I'm having a sabbatical from the tv."

"Well, you'd better switch it on and keep listening. Plenty of people getting out of town while they still can."

There was a cough of impatience from the person immediately behind Schwarzesloch in the queue.

"Put a couple of bottles of vodka in there as well, will you?" he asked.

"Sure thing. You done with that last lot of whiskey?"

"Almost."

"It's not the answer, you know."

He looked at Schwarzesloch with a concerned expression. Seeing the same customers week in, week out, Albi knew a little about their lives. He knew the pain that Schwarzesloch was going through. Albi had lost his only son in an auto-wreck on the I-10 some fifteen years earlier, but hardly a day went by without Albi thinking of him.

"I know," said Schwarzesloch, his voice quiet.

There was another impatient cough from behind.

"Now you keep that noise down there!" said Albi, leaning around to give the queue a hard stare. "Everyone'll get their turn! There's never such a rush that manners go out the window!" He bagged up the groceries and Schwarzesloch paid.

Just before he turned to leave, Schwarzesloch asked: "What are they calling this one?"

"Katrina."

"That doesn't sound like a bad name."

"I hear it's gonna be another Betsy."

Everybody in these parts remembered that storm with awe, one of the worst natural disasters to ever happen on American soil. Everybody knew that one day, something worse would come along.

"We'll see," smiled Schwarzesloch. "See you in a couple of days."

"If I'm back by then. I'm shutting up shop and getting out of here tonight. Got a sister in Baton Rouge, she'll see me alright. You take care now."

Schwarzesloch placed the grocery bags into the footwell on the passenger side and drove the short distance to his house. A couple of neighbours were already fixing shutter boards across their windows. High above, the sky was overcast, the air a little muggy.

Schwarzesloch parked the car, grabbed the bags and walked up to his house.

He had a lot of work to do.

It was time to begin again.

# EXPERIMENTS WITH HUMANS

*In light of recent events, I thought it best to prepare some sort of defense case. Not that I can be blamed in any way for the carnage in the news this week, but if they catch her and she ever learns to talk....*

*I've posted this to you to keep safe, in case I suddenly go missing or turn up on a park bench full of ricin (you know how this sort of thing works). It isn't much but it's all I have. The following account has been taken from my own personal diaries – the official reports were handed in at the time and I have no idea where they went. If anyone is interested enough to look, they are all stamped with a blue butterfly symbol.*

*I have also been unable to contact Bathgate. He could be anywhere. He could be anything. He could even be dead.*

*What a mess.*

**16-MAY-1972**

I received a confirmation letter for an interview today, which came as something of a surprise, mostly on account of my never having applied for the position. As it happens, I *am* in the market for a job, so maybe the universe is giving me good karma in the form of a clerical error. I'll go along and see what happens.

**19-MAY-1972**

The interview was today, held in a large, nondescript building in the city centre. I think I saw a 'Ministry of Defence' logo on some of the receptionist's paperwork. I took the lift to the second floor, where I was met by a Mr Billington, a smallish figure with a very firm handshake. He led me down a corridor to an office, asked me to sit down and waited as I answered a series of written questions. After, he took the paperwork and left me alone for a while.

"The position is front line stuff," he said upon returning. "The job will involve research at the very frontiers of science. You'll need to sign a confidentiality agreement, of course."

"No problem," I told him.

He ended up offering me the job. Easiest interview I've ever had. I still have no idea what this is all about, or why I've been chosen.

**24-MAY-1972**

Long day. I drove across the country, following a set of posted directions. The motorway fed into an A-road, branched off into a country lane and went through a small hamlet called Wexley, where a narrow, almost unnoticeable farm track with forest on either side led into a pocket of woodland. I pulled up in a clearing. There was a small, blocky building with a door. With accommodation being part of the deal, this would be my new home for the foreseeable future. I wasn't impressed.

A flight of stairs led underground, down into the darkness. From such inauspicious beginnings, the interior of the rest of the building was startling. I found myself in a sort of chamber, full of desks and filing cabinets and banks of equipment with thick black wires coming out of them. There were tinted windows embedded into every wall. Looking through one of them, I saw there were large, empty rooms below.

A second door opened and in stepped a thin man, pinched-faced and balding, dressed in a white laboratory coat. This was my new boss, Bathgate.

"From this point on, everything we discuss will be of a classified nature," he said. "There are things you will see during the course of our work that will disturb you, even though your psychometric tests revealed borderline sociopathy."

What the fuck was he talking about?

"Don't look so startled, it's why you were chosen. We can't give this sort of work to just about anybody. Now, listen: There are four test areas down there," he said, "and each is completely isolated. The walls are three feet thick. There will be no sounds, vibrations or smells in those rooms unless they are generated by us. The rooms will be lit twenty-four hours a day. Do you understand?"

"I think so."

"Tell me about the last project you worked on."

"We were studying infants, attempting to quantify the psychology and entymology of language origination. There was some parallel work with monkeys, sign language and so forth, and some surgical procedures for which I would analyse data."

"You were lucky to get that sort of work – most graduates end up stacking shelves."

"I'd like to think the quality of-"

"And you were dismissed for a lack of empathy towards the subjects," he interrupted.

"How do you know that?"

"Don't be ridiculous. Do you think this is amateur hour? You were chosen for this project, by me personally. Did you think I send out interview requests to just anyone? Come, I'll show you to your room."

I followed him through a dingy corridor to a series of small rooms. The first was mine. There was a bed, an empty bookshelf and a chair. It felt like a prison cell.

**1-JUN-1972**

I've been incredibly busy with preparations. Deliveries including sand, plants and gravel all have to be wheel-barrowed into the test rooms and distributed. Endless amounts of jars and tinned food were stored in the larder rooms, by the look of it enough to survive the end of the world.

The facility is deceptively huge. Each room has almost a thousand square feet of floor space, bitten into by the central column that rises up to form the observation tower. There are vents and pipes that affect the climate and air quality.

The more I am with Bathgate, the less I like him. He's abrupt and often ill-tempered. At times, I think about punching him in the face and driving home.

**8-JUN-1972**

Bathgate visited my quarters this morning and explained the nature of our work here. Finally!

The test subjects will be four newborn babies, two male and two female, all orphaned and procured from various channels within Eastern Europe. It will be our job to ensure their survival and study them.

Never before has human development in such acute isolation been so strictly controlled, and the facility was built specifically for this purpose. The ultimate questions – *with minimized external influences, what is the true nature of our species? - How does a human develop in its 'purest' form?* – will be answered.

Whatever.

There are hundreds of tests and experiments that are already set out, and we must conduct these to the best of our abilities. Most of them can't begin until the subjects are old enough to provide any sort of measurable validity, so the first few years will be more about maintaining the environment and keeping the subjects in complete isolation. Any experimental results must be thoroughly documented, which will be my main role.

Ethically and morally it is wrong on every level. We will be depriving these babies of the world, of the lives they could have lived. Bathgate says that these children wouldn't have survived for very long in the orphanages they came from, that we have effectively saved them from an early grave. He also told me that these babies have been certified as dead in their countries of origin. They no longer exist.

For the record, I have no misgivings.

**12-JUN-1972**

The subjects arrived today, packed into incubation tanks in, of all things, the back of a white transit van. The driver wore a tracksuit and spoke very little English. It all seemed a bit underhand considering this was supposed to be a government backed operation.

We took them inside and deposited one in each room, leaving them naked, alone and crying. One, with a wisp of reddish hair crowning its head, looked right at me as I closed the door.

**15-JUN-1972**

This is ridiculous! I've spent the last few days mopping up baby shit and heating milk. We put an anaesthetic into the air and clean up when the subjects are asleep. Each time they wake up, their environment is reset. I doubt they're aware of what's happening.

**30-JUN-1972**

No change. Nothing to report. All they do is sleep, drink a little milk, poo everywhere and then spend hours crying. I dutifully write all this up and hand my reports to Bathgate. He stamps them with a little blue butterfly symbol and puts them in folders in the archive room.

This job is going to be very boring.

**17-JUL-1972**

That bastard Bathgate has got me looking at a plumbing leak in the toilet. This isn't in my job description! I tried to argue but he just won't listen to reason. So not only do I have to clean up the mess from the babies, but I have to clean up our stinking piss as well. I'm not happy.

**02-AUG-1972**

Boredboredboredboredboredboredbored.......

**06-AUG-1972**

I have given the subjects names - Lena, Rula, Miko and Pog. Pog is a bulbous-headed little fucker, perhaps the ugliest child that's ever been born. He seems happy enough. Perhaps it's best that he's hidden away from the world, looking like he does. Lena has a fiery mop of red hair and seems the most active of the bunch. Rula stares into space a lot and might be a little backward. Miko likes crawling through his own shit and is a nightmare to clean properly.

This experience is really putting me off ever having kids of my own.

**09-MAR-1973**

Lena sat up straight today. *Whoopee-do.* It's the most exciting thing that's happened in the last 9 months, discounting the fact that we've started adding rusks to their diet.

**14-APR-1973**

Pog is ill, coughing and crying all the time. I told Bathgate that we should get a doctor in to take a look but he's insistent that the experiment remains untainted by any external influences. I argued that we are an influence, just by ensuring they remain fed and clean, but he shot me down with a withering look. He hates me, I think.

Lena is crawling around and trying to stand. The others aren't doing much.

**16-APR-1973**

Pog is in a bad way, lying on the ground shivering, occasionally whimpering. This afternoon, Lena crawled over to the wall that divides their rooms and sat there with her hand against the concrete. It's almost as though she knows something is wrong.

**18-APR-1973**

Pog is dead. After a post-mortem, we burnt the body in the incinerator and I wrote up a report. Bathgate told me that the subject will not be replaced, that this room will now remain empty for the duration of the experiment. I asked how long that might be. He shrugged and asked: "How long is a piece of string?"

I've thought a lot about leaving, but where would I go? What would I do? This job might be incredibly boring most of the time but it's better than flipping burgers or laboring on a building site. I don't think I'd get a job involved in any other kind of scientific research, not if I'm honest with myself (and especially after taking a sneak look at my psychometric test results, stored in the archive). At least here I get to sit around and drink coffee all day, and there's a regular, decent wage. I suppose I should count myself lucky.

**1973-1979**

The remaining subjects develop normally, taking into account their circumstances. During sleep, we monitor their physiology, take blood samples and so forth. From time to time we place new objects in their environments, and they all display signs of curiosity and interact with whatever they're given. Only Lena seems to look around and wonder where these things come from, sometimes searching her chamber thoroughly for anything new.

Growth, intelligence, spatial awareness *etc* seem to correlate with expected development of 'real world' infants. Of course, were we able to test for social skills and group psychology, one would expect severe retardation.

All the time, we wait for signs of abnormal behavior. Quite what we're looking for, I don't know. Sometimes, the rather abstract nature of the experiment makes it all seem rather pointless. Still, the wage envelopes are delivered every month and my own isolation means I can't blow it on stupid things I don't really need. My savings account looks very healthy.

**01-FEB-1980**

The subjects continue to display divergent traits of character. Miko runs around a lot, shouting nonsense words that Bathgate has me trying to spell accurately. He's poring over entymology texts looking for similarities, as though he expects Miko is somehow pulling language from a sort of collective ancestral mind-pool.

This is the sort of thing we've been waiting so long for. Until now, the test subjects haven't displayed any sort of behavior that wouldn't be expected from similar children in a normal, social environment. As they get older, though, Bathgate is taking even more of an interest, watching them closely.

I'm not sure what he expects. Does he really believe that Miko, separated from all contact with any other humans for the duration of his life, will start spouting grunts forgotten since the days of cavemen? As if there are parts of the brain, never needed by modern man, that retain such knowledge? And, more to the point, even if this was the case, is such knowledge useful?

For the thousandth time, I question the validity of this experiment, and my involvement in it. But not too deeply. When it finally ends, I'll have enough money put by to go travelling and avoid the need for any other kind of employment for a few years. So I'll just keep quiet, keep filing the reports.

Rula sits in silence for long periods. She's so boring it's killing me. She's about what I expected out of the experiment – deprived of contact, lacking any sort of social skills, retarded through a lack of interaction and any sort of real mental stimulus. Little more than an empty shell, bumbling along on instinct. Sometimes, I wish it was Rula that had died instead of Pog, at least he had the potential to be a little bit more interesting.

Lena, though, is doing interesting stuff all the time. She sometimes stands with her hands outstretched. It was a few days before we noticed that each hand points directly at the other subjects. When they move, Lena's hands move as though following them. This is clearly impossible, but we haven't come up with any sort of explanation as yet.

**29-MAR-1980**

A strange day. Lena did her pointing thing and Miko pointed back, which was weird enough, but then they both walked to their dividing wall and touched it. Looking down from the observation tower, they were adjacent to each other, and if there was no wall between them they would have been in line to touch each other.

I've tried to think of an explanation to rationalise such behavior but can't come up with anything. Bathgate is tremendously excited about the whole thing, urging me to pay close attention and describe things in my report exactly as they have happened. Which, of course, I'd do anyway – after so many years of writing these dull reports, I have a clinical eye for detail. But this episode has me confused, and I'm not sure I understand it.

Can they possibly know of each other's existence?

**13-NOV-1980**

Lena has taken to sitting for long periods, as though meditating. Miko copies the behavior. Bathgate is calling it 'sympathetic resonance'. I asked him to explain and he started talking about ants and tuning forks and, in the end, I had no idea what he was banging on about. I just let him talk himself out, nodding whenever I thought it appropriate, until he was done.

**27-NOV-1980**

In the room diametrically opposite Lena's, Rula has started hiding herself away in the plant area, as though afraid of something. She's a nervy child, always looking around with wide eyes and displaying caution whenever she roams the outer limits of her environment, but something is making her even more jittery than usual these days. We're picking up on something as well. There's a funny feeling in the air, an unsettled atmosphere.

It feels like we're all waiting for something to happen.

**17-FEB-1981**

Today, Lena meditated and slumped over. At the same moment, Miko stood up, an expression of wonder on his face. He reached out and touched the air. He was seeing something that we couldn't.

I hissed at Bathgate to come and take a look.

Miko started running around, and for the first time we heard the sound of laughter. As we looked down, it seemed as though Miko were engaged in play with another entity, as though another child was in the room with him. This lasted for almost fifteen minutes and stopped abruptly.

We moved around the chamber and peered down to see Lena stirring. She stood and looked around her room. Bathgate was so fascinated, his face was actually pressed against the tinted glass.

And then Lena looked up, right at us.

I'll admit I felt a shiver pass through my body and had to look away.

These days, it seems more and more things are happening that make writing a detailed report problematic. It's not my job to theorise, simply to create accurate reports. But it's hard to remain completely objective in the face of such weird behavior. *Something* is happening, right before our eyes. But what is it?

**21-FEB-1981**

Bathgate has spent days on the phone, arguing with whoever is funding this experiment. He wants an MRI scan of each subject but insists it must be done in situ. Whoever he's talking to doesn't seem to want to buy us the equipment, brand new technology that is just coming onto the market. At one point, he screamed into the phone. He seems to forget that our smoked glass isn't as soundproof as the concrete walls down in the test rooms. I was horrified to see that all three subjects were looking up at the observation tower.

Idiot!

**28-APR-1981**

We're now convinced that Lena is somehow making her presence felt in the other test rooms. Miko continues to play with an invisible 'friend', but Rula runs away screaming, terrified. Still, I can't make any mention of what we think in the reports – Bathgate is adamant about this. The episodes only happen when Lena is meditating, when she has slumped over and appears to be lifeless. And then, the effects are only observed in one other chamber at a time. If Miko is playing with his imaginery friend, Rula sits quietly, and if Rula gets a case of the terrors and runs around screaming, Miko stands around looking disappointed, as though wondering why he is alone.

When she's not meditating, Lena spends long periods staring up at the observation tower. I know she cannot see us but meeting her gaze makes me feel uncomfortable... I get strange thoughts, memories of traumatic times from my childhood. The time I fell off my bike and scraped my face along the road. Falling out of my first floor bedroom window and landing on the outhouse, breaking my arm. The time I lost my mother in a supermarket and stood there screaming and crying until she returned. Horrible little moments, snapshots of misery and fear. Things I haven't thought about in years.

**12-MAY-1981**

Bathgate spends most of his time shouting down the telephone, arguing about funding. It's prompted a renewed interest in the project and we are under scrutiny – I have been asked to prepare a series of reports summarizing our key achievements. It means extra work and Bathgate is on my back all the time, urging me to get it done. I've had quite a few nights in my room, working late, and without any overtime pay. I'm not happy about it but it needs doing.

If I'm being honest, I've had a change of heart about the experiment. During the last year or so, things have certainly become a lot more interesting. I wouldn't go so far as to say that I'm now enjoying my job, but with all the weird occurrences I'm finding it easier to stay interested, to the point where I'm actually rooting for the MRI money to come through because I actually want to see the results.

I've spent years thinking the experiment was a waste of time, just an easy way to pull in a decent wage, but now I really feel like we're doing something important. We are getting unusual results and we are on to something here. I don't know what, exactly, but the way things are developing we may begin to see even more startling results. I get a feeling that the really freaky stuff is just around the corner.

**02-JUL-1981**

I'm finding it hard to stay focused. Every time I look down at Lena she stops what she's doing and looks back at me. It makes the hair on the back of my neck stand on end. I know she can't see through the tinted glass so what could the explanation possibly be? How does she know when we're looking, and how does she know exactly where to look to make direct eye contact with us?

This can't go in my report, but I'm beginning to think that she has some sort of extra awareness, some kind of ability to process the environment in a way that we don't yet understand. The closest thing I can think of is when you are amongst a group of people in a social environment and suddenly turn your head to look straight at some stranger who happens to be staring at you. It's not that uncommon an occurrence, but there hasn't yet been a rational explanation for it. Even so, Lena's ability to do this every time we observe her is really unsettling.

Bathgate is more irritated than usual and there's an atmosphere in the chamber. A *tension*. Today, we hardly said a word to each other.

**11-JUL-1981**

This is going to sound crazy, but sometimes I feel like we are the ones being observed. I keep turning around, expecting to see Bathgate behind me, only to find that he's on the other side of the chamber, or sometimes even somewhere else entirely.

During the afternoon, when I was alone, a pen suddenly rolled off the edge of one of the desk and the sound of it hitting the floor made me jump with fright.

**17-OCT-1981**

At just before 3am, I woke in my quarters, convinced that someone was in my room. There was nobody there, of course, but the feeling stayed with me and I couldn't get back to sleep. I lay there thinking for a while, and the feeling of unease seemed to grow until it was replaced by fear and I had to get up.

I made a cup of coffee and went to the observation chamber. Miko and Rula were asleep. I couldn't see Lena. After fifteen minutes, panicking, I went and woke Bathgate, who was enraged at being disturbed.

When we returned to the chamber and looked down, Lena was standing there looking up at the tower.

She was laughing.

**22-NOV-1981**

Lots of bad dreams lately, a churn of horrible memories and vague terrors. Bathgate has them too, I think – I hear the odd cry from his room now and then. The feeling of being watched is almost constant, and judging by our observations of Miko playing with an imaginery friend, it's hard not to postulate that Lena is somehow managing to initiate out-of-body experiences at will. We discuss it, but Bathgate warns me not to write such theories in my reports, insisting that I must simply describe what we are observing without providing any conclusions.

"What are we doing all this for, if not to provide our own conclusions?" I asked.

"We're here to collect data and ensure the smooth running of the experiment," he warned.

"Do you think Lena is somehow leaving her body and travelling into the other chambers?"

"It doesn't matter what I think."

I know he agrees with me but he won't come out and admit it. His biggest fear, I think, is that the experiment should become tainted by our personal opinions. Scientists aren't meant to influence their experiments in any way, merely to let them play out and observe what happens. I do agree with that, but it's frustrating that he can't drop the professionalism for a moment to have a frank conversation about what's been happening lately.

**18-DEC-1981**

Lena broke a stalk from one of the larger plants and started drawing in the sand area. As we watched, a curved line became the top of a head. She drew eyes, a nose, a mouth. Bathgate remarked aloud that she was displaying signs of self-awareness, until I pointed out that she had never actually seen herself and had no basis for drawing a face. Only when Lena added spectacles did the truth dawn on us – she had drawn a picture of Bathgate.

"How is this possible?" he asked.

"She must have seen you, somehow."

"You know that isn't possible!" he raged.

"Then you tell me what you think is going on!"

"The glass.... She must be able to see through it. It's the only possible explanation. Maybe, when it's dark in the chambers and we have the lights on up here..."

"Bullshit," I said. "She can't see anything."

Clearly, our experiment was heading towards areas normally labeled 'paranormal'. We must be cautious. Misreading any further signs may open our eventual summaries to ridicule, I understand that, but there are things happening here that simply cannot be explained by our current understanding of the world.

Is this what Bathgate was expecting from the experiment? Would it be so wrong to postulate that humans are born with certain abilities that, if left to mature of their own accord and aren't prone to the distractions of other stimuli, border on what most people would consider 'paranormal'?

**08-FEB-1982**

An unexpected visit by the 'money men'. Six of them, some in military uniform, arrived just after nine and demanded to be let in. They nosed around the complex and asked lots of questions.

They seemed disinterested in our work and I heard one mutter something about 'wasted resources'. It was one of those days where the test subjects did nothing but lie around and sleep all day. When they left, Bathgate went to his quarters and didn't emerge for two days.

**24-MAR-1982**

We had a powercut today. The whole facility was plunged into darkness. Bathgate went down into the maintenance area to start up the backup generator. When the lights returned, I immediately checked the subjects.

Miko was curled up, his hands over his face.

Rula was hiding.

Lena was standing with her arms outstretched.

Her feet weren't touching the floor.

She was *levitating*.

Her powers, whatever they are, are getting stronger. There can be no doubt, this is new territory. This *is* paranormal.

**26-MAR-1982**

There can be no doubt. We are in over our heads. This morning, Lena put out her arms, closed her eyes, and concentrated until her feet rose from the floor and she lifted herself into the air. As we watched, open mouthed with horror, she rose to the height of the observation chamber and levitated before us, some twenty feet or so off the ground.

She opened her eyes.

She looked right at us.

She smiled.

Her red hair floated around her head, as though caught in a stiff breeze. As I watched, a powerful surge of dark thoughts flooded my brain, horrors both real and imagined. A memory of being bitten by a neighbour's dog, which left me too frightened to go out of the house for months afterwards. I remembered, in vivid detail, the time when my mother was seriously ill in hospital with kidney stones and I was convinced she was going to die. Back in the present, I imagined that my flesh was crawling with spiders, perhaps my worst fear of all.

Terrible, horrible thoughts and feelings.

She was doing this to me. Turning my worst fears against myself. I forced myself to stand and looked at her through the tinted glass. Her face seemed blurry somehow, as though her features had become fluid and indefinable. The harder I looked, the less sense I seemed to make of the figure before me.

Across the chamber, Bathgate was rolling around on the floor, moaning, suffering his own private agonies.

And then, suddenly, the fear lifted and I looked out to see Lena slowly sinking, using the last of her strength to safely deliver her back onto the floor of her chamber. She slumped, unconscious, her red hair plastered across her face, dark with sweat.

Whatever it was she'd just done, it seemed to have used up all her energy (and it would take her days to recover). But the message had been clear – her powers were getting stronger. I began to wonder how we would be able to contain her if this continued. With practice, with maturity, what would this girl be capable of?

**02-APR-1982**

We are at war with Argentina over the Falkland Islands. War! Where did that come from? I've never even heard of the Falkland Islands, and all of a sudden they're the country's top priority. I can't help but feel that this is going to have a negative impact on us, especially after the recent military visit. Other eyes are on us now, we are on somebody's radar.

Bathgate has spent hours on the telephone screaming and shouting. It sounds bad, like they're ready to plug the plug. I've seen him angry, lots of times, but never like this. I stayed out of it as much as possible. It's not as if I have much of a voice in this project – I'm just the guy that writes stuff down. Nobody listens to what I have to say.

**05-APR-1982**

We are being shut down. The facility is to be decommissioned. Our funding is being diverted to the war effort. Just like that, the experiment is over. Bathgate was so furious, he started smashing up the observation chamber until I managed to calm him down.

I tried to make sense of it all but some things are just beyond rationality. Obviously, the people behind the scenes, the ones providing the budget, have decided that they no longer want to continue. From their perspective, I suspect they think it's all been a waste of time. All of our research, wasted. All these years, all of our efforts rendered useless.

And can I blame them? What have we discovered, really? A girl who can float? Was it all worth it? I can only answer that question on a personal level. The experiment has kept me in work for the last ten years, and I haven't had to worry about any of the things ordinary people worry about. I haven't paid any rent, or any utility bills, and I've managed to save up a serious amount of money. So for me, the experiment has been worthwhile. But now what? Where do I go from here? I'm going to have to go back out into the world and find my place again. The thought of it makes me uneasy. All those people. The pace of modern life. The frenzy.

"What do we do now?" I asked Bathgate.

"Back everything up to floppy disk," he said. "Now they've fucked us over, I'll probably have to write a book about the whole thing."

**10-APR-1982**

We let the children go. We had to. There was no provision for anything else, no funding to have them returned to their countries of origin. Besides which, they didn't officially exist, having originally been signed off as dead. There was no way we could see them integrated into the care system here – it would raise all sorts of questions about where they'd been for the last ten years.

I opened their doors and we waited outside for them to join us. I could only imagine how they were going to feel at the sight of a larger world outside of anything they had ever known. If the thought of rejoining the world left me feeling uneasy, it will be a million times worse for them.

Miko emerged first, blinking at the sunlight and holding a hand up to shield his eyes from the glare. They had never even seen daylight before. Would they have any concept of the sheer scale of things out here? Would they know what the sky was? We watched as Miko slowly stepped forwards, looking around at the grass, the trees, back at the building itself.

"This doesn't feel right," I said.

Bathgate ignored me.

Miko looked at us and walked forwards until he was just a few feet away. He reached out and leaned forward, touching Bathgate, poking him in the chest, presumably to see if he was real. Bathgate looked on, expressionless. Miko then came to me and held out his hand to touch my face. I let his hand wander across my features, his cold fingers getting their first contact with another human's skin. He smiled and muttered something unintelligible before running off into the surrounding forest.

"Where the fuck is he going?" I asked.

"Who cares?" said Bathgate.

He was a cold bastard, there can be no doubt about that. And, back at the beginning of all this, he'd had the nerve to suggest I was a borderline sociopath!

Rula made it only as far as the doorway, terrified of what lay before her. She slumped across the threshold and buried her face in her hands. She lay there sobbing as Lena stepped over her and took in her first view of the outside world. She slowly turned her head as though confirming what she thought was out here. For all we knew, she had already sent her mind out through the walls of the facility, and this was a scene she'd looked at many times before.

However, it turned out that this wasn't the case. Her out-of-body experiences must have been limited to the building itself, because she suddenly let out a scream and glared at us. She shouted something, but there were no words for her to draw language from and she sounded like an angry cat. It would have been funny were her eyes not filled with so much hatred, and I took an involuntary step backwards, suddenly afraid.

Out here, we had no idea of her powers. She could be capable of anything.

With a final scream of rage, Lena ran back into the facility, slamming the door behind herself.

The force of it decapitated Rula, still sprawled across the threshold.

"Jesus Christ," said Bathgate.

We stood there for what seemed like an eternity, silently mulling over the sight of Rula's head on the path in front of the door. If Bathgate told me to pick it up and get rid of it I would punch him. Thankfully, he said nothing.

"Now what?" I asked at last.

"Now we move onto new pastures," he said.

"Are we just going to leave her in there?" I asked.

"Do you have a better idea?"

"She's dangerous!"

"That's not our problem."

"What if someone finds her?"

"This is MOD land. Nobody will come."

"You can't be sure of that. There's a bloody village less than half a mile away."

"And the perimeter of the facility is clearly marked. I'm sure someone will come and stick a big fence up. But, like I said, that's not our problem. Goodbye, Henderson."

Bathgate climbed into his car and drove off. Ten years and the prick didn't even shake my hand.

I stood in the cold, wondering what to do next. What *could* I do? Nothing.

I drove away, glancing back at the facility through my rearview mirror until it disappeared from view.

# FISHES AND ENGINES

Jack MacReady was a dour, miserable bastard, come from a long line of dour, miserable bastards. He knew it. Everybody on the island knew it. Even God knew it. Like his father before him, and his father before that, MacReady fished the waters off the northern coastline of the island. He loved being at sea, even when there was a gale blowing and the boat bobbed about like a cork in a maelstrom. The smell of the brine was in his blood. Cut open a MacReady and salt water would spill out.

His battered trawler had spent countless thousands of nights out on the waters, waters sometimes so ferocious that he had wondered many times whether certain stormy nights would be his last. But always he returned. The MacReady's were famous for their hardiness.

He worked alone and preferred it that way, despite the fact that he had to do everything himself. Other people just got in the way. He'd once been persuaded to take on an apprentice, a young island lad fresh out of school, and he'd been useless. Couldn't tie a decent knot, didn't know his aft from his elbow. Jack tolerated him for two days before sending him packing back to his mother, the Post Mistress who'd forced him onto Jack in the first place. Things had been a little awkward since then, and Jack rarely visited the Post Office anymore.

He didn't mind. He was happy with his own company. His tolerance of other people in general was poor – sometimes it would be months between talking to anybody else, although Jack would think that even this length of time was not long enough.

He had no need of friends. He'd once owned a dog, a stupid clod of a beast that used to get seasick and would throw up all over the deck. Jack had simply turned him loose. A week later, he'd seen the remains by the side of the road. He felt no remorse. If the dog didn't even have enough sense to cross a road that had no more than one or two cars a day passing by, it was for the best that it's time on the Earth was brief.

He fished for himself. He rarely needed money, although there was a considerable sum stuffed underneath his mattress. Sometimes, he scooped it all out and counted it, a methodical process that brought joy into his drab life for a few hours. Spending cash brought on a discomfort bordering on physical pain. If he had to go shopping, he haggled mercilessly with the shopkeepers, and they were always glad to see the back of him. He was relentless, and drove a hard bargain.

The other island fishing family, the Buchanans, had called it a day just the previous year, and had wound up the business and moved to the mainland. The last he'd heard, they were thoroughly regretting it, living in a suburb of Dundee, surviving on State handouts. He was secretly pleased, even though he had time for old Ike Buchanan. Less competition meant more fish for him.

He ate what he caught and salted or smoked the leftovers. Sometimes, if he was feeling up to it, he would drive into the village and set up a stall, and sell what was leftover, but he sometimes struggled for enough fish to justify the bother. Fishing was a hard business, and age wasn't making it any easier.

His house was bare, with just a few bits of furniture and an old tv set in the corner that hadn't been switched on in years, since they'd cut off the electric supply. He knew that the modern world had moved on, and the set would no longer work as it used to even with power, but he hadn't yet gotten around to throwing it away. During the rare times he'd watched television in the past, he would look at the idiots parading themselves for the purposes of entertainment and snort with disgust.

The house was functional in a primitive way. He burned driftwood, and if he couldn't find any he went cold. He cooked his dinners, usually fish broth, in a big black pot in the hearth. He got all of his water from a well in the back yard. He had no telephone. The house was a weather-beaten, isolated building on the northern tip of a weather-beaten, isolated island, and Jack MacReady was about as far removed from modern society as it was possible to be.

One bitter morning in March, as MacReady was driving the short distance to the sheltered harbour where he kept his trawler, there was a streak of white light in the Heavens and a heavy object fell from the sky and smashed into the bonnet of the car. The noise was horrendous, a crash that must have reverberated around the entire island. MacReady sat in a stunned silence for a few moments, waiting for the smoke to clear. When he was ready, he clambered out of the car and stood with his hands on his hips, surveying the damage. It was catastrophic. Something had punched a great hole through the bonnet and had wrecked the engine.

"Bastard!" he said.

He looked up at the sky, wondering where the falling object might have come from. There was nothing else up there. He surveyed the empty landscape. He doubted anybody else would drive up this way for days.

There was only one thing to do, and he started walking back the way he'd come. A mile down the road, he passed his house and kept walking. The town was only three miles away. A brisk pace would see him there within the hour.

At MacDuff Auto Repairs, brothers Andy and Cathal were chatting about which of the island's two pubs they would frequent that evening. It was a conversation they had engaged in many hundreds of times, and the result was always the same. They would go to The Hungry Cow first to check out the talent for Cathal (usually none, new women only came during the meagre tourist season) before heading off to The Swan to get suitably drunk. It was the same routine three times a week, but they never seemed to tire of it. Once upon a time, before Andy had married Louise and they'd had a daughter, it was seven nights a week. Now, all Cathal wanted to do was settle down and start a family, like his brother.

Cathal looked up to see MacReady walking towards the garage.

"Aye, aye," he said to his brother. "You can deal with this old bugger. I'll go make some coffee."

Cathal disappeared and the old man walked straight over to Andy.

"My car's fucked," he snapped. MacReady wasn't known for his convivial banter.

"Is that so?" asked Andy, wiping his hands on a rag and setting it down.

"Can you come and take a look at it? Have you got much on?"

"We're pretty busy," said Andy, a stock response made more out of habit than anything else. Cathal reckoned that you could always add a bit extra to the bill if the customer thought you were doing them a favour by doing their car first.

MacReady peered over his shoulder and looked as though he didn't believe him.

"Okay, okay," sighed Andy. "Where is it?"

"Top of the island."

"Wait here a minute."

Andy went and spoke to his brother and shortly afterwards he was driving MacReady back along the narrow roads towards the northern end of the island. The drive was conducted mostly in silence, the one brief conversation consisting of:

"Have you any idea what's wrong with it?"

"I already told you. It's fucked."

They reached the broken down vehicle and Andy parked up behind it. MacReady watched as Andy bent over the bonnet and took a good look at the damage. Eventually, he stood back and gave his judgement.

"You're right. It's fucked."

"Didn't I tell you?"

"What happened?"

"Something dropped out of the sky and hit the bloody thing."

"What, like a bit of a plane or something?"

MacReady shrugged. Andy reached inside and put the gears into neutral, and then pushed the car forward a length. After pulling on the handbrake, he returned and looked at the ground. MacReady walked over and joined him. The hole went down for an undeterminable depth. Whatever it was, the falling object had gone straight through the car and carried on through the soil. Andy leaned over and spat down the hole.

"Can you fix up the car?" asked MacReady.

"No. It's ready for the knacker's yard."

"There's no more miles in it, you say?"

"Only if you want to start pushing it everywhere."

"Damn and fuck!"

Andy gave the rest of the car a cursory inspection. It was a creaking old rust-bucket, ready for scrapping. He was amazed the old duffer had kept it running for so long.

"What about getting a new engine?" asked MacReady.

"I can, but wouldn't it be better all round if you just bought a new car?"

"Do you think I'm made of money? Besides, I don't know how many days I've got left on this Earth. If I drop down dead tomorrow, what'll be the point of having a new car?"

"I meant second hand new, not new-new."

"Just talk to me about the engine. Can you get one scrap, still working?"

"I can, but it still won't be cheap."

MacReady grunted, as though the words had stung.

"What sort of money do you reckon you're talking about?" he asked.

"A few hundred, at least. We'll have to get a second-hand engine imported from one of the scrap yards on the mainland."

"Jay-sus." MacReady felt dizzy, and leaned back against the car for support. Andy watched him carefully, wondering if the old fool was going to have a heart attack.

"Are you OK?"

"Just getting my breath, son. You've given me quite a start."

They waited whilst MacReady regained his composure. Every now and then, the old man would glance over at the youngster as though about to speak, but instead he would clear his throat loudly and say nothing. Eventually, though, he did speak.

"What do you think of a trade?" asked MacReady, his eyes narrowed.

"What sort of trade?"

"How about you fix up my car in return for something that wasn't money?"

Andy's face creased with a smile. He'd heard about the old man's legendary bartering skills, and now it was his turn to be subjected to them. It was a rite of passage, something that all of the islanders encountered at one time or another.

"I'm not sure," he said, shaking his head. "Money works well enough for me. I've a family to support, as you well know."

"Aye, and I'll bet you spend a pretty penny every week on your shopping, eh lad? I know how much food costs these days. How about I give you the cream of my catch, every week from here on in? Think of all that lovely fish you could be eating, all for free. You know how good fish is for a growing bairn – all those omega oils and all that. What do you say?"

Andy thought it over. The weekly shop did put a huge dent in his wages, and he did love eating fish. Plus one of the lads working in the scrap yard owed him a favour – he might even be able to get a replacement engine for the cost of a few beers. No need to let this old fool know that. So the trade would be mostly for the labour, a bit of welding and the like.

"Every week?" he asked. "The best of the catch?"

"Every week. Cod, mackerel, plaice. Sea bass when I get it. The biggest and the best. What do you say?"

Andy knew that Cathal would call him an idiot but there was a certain appeal to the trade. It would cut down on the shopping bill and one could never eat enough fresh fish. Especially if it was free. The wife and bairn might not be so keen on fish, but it'll keep me in lunches and supper, he thought.

"Go on then," he said. "But you'll have to pay for the parts – the trade's only for my labour."

"Aye, if you insist. Just one last little thing," added MacReady, his eyes twinkling beneath his bushy white eyebrows. "I'll pay for my MOT's with cash, as usual, but if you could keep your eye on the old beast and fix up anything minor for free, that'd seal the deal."

"Bloody hell. All right."

MacReady smiled. That was what he was really after – a deal to lock the little bastard into keeping the car in shape forever. He held out his hand and they shook.

A week later, MacReady was back on the road, the replacement engine purring away under the bonnet like a contented panther. After two days at sea, he returned with a decent load, and before he did anything else, he sorted out a plastic crate full of the best fish and packed it with ice. He drove down to MacDuff autos and handed the crate over to Andy, who looked ecstatic with the bounty.

Week in, week out, MacReady returned from the sea and sorted out the best of the catch and packed it into a crate for Andy, who accepted it gratefully. It was a very pleasant deal for everyone. If the trip had been a good one, MacReady would take a second crate to the market and sell from his stall, and any money he made would be added to the pile beneath his mattress. Less money than usual, which he didn't appreciate, but when he thought that his car problems were now effectively over, he felt a little better.

This continued for months.

The car had been in tip-top shape – as much as an old banger like that could be – ever since Andy had repaired it. Nothing else had gone wrong, and MacReady began to feel a bit short-changed, as though Andy hadn't done anything additional within the terms of their agreement.

One day, in a fit of miserableness that was low even for MacReady, he sat down at his kitchen table and worked out how much giving away all of this fish was costing him. With a pencil and a scrap of paper, he worked out how much he could have sold the fish that had so far been given to Andy for free. Nigh on five hundred pounds at top prices, perhaps enough to have paid for the car repairs and be left with no obligation at the end of it.

From that point on, every time MacReady drove down to MacDuff Auto Repairs with a crate full of fish, he felt anger welling up inside him, strong enough to give him an attack of bile. Each week, it got a little bit worse. Andy would accept the fish, seemingly oblivious to the old man's distress, and MacReady would drive home, cursing all the way.

Another two months passed by. After one particularly rough trip at sea, MacReady sat at his kitchen table, fuming, devastated that he'd have to keep on handing over fish to the manky little bastard of a mechanic. He knew he'd made a huge mistake in trying to save a few pounds. He wanted to cancel their agreement, but couldn't see any way out of it without the whole island eventually finding out that he'd broken his word.

Instead, he took the best of the catch to market and sold it off. Afterwards, he drove down to MacDuff Auto Repairs and handed Andy whatever was unsold. A couple of undersized cod, some rockling, goby and the odd weever – an ugly fish that didn't taste particularly nice and needed more work to make into an enjoyable meal.

"There's not so much of the good stuff around at the moment," MacReady explained. "Those bloody Norweigans are taking it all."

Week in, week out this continued. As the days grew a little hotter, by the time the market was over the unsold fish was starting to get a little smelly, the ice having melted hours before. MacReady would begrudgingly spend a pound at the local supermarket for a bag of ice to scatter across the top but it did little to mask the smell.

Once, Andy made a comment about it.

"It's just the crate," snapped MacReady. "I'll give it a swill, if you like."

Each time he saw him, Andy looked a little bit the worse for wear. As though a cumulative effect of eating slightly off fish was having a detrimental effect on his health. About six or seven months after the agreement had started, MacReady delivered his crate to find Cathal talking with Andy's wife. MacReady observed them for a few moments. They looked awfully comfortable with each other.

"Is Andy here?" he asked, interrupting them

Cathal coughed, clearing his throat. He looked as guilty as Judas.

"No," he said, "he's ill."

"Anything serious?"

"Scombroid poisoning, with a dose of salmonella thrown in for good measure. It better not be your bloody fish!"

"How fucking DARE you!" snapped MacReady, feigning outrage.

"I'm sorry," said Cathal, immediately backing down. MacReady slammed the crate down onto the floor and stormed out of the garage.

A week later, whilst drinking in The Swan, he heard the news that Andy was dead. Weakened by the scombroid, the Salmonella had unexpectedly finished him off.

The funeral was on a Friday, and most of the islanders attended, including MacReady. The church was full, and afterwards a large contingent of mourners made their way into the graveyard and watched in silence as the coffin was lowered into a hole in the ground. His young widow stood weeping, holding their baby girl. Cathal stood next to them, his arm around the widow in a comforting gesture. He threw an odd, occasional glance at MacReady, partly accusing and partly, MacReady thought, grateful.

It looked like Cathal, the lonely brother MacDuff, had inherited an instant family.

After the funeral was over, MacReady walked down the narrow road a little while, to where he'd parked his car, half on and half off the verge. Clambering inside, he started the engine and gently lowered the vehicle fully onto the tarmac. At the bottom of the hill, where a T-junction sent the road west towards MacReady's house, and east towards the town, MacReady touched his brakes to bring the car to a halt and found that nothing happened. Further pressure on the brake pedal had no effect. The car continued straight across the junction and ploughed into a low wall on the opposite side.

Shaken, he clambered out of the car and surveyed the damage. The bonnet was badly crumpled, and it looked like the front axle had snapped.

MacReady stood there with his hands on his hips. Nobody else was around. The bleak, empty landscape stretched off in all directions.

It started to rain.

"Bastard!" said MacReady.

He started the long walk home.

# MR X

It came to be known as the Christmas Day Slaughter. A family of four, stabbed with the knife they were using to carve up the turkey. A stack of newly opened presents strewn around the lounge, covered in blood. The furniture, the walls, even the ceiling – all streaked with crimson. A front door kicked in, signs of a forced entry. A mother and her two little girls, murdered.

The father, the husband... the only survivor.

Emerging from a coma after three months, the father is questioned by police. The incident, faded in the minds of newspaper readers, gets fresh life and hits the headlines again. The Christmas Day Slaughter. Can he remember anything? Does he have any idea why a stranger would want to murder his family?

He remembers nothing. Not the days preceding the incident, not the horror of the attack. When the police tell him the details, trying to force the memories to return, he learns again of their terrible injuries. He breaks down, and the doctors ask the police to leave. Come back when he's feeling better, they say.

He never will feel better, but they'll come back anyway.

Fripp enters the nondescript building and climbs the steep staircase. At the top is a door, inset with a small window, and a button. He presses the button and waits. Presently, a serious face peers through the window and looks him over. Fripp holds up a small blue card. The door is opened.

He enters the Pandemonium Club.

Inside, no expense has been spared with the fixtures and fittings. Every inch reeks of opulence, from the crystal chandeliers to the hardwood lining the walls. It is a gentlemen's club, and no women are allowed to pass through the door. Men wander around, dressed in black suits, holding wine glasses and talking quietly amongst themselves.

He walks around, searching the rooms until he finds what he's looking for. Alone, a man sits at a table by the window, reading a battered, antique book. He recognises the man from his picture in the newspapers.

"Professor Cardew?" he asks.

The other man looks up and nods.

"James Fripp," he says, stepping forward.

"Can I help you?"

"I very much hope so. I would like to offer you a proposition."

Cardew looks him over. He closes the book and places it to one side. He beckons him to sit.

"Go on," says Cardew.

"I have money," says Fripp. "As much as it takes."

"I don't doubt that, if they let you join the club," says Cardew, a flicker of disgust on his face.

"It's not as if I can take it with me."

The attempt at humour falls flat. Cardew lets slip a heavy breath of irritation. "What is it that you want?" he asks.

"I want you to build me a time machine."

Cardew stares at him for a few seconds and then hoots with laughter.

"I know you can do it," says Fripp, his voice quiet but bristling with anger. "I've seen what you can do. I read about your wormhole, the thing you put into space. I know about the other professor – Carr, wasn't it? I know how you made him disappear."

"Who told you that?" growls Cardew, his fists clenching.

"There are no secrets here," says Fripp, gesturing towards the rest of the club. "Everybody knows everybody else's business, isn't that right? Isn't that how this all works?"

"So it would seem."

"I have more than enough money to pay you. You can have everything I own, if that's what you require."

Cardew's face turns dark. He sits and studies the man before him. Obviously not an academic but one of the new intake that bought their way in. Standards were slipping. There was a time when you had to be a special sort of person to become a member of the Pandemonium Club, one with the ability to change the world in some way. It was an institution that had survived for hundreds of years, all but unknown to the common man. And now it was going rotten from the inside out by the corrupting force of money. Prime Ministers, men of power, Nobel prize winners and even royalty were the core of the institution, forging a network of links behind the scenes and influencing the way the world went about its business. Now, they were letting in anyone who could buy a membership, regardless of their talents. They were even letting the bloody Freemasons in.

"I'm not interested," says Cardew, returning to his book.

Fripp startles him by taking a firm grip of his arm.

"Hear me out," says Fripp, his eyes flashing with anger. For the first time, Cardew feels like he isn't the one in control of this situation. There's something about Fripp that makes him nervous. The fierceness of his resolve, the hatred and the anger in his voice, and in his eyes.

"Go on," says Cardew.

A man wakes up in a white room, harshly illuminated by spot lights embedded into the walls. He is alone. He is naked. He tries to remember how he got here, what events led to this place. He remembers nothing, not even his own name. He is a blank canvas, a man with no history.

He stands and looks for an exit.

A voice disturbs him, seeming to come from everywhere at once. The room is filled with it.

"Your family has been murdered," says the voice. He can feel it reverberating in his bones. "You have no one left. Your life has been destroyed. I am the only one that can help you now."

"Who are you?" shouts the man. "Where am I?"

A wall fills with the projected image of a well dressed figure.

"This is the man who killed your family," continues the voice. "I can help you find him. I can give you the tools to take your revenge."

A section of a different wall falls outwards to form a shelf. On it are a bundle of clothes. The man walks across and examines them. Underwear, black trousers and a black shirt. Cold, shivering, he quickly dresses himself. There is a long black coat. A fedora hat. A pair of sunglasses. He dresses and puts on the sunglasses, finding some relief from the harsh lighting. There is a gun, with a photograph next to it. The same photograph that is projected onto the wall. He picks both items up.

"Find him," says the voice. "Find him and kill him."

The lights are extinguished and he stands in a room that is perfectly dark. Thin strands of blue lightning creep up the walls, filling the air with a sizzling sound. A deep thrumming noise begins to shake the floor. *I remember this,* thinks the man. *This has happened before.* He screams as the blue lightning flickers out from the walls and wraps itself around his body. He quickly becomes surrounded by it, enveloped by it. The noise and the lightning build to a crescendo and at the end of it, the man is no longer there.

The room is empty once more.

"He must remember nothing of his former life," says Fripp. "Only the search is important now. He must live from moment to moment, his only focus on finding the person in the photograph. Can you make that possible?"

"Anything is possible," says the Hypnotist.

"He must only remember everything when certain words have been spoken. And then I want all of it to come back."

"Just like you said. You're certain you have the right man?"

"I know it's him," says Fripp, his brow creasing with anger.

"This would be a horrendous thing for someone to go through if they were innocent."

"It *must* be a living nightmare. For what he's taken.... It's the only punishment."

"Wouldn't it just be easier to kill him?"

"No, he must suffer something worse than death."

"This will do it," says the Hypnotist, smiling.

"And you will need to record something I can replay, every time he remembers. When he returns. I'll need to reset his mind. Before it begins again."

"I can do that. It's not a problem."

The man in the fedora hat looks around. He is standing in a strange street, unknown to him. He has no recollection of arriving there. He looks down at himself, at the clothes he wears. The long black coat, the black trousers. These are not his normal clothes, but he doesn't know why he knows this. He can feel the hat on his head, and lifts it off to inspect it. He searches the coat pockets, deep enough to plunge his hands in above the wrists. He pulls out a gun and quickly replaces it.

He pulls out a photograph.

Now he remembers, if only a little. *This is the man who murdered my family,* he thinks. *I will find him and I will kill him.*

He starts walking. The streets are empty. A chorus of young voices are shouting from behind a fence and he follows it to the entrance of a school. Children are playing a football match and their parents stand around the touchlines.

He walks over and holds up the photograph to the first adult he comes to.

"Excuse me," he says. "Do you recognise the man in this picture?"

"I will help you," says Cardew. "But it won't be cheap. And there's one obvious question I need you to answer."

"Which is?"

"Why hasn't be been arrested? After everything you told me – the violence, the abuse – surely he's the prime suspect? We can't go near him if the authorities are interested in him. For all I know, he could be under surveillance."

Fripp shakes his head.

"Caroline never reported any of it. I kept asking her to, but she wouldn't listen. There is no official record of abuse."

"You didn't mention it yourself?"

"I thought about it. When they spoke to me, I almost came out with it. It would have been my word against his, of course, and there was no way of knowing they'd believe me. Even if they did, and he was found guilty, he would've been sent to prison and lived a comfortable existence for the next however-many-years until they let him back out again."

"You don't have much confidence in the judicial system?"

Fripp laughs, bitterly. "Does *anyone*? These people are incarcerated but they only lose their freedom of movement. They can still find some enjoyment in their existence. The prisons no longer seem to operate under a punishment culture, more a rehabilitative one. I don't want to see the bastard rehabilitated – I want him punished. I decided to deal with him myself, once the police had stopped sniffing around."

Cardew thinks for a moment.

"So they think he's a victim," he says.

"Last time I spoke to the police, they told me they were looking for an intruder."

"But you say he ended the episode by stabbing himself?"

"Yes. What of it?"

"There are ways of revealing this – the angle of blade penetration and so on."

"If he had died, and they did an autopsy, then maybe. I don't know."

"Maybe," says Cardew, thinking it over. Fripp waits, inhaling the scents of the club – stale tobacco mixed with furniture polish, and a hint of citrus coming from the short glass vases of pot-pourri scattered around. Eventually, Cardew speaks again.

"Very well. But we will need help."

Fripp leans back in his chair and feels his body relax. Giving his account to Cardew was more exhausting than he'd anticipated. The feelings are still raw. His eyes are glazed with tears.

"What sort of help?" he asks.

"Mind control. For your plan to succeed, and keep succeeding, the subject will have to be programmed before the first event."

"And you know somebody that can do it?"

"He's a member of this club. One that has real power. His company creates software that plugs into corporate systems and distributes mind control messages through audio channels. He's moving into television and film. Pretty soon, we'll have a world filled with mindless automatons, doing the bidding of a few."

"And he will help with this?"

"I think so. If I ask him."

"I don't know how to thank you."

"You don't have to thank me. You just have to pay me."

Langton Matravers finishes his coffee and slams the empty mug down onto the kitchen worktop. He can feel his temper getting out of control again, feel the blood beginning to boil in his veins. He storms out into the hallway and shouts up the stairs.

"Will you get a move on? I'm going to be late!"

Caroline appears at the top of the stairs, looking harassed.

"Effie's just brushing her teeth."

"And Dawn?" he snaps.

"Putting on her uniform."

"Well, just hurry them up."

She disappears and he returns to the kitchen to wait. He forces himself to take a few deep breaths. Now would not be a good time to lose his temper. The last time, so Caroline had told him, he had punched her so hard he'd knocked one of her teeth out. He remembered nothing. Every time he lost control, a new gap appeared in his memory. He needed help, he knew that.

The children hurry down the stairs and wait by the front door. They throw furtive glances at him, as though afraid. Caroline joins them and tries her best to smile. Even down the length of the hallway, he can see the fear in her eyes. He walks towards them and, as he reaches up for his coat, Caroline flinches.

Fripp listens to his daughter and feels his own rage building. The physical and mental abuse. The way the children are in danger. He feels like driving over to Langton's place of work and dragging him outside to administer a beating so severe he'd never lay a finger on his family ever again. But Fripp is too old for that kind of thing. A few years ago, maybe.

"It's not safe for you to stay," he says. "Or the children."

"He's promised never to hurt us again."

"And how many times have we heard that?"

"Dad, please. You're not helping."

"What do you want me to say? Do you want me to pretend that everything's normal? To just accept that my daughter and my grandchildren are victims of domestic abuse and carry on and smile as though nothing's happening?"

Caroline wipes tears away from her eyes and stares at the floor for a few moments.

"I don't know…." she says in a quiet voice.

"He'll keep doing it," says Fripp, unable to hide the anger in his voice. "And it'll get worse. And then, one day, he'll end up killing you."

"Stop being so dramatic, Dad."

"Listen to yourself. It's like you're in some sort of denial."

"I love him! He wasn't always like this. You should see him after he calms down… he cries like a baby and promises he'll never do it again. I believe him."

"Carrie….."

"We'll get back to normal, you'll see."

The white van pulls up outside the Fripp residence and two men clamber out. After getting their toolbags from the back, they ring the doorbell and wait. Presently, the door is opened by a man in a beige leisure suit.

"Morning Mr Fripp!" they chime.

"Good morning," he says, stepping aside to let them in. They are led through a hallway, past the lounge and dining room, and into the kitchen. A new annexe is nearing completion at the far end of the house. They walk inside and look around.

"Should be just another day or two now," says Charlie.

"Just the finishing touches," says Dave, nodding.

"Excellent," says Fripp, smiling.

They are interrupted by the loud ringtone of Charlie's mobile phone. Notes from Grieg's *'In the Hall of the Mountain King'* bounce around the freshly plastered walls of the extension. There are gaps in the plaster, waiting for some kinds of fitting. There are no windows. In the corner are a couple of tins of white paint and some sealed boxes. Charlie excuses himself for a moment and answers the call.

"Hello Mr Knapp," he says brightly. He listens for a few moments before speaking again. "Not a problem. Yes, hopefully tomorrow afternoon, the day after at the latest. OK then. Bye."

Fripp looks over with a curious expression on his face.

"Was that *John* Knapp?" he asks.

"It was, yeah. Got a leak in his swimming pool. You know him, then?"

"We're members of the same club," says Fripp.

"Golf?" asks Dave.

"More of a gentlemen's club."

"Say no more," says Dave, doing a passable Eric Idle impersonation.

"So," says Charlie, putting his phone away, "you want the lights and speakers fitting, then a kind of ledge-stroke-table in the wall here?"

"Yes."

"The projector goes up top and then we'll fit and cover those circuit board things before everything gets painted white – is that right?"

"That's correct," says Fripp. "And the circuit wires come through to the kitchen."

"Are we fitting something on the other end?"

"No, I have a friend who will attend to that."

"Fair enough."

"And remember not to put any handles or markers on the inside of the door. I want the walls to blend."

"Not a problem," says Charlie.

"Well, I'll leave you to it," says Fripp.

After he's gone, Charlie looks at Dave and smiles.

"Miserable old bugger could offer to make us a cuppa. I could murder a coffee."

"Whose turn is it to walk to Costa Coffee?"

"Mine. Do you want to get started on fitting the lights? I'll be back in twenty minutes."

Before he leaves, Charlie takes out his wallet and checks the contents.

"Spot me a tenner, will you Dave? Looks like the missus has rifled my cash."

"No worries."

Dave pulls out his wallet and opens it. A piece of paper flutters out and drifts across the room to land at Charlie's feet. He picks it up and gives it a cursory inspection.

"A Holiday Inn receipt, Dave?"

Dave coughs and looks a little embarrassed.

"Hand it over, Charlie."

"You been arguing with the missus again?"

"Something like that."

"This is for last Tuesday. You could have stayed over at mine. The missus was out for the night at an old college friend's, playing bridge or whatever it is that they get up to. We could've had a few beers."

"Thanks, Charlie. It's all good now though."

Charlie hands over the slip of paper and smiles. He walks around to the garden gate, heading for the nearby shopping precinct. Dave watches him go and then crumples the receipt before stuffing it into his pocket. *That was a close one,* he thinks. *One day, he'll put two and two together.*

Fripp sits in his kitchen, a half full tumbler of whisky on the counter in front of him. Next to it is a small electronic Dictaphone. He takes a sip of the whisky and clears his throat. Reaching down, he picks up the Dictaphone and presses the record button.

"Your family has been murdered," he says. "You have no one left. Your life has been destroyed. I am the only one that can help you now."

He presses the button again, halting the recording. He should have let the Hypnotist take care of this aspect of the plan. Matravers was going to recognise his voice and he'd begin to understand what was happening to him. Fripp finishes off the drink and deletes the recording before starting again, this time in a deeper voice.

"Your family has been murdered. You have no one left. Your life has been destroyed. I am the only one that can help you now." He pauses for a moment before continuing. "This is the man who killed your family. I can help you find him. I can give you the tools to take your revenge."

He presses the button and flicks through the menu to replay this latest attempt. He listens as the cold words echo around the kitchen.

"Do you recognise the man in this picture?"

The woman studies the photograph for a moment before handing it back.

"I'm sorry," she says, "I don't." She picks up her shopping bags and walks away. The figure in the black coat watches her go. He feels his shoulders slump in despair. She was the fiftieth person he'd asked, just another in a long line of people who are unable to help.

He couldn't give up. The need to find the man in the photograph is all he can think about. Every moment is consumed by the desire to hunt him down. He looks around at the interior of the mall, a huge complex swarming with people. One of them must know who is in the picture.

He approaches a short, stocky woman and holds up the photo.

"Do you recognise the man in this picture?" he asks.

The woman leans forward for a better look and squints. After a moment, she leans back and looks at him.

"Can you take off your hat?" she asks.

"My hat?"

"Yeah. Let me get a better look at you."

He obliges and waits.

"It's you," she says.

At the sound of those words, images fire up in front of his vision, projected somehow onto the inside of the lenses of his sunglasses. He sees his dead wife lying on the floor in a pool of blood, her body ravaged by stab wounds. The image is replaced with another, this time of his daughter Effie, her throat slit. She's still wearing a paper crown from a Christmas cracker, the gold foil splattered with her blood. There's a picture of Dawn, his little angel. What he sees makes him shake with a sudden sob of anguish. The pictures are replaced by others, all equally as grisly.

And he *remembers*.

He remembers killing his family, hacking them to pieces with a large knife. He remembers coming to his senses and realising what he'd done. Searching for a way to undo the carnage. He remembers opening the front door and closing it behind himself before turning around and kicking it through in the hope that it will look like an intruder has forced his way in.

Finally, he remembers plunging the knife into himself, over and over before collapsing.

So he was the murderer. All of this time spent searching for himself. He remembers the gun in his coat pocket and pulls it out. As the woman before him screams in horror, he raises it to his temple and pulls the trigger.

The world is instantly consumed by darkness.

As he exits the house, closing the new front door behind himself, he's approached by two men in dark clothing. They are both wearing beeny hats and look like hired muscle.

"Langton Matravers?" asks one.

"Who's asking?" he says, and before he knows what's happening the man who asked his name throws a punch and sends him reeling. A follow-up punch renders him senseless. Unconscious, he's picked up by the men and carried to a battered, pale yellow transit van. They open the rear doors and throw him inside. One climbs in after him and closes the door. He secures Matravers' wrists and ankles with cable ties, and tears off a strip of duct tape to cover his mouth.

Shortly after, the van pulls up alongside the Fripp house. After a brief check to see nobody is looking, they drag the still unconscious Matravers from the van and carry him through to the new extension. They lay him on the floor and leave.

Fripp is waiting, along with Cardew and the Hypnotist.

"This is ground zero," says Cardew. "Where it all begins."

A muddy field is being used as a car park. Half of it has been covered with tarmac, and the unfinished work looks a mess. To the side, a hot dog stand squats, taped off and out of business. The man in the black coat and fedora hat walks up to people, holding up a photograph. Nobody can help. He feels his shoulders slump with despair.

He comes to a young man and asks the question. Always the same question.

"It's you," says the young man. "Even without the hat and glasses, I can tell it's you."

Moments later, the man in the black coat and fedora hat produces a gun, raises it to his temple and pulls the trigger.

"So it's a real gun?" asks Fripp, turning the revolver over in his hands.

"It is," says Cardew, nodding. "With a single bullet. Once he hears the trigger phrase, he'll only need the one."

"And you say it's actually a part of the time machine?"

Cardew nods again.

"This gun is more than just a way of firing a bullet – once it's fired, as well as doing the obvious, it also remotely initiates the recall system back in the charge room. It's all connected – the gun, the hat, the coat, the sunglasses – it's all a way of getting him to carry around this part of the machine without him knowing it."

"I see," says Fripp. "So blowing his brains out can be undone, every time?"

"Of course. The whole thing would be pointless if he could only kill himself once. The firing of the gun is the end of the loop. At the beginning of the loop, he will be intact."

"Back at the charge room?"

"Yes. He won't know it but there will be circuitry sewn into the clothing. The hat will act as a GPS, so he can be constantly tracked until the moment the gun is fired and he's brought back to your house. The sunglasses will, upon hearing the trigger phrase, bombard him with images from the crime scene and bring back his memories. The memories lead to the gun. The coat contains components that are integral to the operation of the machine. Everything is tied together."

"And when he's blown his brains out? The machine puts him back together again, is that right?"

"Strictly speaking, it's not a time machine," explains Cardew, using the tone of voice he usually reserves for his slower university students. "The equipment will generate a variable time loop, a closed circuit that repeats once the gun has been fired. Wherever he is, he'll be brought back to this room intact, ready for the priming sequence to begin again. This will go on forever, or until you think he's had enough."

"Forever isn't long enough."

"That's your prerogative. How are you going to get him to come here, initially?"

"I know a couple of bruisers that will help me out," says Fripp. "I'll make sure the Hypnotist is with us. How long before you're ready?"

"I have a couple of builders coming to finish off the charge room tomorrow."

"Have they any idea what they're putting together?"

"They think it's a cinema room."

Cardew smiles.

"Let me know when they're finished. I have the control panel, so once they're done I can wire that up to the system and we should be ready to begin."

It is Fripp's turn to smile. He can't wait to get started.

Caroline Matravers carries the turkey through to the lounge and places the tray onto a raised metal grille. Langton sits in silence, watching her. She sits at the end of the table, opposite her husband, the children on either side. Around the room, opened presents lie stacked up in little piles. The girls, innocent to the tension between their parents, have had a wonderful morning, rising early and pulling their mother out of bed to come downstairs and open their presents.

Langton had remained in bed, listening to their laughter, angry that they were keeping him awake. It wasn't even seven o'clock before the girls rushed in and woke them up. At eight, unable to get back to sleep, he'd got out of bed and dressed. He went downstairs, straight to the kitchen, and opened a bottle of wine. He downed a large glass before refilling it.

Six hours later, as he sat before the feast Caroline had patiently spent the rest of the morning preparing, his head was pounding and he struggled to contain his anger. All this noise! Children squealing, cutlery clanking, the television blaring away in the corner of the room. Everybody moving, nobody staying still, not even for a minute.

"Shall I carve the turkey?" asks Caroline.

"What?" he says, irritated beyond belief. All he wants to do is go somewhere and lie down. Somewhere far away, where there are no children, no bitch of a wife to keep nagging him. Somewhere where the endless bills can't reach him, where he can escape the relentless pressure, the endless grind of crawling through each new day his world brings. How did his life turn out this way? Bogged down with a family of cretins, swamped with debt, living a life he loathed? His head swam, anger pulsing in black waves, his skull feeling like it was about to explode.

"Langton? Shall I carve the turkey?" asks his wife in a nervous voice.

He looks at her. He reaches out for the carving knife. He stands there, gently swaying for a moment, trying to clear his mind.

*Do it!* says a voice inside his head. *Kill them.*

His grip tightens on the handle of the knife.

He wakes up naked, in a room he doesn't recognise. His head pounds and he reaches up to dab at a tender spot around his jaw. The pain makes him wince.

"Hello, Langton," says a voice.

He turns around and sees a man sitting on a stool, watching him.

"What is this?" asks Langton, standing up. "Where am I?"

"You are at the dawn of a new life," says the man.

Langton looks around the room, searching for a way out. There doesn't appear to be a door. The room is white, with no furniture apart from the stool.

"What the fuck is going on?" he asks.

"Relax, Langton," says the man with the soothing voice. Just hearing him speak those two words makes some of the tension leave his body.

"What do you want?"

"I want you to empty your mind of all thought."

"Why? Let me out of here. I don't know what this is but I'm warning you-"

"Please, Langton. Relax. Take a few deep breaths. Once you listen to what I have to say, you can go."

Langton feels himself relax. There is something about the man's voice that makes him want to listen. Something about his eyes that demands a calm silence.

"I want you to listen to my voice," says the man. "Nothing else matters. There is only my voice. Empty your mind of all thought."

On the other side of one of the walls, Fripp and Cardew stand in the kitchen, watching the Hypnotist go about his work on a small monitor. The sound has been muted. The Hypnotist warned that they shouldn't listen, in case they inadvertently start following the suggestions being made to Matravers.

Fifteen minutes pass, in which Fripp makes them both a cup of coffee and smokes a cigarette. During this time, they see Matravers become more and more relaxed, totally under the power and influence of the Hypnotist. Fripp knows roughly what is being said in that room. Matravers' mind is being wiped, cleared of all memories except for one – the day he killed his family. When the Hypnotist has finished, Matravers won't remember anything except the brutal murders, but even this will be buried.

Even this will only be recalled when Matravers hears the trigger phrase.

*It's you.*

He won't remember anything else from his personal history, or even his own name.

Langton Matravers will be a blank canvas.

Unknown to himself.

Mr X.

The Hypnotist will then begin the programming. He will instil an all-consuming urge to find a mystery man, the one who killed his family. Nothing else will matter. Only the search. And once the programming is complete, the Hypnotist will tell Matravers to fall asleep, and to wake only at the sound of the single toll of a bell.

When it's over, Matravers is lying on the floor, asleep. Fripp opens the door and they return to the kitchen. He nods at Cardew, who immediately begins pressing buttons on a small wall panel. A minute later, Cardew looks at Fripp.

"The loop is now open," he says. "Turn up the volume and listen."

They stand in silence. From the room next door comes the automated sound of a bell tolling. On the small monitor, they see Langton Matravers wake up and look around, wondering where he is. A recording of Fripp's voice begins.

"Your family has been murdered....."

It could be anywhere in the country, the starting co-ordinates are random. But they can be over-ridden. Sometimes, Fripp manually sets the co-ordinates and heads out in his car to meet him.

It's the same every time.

Fripp walks around until he spots the man in the fedora hat. The long black coat. The sunglasses. He watches him for a while, holding up a photograph to strangers, asking them the same question, over and over.

And, every time Fripp walks over, the man spots him and approaches.

Fripp cannot see the man's eyes behind the sunglasses, but he can hear the desperation in his voice. The need to find the man in the photograph is apparent in every tired gesture. Sometimes, Matravers can go for more than a week before someone sees the photograph for what it is.

"Do you recognise the man in this picture?" asks the man in black.

Fripp pauses, preparing himself to savour what comes next.

"It's you," he says at last.

# PLANET OF MANIACS

Oh, it's a disaster, there's no other explanation for it. An unmitigated, ten-star disaster on a scale never seen before, even taking into account Man's grand history of ineptitude since we became sentient beings.

And it's all my fault.

Well, almost all. The idiot who put a wormhole out there in space, about half a light year from Earth, also has to be accountable to some degree. I mean, I might have doomed us but he sped the process up.

I have two things going for me. One is that my great blunder remains undiscovered. The second is the fact that I am getting old, and I have no children - by the time the Mungotians arrive, I will most likely be dead.

The End War, if it comes, will happen without me.

Let me tell you about the Mungotians. They are a race of technologically advanced life forms that are moving across the universe leaving a trail of destroyed planets in their wake. We have never seen them, and don't even know whether their basic chemistry is carbon or silicone, but we know they are out there from the data collected by our interstellar telescopes. And we know they are heading more or less right for us. In just a few short years, they will reach our inner solar system and humans will have to fight to keep Earth from becoming just another ruined planet, yet another victim of this alien terror.

When the threat was acknowledged as very real, it was decided that an army needed to be built. Not born, and trained, because despite Earth having an abundance of bodies suitable for creating an army, the cost of sending them out from Terra Firma was too prohibitive. Fifteen billion people were already starving and dying of water-borne disease, and we couldn't even spare the money to keep them from perishing, let alone turn any of them into an advanced fighting force.

The world's best scientific minds met for a conference in Geneva, and the Hyper Soldier plan was hammered out over a matter of days. That may seem rather quick, but the plan needed to get started right away. We needed to implement the technology and create the fully-formed bodies necessary to fight on our behalf as a matter of urgency. Our new soldiers – our saviours – also needed to grow into adulthood, and needed years of training.

We selected the world's best soldier – a middle aged Afghan man with decades of combat experience, a man who had been a mercenary for most of his life. The Americans wanted one of their own, a gung-ho patriot bristling with their inane ideals and core values. The Chinese also wanted the honour of providing Soldier Zero, and a number of other countries also nominated men of their own. The men on the shortlist were invited to a facility buried beneath the Swiss mountains for physiological and psychological testing.

There was quite a hoo-ha. Even though the goal was to unite the planet against a single, common enemy, it was all we could do to keep the individual fighters on the shortlist from tearing each other apart. During the course of their military careers, each had killed dozens, sometimes hundreds of men from the other nominated countries. The political arguments were monumental, and threatened to derail the entire project. Even in the face of certain death, we were acting like schoolchildren.

Soldier Zero was chosen. Badr udeen Madina, a deeply religious man with a strong moral code. A freedom fighter, or a terrorist, depending on which side you viewed him from. When not killing his fellow humans, he was a loving patriarch, a man totally committed to his four wives, seventeen children and twelve grandchildren. He was as fit as a fiddle, lean and in better shape than men half his age. There were no serious medical issues, either present or looming. Despite his religious beliefs, he was otherwise a rational and intelligent person. He ticked the boxes necessary for spawning an army. One afternoon, when all of the other candidates had returned to their respective countries, he was given an empty plastic vial and instructions to fill it with semen. The results were put into cryo-storage, which is where I enter the story.

Let me state right now that I am a very capable administrator. Of the thousands of people that were ultimately involved in the Hyper Soldier program, I was no more than a tiny, tiny cog in the machine. Not even a cog, really. All I had to do was ensure that the sperm of Badr udeen Madina remained in cryo-stasis until it was time to launch. While my colleagues set up the mechanisms, built the hardware, tested the launch craft and finalised plans for terra-forming HSD-EX001 (a suitable planet that was about a quarter of the way between Earth and the best estimate location of the approaching Mungotians), I monitored the operating system of the storage facility and waited.

It was a phenomenally boring job. Our facility was little more than a couple of rooms in one corner of the overall project site, deep in the mountain. Sometimes, my boss was present, checking this and that, but mostly it was just me and the daily visit from 'Donk', the janitor. I had no idea what his real name was – he was Polish and spoke very little English, but he was the sort of man that kept himself to himself anyway and it's doubtful we would have conversed that much even if he were blessed with the full lexicon of my own language. He mopped the tiled floors, dusted here and there, cleaned out the toilets and occasionally grunted something in return whenever I wished him a good morning.

Of course, I had other duties – my entire job was not about keeping the Afghan's sperm in constant permafreeze, that could have been a fully automated process. As is the nature of such roles, I was involved in a great many projects, and had to compile monthly reports and statistical charts for all of them. On a grander scale, the 'Ark' project – also top secret – involved keeping the DNA of as much of the Earth's biodiversity in cryo-storage and monitoring the requests for partials to analyse on a global basis. I was essentially a shopkeeper, controlling inventory. If the end of the world ever came about, a new world could one day begin using the genetic materials stored in this mountain, whether that was on our own planet or another. So far, HSD-EX001 was the only planet yet discovered that was near enough to be practical (orbiting Proxima-Centauri, just over 4 light years away) and enough within a 'Goldilocks' zone to be viable (with some terra-forming).

The Hyper Soldier plan was fairly straightforward, as much as anything involving space can be. Atmosphere Bombs were launched at HSD-EX001, followed two years later by terra-forming biology and seed micro-payloads. No great machines needed to be built, everything could be done by nanobots and microbes. The entire apparatus needed to transform the planet into an environment capable of sustaining human life could be fitted into a medium sized removal van, and made for an affordable overall payload.

Madina's ejaculate contained just under a billion sperm. A sort of egg copying machine was created – I don't know the full details of how it works – which racked up a billion eggs ready for fertilisation. During transit, everything would remain frozen, until touchdown on HSD-EX001 (in forty separate locations), whereupon apparatus would unite each single sperm with a single egg and suck atmospheric nutrients into a polymer membrane before being spat out and left to gestate. After a five month gestation period, the foetuses would break through the membrane and would be left to crawl around looking for their own sustenance. This is not as fantastic as it might first sound. With an atmosphere and nitrogen rich soil, engineered and managed by the self-replicating nanobots and the spread of microbes across the planet surface, a variety of fruiting food sources would develop. It's factually correct to state that such a diet would be far superior to the diet currently consumed by more than 10 billion humans on our own planet.

After a further seven years, men would travel to HSD-EX001 to begin formal training. A billion young sons of Badr udeen Madina would be turned into an effective fighting force capable of defeating the Mungotians. There would be all military classes, and 3D printers would create equipment and the means to travel into interstellar space and fight the battle before it came anywhere near us.

Everything was progressing beautifully. The Atmosphere Bombs were launched on schedule and, two years later, the terra-forming biology. A deep space telescope relayed imagery back when the bombs exploded, and the Earth held it's breath until the dust cleared and spectroscopy readings confirmed the chemical chain reactions to have played out exactly as anticipated. Two years later, the terra-forming biology reached the planet and started to make the environment habitable. While this was happening, the final payload was prepped for launch.

All of this activity couldn't be kept a secret – even amateur astronomers were picking up significant disturbances on the surface of HSD-EX001, and the Hyper Soldier plan was finally made public. The threat of the Mungotians was revealed and the people of the Earth seemed to accept the plan as the right decision to deal with the approaching disaster. Humanity became united and the Earth entered a Golden Age of peace. Inevitably, Badr udeen Madina became a household name, a celebrity, and student walls the world over became emblazoned with pop art posters of his face. Despite all of the killing he'd committed over the years, during many wars with many different enemies, he was awarded the Nobel Peace Prize and feted for his services to humanity.

Unfortunately, the day before his sperm was due to be launched, I discovered an electronic fault in the storage facility. Despite the computer readings displaying a continued temperature well within the safety tolerance, when I physically had to move the frozen sperm into the launch module bay, I discovered that the stuff had thawed out and dried up years before and the sperm were all quite dead.

I could have admitted this, of course. There was a brief window where something could have been done, but I was more concerned about avoiding any sort of blame and keeping my name out of the newspapers. The fate of the world had just been sealed and it should have been something spotted with my manual checks. But, with the Ark project escalating, I had simply been too busy to properly attend to my duties. I though that Madina's sperm remaining frozen was a given, something reliably protected by the computer systems that governed this part of the facility.

I was in something of a quandary. I had to get a vial full of sperm into the payload bay, but I was so shaken by the discovery that there was no way I could have filled the vial myself. The only other person around was 'Donk', and I offered him fifty pounds to head off into the toilets and fill it with his junk. Ten minutes later, the deed was complete and I flash froze the sperm and handed it across to the payload engineers. Two days later, we launched.

During the next four years, as the final payload made its way to HSD-EX001 at just under light speed, something rather significant happened. 'Donk' – real name Pawel Soszynski – was arrested for a heinous series of crimes committed during the previous fifteen years that included rape, murder and cannibalism. Apparently, his favourite way of spending a Saturday night was to pick up a prostitute, subject them to a horrifying ordeal of rape and torture, kill them in the most horrific way imaginable and then partially eat the remains. He was caught during a routine traffic-stop where the police found a bone saw, a collection of bloodstained knives and a woman's foot in his hatchback. The man was a complete maniac. And a billion of his sperm were winging their way through space in order to build an army.

The next few years were rather tense for me. While the rest of the world, now united and in a previously unthinkable phase of openness and friendliness all celebrated this new age of humanitarianism, I lost weight, started taking medication for depression and watched the hair on my head turn grey, and then white. While Israelis and Palestinians danced on the Gaza Strip together, while Sinhalese hugged Tamil, while hardline Muslim clerics shook hands with fundamentalist Christians, I deteriorated into a reclusive mess, and slowly withdrew from human contact.

I watched as the news programmes – now all seemingly focused on our common, planet-wide goal of raising our army of saviours – beamed back footage from HSD-EX001 as the embryo distribution units landed at scattered locations and the mixing of sperm and eggs began. We saw images of polymer eggs being spat out onto the blossoming soil. Five months later, we saw the first proto-soldiers scratch their way out of the eggs and crawl around on the planet surface. There were parties from

Anchorage to Zanzibar, fireworks and revelry, and countless reaction shots of people weeping with happiness.

We all knew something was very wrong when the tiny little beings started attacking each other. When they were old enough to grow fingernails and teeth, they started clawing each other's eyes out. They crawled around, wild eyed, teeth gnashing, biting and eating, and the planet surface turned red with blood. The people that had once wept with joy now wept with horror. The overwhelming air of unity turned sour. Muslim attacked Christian. Singalese attacked Tamil. All of the old hatreds came back, more powerful than ever.

Wars broke out and the Earth was thrown into turmoil. It seemed that should the Mungotians ever arrive, they would find nothing left to destroy. Countries burned. Societies collapsed. Still the footage came back, sent from cameras in geostationary orbit around HSD-EX001. The Hyper Soldiers were children, running around wide eyed and screaming, tearing each other limb from limb. Mountains of dead bodies littered the landscape, piles of dead and rotting flesh. Each child, one of a billion, was a homicidal killing machine, a lunatic in a world of blood and death.

We had made a planet of maniacs.

**Afterward**

The failed plan was our only hope. And, regrettably, death did not come for me in those tense years before the Mungotians finally arrived. Shortly after poor Badr udeen Madina was hunted down and publicly slaughtered by an angry, baying crowd (all the while protesting his innocence), we started getting more and more data on the approaching Mungotians, and eventually they came close enough for us to get visuals. My God, their ships were enormous. Our scientists estimated that there were billions of these bastards on board.

It's a small comfort to know that our new army, had it not slaughtered itself, would not have been enough anyway.

They came, sending down their war robots to clear the way for their terra-forming machines. As the huge ships waited some distance from our planet, smaller invading vessels breached our atmosphere. Our attempts to shoot them down were futile. From the bellies of the ships came the enormous robotic ant-like *things* that terrorised the major cities and cut down anyone who tried to stop them. If their red laser beams of death didn't get you, their massive steel mandibles would tear you apart.

The newspapers, while they lasted, called these war machines 'Terrorzoids', whipping up the horrified population into a state of terror and despair.

The tv stations, while they lasted, reported on hasty preparations for the only plan humanity had left – to fight these alien scum with nuclear missiles. They screened information programmes, telling us to paint our windows white and hide under our kitchen tables until it was safe to emerge. Honestly, that didn't wash the first time around. Even in a major crisis, the government was still willing to treat us like idiots.

I stood on my doorstep and watched as our own bombs dropped down onto London, filling the sky with a blinding flash of light and then sending up great mushroom-shaped clouds of debris and radioactive material. I could see the carnage from over fifteen miles away.

There was nothing I could do – or any of us could do – to stop them. Even as our major cities were obliterated by our own hand, the Mungotians kept sending down their gigantic robotic ants and, eventually, their terra-forming machines.

And now I sit in the road and wait for my death. I ate my last can of tinned peaches this morning. The water supply has stopped. The air is filled with radioactive dust. I have developed a cough. All around, the country burns.

Where London once stood, giant machines are now drilling.

The insides of the Earth are rising up, into the sky.

There are no cars. No people. Except this one, approaching me now. Dressed in a long black coat, wearing sunglasses and a black fedora hat. If there's a figure that could possibly represent a survivor of the apocalypse, this is it. He walks towards me and reaches for something in his pocket.

It's a photograph. He holds it up in front of my face.

"Excuse me," he says in a sad, tired voice. "Do you recognise the man in this picture?"

# TINY WONDERS

# JAM

Nigel and Peter had always been competitive; it was a core feature in both of their personalities. At school, they were the two best runners, always taking the accolades at the annual sports day. One year Nigel would win, the next it would be Peter. Whenever one found an edge, it would spur the other one to better himself with improved results. This common desire to be the best brought them together, uniting them into becoming best friends.

After school, the desire to outdo each other continued into their adult lives. When Nigel found a pretty young girlfriend, Peter found a (trainee) catwalk model. When Peter gained a management position at a local newspaper, Nigel started up his own publishing company.

And so on.

On the launch day of the new Compact Disc player, Nigel blew a substantial sum of money on a new stereo system and spent the evening unpacking it and putting it together. At some point, Peter turned up and, over a few cans, they finished setting it up and put a disc in to listen to it.

Nigel speculated that this was probably the best that music would ever sound on a home stereo.

Peter shrugged and commented that it lacked the depth and resonance of vinyl.

"Resonance?" asked Nigel. "What the fuck are you talking about?"

Peter seemed not to be listening. His face had lit up. "Have you got any jam?" he asked.

"What, do you want a sandwich or something?"

"I read all about these CD things. They're supposed to be indestructible. You're supposed to be able to cover them in jam and they'll still play."

"That can't be right," said Nigel.

"Let's try it!"

"Don't be stupid. I'm not putting jam on my new Whitney CD."

Peter was already walking off towards the kitchen.

"Seriously," shouted Nigel, not happy about where this might be going.

Peter returned with a pot of raspberry jam.

"Come on, don't be a spoilsport," he said.

"Absolutely not," said Nigel.

Peter badgered Nigel until he eventually caved in. With mounting apprehension, Nigel watched as his friend covered the CD in jam and put it into the stereo. Peter pressed 'play' and they heard the disc start to spin. After a few clicking noises, the speakers gave out a weird burst of static and the display came up with 'ERROR'.

"I told you it wouldn't work," said Nigel.

He opened up the disc drawer and was horrified to discover that jam had been thrown all over the inside of the stereo. It never played another disc. The next day, when he took it back to the store, the cashier, and then the store Manager, told him that he had violated his warranty and they wouldn't be able to issue an exchange or a refund.

As he left, Nigel was sure they were laughing behind his back.

He was furious. Peter seemed to shrug the incident off. When Nigel got angry and brought it up one night, Peter said "You wanted to see it just as much as I did!" and they got into a big argument. After a while, a couple of months or so, the dust settled but Nigel couldn't get the incident out of his mind. And then, one day, he had an idea.

Peter had recently bought himself a new car. It was his pride and joy, and he could often be found washing and waxing it on his front drive, even when it was already clean and polished.

One night, when Peter was in bed, Nigel turned up with a recovery vehicle and loaded Peter's car onto the back of it. He drove to a disused factory unit, used a remote control to open the roller-shutter door, and drove inside. A man was waiting for him, standing next to a metal tank and a small pump on the back of a low-loader. All of this had taken quite a bit of arranging. Perhaps the hardest thing was convincing the manufacturer that he really did want three thousand litres of raspberry jam.

With a special bit, Nigel drilled a hole in the roof of Peter's car. After this was done, he placed a hose through the hole and nodded at the other man. Buttons were pressed. Switches were flicked. With a chugging racket that echoed around the otherwise empty unit, the pump started draining the metal tank. As they watched, Peter's car began filling with jam. Right to the brim it went, until not another spoonful could fit.

Nigel drove back to Peter's house and unloaded the car back onto the front drive.

The next day, a furious Peter stormed into Nigel's office and beat the shit out of him. It was so bad that Nigel had to go to hospital for a couple of days, and received treatment for broken ribs, a broken orbital bone and a fractured wrist.

This was the time when their friendship ended and became something else altogether. Friendliness festered and turned to hate. There was no contact and they both tried to move on with their lives.

But Peter couldn't let it go. Even though the car had been emptied and fully valeted, every time he got in it he could still smell raspberry jam. It drove sluggishly. It was not the same car. It had been ruined. He couldn't shake the thought that Nigel had got one over on him, had trumped him in the jam stakes. It was a stupid thought but one that nevertheless ate away at him and started to destroy his sanity.

One day, Peter's wife Julia told him that Nigel and his wife Stella had gone on holiday. The two women were still friends, despite their husband's absolute hatred of each other. Peter spent the next few hours making phone calls.

Just over a week later, after a long night-flight and a dawn taxi ride home from the airport, Nigel opened the front door of his house and was knocked over by a tidal wave of raspberry jam. Tons of the stuff spilled, and then slowly oozed, out of the house. Peter had filled it to the brim. Every room, even the attic, full of jam. Nigel slopped through the lounge, staring in disbelief. Everything was ruined – every appliance, every last bit of decoration, everything.

"I'm going to kill him," said Nigel, in a voice that showed he meant it.

It took Stella a full week to convince him otherwise. Whilst he returned to the business, she organised the clean-up operation and every night he came home to something that slowly began to resemble the house before the holiday. Thankfully, they claimed on their insurance and the Crown Prosecution Service opened a case file on Peter and began proceedings for malicious damage of property.

But this wasn't enough for Nigel. Dark, ugly thoughts filled his head. He couldn't let it go. His anger grew inside, a corrosive force that revealed itself in exterior ailments such as eczema and a spray of weeping spots across his forehead. It seemed that he could think of nothing else, that real life had faded behind a fuzzy black cloud of rage.

Time passed. Three months, then six. Peter and Julia had a baby boy and moved to a different area. Stella went over to see them. There was no mention of Nigel. Privately, Stella admitted to Julia that she was thinking of leaving him. This business with the jam had changed him. Julia said she thought the same thing about Peter, until the pregnancy.

Later, Stella suggested to Nigel that maybe it was time to forgive and forget. He exploded with rage and, for the first and last time, he struck her. She packed her bags and left that night. After smashing the house up, Nigel sat of the floor of the lounge and swigged down a third of a bottle of neat whisky.

And then he had another idea.

Peter will always remember the day he came home and found his wife and son, dead. They were laid out in the lounge, raspberry jam leaking from their eyeholes, their nostrils and their mouths. Later, the coroner would report that the tops of their heads had been drilled open, that their skulls had been excavated out and filled with jam.

He collapsed on top of them, howling.

It was an hour before he could even compose himself enough to call the police.

Nigel was tried and convicted for murder, and sentenced to life imprisonment. On his first day, at breakfast, he was given a metal tray and a ball of porridge was slopped into the recess. He looked up at the man serving him, a huge, bald mass of muscle with a spiderweb tattooed across his face.

"You want a bit of jam with that?" asked the man, nodding at a small jar on the counter.

"No, thank you," said Nigel. "I can't stand the stuff." With that, he found himself a seat and started eating the porridge. It was horrible.

## CHOLONGOV

Preparations for the festival had been underway for over a week. The village streets were thoroughly cleaned, the houses washed down and the kerbstones scrubbed. All of the cars had been removed to one of Marston's fields for the big day itself.

On the morning, bitterly cold and grey with cloud, the unlit fire baskets were set out along the High Street and the shops were shuttered. People stayed at home, their hearths blazing, until seven o'clock in the evening and, all at once, poured out in their costumes ready for the night to begin. The fire baskets were lit, bathing the street with a flickering, orange glow and filling the alleyways with moving shadows. From the nearby sea, a freezing fog rolled in.

Even though everybody wore a costume, the villagers were all recognisable to each other. The short, squat dragon was Mrs Beet (who had used the same costume for over forty years); the tall thin crow with a limp could only have been Marston the farmer; the two small penguins were Marlie and Wiskie Drover, the young twins who spoke their own language and laughed with a sound like magpies fighting. The costumes weren't for anonymity – they were just a part of the festival, and had always been worn.

Dressed like a turnip, after being convinced it would be a good idea (it wasn't, he knew that now he was sober), Cliff Dunge waddled along the High Street, his face bright red despite being covered up. He looked like a proper idiot – Jeff and Malkie would be taking the piss out of him for months after this. Still, he couldn't see the Cholongov girl being attracted to a turnip, so at least there was that.

Once a year, the Cholongov girl was wheeled down to one of the six villages owned by her family. It could be any of the villages, nobody knew for certain beforehand. Nobody knew how old she was but this ceremony had been happening every year for as long as anybody could remember. Some said – in whispers, in confiding tones – that it wasn't always the same distorted figure of a girl who was brought, that the Cholongovs spawned one for every generation. Some said they had been cursed.

Their arrival marked the culmination of each of the village festivals, though only one village would hold the final ceremony. Through her one good eye, she would watch the villagers dance, surrounded by the baskets of fire (now being swung on the end of poles, casting burning flakes of charcoal into the night sky), and the men would separate themselves off to one side and wait. Eventually, with an animal grunt of pain, she would raise one of her thin, grotesquely twisted arms and point. Whomever she pointed at would be her companion for the next twelve months.

Previous companions, upon returning to their villages, were never the same again. They came back with a haunted look on their faces. Billy Riddip had committed suicide after his turn, hanging himself from the old railway bridge. Jake Hidgen had gone mad and was carted off to the city, never to be seen again. Whatever happened up there, at the Big House, was never openly discussed but the villagers suspected many things, all of them unspeakably awful. It was fair to say that all of the men in the six villages, even the married ones (the Cholongov girl had no regard for the sanctity of the marriage vows), spent the weeks and even months leading up to the festival in a state of rising dread.

Cliff met up with Jeff and Malkie, the fog swirling around them as they greeted one another with childish insults. The pair ridiculed Cliff for agreeing to the terrible choice of costume and then, their faces tightening, walked back down the High Street. Jeff handed him a small metal hip flask and, after some considerable trouble getting it inside his costume so he could take a swig, Cliff handed it back. Despite being surrounded by laughing children and the general happenings of the festival, their mood was downbeat.

Should she come to their particular village, each knew that they might be chosen and be taken up to the Big House, away from family and friends for an entire year. Jeff felt sick to the bottom of his stomach just thinking about it. Malkie, although appalled by the idea, at least harboured a morbid curiosity as to what would actually happen up there, a subject he'd tried to broach with the others a few times before but they'd always gone very quiet and made it clear they didn't want to discuss it.

A procession of instrumentalists marched slowly along the High Street, the disjointed notes of music echoing off the buildings and spiralling into the cold night sky. People danced, strange and awkward figures in their costumes, and the swirling fog glowed and dimmed with the swinging of the fire baskets.

Cliff could feel his stomach tighten as the minutes went by. He was overcome with dread, a terror that tonight they would come to his village and it would be his turn. He'd never been more certain of anything. Like the rest of them, he was trapped, caught by the generous rental discounts offered to their tenants by the Cholongovs. There was no way any of them could afford to leave. It was a beautiful, if harsh part of the world they all called a home, marred only by the vague threat that one day the twisted finger of the Cholongov might point your way. It was a risk worth taking. The chances of being picked were fairly small.

The crowd suddenly went quiet and Cliff's stomach lurched as he realised the Cholongovs had arrived. Tonight, they had chosen his village, as he knew they would. He wanted to run but his legs had become weird and unresponsive, like the time he had stood on that ladder whilst helping his father to clean out the gutters one day.

"Jesus," said Malkie in a quiet voice. "Look at them."

Five figures slowly walked down the High Street, pushing something in a wheelchair before them. The five were dressed in black, with velvet cloaks hanging across their backs. A couple of them, maybe female, wore bonnets and their faces were covered with black lace. The men looked back at the crowd. Cliff couldn't tell how old they were - the flickering orange firelight seemed to play tricks with his vision. One moment these strange men looked a little older than him, and the next they looked so old that they might have been nearing a hundred. Their features seemed to drift and melt with each passing second and the sight fascinated Cliff, at least until one of the figures looked directly at him and it was like being drenched with a bucket of icy water. Those eyes locked with his for the briefest of moments but it felt like an eternity, and it felt as though his mind was being scoured. He wanted to scream but couldn't move, frozen to the spot in terror. The figure looked away and Cliff felt his body relax. He might have groaned, though he couldn't be sure.

The figures passed by and Cliff felt his gaze linger on the thing in the wheelchair, drawn to it despite himself. Beneath a collection of blankets and shawls, a figure writhed with soft mewing noises. He saw a hand, bony and clenched. He saw a foot, attached to a thin, grey leg at an impossible angle. He tore his gaze away, shivering.

"Fuck," said Jeff, simply.

The figures stopped outside the butcher's shop and waited. Beneath the blankets, the Cholongov girl moved and a small part of her face was revealed as she sniffed the air, perhaps catching the scent of old blood or meat. The band members, suddenly everywhere amongst the crowd, started to play and the villagers danced. Cliff and the others joined in, moving with the other bodies, self-conscious in their movements but too afraid to stop and draw attention to themselves.

After a few minutes, the music stopped and the men withdrew from the women and stood in a line on the opposite side of the street.

They waited, the night air around them utterly silent.

There was a palpable tension as the girl struggled to lift one arm.

Cliff was convinced that the girl was staring his way.

Groaning, she pointed.

# TWO SOLDIERS

It could have been any of the thousands of gods people have believed in, fought for, murdered for over the millenia. All of them, at some point, have had followers mad enough to spill blood on account of some made-up rules in some sacred book. It just so happens it was this god that came out on top, at this particular place, at this particular time.

Two of His soldiers, young men with histories of alienation, anger and a disenfranchisement with the society they found themselves in, surveyed the ruins of the battlefield. Essentially, most of the country they were in had been blown to smithereens in a determined effort to eradicate the unbelievers.

Unbelievers were dangerous. They used logic and facts. They used science as a tool to argue with. They tended to favour education and democracy. They gave women equal rights. All of these things meant nothing if you had the Faith. Faith, an unshakeable belief in something that has never been proven, that pits tribe against tribe depending upon the object of one's Faith. And, of course, all of those other Faiths are misguided. Deluded. Wrong. And wrong things cannot be allowed, they must be stamped out.

Bloodshed and violence are hardcoded into the very core of the belief system.

The countryside was stripped of vegetation, absent of living things. There were no trees, no bushes or shrubs, only occasional blackened, splintered trunks to show where once something grew. Nothing flew, nothing crawled. The landscape had been shelled so often and at such density that only a sea of churned up mud remained, visible in all directions as far as they eye could see. Up and down the country, every village, every town, every city looked like this now. Mud and rubble with no sign that people once lived there.

And the people? Cut down, shot to pieces, blown up and vaporised. Millions of them were now spread out across the country like so much fertilizer. Little remained intact, perhaps the odd large bone or a stray limb that had started to rot. Not even the rats came for them. Perhaps there were no rats left.

"We did it," said one of the soldiers, lighting up a hand-rolled cigarette. His hands were stained with months of mud, oil and blood, as were his face and clothes. The only clean looking things left on him were his glittering eyes, shiny and bright. A wisp of smoke drifted skyward.

"We got them all," said the other.

They stood in silence for another while, surveying the destruction. Shivering a little inside at the desolation.

"Now what?" asked the first.

"What do you mean?"

"Now we've killed the unbelievers, what are we going to do?"

"No idea. Rebuild, maybe?"

When the tens of millions of artillery shells rained down over the course of the war, it wasn't just buildings and people that were obliterated. Services, utilities, warehouses, hospitals, emergency response teams, farms, shops, offices – all of these things disappeared too, the entire infrastructure of the country. And this country was only one of dozens that had succumbed to the onslaught. There were more powerful countries that they hadn't yet destroyed but they had problems of their own for now. Different Faiths, different made-up rules, different reasons to subjugate and control the populations. But they would fall, one day. It was the will of the thing in the sky, made known through the stilted imaginations of dour men who studied the arcane, thoroughly invented field of theology.

But here and now, they had won. The unbelievers were dead. The educated, learned unbelievers who knew how to make things and keep society from collapsing. Engineers, doctors, teachers. People who could operate power stations and water treatment facilities. Surgeons who could save lives. Culinary greats who could make more than the basic slop needed to fuel a body. Visionaries who made films that examined what it means to be human. All of them gone, all dead now.

"I was thinking more of the next week or so. I'm so tired. I just want to relax and unwind."

"We'll have eternity to do that."

The first soldier finished his cigarette and flicked it down into the mud.

"Do you really believe that?"

"What are you saying?"

"Remember before we joined up," he said. "Where we grew up?"

"Yeah. And?"

"Don't you sometimes miss those days?"

"No I don't. They were shit. That's why we left."

"I know, I know. But remember that pub we used to go in? And that night we met those two girls?"

"Why are you thinking of that now?" asked the other, suspicious.

"I'm just saying."

"They were slags," said the other, angry.

"Yeah," said the first. "They were." The corners of his mouth turned up in the tiniest of smiles. "I had a great night. I think that was the last time I laughed. It was years ago."

The second soldier turned to face his old friend. "You shouldn't be talking like that," he said.

"I can't help it. Don't you feel it? Come on, I've known you since we were children. You must be feeling it."

"Feeling what, exactly?"

"Look at this. There's fuck all left. Of anything. Is that what He really wants?"

The second soldier's hand drifted unconsciously to rest on top of a handgun holstered in his waistband. "I'm telling you, you shouldn't be talking like that."

"There's only us here," said his friend. "Nobody can hear me."

"He can hear you."

"Ah, yeah. Of course." He looked up and searched the heavens with his glittering eyes. "Is this what you want?" he shouted at the sky. His friend backed away and drew the gun, pointing it at his friend. "What the fuck are you doing?" he asked.

"Have you lost your Faith?"

He sighed. Eyed the devastation, imagined his future.

"Yes," he answered simply.

Half a second later, his brains were fertilizer.

"Fucking unbelievers," snarled his old friend, holstering the gun before walking off towards the sunset.

# HEAVEN IS CLOSED

Samantha Willetts was what you would call 'a good Christian woman', always helping others and generally being as fine a person as she could be. She lived a selfless life, always putting herself out for those less fortunate. She volunteered at a homeless shelter, at the local charity shop and, time permitting, even put a few hours in at a soup kitchen at the weekends.

She donated a small amount of her weekly pension to good causes. Sometimes, she even suffered unnecessary hardship after donating more than she could afford whenever some international crisis resulted in celebrities appearing on her television asking for money.

She was a do-gooder, well-liked and respected.

So, when she was accidentally flattened by a road-sweeping vehicle one day, the shock in the local community was genuine. Hundreds turned out for her funeral. She would be missed, that much was certain.

Being quite dead, she missed out on seeing how much she would be missed. In the moments following her unfortunate squashing, her soul slipped from her mortal shell and ascended Heavenwards, up through the clouds until, with a dream-like quality saturating her every sense, she found herself standing before the Pearly Gates.

She waited patiently, peering through the bars at Heaven beyond. Not that she frequented such places but it seemed to look more like a nightclub than anything else. Presently, St Peter appeared.

"Yes, love?" he asked.

"I think you might be expecting me," she said, smiling sadly.

"Really? Name?"

"Samantha Willetts."

St Peter pulled a mobile phone from his robe and booted up an App. He scrolled through a few pages of text and shook his head.

As she waited, a new figure rose up and stood next to her. She turned to nod hello and saw, with some surprise, that Jimmy Saville was standing there. St Peter looked up from his phone.

"Jimmy!" he cried, opening the gates. "Come right in! We've been waiting for you!"

With a smile and a nod, Saville walked through and the gates were closed behind him.

"Sorry, love," said St Peter, turning away. "Heaven is closed."

"Really?" she asked, confused. "Surely there's been some sort of mistake!"

Sighing, St Peter turned back.

"That's what they all say," he said, more to himself than to Samantha.

"I've been a good Christian all my life," she said. "Always helping others, never harming anyone or anything."

"Well, there's your problem right there," said St Peter.

"I don't understand...."

"No, you people never do. Listen, Jimmy Saville's just come in.... I'm going to have to.... you know. Go. Get ready for the drop, love."

"Wait!" she cried.

"What?"

"I demand to be let in! This is what I was promised!"

"Sorry, but it ain't happening."

"Then I demand to speak to my maker!"

St Peter sighed again, clearly a little exasperated. He produced a small walkie-talkie from the folds of his robe and pressed a button.

"Yeah?" asked a voice.

"Send the Big Man out."

"He's a bit busy right now. You'll never guess who's just got here?"

"I know who's just got here, you fucking idiot! I let him in!"

"Oh yeah."

Samantha was quite appalled at the turn of phrase used by St Peter. She waited, dark thoughts creeping into her mind. This didn't seem at all right.

Presently, God came down the stairs and walked across to the gates. He was surrounded by a posse of hangers-on. She recognised some of their faces. Saddam Hussein. Kim Jung Il. Fred West. Myra Hindley. George Sanders, her old solicitor. Osama Bin Laden! What were they all doing here?!

She stared at them, open-mouthed.

"What is it?" asked God, irritatedly.

"She wants to come in," said St Peter, pointing.

God waved a hand at the others, excusing Himself, and walked over. For the first time, Samantha noticed how He seemed to exude a soft, radiant light. He was more beautiful than anything she could have imagined.

"Well?" asked God, staring at her.

"I'm so sorry to be disturbing you, but...." She stopped talking, unable to find the words. None of this made any sense. What was He doing with these evil people?

"Look," said God, His face reddening with anger. "You've already been told you're not coming in. What more is there to say?"

"But... but I deserve to come in!"

"Do you," said God, although it wasn't really a question. "Tell me, how many have you killed?"

"Killed? I haven't killed anybody! I don't know what you mean."

"Always the same," snapped God. "Don't you people read the Old Testament any more? Don't you see how much I love killing? Didn't you read how I once sent two bears out to kill forty-two children for calling one of my messengers 'baldy'? Or how I killed a man for touching the Ark of the Covenant when he attempted to stop it falling from a donkey? Or any of the millions I smited? Ah, those were the days!"

God's eyes glazed over with the memory of all that lovely smiting.

"But you're a loving God!" said Samantha, close to tears.

"I'm a jealous, monstrous bastard and don't you forget it!" snapped God. "These guys get it," He said, gesturing behind Himself. He turned and walked away.

St Peter shrugged apologetically and clapped his hands, twice.

Immediately, Samantha plummeted like a stone, down through the clouds, down through the Earth's crust, deeper and deeper until the world around her grew unbearably hot and the screams of billions filled her ears. She saw a Hell of brimstone and fire, and all manner of twisted perversions of human misery.

She wandered this place for the rest of eternity. Early on, she saw somebody else she recognised and crawled through the flames and putrid dog shit until she was close enough to speak. But Mother Teresa wasn't listening. Her limbs aflame, she ignored Samantha and bumbled about whilst repeating the same phrase, over and over:

"I had it all so wrong.... so wrong."

# THE WOOLLY SNIRKLEBEAST

They say the woolly snirklebeast is a heartless predator with no redeeming qualities but some would try to eloquently argue that this isn't entirely a fair summation. The creature, with its two rows of dagger-like teeth and black eyes reminiscent of a great white shark, is a merciless hunter and pretty much anything it decides to eat will not escape (including the odd human). In their world, they are apex predators. But dominating the food chain is more of a delicate balancing act than one would suppose.

Remove the woolly snirklebeast from the equation and their favoured prey, the hooded gruntle, reproduces so profusely that without anything to keep them in check they destroy their environment by overeating the plant life, which eventually brings desertification to the landscape and annihilates the lower levels of mammals, lizards, birds and insects that live in, and themselves prey amongst, the otherwise lush foliage. Environmental ecologists call the process a trophic cascade. When wolves were removed from US national parks, the elk ravaged the environment so badly that it even caused the river to reroute and silt up.

The danger of a trophic cascade does not deter the hunters. They come, with loaded guns, and ruthlessly hunt down the snirklebeasts, who have no chance against such lethal technology. Their numbers have dwindled so much that they are shifting from endangered status to critical. On the black market, a woolly snirklebeast pelt is worth a thousand dollars, twice that if it isn't peppered with bullet holes. Their mounted heads line walls of trophy rooms on every continent except Antarctica.

The general public doesn't care much for the decline of the snirklebeast, in much the same way as it doesn't much care for the 100 million sharks that are slaughtered every single year from the oceans. The perception is that the world might be a better place without such creatures, a safer place. The average person turns a blind eye to the horror and cruelty involved in their extermination. Between them, the shark and the snirklebeast kill less than fifty people a year, a fraction of one per cent of our tally, but humans still fear them unduly.

Roger Hartlebury was not your average person. He knew the plight of the snirklebeast and though not an active campaigner for their protection he felt empathy for them and occasionally donated to the cause of those that did. He trod the same earth, a keen long-distance walker whose rambles often veered through snirklebeast territory. He knew that, unless he was really unlucky, the chances of being attacked without provocation were virtually non-existent. They tended to shy away from humans, perhaps knowing the danger our kind represents.

So when Roger came upon an injured snirklebeast one day, laid prone and breathing with a terrible rasping sound as blood leaked from a number of wounds in its haunches, he cautiously approached to see if there was anything he could do for the poor creature. He saw movement in its eyes as he drew nearer, and knew the beast watched him helplessly.

Roger had never been so close to one before. It was magnificent, three tons of bulk and muscle, the raw machinery of life and power now sadly laid waste. He looked into its eyes and they both knew the truth. Roger sat down next to the creature and laid his hand gently on its muzzle. The lips reflexively parted to reveal yellowed teeth the size of kitchen knives. It blew air through its nostrils, spluttering bloodied foam.

There wasn't long left. It seemed grateful for his presence. Roger gently stroked the head and spoke words of comfort. High above, the sun beat down. It licked dry lips and blinked a few times before closing its eyes.

Presently, there came the sound of voices. Excited, clamorous voices. Through the foliage came three khaki-dressed hunters, elephant guns leading the way. They saw Roger and the snirklebeast and quickly walked over.

"Is it dead?" asked one of the men.

"Bagsy my kill if it is," said another.

The third said nothing, looking over Roger with a flicker of disgust.

Roger couldn't help himself. Even though he knew the danger he might be placing himself in, confronting three armed strangers, he let them have it.

"You should be ashamed of yourselves," he said, standing up and shielding the snirklebeast. "Look what you've done to this poor animal."

"Get out of the way," said the first. "We need to finish him off."

"I'm not going anywhere. You three can bugger off and let this animal die in peace."

"I'm warning you," said the man, stepping forward and raising his gun.

"Henry!" snapped the one who hadn't spoke. "What the fuck do you think you're doing?" Henry seemed to come to his senses then, realising how out of hand the situation had suddenly become. "Leave it be," he continued. "We can come back later."

The men left and Roger breathed a sigh of relief.

"That was a close one," he said to the beast at his feet, once again sitting to take his place by its head.

He made the mistake of being complacent, of sitting just a little too close.

With a sudden burst of life, the snirklebeast shifted position and lunged at Roger, grabbing his arm in its mouth. In a second, it had sheared off cloth and flesh and Roger screamed with shock and pain. Caught up in a blood-frenzy, the snirklebeast lunged again, pinning Roger with its weight and using those enormous, razor-sharp teeth to rip off his face, and then his head.

It had decided on one last feast before dying.

In less than a few minutes, there was nothing left or Roger apart from some bloody rags and a dark stain.

They say the woolly snirklebeast is a heartless predator with no redeeming qualities and it's probably fair to say that Roger, had he survived this fateful encounter, would have changed his mind and would now agree with the general consensus.

## ANTI-CLAUS

When December came, everything in the village changed. Once vibrant voices grew hushed and the tinkle of laughter fell away. Joy was forgotten. A blanket of fear descended, heavier even than the prodigious snowfall. People hurried through the streets, afraid to be out alone after dark.

***He*** was coming.

*Santa Claus.*

Every year it was the same but the burden never got any easier. In the summer months, when the bright sunshine reigned supreme, there was always a little knot of fear in the villagers' stomachs, knowing that the reprieve was only temporary. Winter would soon come, and with it the iron grip of the cold and the infinite darkness.

With two weeks to go, final preparations began. All decorations and ornaments were taken down, boxed up and hidden in attics. The indoor trees, situated in the corners of every village house and nurtured throughout the year, were taken outside and left to fend for themselves until January broke. The favourite toys of all the children were put to one side of the chimneys and left untouched. So too were the items most prized by the adults.

When the time came, in the dark and early hours of the 25th of December, Santa Claus would crawl down their chimneys and take what he wanted.

Lily Tomlinson had been badly-behaved all year – bottom of the class in virtually every subject and always forgetting to do her homework. She'd not once helped her mother with the housework, despite being asked often. Her face was usually scrunched in a scowl and she was always climbing trees and coming home covered in muck. At least once a week she'd be involved in a fight, usually with one of the boys. She was getting a bit of a reputation.

When summer was almost over, her parents had bought her a puppy, in the hope of turning her into a good little girl. Quite how this was to be achieved they had no idea, but they nursed the forlorn hope that the tiny dog would bond with her and somehow bring out an angel that hadn't yet materialised. There could be no doubt that Lily loved that puppy with all her heart, and that the feeling was wholly reciprocated, but having a new, constant companion didn't change her behaviour one bit.

Her parents despaired. They had, in their foolishness, given her the one thing that Santa Claus would certainly take, which would only make the following year even more unbearable.

But there was another fear, lurking in their bellies. Every year, the most badly-behaved of the villagers was lashed to death out on the village green, their skin flayed in great strips as Santa's reindeer-hide whip gouged deep crimson wounds and sent blood flying across the pristine, white snow. The others, even the children, would peer through the gaps in their curtains, cold sweats on their own skin, until the deed was over. Only when Santa Claus was gone would they come out and tend to the body, which would be buried at noon the next day. The name of the deceased would be added to the list of Terrible People, carved into the stone marker at the crossroads.

There could be no greater disgrace.

Her parents hoped that this year, it wouldn't be Lily out there.

On the 25th of December, in the early hours of the morning, a clatter reverberated through the house as something large forced its way down the chimney and into the Tomlinson's lounge. Awake, too frightened to move, Lily's parents cowered under their blanket and listened, their ears straining. They heard Santa Claus rummaging through their belongings, and a short, deep growl of appreciation when he found something he wanted.

And then came the sound of his footsteps on the stairs.

*Clump-clump-clump.*

Heavy footsteps, a grunt accompanying each one.

In her bedroom, Lily was awakened by growling. Pongo was standing at the end of their bed, his hackles raised, staring and snarling at the door. Lily sat up and listened. Footsteps made their way along the landing.

He was outside.

The bedroom door opened. A bulky figure stood in the doorway, somehow blacker than the darkness around it. The dog let out a small whine and was silent. Lily felt her feet grow warm. Pongo, in his terror, had wet the bed.

Santa Claus stepped into the room. He waited, saying nothing, only the sound of his heavy breathing in the darkness.

"What do you want?" asked Lily, her voice barely more than a croak.

"The dog," said Santa. His voice was deep. Gravelly. Very, very old. "Give it to me."

Lily reached for the dog and pulled it under the duvet.

"Never!" she screamed.

The defiance was only temporary. Santa ripped away the duvet and flung it across the room. With a roar, he grabbed Pongo by the scruff of his neck and, with his other hand, delivered a blow that sent Lily flying from the bed and into the wall. There was a sickening crunch as her neck broke and she lay there, quite dead.

With Pongo whining in terror, Santa clumped his way out of the room and down the stairs. Outside, screams rang through the streets as one of the men-folk was dragged by his hair and tied to the village whipping post by half a dozen small figures dressed in black robes.

"Please!" he wailed. "I haven't done anything wrong!"

"Ho ho ho!" laughed Santa, his deep voice echoing around the village square. "Hasn't done anything wrong! Listen to him!"

With a quick flick of his wrist, he snapped the dog's neck and threw the body into his sack. People were staring through their windows, watching the scene unfold. Some of the braver souls had come out onto the square.

"Let him go!" shouted a woman, but her defiance was fleeting as she fled when Santa turned his gaze on her.

"Listen to me!" he boomed, reaching for his whip. "Thomas Kelp is the worst of all of you, and that is saying something. You people just can't be good, can you? Even though you know I come to punish you, every year without fail, you still think you can get away with whatever you like."

He rolled up his sleeves and tested the whip. The tip broke through the snow and smashed against the cobbled stones, sending a loud *crack!* through the streets.

"What has he done?" asked another voice.

Santa laughed again. "I'll tell you," he roared. "He stole a loaf of bread from his employer. He hit his wife and made her bleed. He lied, just now, about not doing anything wrong. But worse than any of this," he said, turning his gaze on the owner of the enquiring voice before looking down at Thomas Kelp, "he told his only child that I did not exist!"

"I didn't want to scare him," pleaded Kelp, his eyes wide. "I didn't want him growing up in fear like the rest of us."

"QUIET!" shouted Santa. He lifted up his arm and brought the whip down across Thomas Kelp's back. It cut through his shirt and left a ragged tear in the man's flesh. Kelp moaned in terror and pain and Santa brought the whip down again and again until Kelp was silenced.

As the villagers watched, Santa kept whipping until the flesh was lashed from Kelp's bones. The whip came away soaked in blood, flinging great dollops of fatty flesh onto the snow at the villagers' feet. The punishment continued long after Kelp was dead, until the man was no longer recognisable as having once been a living person.

When it was over, Santa held out the whip and it was retrieved by one of his little helpers. He turned to look at the villagers one last time.

"I will see you all again, one year from now," he said, bowing his head. And then he left, walking into the darkness surrounded by his little helpers, off to where they had parked up the sled. In moments, they were flying through the air to the next village.

It was a long night.

## GLITTER

I've been seeing it for years, ever since I was a boy. Dog shit sprinkled with glitter, out on the streets of my home town. I'd see it so often that I didn't even think it was unusual. Back when it was crumbly white, that's how long ago I'm talking, although you don't see it these days. But shit is always lying around, despite the fines handed out to owners who don't clear up after their pets. Some of them just don't seem to care.

It's not something I pay much attention to, the shit and the glitter, not really. I mean I see it, and sometimes muse on it, but not for long - it isn't something I think about in any great depth. You know that life sometimes has little mysteries that you just accept? Like the way birds sometimes fly into windows, or the way it can rain on one half of the street and not the other? It's like that.

Or rather it was. Because this morning, the mystery was solved. I saw him, this old man, stooping over to pour a little bit of glitter on a fresh turd. It stopped me in my tracks, the craziness of it. And for some reason I needed to know what this was all about. So I followed him.

He did it twice more before he suspected that he was being followed. I'm no sleuth and I wasn't very good at concealing myself. He turned and looked at me for a long time before moving on. At that point I could've walked away but I decided not to. I don't know why. It wasn't really any of my business but now that I'd seen it happening, rather than just seeing the aftermath, my curiosity was piqued. I kept following him, into town, even though this was going to make me late for work.

Eventually he stopped and waited for me to catch up.

"What are you looking at?" he asked.

"Nothing."

"Don't lie. You've been following me. I ain't stupid."

I'd been caught red-handed, there wasn't much point in denying it.

"OK," I said, "you got me. I'm curious, that's all. About the glitter."

"You want me to tell you why I put glitter on the dog shits?"

"Yes."

He looked me up and down and sighed.

"No-one's ever asked before," he said.

"Really? But you must have been doing it for over twenty years."

"More like sixty years, son. Ever since I was a boy." He looked around and pointed at a small café. "Why don't you buy us a hot drink and I'll tell you all about it."

The café was fairly dingy inside. I'd never been there before, never even noticed its existence. We were the only customers. I ordered a tea for the old man and a coffee for myself. The young girl behind the counter (who was very attractive, I noticed) told me to sit and she'd bring them over.

We sat by the window, looking out onto the street. The old man sat quietly, waiting for his drink, occasionally looking my way. He seemed unsure now, as though maybe he thought he'd made a mistake. The drinks arrived and we each took a sip.

"Do you like Christmas, boy?" he asked.

"Yeah. I mean, who doesn't?"

"Not everyone does. If you haven't got any loved ones, or any money, Christmas can be a hard time. The suicide rates go right up at Christmas, did you know that?"

"I think so, yeah."

"It's terrible really. Should be a time for celebration, not for death. You get lots of presents, do you?"

"I used to. Not so much now."

He smiled. "I never used to care much about presents," he said. "My family was dirt poor and I'd be grateful for a fresh orange on Christmas Day. Can you believe that?"

I didn't know what to say. I've never been grateful for a piece of fruit in my life. They're sort of everywhere. I'd have been heartbroken if my parents had fobbed me off with an orange.

"I don't suppose you can," he said, still smiling and looking at me until I had to break eye contact and feign interest in something outside the window. "Youngsters these days get everything they want. It's a different world from the one I grew up in."

I began to wonder where all of this was going. I was conscious of the bollocking I'd get for being late for work – it would be the second time in a week and my boss was only going to take so much. I got the feeling that this old man was a bit lonely and, grateful for company, could sit there talking for hours. As soon as that thought crossed my mind I felt guilty for wanting to get away and deprive him of some human contact.

"I'll tell you about the glitter," he said, as though sensing my thoughts. "Have you ever been to the North Pole?"

"Er, no."

"I have. I loved Christmas so much that I begged my parents to take me. They couldn't afford it, of course. But when some distant relative died and left my father some money, he took me. All those years of thanking him for the oranges must have eaten away at him and this was his was of making amends. We caught a flight up to Lapland on the twenty-second of December and did the whole tourist thing. At least that's what I thought it was – Santa and all his reindeer, all the elves rushing about with toys. Even as a child I knew this was all make-believe. Isn't that right, son?"

"Isn't what right?"

"That it's all make-believe? Some tour company dressing up their employees to make a bit of money from people's stupidity."

"I guess so."

"Wrong!" he said, adding a cackle for good measure. "It's all real! That man I saw really was Santa Claus! They really were elves. And the reindeer, the beautiful reindeer.... They were always my favourites. Rudolph, Dasher, Dancer, Prancer, Vixen, Comet, Cupid, Donner and Blitzen."

"You know all their names from memory?" I asked. "I can never remember more than a couple."

"They were my favourite part of Christmas," he said, his eyes turning misty with nostalgia. "More than the presents, more than the elves, more than Santa, even.... I loved the reindeer and spent most of my time in the North Pole petting them. They were magnificent beasts. Anyway, as things turned out, there was something wrong with the plane that was supposed to fly us home so we ended up staying another couple of days until they sorted it out. We saw Santa and his reindeer fly off on Christmas Eve to deliver the presents. And we were still there when they came back."

He trailed off and I noticed that his eyes were glazed over. A single tear rolled down his cheek.

"What happened?" I asked.

"The reindeer had aged terribly overnight. They were so exhausted from flying around the world, delivering all those presents, it had taken everything from them. One by one, as I watched in horror, the poor creatures dropped down dead in the snow. My father tried to drag me away but I ran over to Rudolph and flung myself across him. He was still warm. I stayed there until he turned cold.

"That's really sad," I said. And it was. I hadn't really thought about it before but I suppose it was obvious that a reindeer's workload was so strenuous that it could only prove fatal.

"I found out that Santa Claus needs to replace his reindeer every year," he said. "He needs the fittest youngsters he can find – only the healthiest will make it through Christmas Eve, but even the strongest cannot live past Christmas Day. The toll on their bodies... it's too much."

"I'll bet that ruined Christmas for you," I said.

"And you'd be right. But it's not the worst thing."

"There's something worse?"

"What do you think happens to them?" he asked.

"The reindeer? I don't know. Do they get buried?"

"No. They get ground up and used for food."

"Really? Santa's reindeer? What, like reindeer steaks?"

"Not food for humans. They've used so much muscle power through the night that their flesh is too tough for people. Even if you slow-cooked it for three days it'd still be as tough as old leather. Santa chops them up and-"

"Santa?" I blurted, appalled.

"Oh, yes. Didn't you know Santa is a butcher? In the old days, his suit was white, all white. But, over the years, enough people have seen him after he's butchered the reindeer that he couldn't continue with white and changed his outfit to red. To hide all the bloodstains, see. The last thing he wants is for a child to see him covered in blood – imagine how *that* would ruin a child's Christmas."

I took a big slurp of coffee and wrinkled my face. It suddenly tasted so bitter. This was the most horrible story I'd ever heard. Santa – a butcher! Chopping up his reindeer! It couldn't be true. But something in the old man's eyes told me it was.

"So what does eat the reindeer?"

"Dogs. They get chopped up and then Santa loads them into a mincer and bags everything up for export. It all ends up in dog food."

"So why the glitter?" I asked.

"A mark of respect. Every bit of dog shit out there contains a little bit of Santa's reindeer. Putting a bit of glitter on the turds is my way of thanking them for their sacrifice."

He sat there and stared at me for a while before lifting his mug and drinking the rest of his tea.

"Happy now that you know?" he asked.

"Not really."

"Well, you know what they say about curiosity. Thanks for the tea, son. I'll be seeing you."

I watched as he shuffled out of the café and he gave a final nod as he passed by the window. I sat there for a while, my thoughts in turmoil. What a downer. This was going to upset me for days. I slowly stood and walked towards the door and the girl behind the counter thanked me for my custom.

I gave her a sad smile. She really was beautiful. I suddenly thought of a way to make the world a happier place, for me at least. Without stopping to consider the possibility that she might turn me down, I opened my mouth and asked her if she'd like to go for a drink somewhere, after she'd finished for the day.

"I'm sorry, I have a boyfriend," she said, looking a little sorry for me. I smiled, nodded, and left the café. It took a few minutes to walk to work and, when I arrived, my boss shouted at me that I'd been late one time too many and sacked me on the spot.

What a horrible day. I didn't think it could get any worse but on the long walk home I stepped in a huge pile of dog shit. I looked down at the horrible brown mess covering the sole of my shoe and noticed that there wasn't even any glitter in it.

# THE PIKE

*Yap yap yap.*

*Yap yap yap yap yap yap yap yap.*

All day, all night, that's what I heard coming through the walls. It kept me awake in the early hours, gritting my teeth in bed and trying to avoid thoughts of kicking down the neighbour's front door and going on a murderous rampage. It got so bad I couldn't think straight any more. Christine – that's my wife – thinks I dwell on it too much, that I should 'live and let live'. Christine, you see, sleeps like a dead thing. I doubted she'd wake up if a nuclear bomb went off, so a few yips from a Chihuahua hasn't exactly bothered her.

It hasn't deepened the worry lines around her eyes the way it has mine.

I'd asked the neighbour – Mrs Tomlinson – to do something about it but she just fake-smiled a mostly toothless grin and told me to "Piss off!" She's a charmer. I can't believe she's made it past eighty without anyone killing her. She's as deaf as a post, so the yapping doesn't bother her either.

It only bothers me. It seems to be my problem alone.

When she moved in, about ten years ago, we thought it might be nice to have a sweet old lady living next door. Christine even baked her a cake as a welcome gift. Christine's not a great baker so maybe that's what did it, or maybe Mrs Tomlinson was already a cantankerous old git when she arrived and the cake made no difference at all. For all we knew, she could have been that way all her life (and that's pretty much what I've concluded).

Whatever it was, any inchoate feelings of friendliness quickly dissipated and we'd only spoken to each other since when any kind of neighbourly dispute came up.

Our garden fence blew down in a gale one night and we got a new one, which, on many occasions, she let us know that she hated. It was the wrong colour, and after we Creosoted it the colour was still not to her liking. She complained to the council about us having overfilled waste bins a few times – once when the bloody bin men were on strike! She even complained when we had a family barbeque one Summer afternoon, standing looking over the new fence and shouting whilst our entire family looked at her angry little face as it sprayed spittle all over the lawn. But all of this paled to insignificance in comparison to the sleepless nights I endured because of that fucking dog.

She had the Chihuahua when she came. Such a pair were never better suited. It was a manky little ball of hate. It even looked the same as her, with little tufts of white hair poking out of the top of its head, the bulging eyes and a mouth mostly empty of teeth. It had enough to draw blood though, that much I knew from direct experience. First time I ever saw it, way back when we were still talking to the old bag, I said *"Aah!"* and reached down to give it a bit of fuss and the thing gave a screech and leapt at my hand, sinking its gnarly teeth into my finger. It took over a minute for the little bastard to let go, and a minute's a long time in a situation like that.

When we got our own dog, about four years ago, we made sure it wasn't a Chihuahua – anything but a little yappy thing because a stereophonic yap would had sent me over the edge completely. We got ourselves a Highland terrier and he's everything you could ever want in a dog. Jack is friendly, always pleased to see you, never shits in the house, chews only the things he's supposed to and hardly ever barks, even when next door's little monster is going at it full tilt.

I called the Environmental Health people from the council and they sent a guy round with some recording equipment. The Chihuahua barked on cue but the man said that although it was an irritant, it wasn't loud enough to be a nuisance.

"You say that when you haven't had a decent night's sleep in ten years," I told him but he smiled apologetically and said that there wasn't much he could do. I couldn't believe this and must have spent twenty minutes trying to convince him otherwise. Finally, in an act of desperation, I asked him what he would do if he were me and the council refused to help.

"Dunno. Get an air rifle?"

I thought about it, I really did. I'm normally horrified at the thought of cruelty of any kind to an animal (with the exception of maggots, which will become clear) but this dog had been driving me to distraction and I was at the end of my tether. I could have shot it from the bedroom window whilst it was in old Tomlinson's back garden and even though it would have been obvious what had happened, I thought as long as I dumped the air rifle immediately afterwards no-one would ever be able to prove it was me. I mean, nobody would seriously investigate the matter to the point of ordering ballistics reports or anything. Mrs Tomlinson might suspect it was me but what could she do about it?

I thought it best to run the idea past Christine. She was appalled that I could even think such a thing was worth considering.

"Have you heard yourself?" she said, looking at me like I was insane. "Shooting a poor little dog? Is this the man I married?"

Of course, I didn't do it. Christine was right. I couldn't bring myself to shoot that odious creature, I just couldn't. Many mornings since, when I'd lain awake since the early hours – *yap yap yap!* – I'd bitterly regretted my decision.

Luckily, I had something that I relied on to calm me down a bit – fishing. That was my Zen space, a few hours a week when I could blot everything else out of my mind and just completely relax. I was a middle-aged man with a healthy disposable income so it goes without saying that I had all of the gear. (So much gear, in fact, that it was starting to do my head in and these days I seemed to leave a lot of it back at home.) I'd discovered I was happy enough with just a rod, a folding chair, a tub of writhing maggots, a couple of lagers and a good book. Quite often that's how you'd find me, sat on the edge of the pool in the old quarry, reading or dozing and generally being as still and as quiet as it's possible to be in today's world.

It wasn't even about the fishing. Of course, it was always a thrill to actually catch one, but it was never a measure of success and even when I did get a bite the feeling of euphoria was short-lived and I'd unhook the little blighter and pop it back in the pool. In my day I'd caught many trout, grayling, tench, roach, bream, a few minnows and the odd eel. It didn't matter much to me what fetched up on the end of the line, a catch was a catch – I never got excited about the size of the fish, as many other anglers do. For me, fishing was more about just finding the time to spend in my own company, away from other people and, even though I love her dearly, that includes my wife. The act of fishing was just an excuse, really, a way to disguise a few hours of genuine idleness.

And it was a way of spending some time in quiet, often beautiful places I'd never otherwise see. Admittedly the quarry couldn't immediately be appreciated as beautiful but, in its own way, it really was. Rock had been chopped out of the landscape here for over a century and that only stopped about twenty years ago, in which time nature had done everything it could to try and reclaim the land for itself. The hardiest of plants, mostly weeds, had split rock after seeding in the most unlikely spots and although weeds have a bad reputation many of them can be quite colourful and pleasing to look at. When it rained, the rock glistened and, if you went looking, you could sometimes find fossils and imprints from creatures that once walked in these very spots some 60 million years ago.

We lived at the edge of town so all this was just five minutes from the house. I could walk there easily enough but always drove to save lugging my equipment by hand.

The pool itself was magnificent. About seventy metres in diameter, the body of water filled a pit whose depths nobody quite knew. The water was so clear – so crystal clear – that you could easily see to a depth of about twenty metres before a blue tinge quickly darkened to an impenetrable blackness. You could see the fish swimming around as clear as you could see the birds in the sky. Lately, there were so many fish it was almost impossible not to catch one or two every visit. Most times I'd been I'd had the place to myself and it's hard to think of a more pleasing spot I'd rather be on a Saturday morning.

Christine had a habit of asking me if I was going fishing even though she always knew the answer would be yes.

"You off fishing today then?" she'd asked this morning.

"Yep."

"Want me to make up a flask?"

"Please."

"Sandwich?"

"That would be lovely, thanks."

It was pretty much the same conversation, *verbatim*, every weekend. I didn't mind, it was just one of those funny little routines that happily married couples have. She didn't have to ask and, come mid-morning, I always appreciated a flask of hot tea and a cheese sandwich.

"Are you going to drop those record's over to Dad's afterwards?"

Gah. For the last couple of weeks I'd been promising to drop off a load of old vinyl at her parents' house but just hadn't gotten around to it. A large plastic crate filled up most of the boot in my car. They only lived a 15 minute drive away but I just hadn't found the right moment. They were her father's old LP's and 78's, mostly ancient crooners, and had been temporarily stored in our loft when they moved to a bungalow. That was three years ago. The way I saw it, it wasn't exactly urgent.

"I might do," I said. "We'll see how it goes."

"You're bloody hopeless.

As Christine walked from the kitchen, her right foot skidded on the tiled floor and she let out a gasp whilst simultaneously reaching for the door frame to steady herself. My reaction times were much slower these days – had she fallen there's no way I would've been able to stop it.

"I thought I told you to take those shoes back," I said, frowning.

"It's not the shoes."

"Of course it is. You don't go slipping and sliding in any other footwear."

"But I like them."

"That's not the point."

"It must have been something wet on the floor," she said, making a show of examining the tiles but we both knew it wasn't.

On the kitchen counter, my mobile phone started to ring. Graham, my younger brother was calling.

"All right?" I said.

"Not bad."

"What's up?"

"Need a favour."

"How much?"

We'd never been big on small talk. Whenever Graham needed a favour it was usually to borrow some money. He'd had a tough time of it lately. As a graphic designer, he'd worked for two magazine publishing companies that had both folded in the last few years and now he was freelancing he struggled to land the contracts. He was brilliant at what he did but wasn't so hot at selling himself and getting work from new clients. He'd borrowed a bit here and there from me and always paid me back when he came into some money.

"Four hundred."

"OK, no problem."

"Don't you want to know what it's for?"

"It doesn't matter, I know you'll pay me back."

"It's for the car. I have an oil leak and need a couple of tyres. Possibly the brakes need doing too."

"I said you don't have to tell me what it's for."

"Yeah, I know, but I don't want you to think I'm spending it on drugs and hookers."

Graham would be the last person I'd expect to blow money on drugs and hookers. He was a real homebody, loved nothing more than sitting down to a good box-set on Netflix and cooking himself a nice meal. Like most things he put his mind to he was very good at cooking – were he not a graphic designer he could easily have been a chef. It's just a pity he has no-one to cook for apart from himself. Sometimes, when we invite him over, he offers to cook for us. We usually take him up on it. The man can work magic with a handful of ingredients and a few spices.

"Sounds more interesting than spending it on the car," I said.

There was a silence for a second or two and then he changed tack.

"I got a new job," he said.

"Well done. Who with?"

"Some advertising agency based in Ludlow."

"Where the fuck's Ludlow?"

"About sixty miles away, that's why I need the car in good shape. It's a staff job. Not a contract."

"That's great! So you're an employee again? Is the money good?"

"It's pretty shit but it'll be regular. I have to learn a load of new stuff. They do a lot of online and social media campaigns. Can you transfer that dosh into my bank this morning?"

"Yeah, I'll do it before I head off."

"Fishing?"

"What else? When do you start the new job?"

"Monday, that's why the car thing is a rush. Listen – thanks, ok?"

"No worries. Good luck for Monday. I'll transfer that money in the next 5 minutes."

"Thanks, Mickey." Of everyone I knew, he was the only one to call me that, had done ever since we were kids.

"Text me Monday night, let me know how you get on."

"Will do."

We hung up at the same time and then I did a bank app BACS transfer to his account. Half an hour later I was fishing.

I could tell immediately that something was a little off. There was a black Land Rover in the scraggy bit of land used as a car park when I arrived and when I walked through with my gear a man in a green jacket and a flat cap was standing at the edge of the pool and peering into the water. He turned and looked at me as I set up my chair and rod and then walked over.

"Spot of fishing?" he asked.

What a question.

"Yes," I said. "I come here most Saturdays."

"Do you now?" he asked, looking me up and down. "Have you asked the landowner if fishing is allowed?"

"I have no idea who the landowner is," I said. "Nobody knows."

"Well, it's me."

"Oh. Right. So... is it all right if I fish here?"

"Of course it is," he said breaking into a broad smile and extending his hand. "Name's Jim."

"Mike."

"Pleased to meet you, Mike."

"So, you own this place?"

"Have done for about 20 years, ever since they stopped quarrying here and the land became useless overnight."

"It's a lovely spot."

"It is, isn't it? I think that's why I bought it. I could see the potential. Anyone else would've had a shopping centre or a block of flats here by now but I've just let it go to pasture, so to speak."

"Are they your fish?" I asked, nodding towards the pool.

"They are. Every now and then I tip a load of small ones in but I haven't done that for a while. In fact, they've been doing rather well here, so much so that I've had to take measures to curb them a little."

That sounded ominous.

"Curb them?" I asked, prompting him to continue.

"Follow me," he said, walking towards the edge of the pool. I did, and we stood side by side looking into the water. The fish were really active today, darting about all over the place.

"What am I looking at?" I asked.

"Wait for it. You'll see."

We waited. A silence enveloped us, broken only by the buzz of a passing fly. A cloud briefly obscured the sun casting a temporary shadow across the pool.

And then I saw it.

A large fish was gliding through the deep waters, sending everything else scattering before it. It must have been three or four feet long at least, three times the size of any other fish in there. It turned and swam the other way, calm and authoritative. This pool was now his.

"What is that?" I asked. "Is it a pike?"

"Correct," he said. "A proper nasty bastard, if you'll excuse my French. I've had it years."

"How did it get in there?"
"I put it in."
"You did? Why?"
"To curb the numbers. If there are too many fish here it will start attracting the attention of more anglers. I don't mind the odd one but I wouldn't want this place over-run. No offence, mind."
"None taken. Won't it eat all the others?"
"It'll have a good go. It'll probably be a few pounds heavier by the time I take it out."
"And then what will you do with it?" I asked.
"I move it around my fisheries, keep all the other fish on their toes, so to speak."
"How do you catch it? With a rod?"
"With a big net and a pound of raw steak."
"Jesus."
"He likes being caught, by me at least. He knows how well I look after him."
*"Him?"*
"He's more like a pet. I shouldn't really admit it but I am rather fond of him."
"So, you have other places? Like this?" I asked, my eyes on the dark shape cutting through the water.
"No, nothing like this. This is more like a hobby, an experimentation pond. I sometimes try different groups of fish together to see how they get on."
We watched the pike for a few minutes in silent contemplation and then he turned to me and extended his hand once more.
"I must be off," he said, shaking my hand. "Nice meeting you."
"You too," I said, watching him go. He seemed pleasant enough and it was nice of him to let me stay. I returned to my spot and sat down on my folding chair. I was hungry already and demolished the sandwich whilst sipping hot tea and staring into the pool. Things were getting a little more frantic. The pike had increased its speed and seemed to be actively hunting. The other fish were zooming about all over the place. Underneath the calm surface the pool was in turmoil. As I leaned forward to watch, the pike started honing in on one particular fish and I found myself rooting for it to get away. Wherever it went, the pike was on its tail, getting closer by the second. It was almost too much to watch. Suddenly, the prey changed direction and started swimming

furiously up towards the surface – towards *me* – and like something out of a 3D movie it broke the skin of water and launched itself into the air, landing in a flopping mess right at my feet.

I jumped up in alarm, spilling hot tea down my front as I did so. I danced around for a few moments, pulling my shirt away from my chest so I didn't get scalded, flapping the material around to get some cool air circulating. I must have looked like a maniac. When I stopped, I could see the fish – a sizeable brown trout – struggling to breathe.

I didn't know what to do. I looked at the pool and felt the blood freeze in my veins – the pike was there, hanging in the water, looking right at me. The evil bastard was giving me the eye. I could imagine what it was thinking: *Chuck that fish back in here or I'll come right out and get both of you.* It was a terrifying, if ludicrous prospect.

I turned my attention back to the trout. It was dying and didn't have long. There was no way I was throwing it back into the pool, offering it up for sacrifice to that monster. If you'd asked me earlier that morning if I had it in me to feel sorry for a fish I'd have laughed you out of my house but now? I did, I really did.

I ran back to the car and opened up the boot. All those vinyl records went onto the back seat and I ran back with the empty plastic crate. I moved along the pool a little bit and dipped the crate into the water to fill it. The pike moved closer to see what I was up to. I heaved the crate out and walked awkwardly back to my chair. Water is heavier than you'd think and I was knackered after just a few short steps. I put it onto the ground, picked up the trout and gently placed it in. For a few moments I thought it might be dead but it started moving and was soon swimming in a very tight circle.

With a look of disgust, the pike finally turned its attention away from me and resumed the hunt. There was nothing I could do for the others but this little fellow was safe.

But now what? What the hell was I going to do with a trout in a crate full of water? I had no idea, at least for about a minute until I had an extremely stupid idea. I'd take it home with me. It could live in the bath, until I worked out a better solution.

I backed the car up as close as possible and then heaved the crate into the boot before returning to collect my things. Before I set off, I tossed a few maggots in.

"You've done WHAT?!"

It's fair to say that Christine wasn't a fan of the idea. Like I said before, my idea of finding some me-space in the modern world was to go fishing for a few hours. Christine's thing was a nice long soak in the bath, preferably with a glass of wine. She stood in the bathroom doorway looking down at the trout and for a moment I thought she was going to have a heart attack. Her face was bright red. Jack was at her feet, circling and sniffing at the air.

"Calm down!" I urged, squeezing past her. "It's only for the time being."

"I wanted a bloody bath tonight!"

"You can still have one."

"With a fish? Are you mad?"

"I can put it back in the crate until you've finished."

She looked at me in disgust.

"The bath will be all slimy."

"Of course it won't. Fish aren't slimy. Okay, one or two breeds can be but this one isn't."

"Get rid of it."

I hated it when she was like this. Being married for so long, I'd seen this mood hundreds of times and it could last for days. One time I bought a motorbike and she gave me grief non-stop, telling me I was an idiot and that I was going to end up killing myself before my midlife crisis was even over. She shouted that I'd come a cropper and fall off it and she'd be left to grow old with only the dog for company. I had to spend days assuring her that it was perfectly safe and that she was being unreasonable. Of course, the very first time I took it out the bloody thing slid out from under me on a rain-soaked corner and I broke my arm. I sold it for half the price I'd paid for it, spent six weeks in a cast and neither of us mentioned it again.

"I will, but only when I have somewhere for it to go."

"What about that pool where you go fishing?"

"Where do you think I got it from?"

"Well, take it back!"

"I already said, I can't!"

"Why not? It's a bloody pool! There's no better place for it!"

I glanced down at the fish and it seemed to be looking up at me apologetically, as though it felt guilty of causing all the commotion. I wanted to bend over the bath and say a few reassuring words but Christine would've brained me.

"The guy that owns the place has put a pike in there and it'll eat him if I put him back."

"Him?"

Jesus, now *I* was referring to a fish as a *'him'*.

*"It."*

"Isn't that what fish do? Eat each other?"

"Yes, but..."

"But what?"

"I just can't. It's a *monster*. You should have seen it."

Christine waved her arms in exasperation and stormed off, followed by Jack, telling me to get the fish out and wipe the bath down so she could use it later. I'd left the empty crate in the bathroom so grabbed it and eased it into the bath, gently scooping up the trout with a load of water. I carried it to the spare room and put a few more maggots in. The trout pursed its lips at the surface of the water and nibbled them down.

"It's all right, mate," I said, crouching over the crate. "We'll sort something out for you."

It turned in a tight circle and looked up at me. I tell you, there's not much expression in a fish's face but I could see the gratitude on his – he knew that I'd saved him from that bastard pike and I'm pretty sure he appreciated my current dilemma with Christine. Fish are smarter than you'd think. That old joke about a goldfish having only a few seconds of memory may just be true but once you start getting bigger breeds their brain size increases too. I'm not saying a fish is ever going to quantify String Theory or anything but they aren't the brainless automatons many people think they are. Dolphins were trained during the Second World War to lay mines out amongst the Japanese fleets. Octopuses are now being considered as one of the most intelligent life forms on Earth, after humans and chimps. Not exactly fish, so bad examples, but you get my point.

Christine had her bath and when she was finished I thoroughly cleaned it with cold water so there would be no trace of soap and then filled it up. The trout was gently tipped back in and he swam a few circuits of the tub before looking up at me and, I swear, *smiling*. I was really starting to like this fellow. I wondered if I'd be able to talk Christine into having a large fish tank installed in the lounge.

I kept checking up on him during the evening, just to make sure he was OK. Christine rolled her eyes and sighed but I think she was secretly pleased to have a husband with a caring nature, even if it was being misplaced on a fish. She might have hated it now but I knew, in time, she'd grow to tolerate it. Sometimes I knew my wife better than she knew herself. We owned a cat once, a miserable old bastard we got from a rescue shelter and it caused mayhem for the year or so it was with us. It pissed all over the settee, tore up the curtains, scratched the hell out of both of us and once shat in Christine's jewellery box (*I'd told her not to leave it open!*). That cat made our lives a misery and she often complained how much she hated it but, when it keeled over one day and died of old age, Christine was inconsolable. She cried for three days straight. Its ashes are still on our mantelpiece, in a pewter urn.

We had a quiet evening, with the exception of the usual yapping from next door and a telephone call just after seven. Christine's boss wanted her to deliver some training on Monday afternoon – the original trainer had come down with something and Christine was the only one he felt was up to the job. He actually said that, knowing that the flattery would win her over. She agreed, and then he told her the job was eighty miles away at another office. After hanging up, she spent ten minutes moaning at me about how the traffic was going to be terrible and that she'd probably be late back on Monday so I'd have to get my own dinner sorted. I didn't mind so much, it had been ages since I'd had a Chinese.

Sunday was a quiet affair. I left Christine in bed and nipped out to buy a length of garden hose and a children's paddling pool. By half ten I was back, inflating the pool and then filling it with water from the kitchen tap with the hose. I took Christine breakfast in bed and, whilst she was eating it, carried the trout downstairs in the crate and gently tipped him into the pool, which was a good deal larger than the bathtub.

He raced round and round it, looking at me every now and then to share his joy. He loved it! I'd never seen a happier fish. I felt so glorious I could burst. This must be what having children is like. I fetched a couple of folding chairs from the garage and plonked them next to the pool. The sun was climbing high in the sky and there was a thin layer of wispy cloud that took the edge off the heat. I'd cut the lawn the week before so the threat of that job wasn't looming over me. At that moment, life was about as perfect as it could get.

Christine wandered out into the garden in her dressing gown, looked at the pool and the chairs next to it and then looked back at me. Jack trotted past her and sniffed at the pool. He could tell something was in there.

"Leave it, Jack," I said in a firm voice. He looked up at me inquisitively and then sniffed at the grass before wandering off to do his business.

"Would you like a cup of tea?" she asked.

You see, progress already! No moaning, no rolling of the eyes, not even a sarcastic joke of any kind. She'd looked over the new setup and it was being quietly accepted.

"Yes, please," I said, offering her a warm smile. "You see," I said to Gilbert after she'd gone back inside – *I don't know why but that name just seemed to pop into my head at that moment* – "you're part of the family already!"

He did a little lap of excitement to celebrate.

It was one of those lazy Sunday mornings, where time slowly – and, paradoxically, all too quickly – drifted by. We were in our own little bubble. Nothing else in the world mattered. Christine got up to fetch a cold drink once or twice and otherwise remained engrossed in a book, Jack curled up on her lap. I was happy enough just looking at the pool and letting my mind wander. I pictured us getting a more permanent sort of pool in the garden, which would be a far better idea than having a big glass tank inside the house. Gilbert wouldn't mind the transition outdoors, truth be told he was more of an outdoors fellow anyway. I could dig a big hole in the garden and make a proper rock pool. It would be a centrepiece and Gilbert would be its crown jewel. When friends came over they would marvel at my creation and when they asked where the fish came from I would tell them of my heroism, facing down that evil pike and rescuing Gilbert from certain doom.

I was cruelly brought out of my idle daydreams by the sound of next door's dog barking.

*Yap yap yap. Yap yap yap yap yap.*

Christine could see me getting agitated.

"Leave it," she warned.

"I'm sick of it."

"Just leave it."

Gilbert had stopped swimming around the pool and was listening in alarm.

"It needs to shut up. It's scaring Gilbert."

"Who the hell is – no. Please tell me you haven't named the fish."

"What's wrong with that?"

"You need help. I'm seriously worried."

*Yap yap yap yap yap yap yap.*

"I'm going to have to have a word."

"Mike, please. Just let it go."

"But it's wrecking our Sunday."

"*You're* wrecking our Sunday."

"*Me*? What the hell have I done?"

"For God's sake!" Jack sprang from her lap with a little bark and ran around excitedly. Christine dumped her book on the floor, got up and stormed inside the house, followed by the dog and leaving me to contemplate the mysteries of the female species yet again. I sat there trying to work out how I was suddenly the bad guy in all of this and, no matter how I turned the last few minutes over in my mind, I came up with nothing but bafflement. I'd been with Christine for over twenty years, would no doubt be with her until I died and I feared I'd never really understand her.

There was no way I could sit there with all that noise. As soon as I thought that, I realised that it had gone quiet next door. Maybe the dog had gone back inside. I waited, glancing down at Gilbert to see him looking up at me, also waiting. A minute passed. Two. It was still quiet. I dared to lean back in my chair and relax.

I must have drifted off to sleep because the next thing I knew Christine was screaming and all hell was breaking loose.

We'd had no idea that right at the bottom end of the garden, behind the shed, rats had been gnawing away at the fence for months (probably years) and had been making a hole big enough to crawl through. It must have been discovered by the Chihuahua and made even bigger. How it did this with hardly any gnashers is a mystery, but it had just enough teeth to complete the job and force its way through into our garden, where it immediately ran to the inflatable paddling pool and bit a hole in that as well.

The water started trickling, then pouring out, and the pool was quickly on the verge of collapse. The Chihuahua started yapping and Christine came out of the kitchen with two mugs of tea, tripped over the hose I'd forgotten to put away, and screamed as the tea went everywhere. Jack barked and ran after the intruder, trying to play.

I woke with a start.

"What the fuck?" I yelled, taking the scene in. "Gilbert!"

The Chihuahua was yap-yap-yapping, running around my feet and trying to take a bite at my ankles, with Jack close behind it in an attempt to get it to engage in some canine play. I almost tripped over the bloody things as I ran to get the empty crate to rescue Gilbert. Christine was running around flapping her arms at the dogs, trying to shoo away the Chihuahua but it was getting even more excitable amongst all the commotion and then, to add a final layer of mayhem to the proceedings, Mrs Tomlinson poked her manky little head over the top of the fence and started shouting at me.

"What are you doing to my dog, you bleedin' idiot?"

From peaceful silence to utter carnage in sixty seconds.

At the sound of her voice, the Chihuahua raced off back to the hole in the fence and in seconds we heard it yapping away next door. Jack had gone after it so I let Christine deal with that situation whilst I raced Gilbert upstairs to the safety of his bathtub.

"I'm really sorry about all of that," I told him once he was back in. He looked a little out of sorts, as though all of this mayhem had been a bit too much. "You settle yourself down and everything will be all right before we know it." He looked at me, unconvinced.

I went back downstairs. Christine had retrieved Jack, who had managed to get his head through the hole in the fence but not much else. I gave him a little tickle on the chin and then sat down at the kitchen table.

"I'm going to have to do something about that dog," I said.

"Look, it's all over with now so let's just forget about it."

"The shock could have killed Gilbert!" I said and knew immediately that I shouldn't. I knew that such an admission would distract her attention from the real issue at hand and that we'd get into a heated discussion about my affections for our new family member. I think Christine knew how this would play out as well, if we let it. Both of us waited in silence, playing an imaginary escalating argument out in our heads. Sometimes, when you know someone really well, you don't have to go through the bother of doing the real thing, it can be done within the confines of your own head. Thankfully, Christine didn't go down the route of verbalising things.

"Well, there's nothing you can do," she said at last. "You've tried calling it in as a noise pollutant and it didn't work."

"I could put a bit of poisoned meat down?" I suggested, immediately regretting that sentence as well.

"Really?" she asked, in a tone loaded with disgust. "Apart from that being one of the most despicable things you've ever uttered, what if Jack ate it instead?"

"I'd be careful."

"You can't go around poisoning people's dogs, Mike, however annoying they are."

"Don't you want to see it gone?"

"Not as much as you. obviously. Give it a couple of years and the thing will die of old age."

"Are we still talking about the dog? Or old Tomlinson?"

She smiled and flicked the switch on the kettle. I sat there stewing as she made the drinks. There was no way I could let this go, something had to be done. And then I had the idea.

Mrs Tomlinson opened her front door and eyed me suspiciously.

"What do you want?" she asked.

I help up a bottle of port. We knew she liked that stuff and there'd been one in the back of our drinks cabinet for years. If she hadn't been such a cantankerous old witch, she could have had it as a Christmas present a long time ago.

"Can I come in for a chat?"

"What?"

"Can I come in for a chat?"

"You'll have to wait a minute," she said, fumbling around with the controls of her hearing aid. After she was finished she looked at me again, with a dash of added contempt.

"I said 'Can I come in for a chat?'"

Her eyes flitted between me and the bottle. It could have gone either way. Finally, with an exasperated sigh, she opened the door and let me inside. The Chihuahua immediately started trying to bite my ankles and I asked Mrs Tomlinson if she'd mind putting it in another room for a little while. She obliged without saying anything. She must have really wanted to get her hands on that port. With the dog yapping in another room, we sat in her lounge. I handed her the bottle and she placed it onto a table without offering to open it.

"What do you want?" she asked again.

"I want to be a better neighbour," I said, trying not to choke on my own words. "And that begins with an apology for this morning's little episode."

She eyed me for a second or two, her expression giving nothing away.

"You should get that fence fixed," she said. "It's dangerous. My Charlie could have been attacked by your dog, vicious little thing."

I mentally took a deep breath and smiled. One pillar of civilised society is that you can't go around punching old ladies, however vile, just because they said something you didn't like or agree with. There was no doubt that she was a horrible woman but I didn't know the history of her life or why she'd turned out that way. She could have had a terribly difficult life, been beaten down by fate until only a shrivelled lump of hate remained. Then again, she might be an old witch simply because she got pleasure out of it. It wasn't my place to judge.

"Of course," I said. "I'll get onto it this afternoon. Is your dog OK?"

"He's fine, no thanks to you lot."

"I'm glad to hear it."

"Apology accepted. Anything else?"

"Well," I said, leaning forward a little to emphasise what I wanted to say next. "Christine and I were thinking that maybe your little Charlie barks a lot and does things like coming into our garden because he doesn't get out enough."

"He has the back yard to run around in."

"Yes, but does he actually get taken for a walk?"

"What business is that of yours?" She looked angry that I would ask about this.

"Listen," I said, forcing a smile. "I'm only trying to help. I know a lovely little place, only five minutes down the road. It's an old quarry and it's perfect for taking the dog. I know Charlie's old, and walking too far might be a stretch, but do you know what the best exercise is for a dog like Charlie?"

"What's that, then?" she asked. Her voice sounded suspicious but I could tell there was a minute thawing in her demeanour.

"A bit of a swim!" I exclaimed, holding my arms out as if this was the greatest idea the world had ever seen. "Think how Charlie would love a little swim! There's a pool in the quarry, you could stand by the edge and let Charlie have a bit of a dip. A swim would exercise all of his joints and muscles and would be far easier on him than a long walk. It's what all dogs would love – he'd really thank you for it."

"He does get a bit restless in the evenings..." she said.

"Then this is perfect."

"Ah, I'm not sure."

"Think about Charlie. What would he say?"

"He'd probably hate it."

"But you won't know until you've tried it. It could be the best thing he's ever done!"

"We'll have to see..."

"I read somewhere that the benefits of swimming include an increase in life expectancy and less chance of joint pains in old age."

"Is that true?" she asked.

"Absolutely," I said. It must be, right?

"We'll have a think about it."

"I'll pop a map of where the quarry is over your fence later."

I stood up to leave. There was a softening in her expression towards me and I tried not to feel guilty. I hoped I'd been convincing enough to get her to take that dog of hers over to the quarry for a swim, even if it was only the one time.

That pike wouldn't need more than one visit.

I dropped the map across to Mrs Tomlinson later that day (when I knew Christine wasn't looking) and prepared for the fallout, whenever that may come. I'd told Christine that I'd reasoned with the old bat and she'd agreed to take the dog out for a walk more often and left it at that.

We had an early night, interrupted by a spate of yapping at about four o'clock, and then we were both up and out early for work. Neither of us had any idea what a horrible day this would turn out to be. Christine left first, heading for her office to do some prep work before heading out again to deliver her training. After she'd gone, I paid a visit to Gilbert to tell him we'd be gone most of the day but not to worry. I told him I'd pop into the pet shop on my way home to get him some proper food – he loved the maggots but it was a bit of a boring diet. With a last look at him, I closed the bathroom door behind myself and went downstairs.

I left Jack on his bed chewing a treat and drove off to my own job.

When I was a child I thought I was going to be an astronaut when I grew up. Then perhaps a fireman. I suppose most kids – boys anyway – say the same things. What actually happens is that we all grow up and end up in jobs that we hate, stuck in an endless spin-cycle of trying to earn more money for better upgrades on the car, the house, the goddamned mobile phone. I'd been through a fair number of jobs and redundancies, and though I'd hated a lot of them I hadn't done too badly. My current job was based in an office a half-hour's drive from the house. I had my own desk, could get a parking space when I needed one, and there was free coffee. My colleagues were all reasonably nice and I think my boss liked me. For a middle-aged man whose dreams had long since turned to dust, it wasn't that bad a deal. It wasn't too taxing, I wasn't terrible at it and the pay kept us afloat. There was a bit left over for saving towards a good holiday every year.

The work was fairly mundane, a lot of admin and looking at invoices and receipts, the occasional mailshot. During the afternoon, I was in the middle of printing a load of address labels when my mobile rang with a number I didn't recognise. I never get calls on my mobile unless it's from Graham or Christine. I'm not sure why I decided to answer it, I guess I knew that something would be wrong.

"Hello?" I said.

"Is that Mike West?"

"Yes. Who's this?"

"Peter Wilmott. I work with your wife, Christine."

My heart skipped a beat.

"Is something wrong?" I asked, panic rising in my chest.

"It's nothing to worry about, just a precaution. She's had a bit of a tumble and banged her head. She's been taken to the hospital for a check-up, we think she's got mild concussion. Can you come over? We think you'll have to drive her home when she's been seen."

I quickly wrote down the details of the hospital and looked around the office for my boss.

I'd warned Christine about those bloody shoes!

En route to the hospital I called Graham.

"I need a favour," I told him. "Christine's had an accident and she's been taken to the hospital."

"Oh, God, no. Is she OK?"

"I think so, she's had a bit of a bang on the head."

"I'm sorry to hear that. What do you need?"

"The hospital's in bloody Telford so it's a bit out of the way. Can you pop by our place after work and feed the dog, make sure he's OK?"

"No problem. Why Telford?"

"She was doing some training over there."

"Do you know what time you'll be back?"

"No idea, late probably. Listen, thanks Gray."

"No worries. Give Chris my best."

"Will do."

I hung up. In all of the panic I'd forgotten to ask him how his new job was going.

Christine was sitting up in bed with a bandage around her head when I arrived. She broke into a broad smile at the sight of me, quickly followed by a sudden rush of tears. I'd say that was the effect I've had on most women I've known. She leaned forward and opened her arms and we hugged tightly for a few moments.

After disengaging I looked at her closely, half-expecting to be able to see any signs of possible brain damage somehow manifesting on her face. Of course there was nothing, no visible sign of trauma in her features.

I loved that face, and now it was older than the one I initially fell for, and had the beginnings of crow's feet around the eyes and tiny bags beneath them, I loved it even more. My wife was the most beautiful person I'd ever seen, to me anyway. I loved the colour of her eyes, the green/grey of deep waters touched by sunlight. I loved her pert little button nose and her thin-lipped mouth, surrounded by an almond-shaped face. I could happily look at that face forever. I would be destroyed should I never be able to look upon it again.

The best thing about Christine's face was that I could see that love reflected back at me.

I reached for her again, hugging her tightly, tears forming in the corners of my own eyes.

"I'm sorry," she said.

"Don't be silly. Listen to me – those shoes are going in the bin, okay?"

"Not the bin, they're too good to throw away. I'll take them to the charity shop."

"Make sure you do. They're lethal"

"I should listen to you more often."

"Can I get that in writing?"

"Piss off."

I sat down on a slightly too small plastic chair by the side of her bed and held her hand. For the first time I noticed there were other beds in the ward and one or two other patients were looking at me. One smiled and nodded and I smiled back.

"How long before I can take you home?" I asked her.

"They haven't told me. I think I'm just waiting for test results. Will I be able to drive?"

"I doubt it."

"What about my car? It's still at the office."

"We can worry about that later. I can come back over with Graham tomorrow, maybe."

"OK." I could see her relax a little, as though the worry about what to do with the car had been taken away from her.

"What about Jack?" she asked, concern furrowing her brow again.

"Everything's fine, stop worrying. Graham's popped by the house to see to him."

"I don't want to be here overnight."

"Well, if you are we'll have to deal with it. Let's wait and see what the test results look like."

The test results were fine. The concussion was indeed mild and, apart from a sore head and a little bruising there would be no lasting effects. The doctor, a tall slim man who looked about fourteen, advised a good rest as a precaution with a couple of days at home doing nothing strenuous.

They said we could go just after half seven and I phoned Graham to update him whilst Christine got dressed. The drive home was quiet and uneventful, the heavy traffic of rush hour long since gone. It was starting to get dark as we turned the corner into our street and we were both suddenly alert as we saw the flashing blue lights outside our house.

"What the hell...?" I said.

We drove closer and saw that the ambulance was actually outside Mrs Tomlinson's. We parked up and got out of the car just as two paramedics brought a stretcher out. Whatever was on that stretcher – an inert lump just under five feet long – was completely covered by a blanket. A wisp of frizzy white hair was poking out of the top.

"What's happened?" I asked one of the paramedics, careful not to get in their way as they loaded the stretcher into the back of the ambulance.

"Heart attack," he said simply.

"Jesus. Is she... is she dead?"

"I'm afraid so. Do you know her?"

"I'm her neighbour."

"You might want to notify any next of kin," he said, climbing back out of the ambulance and closing the doors. His colleague walked around to the front of the vehicle and got inside.

"I don't think she had any. Do you know how it happened?"

"Hard to say. Probably had a shock of some sort."

*Oh Jesus, no.*

"Is there a dog inside her house?" I asked him, my throat dry.

"We didn't see a dog."

With that he too clambered into the front of the ambulance and, with the flashing lights suddenly extinguished, they slowly drove away. I walked back over to Christine, waiting by the garden gate.

"Is she dead?" she asked.

"Yeah."

"Poor old bag."

We heard a noise and saw Graham poking his head through the gap after partially opening our front door. He came out to join us.

"They've gone then?" he asked.

"Yes," said Christine.

"I heard this moaning sound about an hour ago, then there was this loud bang. I knew something was wrong."

"Did you call the paramedics?" asked Christine.

"Yeah. How is she?"

"She's dead." I said.

"Ooh. Dear."

I was feeling terribly, horribly guilty. I could just imagine what Mrs Tomlinson's last day on Earth had been like. Believing all my guff about swimming, she'd walked her dog – *Charlie* – to the quarry and had let it swim in the pool, where a monster had been waiting. She'd bore witness to her pet being pulled beneath the surface, violently snatched away and killed. She'd probably fallen to her knees, howling, maybe even entered the pool in an attempt to rescue her beloved pet.

The walk home must have lasted an eternity. Then, she'd have sat in her lounge, thinking about nothing else. The anguish must have torn her heart in two, and it had given up on her. And I'd done this. I'd killed her.

That pike wasn't the monster, I was.

"How are you, Chris?" asked Graham.

"A bit sore. Fine, compared to her."

"Come inside, both of you. I've got just the thing to cheer you up."

I followed my wife and brother up the path to the house.

"How come you're still here, anyway?" I asked him.
"You'll see."
As soon as we entered the house I could smell it. Graham had been cooking again. The most delicious aromas teased their way up my nostrils. Until that moment I hadn't realised just how hungry I was. My God, it smelled amazing.
"Sit yourselves down," he said, taking our coats and hanging them on the hooks in the hallway. We went through to the dining room. The table was already laid out. All around, the smell of delicate herbs and spices filled the air with warmth and joy – home cooking, done exceptionally well, is one of the most pleasurable things to experience. Graham was a magician with food.
"What is it?" I asked, sniffing the air.
"Wait and see."
He disappeared off into the kitchen and we heard the clatter of things being unloaded from the oven and trays being put onto racks.
"We should invite your brother over more often," said Christine. At that moment, sitting there smiling at me, her head wrapped in a neat bandage and her face slightly droopy with tiredness, I don't think she'd ever looked lovelier.
Graham walked in and placed a large roasting tin down onto the heat-proof mat at the centre of the table. Our meal was revealed. Scattered with herbs and resting in a thick sauce was a fish. A trout. Graham stood there with his hands on his hips, beaming at us. He couldn't have looked more pleased with himself.
I slowly lifted my head to look at him. Then, with my insides crawling and dread filling my veins with ice, I asked him a question.
"Gray - where did you get the fish?"
"What do you mean?"
"This fish, Gray, the fucking FISH! Where did you get it?"
I was hoping he'd say he picked it up on his way over but I already knew that he hadn't. I felt a sharp pain spreading along my left arm and my chest hurt like I'd been punched in the solar plexus. I felt breathless. The room span and I placed my hands on the table to steady myself.
"It was in the bath upstairs," he said. "What's up with him?" he asked Christine, nodding at me with a puzzled expression.
Everything seemed to catch up with me all at once and I keeled over, clutching my chest. Later, we would discover that it was nothing more than a panic attack but at the time I thought I was dying. At the time,

curled up on the carpeted floor with my wife and brother reaching out for me, I wondered if this wasn't what I deserved and that somewhere in the room, invisible, two ghostly figures with perhaps half a dozen teeth between them were watching me suffer with grim smiles of satisfaction on their faces.

# THE HUNT

# THE HUNT

When fox hunting was once more a legal pursuit there was a big party up at the Crabbe house. It was attended by friends and family, all of whom were in favour of what they considered to be a traditional countryside pastime. It had been a long while since they had donned the regalia and set forth on a hunt and the party was merely a preliminary event for the following day.

August Crabbe welcomed his guests with a hearty laugh, sometimes a hug, and a large glass of whatever it was they felt like imbibing that night. There was plenty to go around. As soon as the political winds hinted that his favourite hobby was to be legalised once more he had started planning the party and began ordering booze. Plenty of it.

A live band played swing music under an awning in the large back garden, the end of which was marked by a post and wire fence, with nothing else to separate it from the fields and forest beyond. It was God's country, Crabbe often remarked to anyone who'd listen. The house, a sprawling twelve-bedroomed, single storey property once visited by Churchill, had been passed through the Crabbe generations for centuries and would be passed to his eldest son when he himself was dead and buried.

He had two sons, the eldest eight and the youngest six. They were bright young things, as could only be expected from the astronomical fees Crabbe stumped up to have them educated. More often than not they were away at boarding school but for the following week they would be at the house, fussed over by their mother whilst Crabbe busied himself with the hunt, the parish council, the village historical society and a hundred other things that filled up the days of a man of leisure.

And he was just that, having never been subjugated to an employer for a single day of his life, answering only to Queen and Country. An inheritor of great wealth, he had never lived by the rhythms of the common man, had never contemplated life in the shoes of one less fortunate. He was a charitable man, having some measure of philanthropy coursing through veins otherwise filled with red blood and even redder vintage wines. He gave often and generously to causes he felt deserving. He wasn't a bad man, by any means, and he was generally well liked and respected throughout the village. That's not to say there wasn't any enmity towards him, particularly from ex members of staff. Crabbe was notorious for acting like a tyrant towards those in his employ, paying minimum wage and expecting them to sometimes work additional hours for free when required. There were a handful of villagers who would have loved to see him taken down a peg or two.

The one thing he loved more than anything else, perhaps above even his wife and sons, was the hunt. There was nothing else like it. Astride a galloping horse, trumpets blaring and dogs baying, the furious stamp of hooves on the ground that flew by beneath him, Crabbe experienced something akin to Nirvana when the chase was on. Since the practice was banned, his life seemed to have been leached of colour and nothing seemed to rouse his excitement levels in quite the same way. He only had to glance at the numerous oil paintings adorning the walls, all of them hunting scenes, to feel a flutter in his stomach, an ache in his soul.

Dusk was encroaching when the party received some unexpected guests. A party of five came marching around the side of the house and into the garden waving home-made signs. The musicians stopped playing and everyone turned to look.

"What is the meaning of this?" demanded Crabbe, storming over.

"You know why we're here," said one of the men, stepping forward. The sign he held said 'HUNTING IS MURDER' and he let it fall to the floor as he squared up to Crabbe.

Crabbe, a well-built man who had some pugilistic experience from his schooldays, broke into a smile.

"You bloody idiots," he said.

"Call off the hunt," said the man. Crabbe recognised him but couldn't recall his name. Sometimes, when Crabbe went down to the local pub and mingled with the rest of the villagers, he'd receive a few deferential nods and hellos from the people he didn't know that well. Others, such as the local constable or some of the farmers, would come over for a chat. The man before him had never spoken but he'd caught him staring once or twice.

"As you well know," said Crabbe in a loud voice, "hunting has been voted back in."

"That doesn't make it right," said the man.

"Of course it's right – it's the bloody law."

"You know what I mean."

Crabbe turned to look at his guests. He spotted Dave Davies and beckoned him over. Davies, a burly man with a wonky eye came and stood next to Crabbe.

"Tell this man what happened to your chickens two nights ago," said Crabbe, folding his arms and maintaining eye contact with the interloper.

"Fox came and killed them," said Davies.

"There you go," said Crabbe. "A fox killed them. How many were there?"

"Just the one," said Davies, scratching his head.

"Chickens, Dave. How many chickens?"
"Oh. 'Bout forty."
"About forty," said Crabbe, still staring at the intruder.
The man looked at Davies and then back at Crabbe. He shook his head, slowly.
"Seems like your friend needs to build a stronger fence," he said.
"Now you listen here-" began Davies and Crabbe held up a hand to stop him.
"Leave it, Dave. I'll take it from here."
With a backward glance, Davies walked away, muttering darkly to himself.
"It's natural for foxes to kill chickens," said the man.
"Not forty in one go."
"I'm not disputing the fact that the fox was out of order by killing them all."
Crabbe hooted with laughter. "Out of order," he said to himself, and it was his turn to shake his head. "You talk as if the fox had any kind of notion of what 'order' is! They're vermin and there are too many of them. They're everywhere you look and that's why they've brought the hunt back. We'll control the numbers."
"I'm not disputing that a controlled cull would be a reasonable solution."
"Then why the hell are you here?" roared Crabbe. "Why are you trespassing on my land with your stupid little signs?"
"It's the way you kill them that bothers me. It bothers a lot of people. Tearing a fox to pieces for sport shouldn't be allowed."
"But it IS allowed, and you don't seem to be getting it."
"Don't you ever think about what that fox goes through? Chased for miles, exhausted, unable to comprehend what's going on. Cornered by a pack of dogs and set upon. Can you imagine the terror, the pain? How would you like to have chunks of your flesh ripped away whilst you screamed for it to stop, knowing that it wasn't going to stop until they'd killed you."
"Don't be so melodramatic."
"You cruel, cruel bastard." The intruder's fists clenched and unclenched by his sides.
"Fox numbers have to be controlled, you moron."
The tension between the two men was quickly rising. It felt like they might resort to violence at any moment.
"It's inhumane," said the man. "You could shoot them instead."
Crabbe sighed with exasperation. He knew the arguments well enough, had heard them all down the years. This idiot was ruining his party and the last thing he wanted was to stand there and debate him all night. He thought for a moment or two and wondered if he should call the police.

"Where are you from?" he said at last.
"What's that got to do with anything?"
"It has everything to do with it. Where are you from?"
"I was born and raised in Coventry, not that it matters."
"Like I thought. You aren't from the country. You don't know our ways. Country people have hunted for centuries. It's in our blood."
"That's no excuse. You bloody toffs think you can do what the hell you want."
"Toffs, eh?" remarked Crabbe, raising an eyebrow. "Are you sure this isn't all about something quite different from a few foxes?"
"What does that mean?"
"You know exactly what I mean. You don't like to see those more well off than you having a good time."
"That's bullshit," said the man. His face creased with controlled anger. "Listen to me. I'm warning you – don't go out on the hunt tomorrow."
"I'll be doing exactly that," said Crabbe, his voice laced with menace. "And that damned fox will be dead by the time you rouse your lazy arse out of your pit. Now, I'm warning you, get off my grounds right now or I will call the police."
The man took a step backwards.
"Don't forget I told you not to do it," he said. "Whatever happens, I gave you fair warning."
"Threaten me again and I'll knock your fucking block off," said Crabbe, finally reaching breaking point. He took a step forward, ready for a fight. The man just smiled to himself and turned away. The group left the garden.
"Someone get me a drink!" barked Crabbe.

In the early hours, whilst Crabbe and his wife were in a deep, alcohol soaked sleep, the man crept back into the garden under cover of darkness. He crossed the wide lawn and walked around to the eastern side of the house, where he knew the youngest Crabbe child had a bedroom. It had been easy enough getting the layout of the house, the information given freely by a disgruntled ex-cleaner after a few drinks down the pub.

It was a warm night and the boy's window had been left open a fraction to let air circulate. Had it been closed, the man had the tools to open it but he was glad that he didn't have to bother. There would have been some unavoidable noise and a risk of the boy waking. Slowly, carefully, he reached a finger through the gap and lifted up the latch. He opened the window and quietly heaved himself up onto the sill.

In seconds, he was standing in the room waiting for his eyes to adjust. He took a Ziploc bag from his jacket pocket and opened it, taking out a cloth handkerchief. He could make out the shape of the bed in the gloom and silently crept over. Gently, he lifted away the thin blanket so he could see the boy's face.

At that moment, the boy opened his eyes.

Before little Julian could open his mouth to scream at the sight of the dark figure looming over his bed, the man forced the handkerchief down onto his face, pressing down firmly to stop any noise escaping. The handkerchief, soaked in chloroform before being sealed in the bag, covered the boy's airways and the chemical rendered him unconscious within seconds.

Gently, stealthily, the man walked back to the window and flashed a torch out into the darkness. A second figure came running across the lawns to the window. The man returned to the bed, peeled away the blanket, reached down and picked up the boy. He passed the child through the window to the second man outside before climbing through and landing back on the grass with a soft thud.

Silently, the two men carried the boy across the lawns and into the darkness of the night beyond.

The boy woke a few short hours later. He was in a windowless room. His body ached and he sat up and looked around in alarm. A man sat on a stool in the corner of the room, watching him. Seeing him wake, the man bumped his fist against the nearby door.

"Where am I?" croaked the boy.

"That doesn't matter."

Julian looked around the room. Apart from a thin mattress and the stool there was no other furniture. The walls were bare except for patches of damp. In another corner of the room, a pile of orange-brown clothing lay in a heap. It looked filthy. The stink of it filled Julian's nostrils, which crinkled in disgust.

"Where are my parents?" he asked.

"You'll see them soon enough."

The door opened and another person stepped into the room. It was same man who had accosted the boy's father the previous day.

"I don't understand," said Julian. He looked like he was about to cry.

"You don't need to understand, just do what we tell you and you'll be home in no time at all."

The man, whose name was Reed, walked over to the corner and picked up the pile of clothing. It was a one piece item and as he held it towards the boy it revealed itself to be a child's onesie. It was a fox outfit, complete with a hood in the shape of a fox face. The whole thing stank of shit, mainly because it had been vigorously rubbed in vulpine urine and faeces.

"Take off your pyjama top and put this on," said Reed.

"I don't want to. It smells."

Reed threw it at the boy.

"Put it on," he snarled.

Julian batted the piece of clothing away in disgust. When he looked up at Reed, his eyes were filled with tears.

"No," he said defiantly.

Reed walked closer and bent over the boy. Without warning, he lashed out and slapped Julian across the face, hard enough to send him sprawling.

"Put it on or next time it'll be a punch."

Julian stared at him in shock and growing terror. He didn't doubt for a second that this man would hit him again if provoked. Julian was used to being bullied, it was part and parcel of attending boarding school for some children, and even at such a young age he knew the world could be a cruel place. But this was different. This was the world of men and the threat of violence was more sinister than anything he'd experienced before. Snuffling, he took off his top, picked up the smelly outfit and put it on. He sat back down on the thin mattress and waited, watching Reed with saucer-like eyes.

"Get the car," said Reed to the other man. "It's time."

After a few minutes Reed grabbed the pyjama top and ordered the boy to follow him. They went up a dingy staircase and entered a dark house that smelled of damp. They went outside, where a Range Rover was waiting. Julian looked around, hoping to see somebody, anybody that he could call for help. There wasn't anyone. Dawn had just broken over the distant, empty horizon. The house was isolated, a crumbling cottage in open countryside. Julian didn't recognise any of it.

He thought about running and immediately thought about the possible punishment if he was caught. And he would be caught, he knew that. He didn't want to be hit again. He realised that the only way he was going to get through this would be to keep quiet and do what they wanted.

"Get in the car," snarled Reed, holding open one of the rear doors. The seats were covered in plastic sheeting. Without a word, the boy climbed into the car and Reed slammed the door shut behind him.

Reed got into the front and the other man clambered into the driver's seat and started the engine.

"Are you sure about this?"

"It's too late to back out now, Pete."

The second man turned around and glanced at the boy before turning back.

"Don't say my name," he hissed.

"It doesn't matter," said Reed. The subtext was obvious to the adults but the boy had no idea of the implication.

They drove for the next quarter of an hour in silence. Julian, despite himself, was starting to doze off in the back. When the car suddenly stopped and the engine was silenced, he sat up straight and looked around. They were still in the open countryside.

"Get out," said Reed.

Julian was left to open the door and climb out. He stood there, in a dirty, stinking fox outfit and waited for any further instruction. The men got out of the car. Reed grabbed the pyjama top, walked over to Julian and rubbed it vigorously against the boy's back. It came away covered in smears of old fox shit. He backed off and the men stood there looking at Julian. Reed lit a cigarette and spat on the grass.

"This is your father's fault," he said.

Julian said nothing.

"Home's that way," said Reed, pointing across a huge, adjacent field. "I want you to run. Don't stop running until you get home. Ok?"

"Okay," said Julian in a quiet voice.

"Then move it!" shouted Reed, lunging forward as if to hit him.

Julian dodged out of the way and sprinted into the field. With tears streaming down his face, he ran.

Reed turned to his companion and passed him the top.

"Take this to the dogs," he said. "Make sure they get the scent."

Crabbe awoke at six with a slight hangover. He climbed out of bed gently, so as not to disturb his sleeping wife, and put on his dressing gown before leaving the bedroom.

After a shower and a quick shave he went downstairs to the kitchen and made himself a coffee. It was too early for breakfast, even for a man of such hearty appetites as Crabbe. He would wait until after the hunt – as far as he remembered, Smith-Wylde's wife Marjhorie had offered to drum up sausage and bacon sandwiches once it was all over.

Despite the dull ache in his head, he felt wide awake and full of beans. This day had been a long time coming and he couldn't quite believe it was finally here.

He drank the coffee and returned upstairs to get dressed. The sun had been up less than an hour and the wan light was slowly warming up the world outside. In silence, Crabbe dressed in his hunting outfit. Just putting it on made him feel ten years younger.

God, he'd missed this.

Fifteen minutes later he was standing in the car park of the village pub amidst the gentle chaos of the hunt preparing to head out. A dozen men stood around wearing the same regalia, talking amongst themselves and patting their horses every now and then to quieten them down.

The dogs were agitated, raring to go. They barked and howled with excitement. Two young farmhands in working clothes fussed about the dogs, trying to calm them. One of the men walked over to Crabbe.

"I dunno what's wrong with 'em this morning," he said.

"They're probably just excited," said Crabbe. "I know I am."

"They've been like this since before we arrived to let them out. Right worked up, they were."

Crabbe smiled.

"They'll run it off. They'll sleep well tonight, that's for sure."

The other hunters kept glancing over at Crabbe, waiting for the hunt to begin. He climbed up onto his horse and reached for the horn.

"Is everybody ready?" he shouted. All heads turned his way, even those of the dogs. "Then let's catch ourselves a damned fox!" He lifted the horn up to his lips and blew hard. The group moved out onto the road, where the young farmhands stood waving them safely over, and into the field beyond. With another blast of the horn, the dogs took off and the horses bolted after them.

The ride was exhilarating. All of the farmers had left their gates open so access across the surrounding fields was uninterrupted. They raced across the tamed wilderness, leaping one or two small streams and coursing through the woods, and Crabbe was filled with a joy so immense it almost made him dizzy. The wind whipped his face, his cheeks turned red and he felt at one with the sleek, powerful beast beneath him. These namby-pamby idiots who wanted to shut the hunt down again would soon change their minds if they joined in and tried the experience for themselves. There was nothing like it on God's good Earth. It was more exhilarating than anything.

After an hour the pace had slowed down somewhat, and the hunt seemed to be floundering. It would be awfully disappointing for it to end without a kill, thought Crabbe. But this sometimes happened, and he supposed it made the times where the hunt was a success even more pleasurable.

The dogs seemed to be confused, sniffing the ground and looking around for something to chase, and Crabbe was thinking of calling it a day when one of the lead dogs started barking frenziedly and raced off. The other dogs quickly followed and Crabbe, who had been the first to notice the sudden catching of the scent, was also the first to head out after the pack. His hunting companions followed, a blur of red and black on horseback, pouring across the field with a sudden, burgeoning excitement.

The hunt was back on.

In the distance, a small figure was running. The dogs, far ahead by now, were almost upon it. Something about the sight caused an element of confusion in the back of Crabbe's mind.

As he raced after them, he saw the dogs bring the fox down and swarm all over it. By the time he reached the pack, they were well on the way to tearing the fox to pieces. Only it wasn't a fox, Crabbe saw that now he was close to it. His stomach lurched and he waded into the pack, grabbing collars and yanking dogs out of the way. They were completely crazed, foaming at the mouths in their desire to tear at the soft flesh of the thing they'd caught, their muzzles soaked through with crimson.

Through a fleeting gap in the heaving mass of canine bodies, Crabbe caught sight of a small face he recognised. As he screamed, he saw a dog lunge and rip a great chunk of that tiny face away from its skull.

He was still screaming as the others reached him, screaming and fighting to keep the dogs away from his youngest child.

## THE FARDA

Dorey was a man who had never known the beauty of romance.
He had never known the caress of a woman who loved him, and had never been gazed upon without ugly thoughts rising in the mind of the observer. Not that they could help themselves. A hundred years ago, Dorey would have been a circus attraction, something for small children to pay a few pennies to stare at.

Dorey weighed thirty-one stones. A man his height should've weighed twelve. Over the years, Dorey had eaten enough to feed three, and had grown so big that some days he couldn't even get out of bed. He'd lie there, sweating into the sheets, tears in his eyes and his stomach rumbling.

He hadn't been out the front door in years. He doubted he could fit through it any more. The only time he felt fresh air was when he opened the back door and stood just inside the step, breathing heavily. The desire to roam the world outside had long vanished. The pain of the memories of the pointing fingers and cruel laughter haunted him, as fresh as though these things had happened only yesterday.

Nobody visited Dorey. He had no friends. His parents were dead, two people whose faces he had started to forget already. They had shown little love for their only offspring, choosing to shower their time and energy into their careers, which had left Dorey with an inheritance too large to sensibly contemplate.

He was all alone in the world, and he knew it.

Thank God, then, for technology.

In a way, Dorey had everything he needed right inside his house. His internet favourites folder held the web addresses for supermarket deliveries, and oversized gents catalogues, and pornography. He ordered the same enormous batch of groceries every week from a saved electronic shopping list. He paid his bills by debits from an electronic bank account. He ordered shirts the size of tents and trousers big enough for a hippo. He had new girlfriends every week, ones that stripped for him and never judged. They would look into his eyes the way a real woman never would – with lust and expectancy for a rubbery cock that had never grown proportionately, a cock that he hadn't seen for years unless it was in the mirror.

He knew all of these things could never compensate for an existence amongst the living, flesh and blood populace that went about their lives just yards from his self-imposed prison, but they were enough to stop him ordering a twin-barrelled Purdey shotgun and blowing his own fat bowling ball of a head into oblivion.

Dorey's favourite food was banana. The other things he ate, the cakes and crisps, the pork chops and chips with garlic and herb sauce, the cheesecakes and ice cream, the southern-fried chicken fillets and goujons and bacon sandwiches, the strawberry milkshakes, the burgers and biscuits and buns and everything else – these things were nice, but they weren't bananas.

Some fat people blamed their glands or their genes, but Dorey knew the only reason he was so fat was because of his greed, and his love for food. When he wasn't eating, he was thinking about food. When he was sleeping, he dreamed he was eating. Often, he would start wondering what to cook for his tea when he was still wolfing down his dinner.

He liked what he liked and varied little from the range of dishes he cooked himself. Many of the meals were the same that he used to eat as a boy, things his mother cooked him such as sausages and mash, and fish fingers and chips, exactly as he remembered them only five times the size. Such meals brought small joys to a largely joyless existence, and yet with them a sadness that was hard to bear. The things that made him happy in life were his memories, and memories of better times brought a melancholy tinge and a bitterness for the present.

When Dorey was a small boy, eight or nine years old and still a mere ghost of what he would become, the small girl across the road (whose name he could no longer remember) once gave him a banana. Thirty years later, he had no idea why such a thing would happen, and sometimes doubted such a thing did indeed happen, but in his memory this tiny slip of a girl held out her hands to him and offered a yellow piece of fruit.

This mere snapshot in time would reverberate down the decades for Dorey, and become an important event for all the wrong reasons. It was a mystery that would never be revealed, the whys and wherefores forever buried in time. This simple act of kindness was an exaggerated event of pleasure in a distorted playground of nightmares and miserable tortures, the ever increasing loneliness of adolesence.

Little does it matter, but the real reason the girl – now a married mother of three who would not remember this incident – gave the fat boy the banana was because she herself did not like bananas, and there is no more mystery than this.

Translated into literal terms, in the present, Dorey absolutely loved eating bananas, for as well as the divine taste they also gave him a general feeling of happiness, of well-being and security. For these reasons, he had two crates of imported, fresh bananas delivered to his house once a week from a local market. Promptly at eight in the morning, every Friday, Dorey would open the front door and receive the crates of fruit in return for a cheque given to the dour faced elderly gent who drove the delivery van.

For years this continued, until one day Dorey found something rather unpleasant in one of his crates. Just as his blubbery arm was pulling out a bunch of bananas, something spilled from the crate and landed on the floor with a gentle thud. Startled, the small black object, about the size of a bunched fist, woke in a fury and stared up at Dorey with its eyes aflame.

It was the biggest spider Dorey had ever seen in his life. Out of instinct more than anything else, he raised one great fat leg high in the air and the spider let out a piercing screech at the sight of its impending nemesis – the underside of a size eleven boot.

'Don't kill me, mon!' screeched the spider, raising a number of legs to cover its eyes.

Dorey halted, stunned, off-balance with one leg still in the air.

'Don't kill me, mon,' repeated the beast. 'I's not worth a killin'.'

Dorey let his foot come back down to the ground, and he backed away.

'What are you doing in my crate?' he asked.

'Was sleepin', 'fore you come an' turf me out. Mercy on me, big feller.'

The two regarded each other, a touch of fear in the air. Dorey backed away another yard, and placed his hands onto his great hips.

'Why were you in my crate? Who put you there?'

'I's hijacked, mon. Put on a fuckin' boat an' brought here. No choice for me.'

'Where are you from?'

'Plenty places. Jamaica de last place, clot.'

Dorey contemplated this for a few moments. He thought about trying to stamp on the little beast before it had a chance to get away and hide, but decided not to.

'What you gonna do wit' me?'

'You'll have to leave.'

'Aah, mon. Cold out there, you know. Be the det o' me. You got no room for a spider in ya house, blud?'

Against his better judgement, and feeling pity for the skanky beast, Dorey decided to let the spider rest in the house for a day or two, though he laid down a few conditions. This was despite the small shiver of revulsion he felt every time he saw the little monster, for no man, however lonely, finds comfort in the sharing of his abode with an arachnid. It was not to go upstairs, nor was it to go back in the crate. Dorey threatened death, in no uncertain terms, should it venture near to his beloved bananas.

'I's a good house-guest,' it said. 'Quiet, like.'

'You'd better be.'

It was the start of a magnificent friendship.

A few days turned into a week, turned into a month. As it turned out, Dorey did find comfort in the companionship of the little visitor, and the relationship quickly developed into one similar to those found between humans and canines. The spider generally kept out of the way during the day, off on little adventures and explorations around the house. But, in the evenings, particularly when Dorey turned on the electric fire, it would come into the lounge and sit watching television with its new master. Before long, Dorey had ordered a small cushion for the beast, and the two would sit together on the sofa and watch soaps and suchlike.

The spider fulfilled numerous needs for Dorey, one of which was an education, of sorts, about the world at large. Having spent so much time indoors, he was mostly ignorant of the goings-on of the globe outside of the boundaries of what appeared on the news. His little friend had travelled all over the Caribbean, it seemed, and told tales of places Dorey knew he would never visit. It regaled its fat host with stories of voodoo, and stews made primarily of chickens' feet. In a hushed voice, it recanted the story of how, when it was just a baby spiderling, it lived for a while in a lush jungle in the middle of a desert, and one day the food ran out and all its siblings had turned upon each other. The beast had paused for a long time, for these memories held much power. Eventually, it had finished the story by telling how it had let loose a great strand of web to catch the wind and lift it skyward to pastures new.

'I's too heavy for that kind of ting now,' it said, and the two stared at each other in a kind of mutual understanding.

The house was a veritable assault course for the eight-legged athlete, a minefield of empty packets and boxes to clamber over and under and in between. Dorey was something of an untidy gent, whose skills at tossing litter towards the tiny waste-basket were in need of honing. Every now and then he would fetch a black bin-liner from the dusty cupboard beneath the sink and spend half a day blubbering around the house scooping up great armfuls of rubbish. This hadn't happened for a few months at least, and the impracticality of living in such conditions soon took their toll on the spider. Before long it tended to stick to the walls and even the ceiling, going about its business whilst keeping well clear of the clutter collected by idleness and gravity.

Occasionally it would wander down to inspect some morsel of food, some stagnating titbit that had somehow missed Dorey's mouth and ended up on the floor, a glittering, pungent leftover of one kind or another swifty heading for a fungal existence of spewing spores and rank fumes.

Mostly though, it kept a lookout for living things, and patiently held out for the summer, when the flies would come.

As the days warmed up, the agents of Beelzebub began making their appearance, groggy and dizzy at first, knocking themselves against windows and light-shades. With the amount of detritus on the floors, no passing fly could resist the trip into the house, where a feast of vomit-inducing goodies lay scattered all around. It was a problem Dorey had kind of learned to live with over the years, though he suffered the visitors with a kind of permanent, inchoate Krakatoa bubbling beneath the illusion of calm. They seemed to tease him, to know intuitively that he was too fat and slow to chase them. Every summer, the little bastards would buzz past his face and perform circuits around his head, daring him to heave himself off his great, lardy arse to chase them. He grew to hate flies, and tolerance came only out of the acceptance that he could do nothing to make them disappear.

So it was with enormous pleasure, one day, that he saw his little friend dangling patiently in the kitchen doorway, waiting for a monstrous bluebottle to come his way. He stopped what he was doing to watch. The fly buzzed backwards and forwards, from the lounge to the kitchen, and the spider stayed hanging, perfectly still as the piece of living shit with wings passed closer and closer each time. Then, when the fly was passing directly beneath it, the spider dropped, catching the fly on its way down.

They hit the floor and rolled, a cartoon explosion of wings and writhing legs. Dorey took great delight in hearing the furious buzzing as the fly tried to get free. Within seconds the commotion had stopped, and the spider enjoyed its finest meal yet on these shores.

'Dat was lovely, mon,' it said when it had finished.

'I'll bet it was,' said Dorey.

'Listen,' said the spider as it walked a little closer. 'I's wondering if I could ax you someting.'

'Go on.'

'I's wanting to put a few webs up around de house, like. Catch de flies widout all de hunting, you know. How's dat sound, mon?'

'I'm not sure. Might make the place look a bit messy.'

The spider let out a hoot and did a small Mexican wave with its hairy limbs.

'You is serious? De place a right mess!'

Dorey was about to take great offence until he realised the beast was right. The house was more like a public tip than a home.

'Are you suggesting I clean up?' he asked ruefully.

'Would not be a bad ting. Might make de place nicer for when de women come round.'

Now it was Dorey's turn to laugh.

'Someting I said?'

'Look at me!' cried Dorey, throwing his arms out wide and looking down at his great belly. 'You think a woman would look twice at a man like me?'

'You's a bit fat, like, but you lose a bit o' de blubba you be fine.'

'You really think so?' Dorey waddled over to the mirror and cleared a film of dust from it with his sleeve. He stared at his forlorn reflection and tried to imagine what he would look like if all the fat was stripped away. His imagination was not so good. He had nothing to work with – he'd never been any possible interpretation of slim.

He turned on the spider, feeling the rage rising up inside himself. All the self-loathing and hatred roiled its way to the forefront of his thoughts, so strong that he felt he might faint with the intensity of the anger.

'Are you making fun of me?' he bellowed, jabbing a fat finger at the beast. Sensing danger, the spider jumped up onto the wall and scuttled towards the corner by the ceiling. It stopped and regarded Dorey with eight glittering eyes.

'No, mon,' it said. 'You's could be a good lookin' feller, if you tried. Have de women knockin' at de door, like.'

'And how do you suggest this thin person materialises?'

'Easy, mon. Exercise. Udderwise you be stayin' fat an' growin' old all lonely.'

And those few words of the spider struck not a chord, but a symphony. It came like an ugly and violent epiphany, the knowledge that unless he changed everything about himself and the way he lived he'd have his worst fears come true: nothing would change. This life he lived would be set in stone, until the day he died. Squalor and blubber, stale air and confinement, Internet shopping and pornography.

'God-damnit you're right!' he cried. He looked at his samaritan and smiled. 'there's going to be a few changes around here,' he said, and he meant it.

The next day, Dorey was up early. He fetched all of the black bin-liners from beneath the sink and spent the entire morning picking up every last piece of rubbish. He found cups with unrecognisable pools of sludge lurking at the bottom, he found plates with things growing on them. All of the empty boxes and packets and wrappers went into the rubbish bags, and one by one he tossed them out through the front door onto the garden.

The spider dangled on a web from the ceiling, watching all of this and occasionally throwing instructions and advice his way.

'Under de sofa, mon.'

'Dat plate a goner. Trow it.'

By the time the rooms were clear, Dorey's clothes were ringing wet with the sweat of his efforts. He flopped down onto the settee and felt like he was going to have a heart attack.

'Already exercising, mon,' consoled the spider. 'Good for you.'

Dorey didn't feel so enthused any more.

'Now what?' he asked.

'Now de real work start. You got de books, mon, wid de pictures in?'

'My porn?'

'No! Tings you can buy.'

'Catalogues?'

'Ay. You gotta get de smart clodes, Babylon.'

'Nothing I wear is smart! They don't make smart clothes for people like me.'

'Den you is order clodes too small for you.'

'And how do I wear clothes too small for me?'

'Easy, mon. You is got to get smaller.'

Over the next month, Dorey followed all of the advice offered to him, despite the fact that it came from an arachnid banana boat refugee. He knew in his heart that these things made sense. He ordered a new set of clothes and hung them in the bedroom so he could see them every day, and felt inspired to keep doubling his efforts until he could wear them.

The spider banished all mirrors from the house, and they were stored in the spare room, faces into the wall. Under his tutelage, Dorey started eating different things. He started to exercise. He threw away his dirty magazines and deleted his numerous two-dimensional girlfriends.

'You get rid of de filt' an' get ready for some real lovin'.'

'Oh, yes!' said Dorey, and he even started to feel a little optimistic.

Another month after this, Dorey had just finished a hundred push-ups when he heard the spider calling him from the bathroom. Covered in sweat, he stood and walked to the bathroom and saw his little friend standing on a pair of scales, its legs patting the metal surface with excitement.

'Weigh yourself,' it said.

'But I thought you told me not to?'

'Dat was a long time ago. Weigh yourself.'

With some trepidation, Dorey ambled across to the scales. He knew he'd lost a lot of weight in a relatively short time, but he had no idea of how much. The spider had kept him so busy, and had made so many changes to his life that Dorey had soon learned not to keep thinking about his own weight – instead he concentrated on the tasks at hand, the changing of diet and the new regimes of exercise and fitness. Then the shopping sprees had taken his complete attention, and he had thrown out his shabby furniture and ordered new suites and things he never even considered purchasing before. New lights with dimmer controls. Vases. Real art, prints in frames with actual glass in front of them.

He stepped onto the scales and the spider stood on a shelf to observe.

'You have to open de eyes, mon.'

Dorey opened his eyes and looked down.

The first change was the fact that he could even see the reading. Two months previously there was a fantastic mound of belly-flesh in the way. With some surprise, Dorey realised he could see his feet again. He hadn't looked down on them in over a decade. He could see the end of his cock. Normal things for most men, but to Dorey this was a bone-fide miracle, an event equal to man walking on the moon.

'Well?' asked the spider.

Dorey looked at the reading. Nineteen stone and two pounds.

'Fuck me!' he exclaimed.

'Aah!' said the spider, much pleased. 'Is good news. But you gotta choice, mon.'

'What? What choice?'

'To continue. Dese tings can escalate. You's good enough for some o' de women like a bit o' de big fellers, but you's still some blubba left to shed. Keep dis up, mon, you's be down another tree stone in a mont. Have all de women look den.'

'I want to do it!' cried Dorey, like a child. This was unbelievable.

'You is okay me sticking aroun'?' asked the spider.

Dorey felt his stomach drop. The intonation of the question almost made him panic.

'What does that mean?' he asked.

'Well! I's been keepin' de house clean of de flies an' that, but is Winter comin' on. Now you's thinnin' an' shapin' up you's may be tinkin' of trowin' me out.'

Dorey felt something that he'd never felt before. It was hard to define. The thought of losing his friend was almost too much to bear. All of the elation fell away to nothing. He held out his hand towards the spider.

'What you doin', mon?'

'Come here.'

Tentatively, the spider walked to the edge of the shelf and looked at the hand for a moment. In all this time the pair had never actually touched. Like a man testing pool water with a big toe, it placed the end of a leg down onto Dorey's hand and pressed against the flesh. Then it carefully traversed the gap until it was standing on the palm.

It was heavier than Dorey expected. Its body was the size of a large orange after keeping the house clear of flies all summer. Its leg hairs were bristly.

'I'm not going to throw you out,' he told it.

'I's just worried, like. Winter comin' soon an' that. And I's got someone else to tink about now.'

'What do you mean?'

'When you been off doin' your exercisin', I been under de floorboards. Courtin', like. I's found me a lady.'

'You have a girlfriend?'

'Please, mon. Embarrass.'

Dorey laughed and bent down to place the beast onto the floor. The motion was fluid and easy. 'Well,' he said.

'You's like to meet her?'

'Why not! We'll throw her a party. How about tonight?'

Later that day, Dorey opened the front door to his house and stood on the step for a long time, looking at the street and the things in it. Dressed in his new clothes, he surveyed the previously impossible, and knew that a new dawn had come.

He stepped over the threshold and entered the real world. He touched concrete with the sole of his new boots. He breathed fresh air and looked up at the immense blue sky.

And then, placing one foot in front of the other, he walked down his overgrown garden path and went to look at what reality had to offer him.

That night, Dorey placed his new plates onto his new table and lit a new candle and poured himself some red wine into a new glass. The lights were dim. Even without redecorating, the place was transformed. Dorey had turned into a human being, and his house reflected that. He could pass for being civilised now.

Whilst he waited for his guests he ruminated on that day when he first found his new friend, and felt sick at the thought of what could have happened if he'd followed his instincts and stamped the hairy intruder into the carpet. This new him would not exist. He had a lot to be grateful for. Everything, really.

He drank his wine in a gentle, reflective silence and waited.

'We's here, mon,' came a voice from the doorway.

'Well, come on in,' said Dorey, turning.

In the darkness, two dark spots of shadow moved across the carpet and came into the glow of the light. The familiar beast had with him a companion. Dorey almost gagged at the sight of her. A great, bulbous body the size of a large plum was suspended on eight spindly, hairless legs. This was the kind of spider that inspired a hatred amongst humans. Different from a solid, hairy beast that could almost pass for a small mammal, she was the epitomy of arachnia, the alien and ugly form of a creature that roams beneath the floorboards and occasionally staggers a homeowner by racing across the carpet at full speed.

'Isn't she lovely, mon?' asked his friend.

'I suppose she is,' said Dorey, trying not to gag.

'She been lookin' fore-wad to meeting wid you. I's told her you's been so good to me, like.'

Dorey watched as the pair climbed onto the nearest chair and then clambered up onto the table, bridging the small gap with effortless leaps. They stood on the table, sixteen twinkling eyes watching him.

'What is we eating?'

Dorey stood and backed away towards the kitchen. 'Chicken for me,' he said. 'I managed to find you two something special.' He disappeared into the kitchen and returned with two tiny saucers, a small pile of dead flies on each. He placed them at the far end of the table and the spiders moved closer to inspect them. There was an unappreciative silence for a few seconds.

'Anything wrong?' asked Dorey.

'We's prefer something movin'.'

'Oh.'

'Dere might be a mot or sometin' in de kitchen?'

'I'll have a look.'

Dorey went to the kitchen and found it empty of moths. He opened the window and waited for the first poor unfortunate to come skitting to its doom. After a few minutes he caught one, large and fat like a very small bird, and returned to the lounge.

The spiders were waiting for him. The female bobbed up and down on her spindly legs, excited about the coming meal. Dorey opened his hands and a disorientated moth fell clumsily onto the table. In a blur of motion, the two spiders fell upon it, and Dorey watched the feast with disgust.

'That was lovely, mon. Is you not eatin'?'

Dorey no longer felt hungry.

'I think I'll just stick to the wine,' he said, returning to the kitchen to turn off the oven.

The summer slowly grew colder and darker, and winter fell upon them. Dorey continued to share his house with his spidery guests, more often than not all three sat together in the lounge where the electric fire made things nice and cosy.

The romance was coming along just fine, and Dorey would sometimes watch the pair chasing each other around the room in a display of energetic courtship. They respected Dorey's privacy enough to disappear beneath the floorboards for their bouts of lovemaking.

Dorey, however, fell into something of a funk over his lack of finding a mate of his own.

'You is down,' observed the spider one night. His own lady, always silent and wary of Dorey even after such a long time of rent-free living in his house, was asleep behind the opaque veil of webbing in a corner of the room.

'I can't help it,' he said. 'I'm still lonely.'

'But you is have a family wid us,' it said.

'It's not the same. I want a woman.'

'Then you is lookin' all wrong.'

'What are you talking about?'

'You is not switched on for lovin',' it said. 'You's not givin' off de right vibes.'

'What vibes? What the fuck are you talking about?'

'When was de las' woman come here? To de house, like?'

Dorey couldn't remember ever seeing a woman inside the house.

'Never,' he said.

'Well! Der it is. You is needin' some nice music an' food. Make de place a lair, like. Be enticin' de woman back.'

'You think that would work?'

'Work for me.'

Dorey took a large glug of red wine and stood up to look in the mirror.

'I need a shave,' he observed.

'Haircut not be a bad ting.'

'Maybe.'

Dorey left the room and reappeared ten minutes later, his chin free of whiskers and his hair combed with some gel in the fringe.

'I'm going out,' he said. 'Don't wait up.'

In the early hours, the spiders were woken up by a loud crash in the hallway and the sound of two voices laughing. Startled, they came out of their web to watch as Dorey and a strange woman burst into the lounge and turned the lights on.

The spiders immediately bolted back into the darkness of their hidey-hole and peered out from behind the edge of the web.

The woman was older than Dorey by about ten years. She was a little overweight, a little weathered, and her laugh was like a chainsaw cutting at stone. She gave the room a cursory once-over with her eyes and moaned at nothing in particular.

'You like the place?' asked Dorey, standing behind her with his eyes fixed on her backside.

'Very posh,' she said, completely giving away a thousand details of her own upbringing.

'Come here,' said Dorey, lunging at her and spinning her around so their faces connected. They all but fell into the sofa and spent a few minutes slobbering over each other. The spiders could see Dorey was in Heaven. His glazed eyes were wide and full of joy, and when his lips weren't fixed limpet-like to the woman's he was grinning fit to split his face in half.

It was obvious he was on a promise.

'I'll get that wine,' said Dorey, standing. The spiders watched as he staggered towards the kitchen, and then all sixteen eyes flicked a little bit to the left. A small moth had followed Dorey and his companion into the house, and now it flittered around the room, circled in a wobbly orbit and flew headlong into the lightbulb. As Dorey disappeared into the kitchen, the dizzy moth spiralled towards the carpet, and in a sudden rush the female spider dashed from the web to hunt it down.

The next few seconds turned the world upside down.

The woman let out a piercing scream, the kind that women make when witnessing the murder of their offspring, and leapt from the sofa. A great stiletto shoe went up into the air, attached to the wobbly expanse of bare, cellulite-riddled leg, and came hurtling down.

Spindly spider legs were strewn everywhere, and that great plum of a body exploded beneath the sole.

Dorey flew back into the lounge, expecting to find some sort of violent intruder, and saw his new girlfriend flying towards the doorway, fleeing the lounge. As he went after her, his eyes flicked down to the carpet and saw the pulverised body of the spider.

'Oh no!' he said, but did not stop to console his friend, who had also run out to take in the scene of devastation.

There was a commotion in the hallway but the spider did not hear it. It looked at the remains of its mate and heaved with a great sob.

Amongst the mess were dozens of half-formed baby spiders, tiny and squashed and dead.

That night, Dorey had his first sexual experience involving more people than just himself. He couldn't believe his luck. But, the foreplay was something he could have done without.

The woman was beside herself with terror, still aghast at the sight of that huge spider running straight for her bare legs. She had trampled the beast out of pure instinct, jumping up to stamp it into the carpet before she even knew what she was doing.

Upstairs, on the edge of the bed, there were tears and lots of smoked cigarettes before she had calmed down enough to even relive the horror for Dorey.

'It was disgusting!' she wailed.

Dorey, who could not tear his eyes from the sight of her hitched skirt, was not really listening, instead his drunken mind was racing, trying to think of the right words to shut her up so he could get his hands on her flesh.

'It was just a spider,' he said, his comforting hands getting a thrill out of touching her, even through her clothing.

At the top of the stairs, the forlorn mate listened to this betrayal, its little heart dealt a second hammer-blow by Dorey's callousness. As the minutes passed and the floor started to shake with the rocking of the human coupling, the spider felt a tremendous rush of anger, and bobbed up and down on its eight hairy legs.

The sun came through the net curtain, splitting into swords of light as it passed through the holes. One vicious lance hit Dorey smack on the eyelid and he groaned.

Slowly, he became aware that he was still alive. The light on his eyelid set off a nuclear meltdown inside his head, and his brain felt like it had expanded overnight. He felt the pressure as it pushed at his skull, trying to burst its way out.

He let the hangover take hold, hoping that it would dim in intensity. The memories of the previous night wormed their way into his mind. The feel of the woman, whose name he had now forgotten. The size of her tits, and the way they felt in his hands.

He sensed a coldness in the bed, next to him.

He remembered the taste of her. He remembered riding her. What the hell was her name? He delayed moving, in case she woke up and it emerged that he had no idea what she was called. Dorey felt it would be extremely bad-mannered not to try to remember.

But something in the bed was very cold, enough to disturb him. He opened his eyes and turned to face her.

He screamed.

Next to him, lying in his bed, the woman lay dead with her nose and mouth webbed shut.

Dorey leapt from the bed and hauled off the duvet. She was naked, and turning blue. He remembered the full events of the previous night.

'Oh no,' he said.

He pulled on a pair of trousers and ran to the stairs, calling for the spider. There was no reply. He felt the panic rising up. There was a dead body in his bedroom!

'You little shit!' he shouted from the landing. 'You'd better be gone when I get down, or I'll kill you, I swear I will!' He stormed down the stairs, in such a rage that he would tear the house upside down to find the little murderer.

He didn't see the thick strand of web running from the banister to the wall, only felt the sudden taut line against his shin and then he was falling, tumbling heavily down the last few steps. The last thing he felt was the thud of his skull connecting with the floor, and then there was nothing but darkness.

Pain.

Dorey felt pain in his head.

He opened his eyes and saw a blur, a dark spot in the centre of his vision.

Slowly, it came into focus. Hanging directly above his face, the spider stared balefully into his eyes. Dorey tried to move.

'I'm paralysed,' he croaked.

'Ay, bumbaclot,' said the spider.

Dorey stared back at the beast. He felt a crawling in his stomach. Fear. Dorey realised that he could still feel his body – he wasn't paralysed.

He was bound.

'You've tied me up!' he said.

'You was comin' to kill me.'

'I wasn't!'

'We boat know you was. Now de question is 'What I's gonna do wid you?'

The spider lowered itself and settled onto Doreys chest. Dorey rolled his eyes down to look at the beast. He saw two little fangs in its mouth, dripping their venom onto his clothing.

'Let me up!' said Dorey, genuinely frightened. 'I thought we were friends!'

'All dat changed now.'

'You've murdered my girlfriend,' said Dorey.

'And you's killed me lady and me little...' The spider trailed off and its eyes grew glassy.

'You mean..?' asked Dorey.

'Dat right. Your woman be killin' de whole family.'

Dorey closed his eyes for a moment and heaved a great sigh.

'So what now?' he asked. 'Are you going to put your web in my mouth too?'

'I was tinkin' more of the venom. In the neck, like. Be a slow det. I don't want to do it, mon. You is like.....'

'Like what?'

'You is like a farda to me.'

There was silence for a few moments.

‘Only one way out o’ dis mess, widout de killin’,’ said the spider.
‘Go on.’
‘You has to promise two tings.’
‘What?’
‘If I’s be lettin’ you up, der be no stampin’ on me.’
‘Agreed!’ said Dorey, sensing a glimmer of hope. ‘What else?’
‘You’s leave de body on de bed, like. Upstairs be mine now.’
‘What do you want me to do that for?’
As if on cue, a fat bluebottle buzzed out of the lounge and circled overhead. The spider turned to watch it, and sat on Dorey’s chest as the fly traversed the length of the hallway and then buzzed its way up the stairs towards the bedroom.
‘You don’t mean...?’
The spider looked back into Dorey’s eyes, its fangs secreting a sudden surge of venom.
‘Ah, mon,’ it said. ‘Now you is getting’ de picture.’

## BONSHER

As an incentive to get young children interested in anything that didn't have a screen, the government initiated a programme of inviting interesting people from local communities into schools to give talks about any subject that the Head Teachers agreed might be informative. This could be on any subject, irrespective of the prospectus.

At the Grange Junior and Comprehensive School this had proven a modestly successful endeavour. So far, the children had been subjected to talks on civil engineering, app design, archery in a sporting context, fishmongery, the prison service, the importance of food hygiene and, in a particularly lively presentation that was boycotted at the school gates by a collective of local traders, the benefits of having a local, major supermarket.

It was not always easy to book a speaker, despite the inundation of offers from corporate interests looking to poison a few young minds early. The Headmaster, Mr Hartlebury (an elderly gent who fondly remembered the days of corporal punishment), struggled to get speakers who could perhaps teach his young students one or two more abstract lessons about life. When he heard about Mr Carter and his elephant through an acquaintance at the golf club, Hartlebury made a special effort to contact him and invited him to share his story.

As a result, frail old Mr Carter walked into the school one Thursday afternoon and shortly thereafter found himself standing, somewhat nervously, in front of a class of 8 year olds. Mrs Staniforth, the teacher, introduced him to the children and then took a seat at the back and watched as Mr Carter cleared his throat and placed a tatty folder down on the desk in front of him. Twenty-five pairs of young eyes stared at him, unblinking, wondering what he was going to be talking about.

For Mr Carter, it had been a hard decision to come along and open himself up like this. Essentially a private person, he had kept himself to himself for all of his life. He had never spoken publicly before and even though the audience was made up of children he was no less apprehensive because of it. He felt a dampness around his collar and on the palms of his hands. Quickly, he wiped them on his trousers and looked back at the children.

He took a small photograph out of the folder and held it up towards them. They leaned forward to see what it was. The photo showed Mr Carter as a much younger man. Standing next to him, coming only as high as his knee, was a miniature elephant. Mrs Staniforth, standing for a moment, suggested that Mr Carter pass it to young Beyonce at the front, who could then pass it around for the rest of the children to see. He stepped forward and, with a smile, handed the picture to the young girl.

"This is – was – Bonsher," he said in a sad voice. "An Indian elephant with a rare form of dwarfism that meant he was rejected from his family and taken into human care for his own protection. Without human intervention, it's likely that he wouldn't have survived more than a few short years."

He paused for a few moments, collecting his thoughts before continuing:

"The zoo that had taken him on was struggling for money, and my father offered to take him off their hands. Zoos don't usually sell their animals but, I suppose, they were desperate. My father told me years later that the zoo closed shortly after he bought Bonsher and the rest of the animals were put down. Anyway, I got him as a Christmas present when I was about your age and he stayed with me for over sixty years. He passed away eighteen months ago and I miss him every single day."

It was clear (to Mrs Staniforth at least) that talking about the little elephant was clearly an emotional exercise for the old man, and the pain of his loss was still raw. He looked such a sad and lonely figure, standing there in his old suit, his eyes growing watery.

Beyonce passed the photograph to the child sitting at the next desk along, a boy called Brooklyn who gave it a cursory glance and tossed it to the adjacent child on his other side. The photo landed on the floor, face down, and there was a scratching sound as it was dragged along before being picked up.

Mr Carter stood there, unsure of how to proceed. There was a lump in his throat. Talking about Bonsher was proving as difficult as he'd imagined it would, stirring up all kinds of emotions and memories. He could still feel the loss of his little pal as an ache somewhere deep inside his chest, a physical manifestation of his grief. That would never go away.

After being contacted by the headmaster, Mr Carter had, after some considerable thought, finally accepted the invitation because he wanted to share his happy memories of Bonsher with the local schoolchildren, an exercise that would keep the little fellow alive somehow, and perhaps be carried forward in the minds of these youngsters after he himself had passed away.

But now the time had come to talk, his mind seemed to have gone blank and he didn't know what to say next.

Recognising that Mr Carter was struggling, Mrs Staniforth called out from the back:

"Tell us about Bonzai, Mr Carter. What was he like?"

"Bonsher," he said, smiling.

She flushed at her mistake. "I'm sorry."

"No, it's fine. Well, he was the friendliest of creatures. He loved meeting people and letting them stroke his head. When he was happy, which was most of the time, he would have this big grin on his face, and I often used to think he was laughing. Sometimes, he'd raise his trunk and let out a sound like a trumpet."

He looked at the children, expecting perhaps a giggle or two at the thought of happy little Bonsher making a trumpeting sound. He was startled by their apparent lack of interest. A few of them were already tuned out, fiddling with their mobile phones. Two others were talking amongst themselves. One was picking his nose and staring out of the window and one more might even have been asleep.

"He was my best friend," he said, his voice barely audible. "We did everything together. We would go out into the countryside, roaming anywhere and everywhere, across fields and through streams. Rain or shine, we practically lived outdoors. I remember his little face the first time he saw snow.... the sheer joy, the sparkle in his eyes. Before long he could gather up a bit of snow in his trunk and sort of blow it out, almost as good as throwing it – we had some pretty good snowball fights, I can tell you...."

He looked up at the children and realised that none of them seemed to be listening. Mr Carter swallowed, his throat dry, and wiped his palms on his trousers again.

"I taught him how to swim in the local quarry, but of course that's long gone now. I think it's where the big shopping centre is. You probably wouldn't remember it, but your parents might...."

He trailed off, aware that he was starting to wander.

"Mr Carter?" asked Mrs Staniforth.

"Yes, dear?"

Her face blanched.

"Please don't call me 'dear'", she said, her smile taut.

"Oh, my apologies. I'm old fashioned that way."

"It's not a problem," she said, though clearly something about the term had niggled her. She shifted in her seat, knowing that she shouldn't have reacted. She knew he meant nothing by it but she also knew that terms like 'dear' were derogatory in this day and age, a condescension towards women that had no place in modern society. Annoyingly, she knew that now she had reacted, the children would no doubt call her 'dear' for the rest of the term. "What did you do for a job?" she asked, partly out of curiosity, partly to keep the talk going a tad longer.

"I worked on the canals for most of my life."

"Really? That sounds very interesting, doesn't it, children?"

Nobody answered.

"Maybe you could come back in and give a talk about that, one day?"

There was a quiet groan from one of the children and a few giggles broke out.

"Well, maybe," said Mr Carter, looking as though he wanted nothing more than to get out of there as quickly as possible.

"Who would look after Bonsher during the day?" she asked.

"He'd come with me! I really did mean it when I say we did everything together. I worked repairing the locks, see, and we could walk to each job along the towpath. People would have a right old shock when they saw the two of us walking along. We were always having our photograph taken. He loved the attention, especially from the ladies."

"So Bonsher was a bit of a ladies man?"

"Oh, I'd say," said Mr Carter, smiling to reveal a gap-toothed grin.

"And did you ever marry?"

"I didn't have the time. Bonsher took up all of my time, there wasn't really room for anybody else. I know that sounds very strange but that's just the way it was. A lot of people don't put much stock in such dotage but to me he was more than just an animal. I loved Bonsher as much as I could've loved any human. More, probably. He never let me down, not once. Through thick and thin, he was always there for me. And me for him."

"And he was with you for how long, did you say?"

"All my life, practically. In sixty years, he never left my side."

She looked around the room. Not one of the children was paying attention to the old man any more. It was such a shame. It was a wonderful story and they were simply ignoring him, to the extent that the atmosphere was getting a little uncomfortable. At least she had taken an interest and she hoped the old man could see that. Still, despite the way the talk was going, the fact that these brats hadn't murdered each other and had at least sat still for the last fifteen minutes was something of a success. She did feel terribly sorry for Mr Carter though. Maybe if he was talking about video games, or Facebook, or celebrities, the little shits might have been a bit more receptive.

"I didn't know elephants lived that long," she said at last.

"Oh, some live a lot longer," said Mr Carter. "Bonsher had a heart condition that developed later in life, but the vet told me that it had always been there and nobody knew anything about it until.... Well, until it was too late."

"I'm sorry." She didn't know what else to say. His sadness was clear to see in the way he stooped, the way his face was starting to crumple.

"He had a good life," said Mr Carter suddenly, voicing his thoughts rather than directly addressing the children. "He was very much loved, and he knew it."

A tear rolled down Mr Carter's cheek. He wiped it away and looked around the room, catching Mrs Staniforth's eye. She could tell that the talk was now over, that trying to prolong it was only going to upset the old man further. She stood up and clapped her hands to rouse the children from whatever daydreams or stupor they were possessed by.

"Everybody thank Mr Carter for coming in," she said in a commanding voice.

There were a few non-appreciative mumbles.

She handed back the photograph – now scratched, with a smear of something distorting Bonsher's little face – and thanked Mr Carter for coming along and sharing his memories. Blinking hard, trying not to show how upset he was, he mumbled something back and fled from the classroom.

He walked as quickly as his old legs would allow him, out of the school grounds and across to the local park. He sat down on a bench and started to cry. He was there for quite a while.

# THE WHALER

### One

I had no business in America. I had come to make my fortune and had failed, miserably. They said there was gold in the hills out West, but I found nothing other than dead things and lawlessness. I gave away my prospecting equipment and gave up on the dream of a new life, heading back to the eastern seaboard on foot, relying upon the kindness of strangers to survive.

I was in New Bedford to try and make my way back home to England, tail between my legs, humbled.

New Bedford was an old town, for this part of the world. The houses lining the streets leading to the harbour were run down, worn out and crumbling from perhaps two full centuries of aging in the salty air hereabouts. The coloured paints they used were faded and flaking. Even the people I saw appeared decrepit and stooped, older than their years.

If I could find passage on a ship I was prepared to work hard and pay my way with labour. My immediate plan was to put the word out with the locals and wait. Somebody, somewhere, would sail for Europe, I was certain of it. If there was a delay in procuring passage, I would look for work until a ship was ready.

As I neared the harbour, the sounds of industry grew louder. There were more people here, not all of them friendly. A beggar shouted something at me, remonstrating with me for ignoring him and not providing him with money. In all seriousness, he was probably better off than I was – perhaps I should have been the one asking him for a handout. I had little more than a few coins in my pockets, and if I didn't find a place on a ship I would probably end up on the streets, a daunting prospect at the best of times, but with a harsh, imminent New England winter it was a prospect that would more than likely see me dead in a gutter within days, frozen solid and covered with a blanket of thick snow.

I was approached by a prostitute touting for business. It had been a long time since I had intimately known another person, and just the thought of touching her skin brought on a sadness that felt like a dead weight inside, a realisation of just how lonely I was. If I'd had money to spare, I would have succumbed to her dubious charms, but I was forced to merely smile, and carry on.

I reached the harbour, and looked out upon the sea. Thousands of miles across that heaving body of water lay my home soil. It may just as well have been on the moon. A number of ships were anchored a short distance out, rolling with the restless waves. The incoming tide smashed repeatedly into the harbour wall, sending up great plumes of spray that settled on a group of low buildings, one of which was a tavern. It had been this way for centuries, and my passing through this place would leave no mark. Long after I had gone, things would be exactly the same.

I entered the tavern and waited for my eyes to adjust to the gloom. It was mostly empty, save for one or two old gents nursing their beers, hunched little men in a room full of stale air and old smoke. They stared at me, openly. One of them was missing an eye, having a dark and empty socket on one side of his face. I nodded and turned away before my own staring became an obvious rudeness. I walked over to the bar, where I ordered a beer from the barman.

'Would you know of any boats heading for Europe?' I asked him.

'No boats going to Europe,' he said, with something of an unfriendly sneer. 'Ships maybe. No boats.'

So I'd found myself an idiot. There are plenty of them in this world, sure enough, and they are all equally tiresome. What kind of a man takes pleasure belittling a stranger simply because of incorrect nautical terminology? Is it really worth the effort? I paid him and grabbed my drink without thanks, and sat on a bench near to the window. Great clouds of spray threw themselves over the harbour wall and settled on the window, making everything blurry outside.

'Heading for Europe, then?' asked a voice.

I turned to see one of the old men staring at me. It was him with the missing eye.

'What of it?' I asked.

'I know of a ship bound for Marseilles in three days. Would that do you?'

'It's a start,' I said. 'I'm heading for England, if there's anything bound that way.'

He shook his head slowly, and smiled a grin made of perhaps three teeth. 'You won't get anything bound for England,' he said. 'There's nothing there worth the journey.'

I had to smile at his directness. It appeared that men were rude around these parts, at least the ones I had met so far, but at least this old fool had a sense of humour about him. Marseilles. It would still be something of a stretch to get back home on my limited funds but I would be on the right continent. Maybe I had been lucky by even finding a ship bound for Europe.

'Then Marseilles will do me,' I said. 'Who do I speak to?'

'My son,' he said. 'He'll be here shortly. Come, sit with me.'

I picked up my beer and joined the old man at his table. It was hard to tell his age, though it was certainly great. His face was as weathered as the facades of the crumbling cottages I'd passed on my way to the harbour. His one eye looked like a black jewel, shining with a fierce intelligence. The other was an empty socket, the eyelid raised and providing no cover for the red, moist hole in his face. It was hard not to stare. His chin sported a thick, shaggy beard, and his hair had been cut short with a severity that left only grey stubble behind.

'You're from the old country, then,' he said.

'England, you mean?'

'Aye. Most of us hereabouts have ancestry buried in England, but not one of us still living would swap for this. You're in God's country now, lad.'

'Is that so?' I asked him, smiling. 'When you have finished pouring scorn on my homeland, would you care for another beer whilst we wait for your son?'

'I would,' he said, tipping the dregs of his ale down his bearded throat. I glanced over at the bartender.

'Another one here,' I said. Whilst we waited for the old man's drink to be brought over, we sat regarding each other in silence for a few moments. His was easy company. Despite his lively tongue, I found myself liking him.

'You want to know about the eye?' he said at last.

I feigned disinterest but he had me. Of course I wanted to know about the eye. Any man who sees another missing an eye is naturally curious, and the more he protests disinterest the greater the liar. The barman set the drink down on the table, disturbing us, and stood hovering. I started searching my pockets for change and the old man looked up at the barman and told him to add the charge to his tab.

'I'm supposed to be buying you a drink,' I said. He waved a hand in a dismissive gesture.

'It doesn't matter, really,' he said, smiling. 'Now then, what do you know of whaling, lad?'

'Whaling? Nothing at all.'

## Two

'You are in the whaling capital of the world,' he said, gesturing at the blurry scenery just outside the window. 'Men from these parts have plied the trade for centuries, and for a long time I was one of them. In the old days, before my time, the carcasses used to wash up on the beach and the Indians would strip them down. By the time I started, it wasn't just the Indians that needed what the whale could give – the whole world was gripped by whale-fever.

'Never was a more useful creature invented by God! Without whale oil, man would live in darkness. There would be no perfume to keep the dainty lady-folk from stinking. Machinery would seize up, and industry would come to a grinding halt. Can you imagine that?'

'I haven't really given it much thought.'

'The disappearance of the whale would cause the very world to end! Ever seen a whale?'

'Once, when I first landed in New York. I saw a group of them.'

'A pod, you mean. Beautiful creatures, aren't they? I've helped to kill hundreds in my time. I did my bit to hold the darkness back and keep machines lubricated, for what it's worth.'

He smiled sadly, and took a sip of his ale. Then, with a little grunt of discomfort, he bent down to his overcoat on the stool next to him, reached into the pocket and pulled out a pipe and a small tin of tobacco. I watched as he went about his pipe-work, a routine that he had obviously perfected over the years. He tapped the head onto the table and inspected it before taking out a pinch of tobacco and pressing it down. He lit a match and sucked at the pipe until the tobacco was lit, and thick curls of blue smoke rose up towards the dirty ceiling.

'I hunted whales,' he said grimly, 'until the waters of New England were virtually empty. Each time we went to sea, we went that little bit further to find them, until we eventually pitched up on the other side of the world. In the end, we were away for two years at a time. How long was your voyage to New York, lad?'

'Five weeks.'

'That's hardly enough time to get the ship wet! It might have felt like a long time but believe me, when you're at sea for two years it'll leave a mark on your very soul. You forget what land feels like, and maybe even forget what it looks like. The entire world is in constant motion, shifting and rolling, up and down, heave and ho! And yet, there are places where the very same oceans are stagnant and still, with nary a sniff of a breeze! I've seen many strange things, in my time, and most of them involve the sea. What about you?'

'What about me?'

'Tell me about the strangest thing you ever saw.'

'Well, your eye is pretty strange.'

He hooted with laughter and slapped the table in a show of good humour. This eruption quickly descended into a coughing fit, and for a moment I thought he was choking to death. I stood, about to do something – anything – but he held up a hand to ward me off and, with a rattle of strenuous hacking, coughed up a thick gob of phlegm and spat it onto the floor. The barman looked over with evident disgust but said nothing.

'Anything else?' asked the old man, now sufficiently recovered to continue.

'I've seen a tornado – does that count?'

'Aye, that counts. I've seen one myself, out on the South Atlantic – a great twisting column of briny water that stretched up into the sky! But it's not the weirdest thing I ever saw. That would be the whale. Yes, I have no doubts about it. We found one with something rotten inside it - rotten and black and alive!'

'What was it?'

'Ha! If only I knew! I was a whaler for the better part of fifty years. Made it all the way to First Mate, and should've had my own ship but I was too fond of the drink and I didn't want the responsibility that comes with the position of Captain. First Mate was good enough for me. Easy enough, if you know what you're doing, little more than keeping log and inventory, and noting down all that things that happen on board. Each whale we caught, it was my job to note down the haul once we'd stripped it down. So, I was a pencil-pusher.

'The men liked me well enough, I think. They're a rough breed, whalers. Some of them would murder you if you looked at them the wrong way. I once saw a whaler gut one of his friends over a derogatory comment involving his mother. Yes, they're very rough characters. And all of them, to the last one, were terrified of the Captain.

'It's common knowledge that the Captains of whaling ships are a breed of men more deranged than most, but Grice was the worst these parts have ever known. Nobody liked him, not even his wife. And he hated everybody right back. He was a stone-hearted bastard, full of hate for the world and everything in it, but he had a special kind of hate for whales. He exulted in their murder. The only time I ever saw him crack a smile was when he was knee deep in whale blood.

'Killing was the only thing that gave him pleasure, and the bigger the thing he could kill, the happier he was. If whales didn't exist, he would have been out on the plains of Africa, bringing down elephants. Or maybe hunting men through the streets of New England. He was that kind of man. Dangerous. Unhinged.'

He trailed off for a moment and took a sip of his beer. We were surrounded by a fug of fresh tobacco smoke, giving the musty air inside tavern a slightly blue tinge, and though I had no time for engaging in the dirty habit myself, I found the aroma pleasant enough.

'Now then,' continued the old man. 'The Nautilus left New Bedford in December '52, and we sailed East, cutting down through the North and South Atlantic and rounding the Horn in a storm that almost wrecked us. After months at sea, we reached our hunting grounds in the South Pacific.

'Now you say you've seen a pod of whales off the coast of New York, and it's likely you'd have seen sperm whales. They are enormous, magnificent creatures. I've seen them more than 60 feet long, and they can weigh 40 tons. Bear in mind that the Nautilus herself was only 87 feet, so we were hunting beasts that were almost the size of the ship. A single whale can yield more than 20 barrels of oil, and by the time we found the whale that did for Captain Grice, we must have had more than 200 filled barrels in the hold, and 6 tons of baleen we'd stripped from smaller whales we found on our route.

'This whale was alone. The lookout spotted it and we dropped the boats into the water. Grice took captaincy of the first. Normally, the Captain would stay aboard the ship and let his men go about the business of killing the whale, but not Grice. I took charge of the middle boat and the Second Mate took charge of the third. We fanned out and approached the whale from behind.

'I could see there was something wrong with it immediately. It moved in a very odd manner. It kept coughing through its blowhole, sick and probably dying already. We were almost upon it before the whale suspected we were there, and the harpooners were readying themselves to throw. We had three of them, one in each boat, and they were all Indians - two Narrangansets and a Wampanoag. They were fearless and no white man could match them for skill with a harpoon.

'Grice couldn't contain himself. "KILL IT!" he screamed, and the Indian in his boat launched a harpoon and it struck home. The whale thrashed and set off at a rate of knots, dragging the boat behind it. A strong adult whale can pull a boat for two hours, bouncing and crashing on the waves in its wake. It's called the Nantucket Sleigh Ride for good reason. It wasn't uncommon for men to be thrown clear in the turmoil. Once, a whale managed to get all of us thrown out and it disappeared with the empty boat, and we never saw it again.

'The kills were rarely easy, even with old or sick whales. In the hundreds of encounters I was directly involved with, there was always something that happened that wasn't supposed to. Sometimes, a whale can turn, and it ducks under the boat and rises up out of the water with enough force to smash it to kindling. If that happens, the whale often likes to come back for the men, and I've seen quite a few killed this way. Thomas Essex was taken in the jaws of one and sunk to the bottom of the ocean, straight to meet with Davy Jones. I remember I had to tell his wife, and she lost her unborn with the shock of it.

'But this one was extremely weak, and happened to be one of those whales that gave us nothing in the way of trouble. After no more than a few minutes it gave up the chase, exhausted. As the trailing boats caught up, Grice grabbed a lance and stabbed it, and a terrible shriek came out of its blowhole. It's a ghastly sound. I heard it many times, over the years, and never did get used to it.

'They have a language to themselves, these creatures – snorts and barks, moans and howls and clicks and coughs – you wouldn't credit a whale with enough intelligence to make their feelings known through sounds, but you'd be wrong, lad.

'When you kill one, you have to aim for the lungs – the heart is too deep and the brain is protected by the skull. Skilled folk can do it with a single blow, but Grice preferred to stab aimlessly, over and over, plunging the lance into the whale with the intention of making it suffer before it died. The sea was turning red and that whale was coughing and throwing up a fountain of blood through its blowhole, vomiting a curtain of half-digested squid and other muck.

Grice kept an axe in his boat for moments such as this. He grabbed it and jumped out onto the whale, striding out until he found a secure position and then he started to swing.

'Now, there's no rhyme or reason for a man to attack a whale with an axe. The beast was dying from lance-wounds, and an axe would make no real difference to its demise. It would only cause it further pain. The men in his boat sat down and watched, and when we drew level we did the same thing. We knew that this was the way Grice was, and there was no arguing with him, no reasoning. He lifted the axe and brought it down into the whale, over and over, gathering speed as the frenzy of violence overcame him completely. His eyes were glazed and he was in his special place, and as the whale rolled Grice kept his footing and started to attack the exposed belly.

'We had to wait until he tired himself out. When he finally climbed back down into the boat, nobody spoke. He dropped the axe with a clatter and sat staring out to sea, as if awakening from a dream. The whale was a mess, its blubber all gouged and hacked, and the men were none too pleased because it makes the flensing an even more difficult job. But nobody remonstrated with him – it was his ship, after all, and it was as plain as day that Grice wasn't right in the head. Anybody who confronted him was likely to end up in the same state as the whale.

'So the other boats hooked up their harpoon lines and we rowed the corpse back to the Nautilus. Sometimes, when we'd killed a strong, healthy whale, it would drag us miles from the ship, and it would be dark by the time we reached her, but this whale didn't make it so far and we had daylight left to get started. We got the mast-hook into the carcass and lifted it up to starboard, and began stripping the blubber.

'We worked through the night and into the next day. That was how it was with whales, you spent days, sometimes weeks looking for them and doing little else besides, but when you found one it was all hands on deck. Strips of blubber were brought onto the ship and chopped into smaller pieces for rendering. This coated the deck in blood and strings of fat, and it would mark the start of a few days where keeping your footing was all but impossible.

'The trywork burners were started up and the blubber was boiled down. It's a business that's almost as grisly as the killing itself. As the blubber starts to render, it gives off a vile, thick smoke, and there's no escaping it. Black and greasy, it settles onto the masts and marks the sails. It stains your clothes and forces its way into your lungs, a stinking, choking mass that settles over the ship for days, hovering like a cloud of doom.

'When that job was finally completed, we cut off the head and brought it on deck, and one of the men drilled into the spermaceti reservoir. This is the mother lode when it comes to whaling – the purest of the oils and the most valuable. It doesn't need processing; it's simply scooped out and poured into barrels. We got twenty barrels of spermaceti out of that whale, and after so long at sea the hold was almost full. We were one catch away from coming home.

'Sharks were circling, waiting for us to let the rest of the carcass fall back into the water. There must have been a hundred of them, thrashing and roiling next to the ship, so densely packed together that it was almost like a single, snarling entity continually turning itself inside out, a writhing beast that stared up at the ship with hundreds of bulging, black eyes, anticipating the meal to come. It's a terrifying sight, but one so common amongst whalers that many simply ignore it altogether, but I never could. Grice would often have a go at harpooning one or two sharks himself, just for the hell of it. There was so many it was impossible to miss. A harpooned shark would be turned on by the others, and as they all began to bite each other, the waters would erupt in a frenzy of blood and gnashing teeth, and Grice would stand and laugh as they tore each other to pieces. Even though I hated what Grice had done, I always watched this bloody spectacle – however hard I tried I just couldn't tear my gaze away from the carnage.

'As he stood on the cutting platform, he called for one of the Indians to pass him a harpoon but then something caught his eye and he lowered himself down onto the carcass. It was slippery and stank to high Heaven, and a highly dangerous undertaking when there were hungry sharks waiting, should you miss your footing. He got down on his knees and poked around amongst the ribs. After a few minutes, he called for the Indians to bring the cutting spades and they set to work on the carcass, chopping out something that the rest of us couldn't see. Grice kept shouting at the Indians, forcing them to keep at it. It was as though they were afraid, but they were more afraid of Grice and kept working.

'Eventually, the mast-hook brought it up onto the deck. We all stood around, looking at it. It was the queerest thing I'd ever seen, a black gelatinous mass about the size of a man, and it seemed to have one large, milky eye that moved and looked at each of us in turn. We could see a black pupil enlarging and contracting as it focussed. Whatever this thing was, it appeared to be alive. When it caught my eye, I felt a shiver of horror and revulsion pass right through me.'

As the old man recounted this part of his story, I saw his posture stiffen at the memory. He shook himself down and blew air through his lips. I took this as a natural break to signal the barman and order more drinks – mine was empty and with a few quick swigs he downed the remains of his. Whilst we waited, he tapped out his pipe and put a fresh batch of tobacco into it. The barman brought over two more beers and walked away.

'Hey,' I called after him. He stopped and turned. 'We appear to be the only people keeping you in business. How about you show some appreciation for that?'

He rolled his eyes and walked off, disappearing through a doorway behind the bar.

"Miserable bastard," I muttered.

The old man smiled, and puffed at his pipe until it shrouded us once more in the sweet smell of burnt tobacco.

'So what was this thing you found?' I asked.

'We thought perhaps a tumour of some sort. Grice ordered it to be taken down into the hold and had one of the men keep watch over it. The Indians had conferred between themselves and stood apart from the rest of the crew, wanting nothing to do with this thing. I think they believed it was the reincarnation of some dark spirit, or some other such nonsense. They have some strange beliefs, Indians.

'Anyway, to all intents and purposes that marked the end of the voyage. Within two days, Grice made the order that we sail home, and for the next two months that's what we did. We caught two more baleens on the way, but Grice's heart wasn't in it. He spent a considerable amount of time below deck, studying this thing we'd found, and eventually had it moved to his cabin. By the time we landed, we hadn't seen him for days, and he left the ship immediately, taking the thing with him in a damned wheelbarrow, covered in one of the spare sails. I was left in charge of unloading the ship, selling off the various oils and baleen, and ensuring the men were paid.

'So began our shore leave. Usually, we whalers get restless after a few weeks, and begin gearing up for a new expedition relatively quickly. You'd think that was strange, and it is, but that's how it is. At sea, with little to do and no human contact apart from the men you share the ship with, you get the homesickness, and then within a few weeks of returning to Civilisation you get the urge to shun it once more, to head back out to sea and let everything else go to hell. It's a paradox we learn to live with.

'After two months, I still hadn't heard anything from Grice, so I went to his house. His wife Bess answered the door and she looked terrible, as though she'd aged twenty years since last I saw her. She told me Grice was unwell, and made me stand on the front step whilst she went back inside and spoke with him. He wasn't up to seeing me, but he gave the order to make preparations for a new voyage, to sail on the first of the following month.

'So that's what I did. I rounded up the crew and we prepared the Nautilus.

**Three**

'On the morning of the first, we waited. The sun wasn't yet up. Everybody was aboard except Grice and we were starting to get impatient, itching to leave. It was highly unusual for him to be so late. There came a point where, after dawn broke and the thin fog lifted from the harbour, I began to wonder if he was dead.

'Eventually, a figure in a long, hooded overcoat shuffled towards the harbour and caught the interest of the men. We watched as it slowly approached the ship. Something about the figure gave me the shivers, but as First Mate I was the one who had to go down and see what it wanted.

'Well, it spoke to me and I almost died of fright on the spot. "Is she ready?" asked a voice from the shadows of the black hood, and I knew then that this shambolic figure was none other than Grice himself. Even though the voice had deepened, and become filled with gravel, there was no mistaking it. He looked like he'd put on a tremendous amount of weight, but with the coat and the darkness it was hard to see what was what, exactly.

'"She's ready, Captain," I said, stepping aside. Grice shuffled up the boarding planks and immediately went down into his cabin. The men stood on deck, looking at each other with fright. The Indians disembarked and refused to board. I had to go down and argue with them for over twenty minutes, and in the end the only way they would rejoin the ship was under agreement that their wages would be doubled. We needed those Indians, we were lost without them. I had to agree to their terms, and I knew that at some point I would have to admit these terms to Grice.

'So we sailed, setting off on the last whaling trip I ever took. Right at the start I knew that we shouldn't have gone, but you can't put an end to your livelihood on the whim of a bad feeling.

'We took the usual route around the Horn, and for once the weather was reasonable. I've seen swells there the size of mountains, and have more than once been convinced of my imminent death. Many ships have gone down in those waters, and I've lost perhaps a dozen good friends there. This particular time, we were lucky, although the Third Mate fractured his arm when the swell pitched him into the tryworks, and he probably wouldn't see our luck in the same light as me. Still, it was nothing a sling and time wouldn't fix.

'Within two months we were back in our favourite hunting grounds. In all that time, Grice hadn't ventured onto the deck. I had to have some dealings with him, and was the only crewman to venture down to his cabin. He kept it in darkness and spoke to me from the shadows. It was a strange business, there was no doubt. I knew, by this time, that there was something seriously wrong with him. His unwillingness to show himself was testament to that, and his voice was becoming harder to understand as the weeks passed.

'We dealt with the normal business of running the ship. He asked our bearings every time we spoke, and made me give him a full report of the happenings on deck, however trivial. He seemed lucid and fully in control of the ship, but it was clear that something was on his mind. As the weeks passed, the pauses dotting his speech grew longer, and he began to sound distracted. Then, one day, he said things that were to disturb me a great deal.

'"I can hear them," he said.

'I naturally assumed he was talking about the crew. Although his presence penetrated every fibre of the ship, the men were now used to working without Grice overseeing them, and had settled about their business in a manner that was somewhat cheerier than normal. Whales were killed without any ugly business involving axes, and the corpses were dealt with quickly and efficiently. After each batch of processing, the decks and the rest of the ship were thoroughly cleaned and the men relaxed for a short while, letting their hair down, so to speak. Some of them had even taking to dancing a jig in celebration of each kill, a new habit that had undoubtedly arisen solely because Grice, a somewhat dour and humourless bastard at the best of times, wasn't on hand to reprimand them for their foolishness. And also, perhaps, because as First Mate I had taken it upon myself to be a little more generous with the rum rations than usual, which I had admitted to Grice and he had let continue.

'It was this that I thought Grice was referring to - the hard soles of the crew's footwear banging on the deck above Grice's cabin as they jigged.

'I'm sorry, Sir – I'll ask the men to stop their dancing.'

'"No, you fool! Not the men..... Them. The whales. I can hear the whales, in the deep. They're talking to each other."

'Now, it's not unusual to hear whales calling to each other, especially when you're below deck in moments of quiet. Water is a very good conductor of sound, and we all knew that the whales were capable of emitting some very strange noises. I was somewhat confused that Grice should have raised the subject – it was something that, perhaps, a new cabin boy would have noted on his first voyage, not something a seasoned Captain would have mentioned.

'"Let's hope they aren't telling each other that we're about the business of hunting them," I joked.

'"That's exactly what they're doing," he said.

'"Sir?"

'"Listen to me, damn it! How many times....? I hear the whales talking to each other. I understand what they're saying."

'You hear a thing like that, and hear the conviction in the voice that's saying it, you quickly realise that the owner of that voice is insane. Grice had been halfway there anyway, but this development made the hairs on my neck stand on end. Remember, we were weeks from the nearest landfall, and completely at his mercy.

'"Captain Grice, Sir," I said. "I hope you'll forgive me for what I'm about to say, but it seems that you aren't quite yourself. As First Mate, I have a duty to enquire about your condition – the safety of the men is paramount."

'A low, guttural laugh came from the shadows. My blood felt like Arctic ice-water, and it was all I could do not to flee back to the deck. I heard various shuffling and scrapings in the darkness, the sound of movement.

'"Light a candle," he said.

'My hands were shaking as I lit a match and held it to a candle on the small table in the centre of the room. The wick caught and the flame guttered a fraction before settling. A dim yellow light brought the rest of the cabin into view.

'I actually cried aloud with horror at the sight of him. Grice was a hideous, deformed version of his former self, and he had doubled in weight. His clothes were in tatters and his overcoat was the only thing that offered cover. And his face....! It was a swollen, lumpy mess, with eyes bulging in their sockets.

'I backed away from him. I was terrified.

'"What has happened to you?" I asked.

He looked at the floor and breathed heavily for a few moments.

'"That thing we found...." he said finally, scratching at a bloated cheek with fingers that seemed to be fusing together. "That thing did this to me. It is me. It became me. I kept it in my house, thinking it safe, not knowing what was to come. It had the bathtub to itself, and a daily change of fresh water.

'"Bess was afraid of it, and begged me to destroy it but I wouldn't listen. She took to barring the bedroom door from the inside, and I laughed at her foolishness. She tried to convince me that this thing was dangerous, but it seemed content enough in the tub, and I came to think of it as something of a pet, even though my end purpose was to sell it, and made certain enquiries to that end. Barnum himself was interested in making the trip up from New York to see it.

'"In the meantime, I studied it. Up close, it was a disgusting creature, a fleshy mass of something jelly-like and yet solid at the same time. There were veins beneath the surface, evidence of a rudimentary blood system, and perhaps a heart. It had that one white eye, large and unblinking, and many times I tried to communicate with it in an effort to determine a level of intelligence. It would fix me with that terrible eye and pulse with life, and though I knew it harboured some secret intelligence it ignored my attempts at communication.

'"It seemed ancient, to me, as old as the Earth itself, old enough to have scoured the oceans for aeons, looking for things to host it. That must have been the key to its survival, for in all the time I kept it not once did it accept food of any kind. It grew smaller, as though shrivelling through a lack of sustenance, and as the days went by it seemed to grow more agitated.

'"Barnum sent word that he had spent many thousands of dollars on the complete skeleton of a sabre-toothed tiger, and he was very apologetic but my creature no longer held any interest for him. I grew despondent and my thoughts turned to killing it. And then, suddenly, my sister-in-law died in childbirth and Bess went to Halifax for a few days to attend to the aftermath. I was left alone with the creature, and my lax attitude to personal safety was my downfall.

'"I didn't bar the bedroom door, and one night I awoke to find the thing on top of me – somehow, it had made its way out of the tub, across the landing and into the bedroom, and had climbed onto the bed, pinning me with its weight. I couldn't get it off! It had spread itself out, pinning my arms by my sides, and nothing I did would shift it from the bed. Only my head was out of the covers, and for a few moments that milky eye hovered right above my face, staring down at me, unblinking.

'"There was no mistaking it, this thing was an intelligent creature, a sentient being with an agenda. It forced its way into my mouth. I bit off great chunks and spat them out, but it simply kept coming and overwhelmed me, pouring itself down my throat. I couldn't breathe, I couldn't move. I felt it travel down my windpipe, down through my oesophagus and into my lungs, into my stomach. This thing invaded me. By the time I could get my breath, every last bit of it had disappeared inside me! It sounds impossible, but I speak the truth. Look at me! And there it remains, inside me."

'He finished speaking and once again looked at the floor. In the dim light, I thought I saw a single teardrop fall, but I could have been mistaken. I had listened to his story with a growing sense of horror, considering it the rant of a madman and a reflection of Grice's current state of mind.

But, the fact was, something terrible had happened to Grice, and his physical appearance was evidence of some massive trauma, of some mechanism of change within.

'"Did you consult a doctor?" I asked.

'"Three of them. They didn't believe me. One tried to put a tube in my throat and the thing reacted with such violence it almost killed me."

'"Maybe we should let the Indians examine you," I said.

'"The Indians? For the love of God, man, why?"

'"They know about these things," I said, not knowing if this was true or not. All I wanted was to get out of that cabin, and any excuse would do.

'"Whether they do, or not, it would kill me, I'm certain. For the moment, we should continue as normal, until I know what it wants. It must have had a reason for using my body."

'I stood there, unsure about how to proceed.

'"Why are you here?" I asked at last. "Why another expedition, in the state you're in?"

'He looked up at me, his distorted face bathed in a genuine sadness. I almost felt sorry for him.

'"Killing whales is the only thing I know. I'm dying, that much is obvious. This will be my last voyage. I would like to die with a lance in my hand, my body soaked with the warm blood of a whale. Do you understand?"

'I didn't understand, not one bit.

'"I want you to speak to the men," he said, his voice suddenly clear and firm. "Prepare them."

'"For what, Sir?"

'"For me. I need to come up to the deck. I've been rotting away in this cabin and I need fresh air, I need to feel the weight of a lance in my hand before I forget how to kill whales. I want the men warned about how I look. I do not want them to panic."

'"Are you sure this is a good idea? I don't wish to sound callous, but the sight of you like this will unsettle them a great deal."

'"Then let them be unsettled! Have you not grown used to the sight of me already?"

'"No, Sir. Not really."

'"Ha! Me neither."

'There was an air of bitter resignation in his voice, and also a great deal of fear. A few months ago, I would have thought it impossible for a man like Grice to be afraid of anything – I'd seen him standing atop thrashing whales in seas of mountainous waves, as dangerous a position as it's possible to be in this life, with little thought to his own safety. But he knew he was dying, and the definitive knowledge of one's own mortality brings a different kind of fear, a terror of certain death, a doom that is inescapable. It was coming for him, and he was perhaps afraid of meeting his maker. Grice had lived a life filled with terrible carnage and maybe he thought there would be some sort of Reckoning for that.

'"I'll have words with the men," I said, welcoming my chance to escape. I left him to his thoughts and rejoined the men on deck.

'I had been down in the cabin a long time, and my emergence into the sunlight made me stop and turn my face to the sun, eyes closed, basking in the heat and light. Something about my countenance attracted the attention of the men – there was probably a tangible air of relief surrounding me. They all cast glances my way, curious. The Second Mate walked over and stood next to me.

'"How is the old coot?" he asked.

'"You'll see for yourself, soon enough. He'll be coming out on deck shortly."

'He looked around in a panic, ensuring everything was shipshape. He needn't have worried – the lack of Grice's presence on a daily basis hadn't led to any slippage in efficiency or standards – all men did their job as surely as if Grice had loomed over them, inspecting every action. Like I said, they already feared him. Surely that fear would only deepen once Grice dragged himself out into the light.

'"Listen," I added. "He doesn't look the same. We need to gather the men and tell them that Grice now looks.... different."

'"How different?"

'"His physical appearance has altered tremendously. He no longer looks like the Grice we knew, but underneath he's exactly the same. This is what we need to make the men understand."

'So we drew the men into a short conference, warning them of what to expect. They looked incredulous, and then wary, unsure of this new business. The Indians remained grim-faced but their eyes betrayed their inner thoughts – they were terrified. Despite my outward confidence, I felt exactly the same.

'Not long after the men had resumed their duties, Grice heaved himself up the galley stairs leading to the deck. He was dressed in his long overcoat and hood, his face and body out of view, but every last man could see that he had grown enormously. He stood on the deck, commanding the attention of the crew by the sheer force of his presence.

'For a long time he stood there in silence, breathing heavily, no doubt drawing fresh air into his lungs and acclimatising himself to the light after so long in his quarters. The men had by now abandoned any pretence of working, and simply stared.

'Suddenly, he took off his coat and flung it aside. There was a collective gasp from the crew, followed by the murmuring of their agitated voices. In broad daylight, Grice looked even worse than the vision I'd seen by candle-light in his cabin. His body was bloated and mis-shapen, covered with lumps, and could barely be contained by his splitting clothes. His face was wrecked, distorted out of shape. His skin, what could be seen, was grey and ashen. Panting, he looked at all of us in turn.

'"What devilry is this?" shouted the Second Mate.

'"Not devilry," I told them all, "but simply misfortune. Captain Grice has been taken with a parasitic disease. Do not worry yourselves, it is not catching."

'The men were clearly not happy at this manifestation of Grice, in their midst. The Indians had removed themselves aft, conferring in hushed voices. The rest of the men, stood where they were, uncertain.

'"Nothing has changed!" I shouted. "We hunt whales, as usual."

'Grice shuffled to the centre of the deck.

'"I am your Captain!" he shouted. "This is my ship! Do not forget it! Now get back to work!" At this, any notion the men had that this strange figure was not Captain Grice was dispelled, yet still they paused, hesitant to surrender to this new notion of normality. Grice turned and slowly shuffled back down to his cabin, and I was left alone at the centre of the deck, with everybody now staring at me.

'"You heard the man," I shouted. "Back to work!"

'Within moments, they were back at their stations.

**Four**

'During the following week, we caught three baleen whales and narrowly missed catching a young bull sperm. Grice took no part in the slaughter, preferring instead to stand on deck and watch. Although the men were now slowly becoming used to Grice being in their midst, they were wary of him, and avoided him where possible.

'The sea air appeared to offer no rejuvenating qualities for Grice. In fact, it seemed to have the opposite effect, because his condition seemed to worsen. If anything, he grew even bigger, and soon resembled a man of perhaps twenty-five stone. His skin, grey like pale granite, came out in splotches of white. His throat grew in size disproportionately to the rest of him, and bulged as though filled with liquid, and this made his voice become even more low and rasping. I struggled to understand him clearly.

'"I hear them," he kept saying to himself, over and over. "Down there, talking to each other. They know I'm here."

'Not long after Grice came out into the light, so to speak, the night terrors began. During the hours of darkness, when the ship was silent save for the creak of old timber and the gentle slapping of the waves against the hull, the most unholy noises began to emerge from Grice's cabin: screams, shouts, and long howls that descended into deep, resonant moans.

'They were the most terrifying sounds I have ever heard, even worse than those made by the whales as we were killing them. The crew gathered on deck, out of their minds with fright. The sounds coming from Grice's cabin were inhuman. They echoed around the hold of the ship, and rang out into the night sky. You would have been able to hear them for miles.

'I calmed the men as best as I could, and told them that it was merely a symptom of his condition.

'"You have to go down there," said the Second Mate.

'Naturally, I argued against it, but in the end they all made me do it. That walk down to his cabin was the longest of my life. I could hardly climb down the stairs because my legs were shaking so much. A belching sound made my hair stand on end, so powerful that I heard things falling from their shelves in the galley.

'"Captain Grice, Sir?" I said in a quiet voice, standing outside his cabin door. I was hoping he wouldn't hear me, so I could retreat. There was a groan from inside. Cautiously, I opened the door and peered in. The room was completely dark. The smell emanating from inside made me flinch. I almost ran screaming when Grice spoke.

'"They are coming for me," he said, his voice barely legible.

'I stepped inside the cabin, lighting a match. There was a fresh candle on the table, and I focussed on getting the flame to catch. As the room lit up in the weak glow cast off by the flame, I looked across at Grice. He was virtually unrecognisable.

'Even as I watched, he flinched with a violent spasm, threw back his head and let out the most horrendous screeching sound. I almost fainted with fear, and my skin was alive with goosebumps. I can still hear that sound in my nightmares sometimes, even now, thirty years later.

'The cabin descended into silence.

'"Who is coming?" I asked.

'"The whales. It's calling them."

'"It?"

'"The thing inside me. I now know what it wants. I thought it was my decision to come out on one last voyage," said Grice, his voice slow and even. "But I was wrong. It made me come. These noises I make, it's the thing calling to them, in their own language. I have no control over it. It tells the whales I'm here, and they want their revenge for all the things I have done. But all of us are naught but pawns! It wants to get back to the ocean, do you understand? It wants to get at those whales, more than those whales want to get at me."

'"Captain Grice, Sir....."

'"Listen to me, damn it!" he shouted, his voice distorting as it increased in volume. "I'm a weak host, and it needs something stronger! It's desperate to get back inside one of those whales, to continue its vile business! And they come, not knowing the truth of what calls them!"

'The parasite inside him, the disease or whatever it was, had taken the last of his sanity. Clearly, there was nothing I could do for him.

'"You need rest, Sir. Is there anything I can get for you?" I asked, backing to the doorway. "Some fresh water?"

'"You don't believe me." he said.

'I couldn't lie to him, so I said nothing.

'"My lance," he said, a flatness in his voice. "Have it ready for the morning."

'I left the cabin and closed the door. Now I was faced with the task of telling the men that our Captain was probably going to be incapacitated in his duties for the remaining duration of the voyage. Whatever madness had hold of Grice, it was filling his head with preposterous ideas, and I grew concerned about the safety of the crew. His condition was worsening, and I already knew beyond doubt that Grice was a man capable of extreme violence. And this maniac wanted me to prepare his lance? Much as I detested the idea, I began to admit to myself that I would soon have to take full control of the ship. For the foreseeable future, I would have to take on the mantle of Captaincy.

'With a heavy heart, I climbed back onto the deck, wondering how I should put my thoughts to the crew. They didn't even notice my arrival. They were all, to a man, standing on port and starboard, looking down at the waters. I called over the Second Mate.

'"What is going on here?" I asked him. "Why are the men not at their stations?"

"Whales, Sir," he said. "As many as I've ever seen in one place, all at once. They've surrounded the ship."

'I ran to starboard and looked down. As far as the eye could see, enormous black shapes cut through the still waters, circling the Nautilus. Grice's words echoed in my head:

'"They are coming for me."

**Five**

'All night they circled the ship. Amongst the inky waters, these leviathans moved gracefully, with only the occasional spray from a blowhole breaking the silence. The sea was calm, and a supernatural peace had settled over everything, at least that's how it seemed to me.

'The men whispered amongst themselves, watching the spectacle, afraid of what it might mean. If things were different, we might have been busy with the business of hunting, for this was a bounty we were unlikely to see ever again, but nobody made a move. The boats remained tied up against the ship. The Indians left their harpoons untouched.

'We waited.

'Just before dawn, there came a sudden loud belching noise from Grice's cabin. At once, the whales stirred into a commotion of activity, spraying and snorting, picking up speed. One or two of them knocked against the ship with enough force to knock men off their feet. The whales circled faster, and closer, and one of them sent up a high-pitched keening sound, the like of which I'd never heard before.

'We all turned at the sound of Grice, shuffling and heaving himself up the steps onto the deck. His transformation from a man into an unrecognisable mountain of grey flesh was virtually complete. He staggered forward on hideously deformed legs, and the men cleared out of his path, terrified. He fixed his gaze down onto the sea, and made a deep groaning sound. The whales responded, all at once. A chorus of moans filled the air. For all intents and purposes, it appeared that they were attempting conversation with Grice. It sounds impossible, but that's how it looked to us crew.

'The Indians were babbling in their own tongue, as frightened as I'd ever seen them. The Third Mate was sitting on deck, his back to the tryworks, head in his hands. He had given up in despair.

'"What is happening here?" I demanded of Grice.

'Slowly, he turned and looked at me. He opened his mouth and spoke, but they were words I couldn't understand, rasping words, twisted into some unrecognisable language. I backed away, horrified, and he turned his attention back to the water. He howled, lifting his mis-shapen head back to expose his bulging throat, and the whales below responded with howls of their own. One of them rammed the ship and sent us sprawling.

'The Second Mate ran over to me.

'"They want the Captain," he said. "It's obvious. Give him to them!"

'I'd known this man for over twenty years, all of them served by his side under the captaincy of Grice. I knew that he had the utmost respect for Grice, and I'd never heard him say a bad word against him, which was unusual because once ashore the rest of us all discussed Grice's antics with a mixture of amusement and horror. He must have been terribly afraid to speak such a thought aloud, knowing that I, as his superior, would be bound to take such mutinous talk with a view to having him arrested. But I stayed where I was, paralysed with indecision. The thought had already crossed my mind of its own accord, but I couldn't let this be known amongst the crew.

'"Hold your tongue!" I warned him.

'But I thought it through. Whatever that parasite was, it had destroyed Grice, for he was clearly dying. I doubted that he would make the journey through to the end, and that at some point he would be going overboard anyway, buried at sea forever. But could I order such an action whilst he was still alive?

'And was this strange turn of events really down to Grice, and his insane theory?

'He had hunted whales for the better part of forty years, and must have killed many hundreds – each time lancing them from the boat and, unless the seas were exceptionally rough, stepping out onto the whales to finish them with his customary axe attack. During these decades, other whales must have seen Grice about the business of killing. Was it possible that he had become known to them?

'Did they afford him legendary status in their kingdom? I had helped carve up enough whale heads in my time, and I knew that the size of a whale brain is enormous. Did that equate to intelligence? Were these creatures actually capable of remembering, and identifying a particular individual from our human race?

'Would it be that great a leap to imagine the possibility?

'Not so, I thought. These things had come for Grice, that much was evident by simply looking at the sea below, and by hearing their grunts, moans and howls when responding to those of Grice. But, there was another thought, and perhaps one more prescient – maybe Grice had also been right about the thing inside him, calling out to the whales with its own agenda. We had found the damned thing inside a whale – was it at all possible that Grice had spoken the truth, that it was merely using him with the sole aim of returning to its natural domain? Who knows how long that thing had lived? In all possibility, it had been killing whales since the very dawn of time, and may even have been a more fearsome predator than Grice himself!

'Either way, tipping Grice overboard would solve the matter, but I couldn't bring myself to do it, not whilst he bore the last remaining vestiges of humanity. It would be murder. Had I known what was about to happen, I wouldn't have hesitated. My decision caused the deaths of a great many men, and I'm sure they will be waiting for me when my time is come.

'So we waited, helpless as events unfolded. The 'conversation' between Grice and the whales grew ever louder and more fierce. The sea frothed with the agitation of the whales as they circled around the Nautilus with increasing speed. One or two lifted themselves from the waters, high until they were completely airborne, and level with the deck of the ship. A living whale out of water is a most unnatural sight to behold, and one that reduces even the bravest of men to a quivering wreck. One of those airborne whales looked into my eyes, and I swear I saw Nature's purest manifestation of rage. They landed in the water, throwing up waves that engulfed the ship, soaking the men and even washing one overboard. We ran to the starboard and watched in horror as our cook was snagged between a set of massive jaws and broken in two.

'Grice shuffled over to the harpoons and held one aloft, throwing back his head and letting out a great belching sound. He held it up for the whales to see, howling his anger at them, and turned back to face the horrified crew. With great effort, he uttered the last words he would ever speak in our language: "KILL... THEM....!" Even then, his one thought was that of killing whales. He attempted to hurl the harpoon down towards the black shapes in the water, and that was the moment our fate was sealed. The harpoon missed, for Grice was now far too bulky and clumsy to wield it in any dangerous fashion, but the whales had witnessed his intent and it sent them into a frenzy. Upon some unknown signal, they scattered away from the ship, heading out to sea in all directions before turning back to face us. Then, as we watched, they began their attack.

'The first came at us so hard that it knocked itself out cold, headbutting the side of the Nautilus with enough force to shunt the entire ship sideways. It rolled over and drifted away, either unconscious or perhaps dead, but the next whale was already coming for us. The Second Mate screamed.

'The whale hammered into the side of the ship and we heard the sound of breaking wood. I shouted at some of the men to go below decks and prepare for bailing duty, and ordered the Indians to grab their harpoons. They were too afraid to move, and I had to run over and shout at them, so close that my face was inches from theirs, covering them with my spit. They were stirred into action, but we were all sent flying onto our backsides by a third strike at the ship. At the starboard, Grice was standing there watching, his gelatinous blob of a body shaking with maniacal laughter.

'There was no time to deal with him, and little point in trying – he had incited the war and it was now too late to stop it. Instead, I focussed on commandeering the men, getting them to aim the harpoons and lances at the approaching whales with the intention of letting them see that attacking us was futile. But it was far from futile, and they knew it. From above, our weapons were useless, even if they struck home. Unless you hit the lungs, such injuries only make the whales angrier. They started coming at us in twos, and I knew that the Nautilus, and all on her, were doomed.

'It was a very short and one-sided war. A whaling ship, however majestic and seaworthy, is no match for a direct attack by such angry, enormous creatures. As whales crashed into the ship, men fell from the rigging into the waters, lost in a commotion of spray, some of them crushed and killed by the whipping of leviathan flukes. Each successive barrage weakened the ship until it could hold out no more. They sank her. There was small, grim satisfaction in knowing that the whale to completely breach the hull was stuck fast and went down with the ship. Men were thrown overboard and others had no choice but to jump. We were floating about in the turbulent waters, smashed by the whales and grabbing anything we could to stay afloat. The Nautilus went down in a matter of minutes, and, sensing their victory, the whales backed off and stopped their attack.

'I could see Grice, a short distance away, floating without the aid of any flotsam, his eyes wide with terror. Nearby, two of the Indians clung to an empty barrel that had somehow made its way out of the hold. I saw more perhaps a dozen bodies floating in various states of death and dismemberment, the crew of the Nautilus, men whom I had sailed with for many years. Close by, I recognised the corpse of the Second Mate. From what I could tell, only four of us had survived the attack.

'I expected the whales to come and finish us off. Instead, they dispersed, and circled at a distance. Now that Grice was in the water, their rage had turned to fear. They knew that something was wrong. Only one returned, an old bull that was perhaps sixty feet in length, covered in barnacles with a lance sticking out of its back. It swam close to Grice and appeared to sniff at him, and with a shriek it suddenly turned and fled. It knew! I tell you, it knew, at that moment, the truth of the matter. And then, so did I. However much that whale wanted Grice, it knew that the thing was inside him, waiting for its moment.'

The old man stopped talking and took a sup at his beer. He looked so very sad, fragile and old and nearing the end of his days. His remaining eye was watery with the memories, and for a moment I thought he might break down and cry. But he took stock of himself, finished his drink and set about filling his pipe once more.

'So what happened next?' I asked him, eager to hear the outcome of this strange tale.

'Well,' said the old man, 'we must have drifted for days. A storm caught us and the Indians were separated, and were never heard from again. I tried to stay close to Grice, but I didn't want to get too close, and by the time they found us we must have been the better part of half a mile apart.'

'Who found you?' I asked.

'The Misquam, a whaler from Nantucket. They told me that an old bull whale with a lance in its back had led them right to us. Well, to Grice actually.'

'So they picked you up and brought you home?' I said. 'That was a stroke of luck.'

'Not quite, lad. There's no sympathy aboard whaling ships, and there was no way they would abandon their own voyage simply to give me a ride home. I was appropriated into their crew, demoted down to Fourth

Mate because that was the only position available to me. It was another year before my feet touched soil.'

'What did they do with Grice?'

'They harpooned him.'

'They did what?'

'They thought he was a calf whale,' he said, smiling ruefully. 'The old bull disappeared and at the sight of Grice, they wasted no time in sending out the boats and hunting him down. I told you, there's no sympathy from whalers, and even a young calf will yield a few barrels of oil. In fact, they even dealt with Grice before they could be bothered to come and pluck me out of the water.'

'I swam towards the ship and by the time I was halfway there, the boats had rowed back and the crew were already lifting Grice out of the water. His clothing had completely fallen away, and all that was left of him was a bulk of grey, marbled flesh. They must have realised that it was one of the strangest-looking whales ever created, but in the heat of the retrieval nobody had looked too closely. They had him up against the side of the ship, cutting into him with the flensing spades before they realised it wasn't a whale at all. I could hear his screams from where I watched in shock, treading water. He was half-butchered and certainly dead when they let him go, and the mess had brought the sharks. I managed to attract the attention of the ship and they finally sent one of the boats out to pick me up.

'And, at the end, even the sharks were afraid of the thing inside Grice. As we watched from the boat, Grice's body collapsed inwardly, and a black mass forced its way out through one of the wounds and slid into the water. The crew of the Misquam cried out in alarm, and the sound brought the milky eye of the creature into view as it looked up at the ship and studied them for a moment. Then, with a high-pitched shriek of triumph, the thing dived below the surface and vanished. Only then did the sharks approach and attack the corpse of Grice with a ferocity that was terrifying. I couldn't get aboard the Misquam quickly enough, I tell you.

'All that happened thirty years ago. It was the last time I was ever out at sea. Since I came back onto dry land, I never left it again.'

We sat there in silence, and the old man looked out through the window at the blurry landscape of New Bedford's harbour. He was deep in thought, and I sat there thinking over his story. There was a certain symmetry to the universe, and the whales had got their revenge after all. Grice had met the end he deserved. All men do, one way or the other.

The tavern door opened and in stepped a young man of about thirty. There was a resemblance to the old man who had talked my ears off for the better part of an hour.

'My son,' said the old man, disturbed from his reverie. 'Here, John – I have a passenger for you.'

'Not a passenger,' I corrected. 'I'm prepared to work.'

The man walked over and shook my hand, and smiled warmly.

'Let me get you a drink,' I said. 'And your throat must be dry as a bone by now,' I added, looking at the old man. 'He has some wild stories, your father.'

'Ah, he hasn't been telling that one about the whale again, has he?'

'How did you know?'

'It's the only story he has – he tells it to anyone who'll listen.'

'It's a good story!' protested the old man.

I ordered a round of drinks, paid the miserable, oafish barman, and sat down again. It occurred to me that I'd listened to the entire story on the pretence that I'd hear about how the old man lost his eye, and that loss was still a complete mystery.

'So how did you lose your eye?' I asked him.

'I have a brother in Fairhaven who farms goats. He wanted help milking them a few summers ago, and as I was behind one of them it lashed out and kicked me right in the eye.'

'So, nothing to do with the whale?'

'No. Nothing to do with the whale.'

# ALL THAT WILL BE LOST

*When his dominions were half depopulated, he summoned to his presence a thousand hale and light-hearted friends from among the knights and dames of his court, and with these retired to the deep seclusion of one of his castellated abbeys. This was an extensive and magnificent structure, the creation of the prince's own eccentric yet august taste. A strong and lofty wall girdled it in. This wall had gates of iron. The courtiers, having entered, brought furnaces and massy hammers and welded the bolts. They resolved to leave means neither of ingress or egress to the sudden impulses of despair or of frenzy from within. The abbey was amply provisioned. With such precautions the courtiers might bid defiance to contagion.*
**'The Masque of the Red Death', Edgar Allan Poe.**

A pestilence was abroad, a darkness spreading across the country and engulfing all it found. People fled in terror, desperate to avoid the blades and bullets of those already affected. A madness consumed the victims completely. Their only aim was to bring others into their sickly fold, to destroy that which was not like them.

The city had been under siege for months. Men fought and killed each other in the streets as the enemy made incursions and citizens rose to fight and defend their homes, their way of life. To look at, the men on both sides were the same, only the disease separated them, the unseen madness bubbling in the brains of the invaders.

Pockets of resistance did what they could to avoid the inevitable collapse of the territory into the enemy's hands. Ordinary folk were frightened to venture out and only did so out of necessity. Shops were running out of goods and people were beginning to starve. Shots rang out at all hours, sometimes in isolation but mostly in frenzied bursts accompanied by shouts and screams before a terrible silence descended. Most days brought a number of small explosions from different parts of the city, followed shortly afterwards by the sirens of the struggling emergency services. The enemy made their own bombs, usually only big enough to take out the odd shop front and a few citizens but once in a while came a major blast, heard across the entire city, demolishing buildings, wiping out dozens of people and rattling the windows of buildings a mile away.

There was a war to the east and the army had gone there to fight. Heavily outnumbered, they were suffering considerable losses. The enemy seemed unstoppable yet the fight was not yet over. There was still hope.

The entire province struggled under the steady influx of refugees fleeing the war, their own lands overtaken. The enemy destroyed everything they conquered, erasing geography and history, so even when driven back there was nothing left for the citizens to return to. In this part of the world, the map was turning black, slowly but surely, as villages, towns and then cities were overcome and wiped away.

This was not a new war but one that had been fought for centuries, for millennia. Where men once opposed each other with swords they now used guns and bombs. Only the weapons had changed. The war had centralised in the East but had taken place across different areas of the globe at one time or another. The enemy had endlessly mutated through the centuries, changing allegiances from one figurehead to another, but their ideology was always the same: be like us, or die.

It was not all despair in the city. A resistance network met regularly to make plans on how to fight back. They pooled their resources to discuss and analyse their situation, to gather weapons and create heavily defended enclaves where safety was guaranteed, for the immediate future at least.

Michael Greaves was part of that resistance. Lucky enough to be born into the sort of wealth that most people strive for but never reach, he had squandered that wealth as a wan and directionless youth, discovering alcohol and women at more or less the same time, indulging in both freely. Although these appetites never left him, he eventually calmed down, bored with his hedonistic lifestyle. He decided that life would be worth living if he could only find something to which to apply himself.

At first, he thought that he'd found that something. Her name was Amy and he fell hopelessly in love with her. For a while his life was perfect and then some incompatibility issues arose. Even though the relationship didn't work out in any traditional sense he still carried a torch and kept in regular contact, but making a life with her had been out of the question.

So he continued his education, more or less abandoned when enslaved by his vices, and with the help of private tutors soaked up new knowledge like a sponge. He emerged into his mid-twenties a new man, well educated and at peace with the world, and considered a number of enterprises from which to launch a career.

The family business held no appeal, not because it didn't interest him but more because he felt uncomfortable with the fact that he'd earned a place on the board only by dint of birthright. He wanted to make his own mark on the world and leave others to run the family concern as they had been doing well for many years. It was hard to pin down what the actual family business was, exactly, because a start in the railroads of Europe had brought about diversification into land ownership and regeneration, property and estate management and the acquisition of factories and rival businesses. Over the years, the various income streams brought many more opportunities and the company's wealth snowballed and gave the owners the freedom to gain a toehold in industries that were previously of no interest. Michael's parents had diversified into technology, medicines and even, as a recent development, into employment and dating agency sectors (they realised that the same database of clients essentially offered the same opportunities).

None of this was for Michael. Although something of a philanthropist, charitable donations weren't the only good that could be done to make the failing world a better place. As his concerns about the distant but encroaching war grew inside, he realised that there were other ways in which to help. Using access to his parents' agency database, a decision which he agonised over for a number of weeks before continuing, he analysed the data and came up with a suitable mailing list to generate interest in his first venture – a magazine aimed at women, offering helpful articles and advice on how to succeed in a male-dominated world. He sought out the best female writers and paid them well, unconcerned about making a loss until the magazine found its feet. He asked Amy, by now a freelance photographer with regular commissions with many of his potential rivals, to send in some pictures.

The first issue was mailed out for free, along with a subscription sheet. More than half of the recipients responded positively and by the third issue sales had gained enough traction to make the venture viable. Women were desperate to be taken seriously, and any information that could help them was eagerly devoured. There was a large group of women out there for whom magazines about fashion, home-making, gossip and celebrity tittle-tattle were anathema to the lifestyles they sought.

Within a few short years, Michael's publishing company turned into a small empire, carving out a niche in the market for intelligent magazines for what were essentially minority markets. One title specialised in articles and advice for immigrants, another for the LGBT community and yet another for scientific research and developments presented in an educated but essentially simple-to-follow manner for those not directly involved in the field. Sales weren't spectacular but they were consistent, enough to keep going and make a decent profit.

As the years went by, more titles were added and his publishing output started winning awards and the company name became synonymous with quality. Michael married and put on a few pounds. Shortly afterwards he divorced and started jogging. His hair thinned out a little. He still saw Amy but met and married someone else and, for a while, thought he was happy. A few more years passed and the second marriage faltered and came to an end. Through it all, the magazines prospered and he focused his energy into the business.

To the east, the war spiralled out of control.

Every year, Michael would organise a gathering at his house. Up to a hundred people would attend, all of them luminaries and contributors to his magazines. Ironically, he became something of a celebrity in the gossip magazines and his lavish parties were reported on, often with the public domain photographs drawn from the social media accounts of those in attendance. Michael became marginally famous. He hated the idea and became concerned that it made him a target for those that would want to destroy everything he represented.

When the war drew closer and with reports of nearby cities falling into enemy hands, Michael knew that the gatherings couldn't continue in their current form. His magazines enraged the enemy. Clips of his publications being burnt by angry people – always men – often appeared on the internet and he knew that danger was drawing ever nearer.

He sold his house and found a new one, and that year there was no party. If they were to continue they would have to be held in secret, with the location and identities of any participants kept out of the public eye completely. The way things were going, the gatherings were in danger of becoming a magnet for dangerous loners. It was clear that individuals from the enemy forces were somehow penetrating into the city to detonate explosives, often killing themselves and many others in the process. The enemy believed that this was not the only life, and by wiping out their opponents they would earn some sort of preferential treatment in whatever life followed. It was a core belief, one that never waned, but the mythical destination of the hereafter changed with a depressing regularity.

The house came with the security of being part of a gated community on the outer edge of the suburbs, with a wooded area to the North (concerning which he tracked down the owner and bought this for an over-generous price). Although he could have easily afforded something more grandiose, his tastes were relatively modest and he preferred the sort of property that any of his contributors could afford. He wasn't one for vulgar displays of wealth. There was nothing to be enjoyed in a mansion with bedrooms in the double figures, especially when he would be alone most of the time. He was happy enough with an older, established property with three bedrooms and a host of features such as the open hearths and high ceilings. The library room was a guilty pleasure although a practical one that doubled as a study and workplace away from the city office. The most attractive feature, however, was the large basement.

Michael's concession to ostentation was a massive extension of this underground area, a project with a budget that rivalled the actual purchase price of the house. It was a necessary addition, a decision he'd made before the contracts were even signed. It was the perfect answer to the problem of keeping the annual gatherings a secret – underground, out of sight. Things could continue as before, away from the eyes of the world at large, away from the eyes of the enemy.

He brought in contractors and Non-Disclosure Agreements were signed before work commenced. Specialist tools were hired to reduce the vibrations so that neighbouring properties were barely affected. If anyone asked he would tell them that he was simply renovating the basement and would apologise for any disturbance. As it turned out, nobody asked and the work continued unimpeded, raising no concerns. Once the main excavation was completed, a tunnel was built, extending north for a quarter of a mile. There, a section of the wooded area was levelled and an access road was built to link to the nearby 'B' road. A squat concrete building was erected, housing a thick steel door. The concrete was cosmetically distressed to make it look old and blend in with the trees behind it, and a small sign with the logo of a national utility company added to distract attention of any curious ramblers that had wandered onto the private land by mistake (or otherwise). The small building was simply the entrance point for the tunnel, and from there onto Michael's underground area.

When his designs had been implemented, he sent out invitations to more than a hundred friends, magazine contributors and business associates. The crème of modern thinking (and a few of the financiers) would attend this inaugural housewarming party, mixing and swapping ideas, forging links for new ventures. Everyone that worked for Michael had the same set of basic principles of working towards making the world a better place. And each one represented something that the enemy despised.

Michael was a beacon of light for those in the resistance, not only for his valuable contributions to the meetings, and any financial aid he provided, but for his sense of vision. His publishing output clearly helped those who needed it, particularly minority groups, and his contributors had strong voices and knew how to get their own message across. Michael's positive worldview represented something to strive for, a destination away from the encroaching darkness. Many thought that one day he might become their leader.

The cars made their way along the access road and parked in rows on the levelled area. The people clambered out and stood waiting. In the near distance a number of rumbling sounds signalled a series of small detonations and the faint clatter of gunfire brought a murmuring from the crowd and a few nervous glances.

Presently, Michael appeared before them, as if from nowhere. The crowd moved towards him and waited.

"Welcome, everybody!" he shouted, looking around at the faces, nearly all of whom he knew well. "You're probably wondering why you're effectively standing in a forest – that mystery will be resolved very soon." He paused at the sound of fresh gunfire, a little closer this time. "Perhaps it's time to get under cover. If you'll follow me, refreshments will be available after a short walk."

They talked amongst themselves as they entered the small concrete building. Four men in black suits stood waiting, automatic weapons dangling by their sides. One of the men smiled and nodded at the guests but the others remained impassive, silently observing the crowd. They gave off a military air. Some of the guests inhaled sharply at the sight of them. Although the war was all around, and all knew friends and even family members who had been maimed or killed, most people hadn't had any direct encounter with the enemy and had never seen a real gun.

"Please pay no attention," Michael called from the front. "They are here for our protection. They will ensure we have no unwanted gatecrashers!" He continued walking, descending a metal staircase into the tunnel, followed by the guests. Once past the entrance, everyone relaxed a little.

Lined with white tiles and brightly lit, the tunnel reminded them of the London Underground, something Michael had anticipated. There were laughs as people noticed the name 'Greaves Central' on the walls, the words in white Johnston lettering on a blue bar with a red circle behind it.

The tunnel opened out into a room and the guests assembled, waiting for Michael to speak. Classical music played from hidden speakers, the volume low. Everyone would surmise this was a recording, unaware at this point that in another room of the basement a quintet of musicians was playing live. The guests looked around at the walls, which were covered in portraits, many immediately recognisable. Marilyn Monroe stared back at them, as did Mother Theresa of Calcutta and Marie Curie. Row after row of faces stared inward towards the centre of the room with barely an inch of wall between each portrait. Florence Nightingale, Maya Angelou, Joan of Arc, Emmeline Pankhurst, Boudicca. Seemingly unrelated figures, captured for eternity in the form of an image, it soon became apparent that there were no pictures of men on these walls.

These were women of great influence, figures who had become part of the fabric of history. They had all changed the world in their own small way, guiding mankind towards a greater understanding of itself, of the universe they lived in. The room was a celebration of these women, of the things they had achieved.

"Welcome, all," said Michael, and the crowd ceased its murmuring. "First things first, I'd like to apologise for the lack of our gathering last year. As we all know, the enemy comes ever closer and now breathes down our necks. Precautions had to be taken and this is why you find yourselves here now."

He smiled and looked around the room before continuing.

"You'll see I've gone to great lengths to accommodate you all this year. We are away from prying eyes, and we are safe. There are security teams at the entrance to the tunnel and in my house, directly above. The work that we do, the beliefs that we have, makes us targets and I want to take no chances. I want you all to relax and enjoy yourselves. I'm sure many of you know each other already and, if you don't, please mingle and introduce yourselves.

"All I ask of tonight is that the candidness of previous years is held in check – for all of our sakes please do not take photographs but, if you must insist, I won't stop you. But keep them for yourselves and please do not post them online. We know the reaction our views get from the enemy – we know that we are sometimes killed for the things we say. At the moment, the world is an extremely dangerous place, and it is one we might not yet survive. So please, let caution prevail. I hope you all understand."

There was a general murmur of agreement amongst the crowd, followed by more appreciative mumblings as a small group of waiters brought round trays of drinks. Before long everyone had a glass in their hand.

"Feel free to explore," said Michael, raising a glass to the crowd. "But please do not venture upstairs as this will mean that our gathering is at risk of being exposed. Everything you need is down here. I will of course be mingling and will no doubt speak with each and every one of you at some point. Finally, if anyone needs to leave for any reason please find me and I will have one of the security personnel escort you back to your vehicle. Now please enjoy yourselves – salut!"

Michael downed the contents of his glass and smiled.

The crowd dispersed throughout the basement area, forming small groups and engaging in lively conversations. Much of the talk was, initially, about the rooms they found themselves in. Michael had gone to great trouble to give the seven rooms a theme and had meticulously prepared each one during the preceding months.

As he moved into an adjacent room, more pictures lined the walls and faces from all corners of the globe gazed upon the revellers. These were not famous faces, not images of women who had made great advancements in their field, but regular people going about their lives, smiling and laughing, their eyes bright and shining. People who lived without fear. A young couple throwing a Frisbee between themselves, the man in a t-shirt and jeans, the girl in a slip of a dress that left her arms and legs uncovered, sunlight warming bare skin. In another picture, an elderly gent sat on a bench with a small white terrier next to him. Elsewhere, a row of laughing African schoolchildren held battered textbooks, one small boy pointing at the camera.

In the background, the music ended and there was a lull before the next movement commenced. The sudden silence brought a pause in the chatter of the guests and, at that moment, they felt the distant rumble of a large explosion – it seemed to resonate in their chests. Above, the small chandeliers rocked gently at the end of their chains. A tension swept into the rooms and was dismissed almost immediately as the band struck up anew. People tentatively resumed their conversations and, within a minute or so, things were as lively as they were before the lull.

Michael stood for a moment and wondered if he should cancel the party. There seemed to have been more activity than usual over the last few hours, as though the enemy were changing gears and mounting a more persistent attack. That last explosion was much closer than he'd have liked.

"This must have cost a fortune!" said a loud voice from behind Michael, interrupting his thoughts. He turned to see Cole Riggs, a prominent advertiser in a number of his magazines.

"Not as much as you'd think," said Michael, smiling and reaching out to shake hands.

"I see you managed to get some decent booze. How did you manage that? We haven't had a large delivery for weeks."

"I had some in reserve," said Michael, aware of the insinuation in Riggs' voice. The truth was that by the time the party was over Michael would be more or less out of alcoholic drinks. He would rather his guests enjoyed it than hoarding it for himself.

Michael didn't particularly like Riggs although he tried his best not to show it. He brought a lot of money into the business, paying for page space to advertise his own business ventures, and Michael was aware that it would be churlish to stop that income stream for the simple reason of telling Riggs what he really thought of him, not that he'd never been tempted. Michael found some of his views a little tasteless, his jokes even more so. Once, Michael was attending a charity event in which Riggs was the host – the crowd was in his hand until he cracked a joke about a test to find out if your wife has Alzheimer's or AIDS (punch line: drop her off in the woods and if she finds her way home don't fuck her). A good enough joke between friends but the charity event was a fundraiser for The Alzheimer's Society and the ensuing uproar still hadn't died down, years later. More than a few guests had cast disgusted glances in Riggs' direction.

It was a quandary for Michael because even though he thought the joke in poor taste his values meant that he defended the right of anyone to say such things (perhaps with an amendment for appropriateness) – such a right was fundamental to the way a modern society should work. Freedom of speech was a cornerstone of Civilisation and only those with dark agendas sought to curb the words of their citizens. This left room for ugly thoughts to be verbalised in public, or tasteless jokes, but the key was not to over-react and create pariahs out of those who exercised this basic right.

The enemy stamped out any freedom of speech a long time ago. The afflicted had become brainwashed into a certain way of thinking, their leaders forcing their own ideas and laws into the heads of their minions. All men were subjugated to a system, it was in their nature, but the enemy's system existed at the expense of all possible alternatives.

The disease they suffered was many thousands of years old. It came from the hills, perhaps, or the rivers or maybe even the moon. As soon as sentient man looked upon a natural feature and wondered who had made such a thing the disease was born. Reason, however basic, was battered into a corner of the developing hominid brain as fear and superstition took hold. Early men were like ants on shaky ground, the living planet moving and changing around beneath them, unaware that such processes were natural because they did not yet have the tools to understand.

So when a volcano erupted, or a river dried away to nothing, men attributed false reasons to these events and made up figureheads who were imagined to control such things. So powerful was the disease, so proficient at appearing ex nihilo in multiple disconnected areas at the same time, that it could be argued that the human brain developed with a disease-shaped hole just waiting to be filled.

Even as brains evolved, enlarging and creating neural networks that gave man the capacity to reach out to the very stars, the disease persisted. What should have become a relic of a bygone age instead strengthened its hold, exponentially collecting victims through the millennia. Virulent and adaptable, the sickness passed down through generations, hiding amongst cranial tissues, protected by bone. Soon, no longer were men content enough to imagine that meddling sky figures controlled their fate, some imagined that they were the Ones who created the world, mutating the disease for their own purposes and becoming figureheads in themselves. Like influenza, there were now too many variants of the disease to count.

"I thought you'd been getting some new stuff, you know," said Riggs, hoping that Michael would suddenly open up and divulge the name of some new supplier.

"I wish," said Michael.

They continued walking, entering a different room. A few red sofas lined the walls, already filled with guests sitting and chatting. Michael spotted Ellie Davis, one of his better writers, sipping her drink whilst listening to someone whose face he knew but whose name he struggled to recall until it suddenly dropped into his mind. Andy WIllman, another advertiser – not a contributor, as such, but another money man who kept the ball rolling. A necessary evil.

Ellie looked up and caught his eye. She saw who he was with and offered a sympathetic smile. He reciprocated.

One of the walls was taken up with an entire picture, this one so big that it had been printed as wallpaper. It featured two men holding hands and walking towards a sunset. The adjacent walls were once again lined with framed photographs and these were all in black and white. Michael took a moment to look around and reflect, momentarily ignoring Riggs' presence. He knew the names of everyone in the pictures, had made sure he committed them to memory as a mark of respect. All of the people were dead, murdered by the enemy. Some had been thrown from rooftops, some hung from lampposts in the street, others doused in accelerants and set on fire. All had died horribly, their lives taken by savages who had taken great offence at some aspect of their victims' lifestyles.

The enemy had a long list of infractions for which a person could be killed. Wherever they went, they left a trail of corpses and their victims were more often civilians than military. This was the cause of the recent influx of refugees into the city. Anyone left behind in an area taken over by the enemy would suddenly find themselves constrained by a set of primitive and ludicrous rules by which to abide. For some reason, this didn't apply to the enemy, who pillaged, raped and murdered at will, excused only by their belief that anyone who wasn't like them deserved such treatment. Suddenly, normal people with their own lives, dreams and aspirations were judged for their apparent misdemeanours and punished with a death sentence. The refugees that turned up at the city were always exhausted, malnourished and filthy, drenched in the evidence of their recent hardship of travelling many miles on foot without any kind of sustenance or provision. And the general news outlets showed them arriving and asked the citizens who would pay for their care, and where would they live. Even a simple photo was enough to dehumanise them, these dirty people dressed in rags, with nothing in their pockets, looking for handouts and medical treatment and somewhere to live.

It was a terrible thing for the media to do but he knew why they did it. They were afraid. And not without good reason – the enemy often disguised themselves as refugees and entered the city hidden amongst the throng, peeling away to meet up and regroup and embark on a spree of terror. The enemy was clearly in the city, its agents moving through the darkened streets, and this was probably their favourite way of getting in.

Even so, the real refugees couldn't be labelled as a hostile threat, not when they were simply fleeing for their lives. Michael did everything he could to reverse the opinions of the general public by using his magazines to shine a light onto some of them. He commissioned interviews so that everyone could read about them and, hopefully, feel some empathy. They were doctors and nurses, office workers, construction workers, engineers, publishers, writers. They were just like everyone else, people with houses and mortgages and all of the usual strife that came with trying to make a life. The only difference between the refugees and the residents of the city was geography. If the enemy continued their advance, soon it would be Michael and all the people in these rooms, and the city above them, that would be arriving somewhere else dressed in filthy rags.

"So what's it all for?" asked Riggs, looking around at the pictures with a blank expression.

Michael turned to look at him.

"What do you mean?"

"All these pictures. There must be hundreds of them and I haven't even seen the rest of the place yet. Why have you done it, why have you spent all of that money?"

It always seemed to come down to money with Riggs.

"Go and see the rest of the rooms and then it'll become clear," said Michael. With a polite smile, he deliberately moved away and melted into the crowd leaving Riggs to stare at the images. It was rude, Michael knew that, but there was only so much of Riggs a person could take in one go. Let him find someone else to mither.

As Michael entered the next room the music grew suddenly louder and the musicians were before him, surrounded by a small, appreciative crowd. He joined them and watched the performance. The quintet was made up of two violins, a viola, a cello and a clarinet and the music had a deeply calming quality to it. He didn't recognise the piece, having no real interest in classical music. Had he followed his heart, he'd have put on a rock band, but that wasn't a practical consideration and he'd dismissed the idea as soon as it had occurred. It would have been too loud for a start. Something about the quintet in these surroundings just felt right.

The ensemble brought the current piece to an end and once again the basement area was filled with a sudden silence, a vacuum of sound that brought nervous glances from the crowd. Whether conscious of it or not, the murmur of conversation dipped and the pause was a moment to reflect on the fighting in the streets not far from where they were, and everybody strained their ears for the next rumbling explosion.

None came. The music started once more and everyone exhaled with relief before resuming their conversations.

Michael looked around. This was one of his favourite rooms, the walls being covered in framed movie poster prints, enlarged book covers, mounted album covers and digital artwork of various computer games. Much of the décor had been on display in the games room of his previous house, his own little bunker where he would retreat to watch the odd film and indulge himself reading or by spending a few glorious hours in some sort of computer generated world. The images reflected a wide spectrum of interests and his tastes were broad, broader than many of the guests who looked at some of the artwork with mystified expressions.

A large reprint of the original film poster for Fritz Lang's 'Metropolis' hung next to one for John Carpenter's 'The Thing', and next to this was a framed print of 'Halo', a launch title for the Xbox and still one of Michael's favourite games. At eye level a run of mounted LP's caught his eye, from the Beatles to Hendrix, The Who, Beck and Jane's Addiction.

Every item represented the different worlds (or sometimes even universes) that had been built by creative people, whether sonically, digitally or through the use of words or celluloid. Each represented countless hours invested by Michael, exploring until he knew them inside out. And though many would disagree, he didn't consider a minute of that time wasted.

He spotted an old friend on the other side of the room and wandered over. She was looking at one of the posters, lost in thought. Michael reached out and gently touched her shoulder. She didn't turn around, knowing his touch.

"I wondered how long it would take you to find me," she said.

"You're rather hard to miss."

She turned then, her eyes meeting his. He felt the familiar rush of adrenaline, a faint stirring of his loins. She was the most beautiful woman he'd ever known and he'd been married twice to other women. She herself was currently married. All of these marriages hadn't stopped them meeting each other once a fortnight for the last twenty years for illicit sex in bland hotel rooms. They were adulterers, both of them, but they hadn't loved their partners any less because of it. As far as they knew, none of the marriages had suffered because of their liaisons and Michael's had ended of their own accord with neither wife knowing of Amy's existence.

She smiled.

"Where's David?" he asked, looking around.

"He couldn't make it. Says he's working late. He isn't. He's fucking somebody from his accounts department like the cliché-ridden idiot he's turned out to be."

"Sorry to hear that."

"Don't be. It keeps him away from me."

Michael was gladdened by those words and felt a little guilty. Although neither marriage had failed because of Amy, it could be argued that he didn't fully invest himself whilst Amy was always somewhere in the background.

He often wondered if they should have tried harder to stay together and maybe should have married each other. But deep down he knew it wouldn't have worked, and she knew it too. Shortly after they had first met they had lived together, for a while, and during that time they had argued and fought, the proximity of being together all of the time too much for either of them. Only when they split did they find a balance, having the room to live their own lives with less passionate people but refusing to completely abandon each other, meeting for sex and sometimes dinner and leaving each other again at the end of it. And it worked, perfectly. But lately doubt had crept in.

As Michael had grown older he thought he'd realised that the idea of family life, of finding a soul-mate, was just a romantic nonsense, incompatible (for him at least) with the messiness of human relationships. And there was nothing wrong with that, he often thought. It was an unconventional view but if nobody got hurt he couldn't really see a problem. But was it all just a romantic nonsense? These days, a little older and more alone than ever, he wasn't so sure. Amy had recently been in his thoughts a lot more.

"Penny for them?" she asked, her eyes wandering over his face, lingering for a moment on his lips before heading back up to meet his gaze.

"You know, the usual. Us."

The room was getting rather crowded as more guests came in to admire the musicians.

"Shall we?" he said, gesturing towards the next room.

He resisted the urge to take her hand and lead her. Instead, he let her through and followed. The room they entered was not so crowded with guests but there was less floor space for them – a number of display cabinets were scattered here and there, each with an item under a glass dome. He didn't need to look, knowing what they were. Under one, a beautiful carriage clock marked the passage of time. Under another, a glass prism appeared to be suspended, pierced by an intense beam of white light and throwing out a spectrum on the other side, onto an opposing wall. When Amy stopped in front of it, she was bathed in the multicoloured glow.

"What about us?" she asked.

"Oh, I don't know."

"Yes you do. What's on your mind?"

"Did you meet up with Julian and get those pictures I wanted?"

"Don't change the subject."

He smiled. Where to begin? Now they were getting older the time they had left was getting shorter – before either of them knew it, they'd be old and their lives would be behind them. Perhaps time had softened them a little, given them the maturity to do what couldn't be done the first time around.

"I miss you," he said at last.

"We see each other all the time!"

"I want more."

He smiled ruefully and she sighed. She seemed to be on the verge of saying something but, for whatever reason, decided against it. There was uncertainty in her eyes. He knew her so well that he could almost read her thoughts, but in a moment like this 'almost' was no help at all.

"Move in with me," he said abruptly.

She laughed, only stopping when she realised he was serious.

"We tried that once," she said. Her voice was calm. Measured.

"And that was a long time ago. We're different people now."

"And you seem to be forgetting that I'm married."

"Divorce him."

"It's not that simple."

"Why isn't it? You hate David, I know you do. He's out there cheating on you right now, you said it yourself."

"And I've been cheating on him since the day we were married."

"You know what I'm saying."

Frustrated, not wanting to argue, he turned and wandered away a few paces. He regained his composure, idly glancing at an exhibit under a glass dome. A model of the double-helix, gently rotating. Amy came over and placed a hand on his chest, not caring if the other guests saw them.

"Do you honestly think things would be different this time around?" she asked.

"I don't know. All I know is that I'd like to try."

There was a long pause.

"All right then," she said at last, taking her hand away. She smiled, completely relaxed, as though a great weight had been lifted from her soul. He looked at her in astonishment.

"Really?"

"I love you," she said simply. "Always have. I don't want to spend the rest of my life with David, I've known that for a while now."

"Just like that?"

"No, like I said, it's not that simple. But, in essence, I've had the same thoughts."

"So why didn't you say anything?"

"For the same reason you haven't, until now."

They looked at each other for a long time, saying no more, letting the moment engulf them.

Above, the chandeliers rocked gently at the end of their chains.

"Come with me," he said at last, reaching for her hand.

"Where to?"

"I want to show you something."

He led her past the other exhibits into the sixth room. It was dark in there, with a number of figurines on plinths, softly lit from beneath. A woman made from stone, with a head formed from two snakes facing each other, watched them pass with dead eyes. The figure wore a necklace of hands and hearts, a skirt made from snakes. Nearby stood a small statue of a falcon-headed man holding a staff. Other figures were spread out around the room. Amy glanced at them as she passed by.

The walls were decorated with murals, their colours muted in the dim light. Bearded men with wings, men with the heads of animals. Figures that were once revered, figures that had caused countless millions of deaths. And now, apart from a few pictures and stone relics, largely forgotten. The civilisations that created these figures were long gone, some no more than a name, their people lost forever to memory. None of the figures in this room had saved their worshippers. They were yesterday's gods, irrelevant and no more than a footnote in the history of Man. Some had lasted thousands of years but all had fallen by the wayside. Nobody worshipped Marduk any more, or Horus, Anu, Odin, Coatlicue or Bacchus or Yamm. One day it would be the same with today's gods. Maybe new gods would come and take their places, or maybe the people of the future would look back and wonder how so many of their forefathers believed the myths and fairy tales with such certainty, with such conviction that they were prepared to kill each other over which of the fairy tales was 'true'.

He led her through to the final room. So far, only two other guests had made it this deep into the basement and they stood engrossed in the spectacle Michael had prepared for them. He led Amy towards the centre and they stood there, holding hands, looking around in wonder.

The walls, the ceiling and even the floor were covered with gigantic high resolution LED screens. They were surrounded by the cosmos, floating in space. The illusion was so encompassing that within moments they began to feel untethered to the Earth, as if they had actually been transported into the belly of the universe.

"This is phenomenal," she said in a quiet voice.

"Isn't it?" he asked, his face like the face of a small boy, bathed in the glow of the screens.

They were surrounded by stars, each one a sun like their own. Many of these suns would be surrounded by planetary systems and many of those would eventually reveal the presence of life.

"We came from the stars," said Michael. "Did I ever tell you that?"

"All the time," she said. He could tell by her voice that she was smiling. Of course he'd told her, he never tired of telling anyone who'd listen because it was all so endlessly fascinating to him. Every human was made up of atoms that had been created in the nuclear furnaces of the stars and spat out into space. These pinpricks of light, trillions upon trillions of them, were all factories for making the materials of life. And nearly every last one of them was further than could be reached in a human lifetime. Michael often mused that if people said they understood just how vast the universe was they were lying.

"We'll all end up there again, one day," he said, certain that he'd told her this before as well. No doubt he'd tell her again, many times before they died. And when they did die, the earth would consume them. The atoms that once made them would be ingested by the worms and excreted, eventually becoming soil. And one day, far into the future, the nearest star would enlarge and eclipse the planet, destroying it, and what was left would drift through the universe until some other galaxy smashed into this one and the resulting mess would birth more stars.

Who could say how many times this would happen before the universe itself succumbed to entropy and was finally silent?

Michael loved the fact that he had been born within a star, and had been consumed and regurgitated in countless forms before coming together in this one, this temporary blip of humanity, his entire lifespan not even registering as a dot in the overall timeline of the universe. Wasn't that so much more beautiful than the made up stories wars were being fought over? Wasn't it more majestic than Heaven, or Valhalla, or Mictlan, or whatever man-made fiction that caused the rest of humanity so much pain?

Michael stood there, holding Amy's hand, becoming lost in the beauty shining from the screens. A warm feeling engulfed him. He turned to look at her, this person that was even more beautiful than the universe, and enjoyed the expression of joy on her face.

Just then, at that moment of perfection, a series of harsh bangs rattled around the basement area. They were shocked out of their bliss. Almost immediately, more bangs followed. Michael realised, with a sick feeling, that the sounds were gunfire. He let go of Amy's hand.

"Stay here," he said.

"Michael – is there another way out?"

He shook his head, his eyes wide and frightened. "There are two ways out from the first room but....." His voiced trailed off, dark thoughts entering his mind. They were trapped. He held his hand out, a signal for her to stay put, and went back through the rooms looking for the source of the gunfire. Hopefully the situation was already over and his security team had dealt with any intruder. Some small part of him hoped that it might not have been gunfire after all, that there was some rational explanation that didn't involve someone trying to shoot someone else.

That hope ended abruptly as more gunshots rang out and the basement began to fill with screams. As he walked forward, almost in a daze, guests started to run past him, deeper into the basement, unaware that there was no way out. He saw Ellie Davis rush past, her face splattered with blood.

He came face to face with the enemy. A man dressed in combat gear carrying an AK-47 walked into the room and looked right at him. Michael was dimly aware of other shadowy figures moving in the background, of gunfire and guests being mown down in a hail of bullets as they ran.

The two men stared into each other's eyes for what seemed like forever, though was really no more than a fraction of a second. A thousand fragmented thoughts rushed into Michael's mind. There was no doubt that he was about to die. The man started to swing the gun in his direction. Michael tried to read the eyes of his murderer, tried to discern any reason why he should be killing his fellow man other than for the crazed beliefs he held. Is this really what his god wanted, to cut down civilians in cold blood because they didn't believe the same thing? If this man's god was real, why didn't it just step down from the sky and show himself, so everyone could choose to believe? Why did it always come down to a loner and a book and a bunch of instructions?

He thought of all the hard work he'd gone into preparing these rooms for his guests. All of the things inside the basement, the pictures and the things they represented, they were everything that the enemy hated. If the enemy had won this battle many years ago, nothing in these rooms would have come about – no science, no medicine, no human advancement. None of us would survive the most basic diseases, or would have any idea of what the Earth looked like from space. There would be no art, no music, no films or games. There would be only one book. Humanity would live in deserts, hiding in caves, evolving no further than the Stone Age.

This is all that will be lost, thought Michael.

His last thought, before a swarm of bullets flew in his direction and destroyed his body, was that even though the enemy had won this small victory, they couldn't win in the end. There was just too much to lose for that to happen. Other cities, other countries would fight and they would win. They had to. The disease would be eradicated, one day, and on that day humans would finally join and make plans to explore the rest of the universe.

Together.

# THE HEAMORRHOID

Wilf blamed Spaniards. The bastards invented tapas, after all. A meal like that, all bits and pieces... it wasn't right. And tapas was ultimately the cause of all his misery. The origin of the disaster. The disintegration of an entire life.

One bad tapas almost half a century before had led to a bout of increasingly painful stomach cramps and an almighty session on the chod-pot. The consequent straining had resulted in the dreadful pile hanging out of his arse.

As a young man in the post-war age, Wilf had ignored his gut instinct to avoid any sort of exotic food and had eaten a platter of foreign muck whilst out on a date with a young shop assistant called Valerie. Or Ivy. Something with a 'V' in it anyway. Marvellous tits, he remembered, even if he didn't get his hands on them. Perky little blighters.

After the meal, he felt bad almost immediately. Like he'd been punched in the stomach, a dull ache that led to stitch and then, as he was driving home after dropping her off, a pain like he'd been stabbed followed by an uncontrollable urge to void his bowels. He only just managed to pull over, scramble out of his car and yank his trousers down before a torrent of brown mush blew out of his arse and splattered all over his best shoes. It was like turning on a pressure hose, a blast of industrial grade slurry accompanied by an orchestra of the Devil's trumpets. And that was just the beginning. After making it home, he spent the night – one of the longest of his life – on and off the toilet, sometimes to force out a watery payload and other times expelling nothing but air and a solemn, low note reminiscent of a tuba. On these particular occasions, he tried to force out solids, hoping that the nightmare would end once his stomach was completely empty. He forced so hard that he gave himself a headache.

He flopped down on his bed for the last time just before dawn, exhausted. After a fitful sleep, he awoke and, with a groan, realised that he needed the toilet yet again. A little bit of something hot and wet dribbled out of his raw backside. When he wiped, a bolt of pain made him gasp. Instinctively, he looked down at the used toilet roll and saw that it was bright red with blood, a sight which made him gasp again, louder this time. Blood! What on earth had happened? His mind raced, trying to come up with a reasonable explanation. He couldn't think of one.

As a young man in the 1950's, he did the same thing as any number of similar men of his generation would do – nothing. He finished wiping, as delicately as possible, and then he pulled up his underwear and trousers and washed his hands. Already, he was putting the problem to the back of his mind, hoping it was some kind of one-off anal disaster that would quickly sort itself out. He had no idea what a haemorrhoid was. Nobody talked about that sort of thing back then. There were no television programmes where fame-hungry idiots bared their anuses for celebrity doctors to share their diagnoses with whatever depraved audiences were watching that sort of thing. Nothing that could educate a young man to the more embarrassing problems his body might betray him with and certainly nothing persuasive enough to make him consider going to his local locum and baring all. This was an age where certain things were still very much taboo, an age before the internet made even the most basic research a simple task. The only way Wilf could find out why he had a sore arse would be to actually go and ask somebody and he was never going to do that. Could you imagine what Mrs Bishop at the chemist would make of it? He'd never be able to look her in the eye again. And old Bernstein the local Doctor? A man rumoured to travel down to London once a month to frequent the parks notorious for men of a certain persuasion – could you imagine what he'd do at the sight of Wilf's young arse opened out in front of him, bent over his examination table? The old pervert would probably stick his finger right up it! Or worse! Wilf would rather suffer in silence.

And suffer he did, for the next fifty years. He learned to manage the pain, and then to tolerate it, but there was always a level of suffering in his daily existence, an unavoidable trauma spike whenever he needed to defecate. There was always a grimace, a careful wipe, a cursory check for blood amongst the debris on the toilet roll.

Over time, the haemorrhoid grew in size. At seventy years of age, the pile now dangled down like a third testicle, a bulbous pendulum surrounded by a menagerie of lesser polyps - a sort of fleshy, exotic flower. Although he didn't realise it, it controlled his gait and the way he walked. After learning the hard way, during a late night wait in a city centre burger bar where he sat down too hard on a plastic chair and frightened all the other drunks with a howl like a horse being murdered, he had to be very careful how he sat down. To a greater extent, it controlled his very life. Never one to charm the ladies, nor having any sort of wit to compensate for his borderline ugly features, any confidence he did have was eroded by the knowledge of the fleshy monster hanging off his arsehole, and he dreaded the reaction of any woman setting eyes on it so much that he never put himself in a position for that to happen. It's why the recollection of Valerie's/Ivy's perky little tits was so strong in his mind, being the only time he ever really got close to the possibility of touching a woman.

He hated it. Wilf's had been a life lived in misery, a broken slave to a tyrannical prolapsed vein, an unspeakable and terrible monster that had all but destroyed any chance of happiness.

When the haemorrhoid began speaking to Wilf, just after his thirtieth birthday, it was in conversations restricted to his dreams. Usually, the beast would loom out of the darkness and taunt him, calling him all sorts of abominable, unforgivable names. In his dreams, Wilf had insulted it, argued with it and even, on numerous occasions, wrestled with it. Without fail, it always got the better of him, and upon waking, a night-time encounter would invariably ruin the rest of the day.

By his mid-thirties, the haemorrhoid somehow found the power to speak to him during waking hours as well, and the second half of Wilf's life suffered under this additional mental torture. Everywhere he went, he would be followed by insults and shouted obscenities, and it was only after a number of dust-ups with startled passers-by that he realised the voice was actually coming from inside his own head. For a long time, he thought he might be going mad. After a little longer, he was certain of it.

Despite all of this haemorrhoid related upset that had cast a shadow over his life, Wilf was, to the casual observer, a perfectly ordinary functioning member of society. Now retired, he had held down numerous jobs and had been a member of various social clubs and organisations. The pile erupting from his backside hadn't completely curtailed any enjoyment that could be wrought out of playing bowls, for example, or (with the right trunks) a spot of swimming now and then. There were a few regrets, of course – he would have liked to go on a cycling holiday, for instance, but such a thing was merely an impossible dream.

He spent Saturday afternoons in his local pub, quietly nursing a pint or two of ale whilst he read or filled out crossword and Sudoku puzzles. The fact that he always brought his own cushion was not particularly remarkable, and the regulars just supposed it was some sort of quaint trait of eccentricity, a thing not nearly as common in modern English gentlemen as it ought to be. Although not overly sociable, he was generally liked and could be relied upon to participate in the general pleasantries that Civilised society revolves around.

It was at the pub that Wilf picked up an admirer, something he noticed long after the other regulars began gossiping about it. Mrs Tobias, an elderly widow with more than a passing resemblance to Albert Einstein, had taken a shine to Wilf, seeing something in him that was perhaps too well hidden for most people to notice.

"Doing your crossword?" she would ask, despite it being patently obvious that he was.

He would grunt in reply, and offer a curious sort of smile – it may have been a response to the sudden attention and a rueful recognition of his wasted life regarding any sort of female companionship, or it may have been a distracted smile brought on by a particularly troublesome clue that simply couldn't be fathomed. It may even have been a reaction against the sudden pain brought on in his nether regions as he subtly shifted his weight upon looking up. Most likely, it was an automatic response to the filth being shouted inside his skull, a smile to show the sprouting monstrosity that it was never going to win.

"Need any help?" she would ask, so often that it became a little ritual.

"I think I can manage," he'd say, followed by a smile that was a little more open.

This continued for months, a little exchange that would see the regulars pause their own conversations to quietly observe any progress before, with a sad little shake of their heads, they would return to their chatter. Possibly, it would have continued this way until death caught up with one of them.

However, one day whilst Wilf was ambling around the supermarket with a few bits and pieces in a hand basket, he bumped into Mrs Tobias and, before he knew it, became embroiled in a conversation with her.

"Fancy seeing you here!" she remarked, her rosacea flecked cheeks glowing a little redder.

"Just doing a bit of shopping."

"Me too."

"Well, this is the right place to go about it."

"It's too bloody big in here! By the time I've got everything I need I must have walked about four miles!"

Wilf chuckled in recognition, having often thought the same thing himself.

"Too much choice," he said. "That's the problem."

"I know! I want a bit of soap and there must be fifty different bars to choose from."

They stood for a moment, enjoying the exchange.

"I was going to call a taxi," said Mrs Tobias. "I wouldn't need to if you would carry one of my bags and walk me home."

The comment caught Wilf off guard.

"Erm..." he said, struggling to think of a response.

"It's only a short walk away. It would be a big help."

"Okay then," he said, realising that there wasn't any good reason to try and get out of it.

They walked around the store together, picking up various items for their baskets and moving along to the next aisle. Against his expectations, Wilf found that he was enjoying himself. For a few moments, he even imagined that this was how his old age might have turned out had he been able to marry. Doing the shopping together, with Mrs Tobias, was one of the most romantic things he'd ever done. Was it foolish to think along these lines? Mrs Tobias was no doubt reading nothing more into it than getting a vague acquaintance to help out with an errand, but Wilf explored the situation a little deeper and, with a bittersweet feeling clouding his emotions, allowed himself to daydream. In another life, maybe they had met at a teenage dance and had spent the last five decades deeply in love. Maybe they had children, successful and doting and with children of their own.

**"You fucking idiot,"** said the voice.

"What?"

"What's that?" asked Mrs Tobias, looking around.

"Nothing," said Wilf, looking at the floor in embarrassment.

Turning back, she reached out for a small carton of UHT milk.

Wilf silenty seethed at the voice, intruding on a rare moment of pleasantness.

**"Ooh, I'm married, with children!"** mocked the voice, taking on a higher pitch than usual. **"Successful children! Yeah, a prostitute and a drug dealer, that's all your kids would be good for."**

*Don't you be so fucking vulgar!* thought Wilf.

The voice laughed. **"When are you going to show me to your new friend?"** it asked. **"Do you think she'd like to pop me in her mouth?"**

Wilf felt like he was going to explode with rage. Mrs Tobias turned back to face him.

"Is everything all right?" she asked.

"Never better!" said Wilf, forcing a smile. When she resumed her browsing, he stood still and squeezed his buttocks and thighs together as hard as he could. It was a little trick he'd learned when in a desperate situation. At once, his head was filled with the muffled choking as the pile, struggling for freedom, found its terrible voice restricted.

*Ha!* thought Wilf, his eyes flashing in triumph. *That's shut you up, you little bastard!* He decided that when he arrived home he would have a hot bath, something the pile hated. It would always squeal and fill his head with curses. Sometimes it even wiggled, as though trying to swim away and clamber out of the bath, back to somewhere cool.

He looked up to see Mrs Tobias, at the other end of the aisle, looking back at him with a concerned expression.

"Coming!" he called, striding towards her. The sound of hyperventilating filled his head as the pile recovered from its ordeal.

**"I'll get you for that!"** it said.

Bags in hand, Wilf escorted the widow Tobias out of the store and across the car park. A narrow path led across an adjacent area of parkland.

"This is very kind of you," she said.

"It's no bother."

They walked side by side in a companionable silence. The day was crisp and bright. They passed a spindly tree and a robin observed them, silently contemplating the encroachment on its territory.

"It's not far now," she said. Even though Wilf had ensured he carried the heaviest bags, her pace was slowing. They left the park and crossed over a street. Wilf almost reached out and took her arm at one point, ready to steady her, but he held off. He feared that a well-meaning action on his part could be interpreted as an erosion of her dignity. Age was hard enough without unwanted help being foisted upon you.

A couple of streets further on she stopped for a rest, placing her bags onto a low wall and catching her breath.

"Wouldn't believe I used to run for the county, would you?" she asked, a rueful smile etched across her weathered face. A slight breeze made a halo of her white hair around the back of her head. Wilf smiled. With a sigh, she picked up her bags and they carried on.

She lived in a ground floor maisonette. As soon as she put her key in the door a series of high pitched barks resonated around the interior hallway.

"Don't mind Jack," she said. "He won't bite."

Wilf followed her into the house and a little brown and white Jack Russell terrier ran around their legs, barking and desperate for a bit of fuss.

"Cup of tea?" she asked, already heading for the kitchen.

"Yes please. That would be lovely."

He sat on the sofa and the dog wandered over. It regarded him suspiciously and growled when he reached down to pat its head. Still, it didn't move away and, edging closer, reluctantly allowed Wilf to pet it. Within moments it seemed to decide that Wilf wasn't a threat and rolled onto its back, offering its little belly for a rub. Wilf obliged and, emboldened, it suddenly leapt up onto the settee and tried to lick Wilf's face. He couldn't help but let out a laugh.

"You two getting along?" called Mrs Tobias from the kitchen.

"We're the best of pals!" he called back. The dog clambered all over him and then it suddenly stopped and sniffed at the air. As if it knew something was different about Wilf, it cocked its head and looked towards his crotch. From that moment, Wilf had to fend it off as it tried to bury its little snout between his legs.

**"Keep it away from me!"** screeched the voice inside his head.

It was scared. Wilf contemplated pulling his trousers down and letting the feisty little dog grab a hold of the pile between its teeth to tear it loose. The pile seemed to shrivel in terror and Wilf briefly enjoyed the rare turning of the tables – for once, he had the upper hand. The fucking thing was whimpering! He deliberately conjured up images of the dog chewing on the pile and his head was filled with its whining pleading voice.

**"You can't consider this!"** it screeched. **"The blood loss will kill you!"**

Wilf had no idea whether this was true or not. But, the very fact that he wondered brought a fresh burst of confidence back to the haemorrhoid. It knew all his thoughts. Even if it didn't kill him, there would be sufficient blood loss to make a right old mess of the carpet. He couldn't do that to her. He couldn't conceivably face a scene where she returned and saw him with his trousers down and her dog hanging off his arse – it would be deranged to give the idea any serious consideration.

He gently forced the dog back onto the floor and looked up as Mrs Tobias came into the lounge with a mug of tea in each hand. She passed one to him and sat in the nearest armchair.

They spent a very pleasant hour chatting and drinking tea. Mrs Tobias – Maude, he discovered -talked and talked and Wilf chipped in whenever she left a brief pause for him to do so. He didn't mind that she led all of the conversation – if anything, it meant there weren't any embarrassing silences whilst he struggled to come up with something to say. Usually, when in the company of a female, he would feel intimidated, not only from his own social anxieties regarding the fairer sex (he'd never had much of an opportunity to get a woman on her own) but also from the torrent of abuse he'd receive from the haemorrhoid, so much it would make his head spin. If there was a particular woman that Wilf had taken a shine to, it would know and it would increase the abuse accordingly.

She talked so much that the pile seemed to go into hibernation in an attempt to avoid listening to her. It must have been bored, but Wilf was enjoying the experience. He found that he was interested in what she had to say, even though shortly after leaving he could barely remember any of what they'd talked about for the last hour.

He realised that things had changed. He wouldn't be able to sit alone in the pub any more, lost in his puzzles. The next time Maude stopped and asked if he'd like any help he would have to clear a space for her and let her sit down and join in. To do anything else would be out of the question. Whether he liked it or not, his routine at the pub had now changed.

And, he admitted to himself, it was nice. He liked this new situation. Mrs Tobias was a very pleasant woman. Very pleasant indeed. He enjoyed her company. During that hour at her house, something flickered into life deep inside Wilf, the spark of a burgeoning friendship. It was obvious that she was just as lonely as he was.

After he said his goodbyes and was walking back down the streets towards the town, the haemorrhoid stirred from its self-imposed slumber. He felt it awake, felt its malign presence come back to life.

**"You like her,"** it said.

*So what if I do?*

**"Ha ha ha! You think she's going to be your new friend, don't you?"**

*What does that have to do with you?*

**"You don't need any new friends. You've got me."**

*You?! You're nothing but a stinking, rotten bastard. You've never been my friend.*

**"I've always been there for you. Through thick and thin, I've always been there."**

*Yes, you have. Ruining everything. You'd better not mess this up for me, I'm warning you.*

**"You're warning me? Ha ha ha! You can't stop me from doing whatever I like."**

*Oh, can't I?*

**"You never have and you never will."**

*Maybe it's time that changed.*

The pile remained silent, the vague threat left hanging. It sensed that there was something different about Wilf. Down the years there had been numerous threats to cut the pile off, or squash it, or even an aborted attempt to obliterate it with a power drill. Empty threats, ultimately, shouted in moments of hopeless fury. But this was different.

The next day, Wilf phoned the doctor's surgery and booked an appointment. Old Bernstein was long dead and he had no idea of who had replaced him. Whoever it was, Wilf was determined to get some help. For the first time in his life, he thought that it might not be too late to sort this problem out once and for all. Regardless of whether any flowering friendship with Mrs Tobias led to any sort of geriatric bedroom gymnastics – and he was undecided as to how he should feel about that, should the issue become a practicality – it was time this evil parasite was destroyed.

Of course, it knew what was happening.

**"No doctor can help you,"** it said, filling his head with its voice. **"You've left me here too long. Any attempt to remove me now will end up killing you. Is that what you want?"**

*You're a liar.*

Wilf ran himself a bath and had himself a long soak. After the pile had stopped squealing at the heat of the water, it resumed its tactics of trying to get Wilf to avoid seeing a doctor.

**"They'll all laugh at you,"** it said. **"As soon as they see what you've got hanging out of your arse they'll take a picture and send it around all the other surgeries so they can all have a laugh at you."**

*I don't care if they do.*

**"Think of the shame! When news gets out, you won't be able to leave the house ever again!"**

*You're talking rubbish.*

**"Am I? So why haven't you thought of doing this before?"**

*I don't know.*

**"It's suicide! You won't survive an amputation at your age!"**

*Then maybe it's better if I don't. At least if I go I'll take you out with me.*

Between his legs, stretched out so that he could see it through the bathwater, the haemorrhoid pulsed with anger. Wilf reached down and pinned it against the bottom of the bath with his index finger. The pain of it made him wince but he knew that the pile hated this more than anything. It squirmed and tried to wriggle to freedom but he held it fast.

"You'll be gone soon," he said out loud. "Nothing but a memory." When he eventually released the little monster, it seethed in silence, saying nothing.

On the way to the doctors, the pile wept blood, staining the back of Wilf's trousers.

**"You'll have to go back home!"** it said. **"People are looking and pointing at you."**

*Let them.*

It jiggled and wriggled, making a ruckus inside his underpants.

Wilf ignored it as best he could.

As he approached the surgery, the pile resorted to pleading.

**"Pleeease!"** it wailed. **"Don't do this! I'll change! I'll be nice from now on!"**

*I'm not listening to you. Cry all you like.*

Wilf was determined to see this endeavour through to the bitter end. Now that he had finally made the decision, nothing was going to stop him. No amount of begging or pleading.

**"Murderer!"** cried the pile.

Wilf entered the surgery and confirmed his name to the receptionist. She asked him to sit down and wait until his name was called. Wilf picked up one of the magazines on the nearby coffee table and gingerly sat down on one of the plastic chairs. Inside his head, the haemorrhoid screamed. On and on it went, a terrible screeching sound that would have had the old Wilf on his hands and knees, begging for it to stop. But this new Wilf accepted the noise with a Zen-like calm and casually flicked through a home style magazine. After a while, the screaming stopped. There was a loud buzz and Wilf looked up at a wall-mounted screen to see his name and a room number.

The doctor was a middle-aged woman and the sight of her made Wilf stop dead in his tracks. He stood in the doorway, still holding the door handle, and seemed frozen to the spot. The doctor looked up and smiled.

"Come in," she said, indicating to an empty chair on the nearest side of her desk.

He didn't know what to do next. The pile waited, holding its breath. After what seemed like an eternity, Wilf stepped into the room. It could so easily have gone the other way. The only thing that kept him going was the certain knowledge that if he left now there would be no coming back and the pile would stay with him until the day he died. And leaving would have handed it victory on a plate, something that it would never let him forget. It was already an intolerable little bastard and he couldn't imagine how much worse it could get if it knew it had won this final battle.

"How can I help?" asked the doctor.

Wilf stared at her and felt his mouth go dry.

"Haemorrhoids," he croaked at last. "Just the one, actually. A big one."

"Well I'd better take a look at it then," she said. "Pull down your trousers and pop yourself up onto the examination table there."

Wilf remained seated.

**"You're not going to let her look at your stinking bunghole, are you?"** asked the pile.

"Mr... Butterby?" asked the Doctor, glancing at the computer screen to remind herself of his name.

**"You can't do it, can you?"** sneered the pile.

*Yes I can,* thought Wilf, standing up.

**"You can't show a woman your shit-hole!"** shouted the voice inside his head. **"You fucking pervert!"**

Wilf slowly walked over to the examination table, unbuckled his belt and dropped his trousers. With some difficulty, he clambered up onto the table.

"If you can just turn towards the wall and lie on your side," said the doctor, walking over to a nearby set of drawers. Wilf watched as she opened the top drawer and pulled out a box. She produced two latex gloves and put the box back in the drawer.

**"She's going to stick her hand through your ringpiece!"** said the voice.

*Then let her. She can do whatever she wants. You have lost any power you had over me. It's time for you to die.*

Wilf closed his eyes. He felt a cold pair of gloved hands separate his buttocks. His cheeks burned with embarrassment and shame as the doctor took a good look at the pile.

"You've had this quite a while then, have you?" she asked.

"Practically all my life."

"Oh dear. And you never thought to come and have it looked at before?"

"I'm afraid I didn't, no."

He waited, teeth clenched, as she lifted the pile and inspected it thoroughly.

"The good news," she said, "is that this sort of thing is easily treated."

"It is?"

"I can sort this out for you in a few minutes."

"You mean I won't need an operation?"

"Not at all. I have the tool right here. Ligation involves nothing more than securing a band at the top of the haemorrhoid and waiting."

Wild felt the pile twitch.

"Waiting for what?" asked Wilf.

"For the haemorrhoid to shrink and drop off."

The pile twitched again. Wilf could feel it growing hot.

"And that's it?!" asked Wilf, incredulous.

**"Don't you do it,"** warned the pile. **"I'm warning you."**

"That's it!" said the doctor, smiling.

Wilf couldn't believe it. He felt his face grow even redder and his ears burned with shame. All of this time, so many years putting up with that rotten pile when it could have all been sorted in just a few minutes. His life could have turned out so very differently. He could have married, perhaps had children. He might have been a confident, outgoing individual who had conquered life instead of suffered it. He felt such a fool. Why didn't he just go to the doctor fifty years ago? Even having old Bernstein touching him up would have been worth it.

**"Pull your trousers up and leave,"** said the pile.

Wilf could hear the fear in its voice. They both knew that this would all be over soon. He waited as the doctor sorted out the ligation tool.

**"I'm serious!"** warned the pile. **"If you do me in, you're coming with me!"**

*Don't be so ridiculous. You have no hold over me any more.*

**"Is that so? Want to test me, do you? I'm telling you, do this and it'll be the end of both of us."**

Wilf ignored it.

The doctor came and stood next to the table.

"Are you ready, Mr Butterby?" she asked.

**"DON'T YOU FUC-"**

"Yes, I'm ready," said Wilf.

The doctor reached down and separated Wilf's buttocks. He could feel the pile pulsing with terror and rage and wondered if the doctor could also feel it. If she could, she said nothing. All the while, the pile screamed obscenities inside Wilf's head, so loud that he thought that there must be some leakage from his earholes, some tiny voice that made it into the world. Wilf winced as he felt a tug and then a pinch right next to his anus and heard a click as the doctor operated the ligation tool. At the same time, the screaming insults from the pile came to a sudden end. Inside his head, Wilf could hear silence.

*My God,* he thought. *It's over.*

Three days later, he sat on a bench in the local park. Next to him, so close that their legs were touching, sat old Mrs Tobias. In front of them, a flock of quacking ducks snapped greedily at the ground, scrabbling for any bits of leftover bread that might have been missed.

Wilf couldn't remember ever being happier. Even something as simple as feeding a bunch of scraggy ducks had been a thoroughly enjoyable experience when shared with someone. It was only after engaging in such pedestrian and banal activities, with Maude by his side, that Wilf realised just how terribly lonely his life had been. That morning, he had taken her to a local café and they had eaten bacon butties and washed them down with a couple of mugs of piping hot tea. She liked it the same as him, milky with just a smidge of sugar. They had bought a small loaf of bread from the baker and fed the ducks and, later, they were heading back to her place to sit together and watch an old black and white movie on the television.

It was perhaps too soon, but Wilf felt the first stirrings of love. And why not? After seventy years on his own, who on earth could accuse him of rushing anything? If the thought of Maude's company sent his stomach into a flutter, and the sight of her smile made him smile as though his head might crack in half, then what was wrong with that?

Bread finished, they stood and Wilf watched as she patted herself down. The ducks eyed them suspiciously, as though they might be hiding a final bit of bread, and then scattered when Wilf and Maude started walking back down the concrete path leading to the park exit. On the way, she casually reached out and took a hold of Wilf's hand as though it were the most natural thing in the world.

Wilf was so happy that his eyes glazed over and a single tear rolled down his face.

When she turned to smile at him and noticed the tear, she asked if anything was wrong. Wilf just smiled and blamed a cold breeze.

After another few days, the pile was about ready to drop off. At home, alone, Wilf got himself ready for bed and, just before putting on his pyjama bottoms, squatted over a mirror to see how things were going. The pile was noticeably smaller now, about the size of a cocktail sausage, and an ugly black colour. Withered. Dying. There was no pain. No more voice inside his head.

After putting a hot water bottle under the duvet and popping his dentures into a glass of water, Wilf clambered into bed. He sighed, tired after another full day with Maude. One day, they would decide that all this going home to separate houses was too bothersome and would simply share the same bed in one house or the other. They would wake up together. With that pleasing thought, Wilf drifted into sleep.

It was a balmy night, and Wilf managed to somehow kick the duvet off himself. He changed position a few times until he was lying on his back. Mouth open, a low snore reverberated around the bedroom.

In his pyjama bottoms, something moved. There was a barely audible *pop!* as the last bit of skin holding the pile in place finally severed and the blackened lump fell away from Wilf's anus. For a short while, nothing moved and the room was silent and still. Wilf had stopped snoring and, in one of those moments between snores that seem to go on forever, seemed to be holding his breath.

The pile moved. Slowly at first, in spasming, jerking movements, it inched along Wilf's pyjama leg until it emerged onto the bedsheet. An ugly, pulsing thing, it waited to regain a bit of energy and then, when it was ready, it hopped along the bed towards Wilf's head. In tiny increments it covered the distance, stopping a few times, seemingly weakening with the effort. For a few minutes, it looked as though it might finally be dead before suddenly bursting into life and, with an audible squeaking sound, it scrunched itself up tightly and then heaved itself up into the air towards Wilf's face.

It landed on his top lip. With a final sigh, it rolled into Wilf's open mouth and forced its way into his throat.

Wilf awoke with a start, coughing and clutching at his neck. Eyes bulging, fighting for breath, he clambered out of bed and stumbled around the bedroom. The glass of water with his dentures was knocked from the bedside table and landed on the floor, spilling the contents across the carpet. In the darkness, in his desperation, Wilf crashed into bits of furniture before finally falling to his knees and keening over with a final gargle of defeat.

Wilf was dead, choked to death on his own haemorrhoid.

Apart from the vicar, Maude was the only person who attended his funeral.

# LOOKING INTO A FURNACE

Cal called in the afternoon and asked if I was going to town that night. Of course, I'd said, why would this Saturday be any different? He thought I was seeing some bird and the truth is I was supposed to but she'd blown me out earlier in the week. I couldn't tell him that though, he'd tell the others and that'd be it for the next few weeks, endless piss-taking. So I told him I'd fucked her off for being too needy and I'd meet him in the Clock for one on the way.

When I arrived, the rest of the gang was already there. Stevie and Dobb were a couple of pints in already. They were both big lads and I'd seen them sink twenty each in a day before so a couple wouldn't even wet their throats.

"Alright?" asked Cal, slapping me on the shoulder. He moved to one side and I saw a fresh pint waiting for me. He's a good man, is Cal. They all are. They're the brothers I never had. We'd all been through a few scrapes together, down the years, and we were still standing. I couldn't ask for better mates.

We knocked back the drinks and started walking into town. We were about a mile off and the walk usually took twenty minutes or so. Stevie would inevitably need a piss along the way and would end up in someone's garden hosing down their roses. On the way back, gone midnight, he'd stop in a garden (sometimes even the same garden) and do it again. A couple of times he'd even put his half-eaten kebab on someone's wall whilst he'd stopped to take a shit. Disgusting, I know, but funny when one of us sends him the YouTube link the next day after a bit of covert filming on a mobile.

Halfway there, we were approached by a young Japanese woman. She was holding a wireless microphone and a drone hovered over her right shoulder.

"Hello gentlemen," she said in a bright voice. "Do you want to be on tv?"

Dobb stepped forward to speak with her, which I didn't think was a good idea. Dobb wasn't much keen on Orientals. He wasn't much keen on anybody who wasn't white and British. He's always been that way. At school, he did himself a tattoo on the webbing between his thumb and index finger of his left hand, using biro ink and a compass. He drew a swastika and although it's faded now it's still obvious. It's cost him at least a couple of jobs, as far as I know, probably more. I mean, who wants a racist working for them? What the interviewers wouldn't know about Dobb is that he has another, much larger and more professionally done tattoo of a swastika covering his back, along with a portrait of Hitler.

"Is that a camera?" he asked, jabbing a thick finger up towards the drone. Her lower jaw almost dislocated itself with a huge grin and she nodded vigorously. "Are we on telly right now?" he asked.

"This just preliminary filming," she said. Her high-pitched voice and fixed grin made her seem like a maniac struggling to control herself. "Tv later."

"What kind of show is it?" I asked.

"Game show. Big prize!"

I looked at the others and shrugged.

"Fuck it," I said. "Why not?"

"Have we got time for it?" asked Stevie. I knew what he was thinking. Stevie's idea of a good night out involved drinking as much as possible, getting into a fight with someone and then finishing off with a curry or a kebab. Quite a schedule and Saturday night was easily the most important part of his week. He was worried that if we did this for a couple of hours we might not have time to fit everything else in.

"Relax," I said. "It'll be fun. And we might win something."

He grudgingly relented. I turned back to the woman.

"We're in," I said.

"Good news!" she squealed and turned to look up at the drone. "Contestants ready!" she cried, throwing her arms up for dramatic effect.

A black van appeared as if from nowhere and pulled up next to us. The side door opened and the woman pointed at the dark interior. It didn't look that inviting.

"What prizes did you say?" I asked her.

"Yes, many prize! Big prize! In, in!"

With a sigh, Stevie poked his head inside for a quick look around and clambered in. The rest of us followed. With a pitter-patter of stiletto heels on paving slabs, the woman ran over and slammed the door, leaving us in darkness for a few moments before a dim red light came on. There were no seats so we were sitting on the floor. A dull rumble swept through the van as the engine started and we felt ourselves being driven away.

"Are we sure this is a good idea?" asked Dobb.

"It doesn't matter," said Cal, his face a Devil mask in the red light. Let's just see what happens."

"If I'd known I was going to be on the telly I'd have made more of an effort," said Stevie, combing over his fringe with a sweaty hand. "Fuckin' hot in here," he added as an afterthought.

We were driven for about ten minutes, by which time I was beginning to lose my patience. Just as I was about to bang on the side of the van, it turned a sharp corner and then rumbled up some sort of uneven road. We stopped shortly afterwards and someone came over and opened the side door.

We stepped out, shielding our eyes from the evening sun. We were parked in front of the biggest warehouse I'd ever seen.

"Follow me, please," said a small Japanese man with a clipboard. He led us to a door, which he opened and we all followed him through. We ended up in a brightly lit room. There was no furniture other than a table with a few shrink wrapped items on it.

"Please, change," said the man, pointing at the table. Stevie wandered over, picked one of the packets up and opened it. He was soon holding up a pair of white overalls. I looked around the room and noticed two cameras mounted to the walls.

"Are you going to record us getting changed?" I asked.

"No, no, not working," said the man. He was grinning like a Cheshire cat. I could tell he was lying as there were little red lights on them so even if we weren't being filmed we were probably being watched. What kind of tv programme was this, I wondered.

Stevie stripped down to his pants and put on the overalls. We did the same.

"No shoes!" said the man.

"Why not?" I asked.

"Ruin equipment!" he said. Reluctantly, we all took off our shoes. "Sock too!" he said.

Satisfied that we were ready, the man walked over to another door and motioned us through.

"Go to end," he said, still smiling. "Wait."

When we'd filed through he closed the door behind us, leaving us alone.

"This is getting a bit weird," said Cal. "I've half a mind to tell 'em to go fuck themselves and get out of here. I'm telling you, these prizes better be worth it."

"I think it's going to be something like Total Wipeout," said Stevie.

"More like Takeshi's Castle," said Dobb. "With all these Japs knocking about."

We followed the corridor to another room. In the distance we heard a series of dull thuds. They were powerful enough to cause the thin metal walls of the corridor to buzz. Boom, Boom! There was a gap of perhaps two seconds before another two thudding sounds. It continued, forming a regular pattern.

We came to another room and were surprised to see a load of people already in there. Nobody was talking. I looked at them. Everyone here was male and aged between late teens and perhaps late fifties. A few had tattoos on their faces and necks. They all turned and looked us over. There was one guy I had to look twice at, a big bastard with close cropped ginger hair and a wonky eye. I thought I knew him from somewhere but the context of meeting him under these strange circumstances was throwing me off. I was about to turn and quietly converse with the others when a television screen burst into life.

"Hello contestants!" said a woman in a pink dress. She looked insanely happy and I recognised her as the woman who had approached us on the street and got us into this thing. "Congratulation on reach first stage. Begin in two minute."

The camera panned back from her a little and we could see that she also had bare feet. There were cartoon bugs crawling around on the floor beneath her. Squealing, she lifted up her feet and did a little dance. Bugs exploded beneath her. "Mashee-mashee!" she cried, laughing.

"What the fuck?" said one of the other guys in the room. He sounded like he was all out of patience. The air was getting tense.

The woman on the screen was replaced with a countdown.

"What do we have to do?" asked Cal. We were still in our own little sub-group.

"Looks like we have to squash some shit," said Stevie. "Maybe they're counting how many cockroaches we can kill or something."

"I don't like it," I said. "Something about this feels wrong."

We waited and watched the countdown pass the minute marker. With thirty seconds to go, everyone in the room jumped as three metal stutters on the back wall slid open and shadowy figures stood there watching us. It was hard to tell if they were real or just cardboard cut-outs – they didn't move an inch.

Cal touched my arm.

"They have baseball bats," he said, his voice quiet. I took a good look and saw that he was right. I felt my stomach sink a little.

On the screen, the counter dropped below twenty seconds.

"Hey, guys!" I called and a few heads turned in my direction. At this point the room was filled with men who were either bemused at what was happening, curious about any particular prizes that might be up for grabs, or frustrated and angry. The counter dropped to fifteen.

"What?" shouted the big ginger bastard.

"These guys..." I said, nodding at the shadowy figures.

I saw his eyebrows rise as he noticed that the figures were armed. "What the-"

His voice was cut off by the blare of a klaxon. A number of things seemed to happen at once. Beneath the television screen, a door opened into a wide corridor. LED's dotted the walls and flashed like runway lights, drawing us forward. Behind us, the shadowy figures stepped into the room and started swinging their bats and attacking us. I saw one guy's head rupture with a spray of blood as a bat connected with his skull and he dropped like a sack of shit.

"Run!" I shouted at the others.

Terrified now, unable to comprehend what the hell was really going on, I knew that we had to get away from the fuckers with the bats. We burst through the doorway and started running. The floor crunched beneath my feet and I had to swat things from the air with my hands. Then I noticed the sharp pains in the soles of my feet and a quick look down confirmed how far this madness was going – the floor was covered with wasps and we were running over them and getting stung repeatedly.

"Mashee-mashee!" screeched a voice, overpoweringly loud from unseen speakers.

Behind, someone was calling my name. I couldn't tell if it was Cal or Stevie – the voice was high-pitched with panic and I was too busy dealing with my own thoughts to try and focus on it. "Keep running!" I yelled, hoping this would be enough.

The booming sound was getting louder. Two loud bangs followed by a couple of seconds before it repeated. I roared with pain as another few stings burned into my feet and realised that wasps were starting to attack my arms and face as well. These bastards were going to pay for this – I didn't care what prizes were on offer, this was the most fucked-up game show I'd ever heard of.

At this point, I still had hopes of getting out of this experience alive. That changed as the corridor slowly curved and we entered a cavernous room and saw what was waiting for us.

Two rows of armed figures dressed in anti-riot gear lined the walls, one or two of them swinging baseball bats in readiness for an attack. I saw a flash of metal and realised that at least one of them was wielding a sword. Worse than this, the far end of the room contained a large opening, and this was the source of the terrible booming sounds. Above, in green neon lettering, was the word 'GOAL'. Blocking our way, two metal blocks came crashing down in quick succession – *Boom! Boom!* – before lifting up and falling down again. The front block came down first, followed by another behind it. But, as I watched, I then saw the second block drop before the first one. There was a pattern there I wouldn't have time to work out, or it could even have been random. Either way we were fucked.

Were we supposed to dash under them and hope we weren't crushed to death? My mind was still racing but I knew that the answer was yes. Whoever was running this madness was definitely prepared to kill us, for reasons I couldn't even begin to fathom. Had killed already, I guessed, as the man I saw dropped in the other room probably wouldn't have much of a skull left.

I'd slowed down without realising and Stevie, Dobb and Cal overtook me. They came to a halt and looked back. Their expressions were confused, terrified, and they looked like they were pleading with me to come up with some sort of explanation. I glanced around, trying to calculate an option. Any option. I had nothing.

The armed figures began converging on us.

One of the other contestants had kept running straight for the opening under the GOAL sign. I watched, fascinated, deliberately ignoring all of the other dangers, to see if he would make it. He ran at full sprint and ducked as he reached the opening, hoping his timing was right. The next second felt like it happened at a thousand miles an hour and lasted a hundred years at the same time. The first block came crashing down and obliterated him, smashing him between metal and the concrete floor in an explosion of gore. I nearly vomited as the block lifted up and I saw what was left.

"Fuck!" screamed Stevie.

I looked around. Some of the other contestants were trying to fight back against the men in riot gear. They were hopelessly ineffectual, their fists being no match for the bats and occasional sword. I saw on guy lose an arm, watched as it was sliced clean off and landed on the floor a few feet away. The guy didn't have time to even scream as a bunch of armed attackers piled into him and kept beating away with murderous intent.

They were going to kill us all.

We had to get out of this room.

"Move it!" I shouted, starting my run. If we were going to get out of this we had to go through those blocks. There might have been some other way but there was no time to assess the situation any further – if we didn't make a run for it in the next few seconds we wouldn't get a chance to do anything.

I developed tunnel vision and everything else was filtered out. All I could focus on was running forward and gauging the pattern of the blocks. Stevie pulled ahead of us all, his determined effort turning him into Usain Bolt, and as we drew nearer the opening I saw him drop to his knees and skid forward. For a moment I thought he might make it. He cleared the first block but the one behind caught him. Stevie was squashed like a bug, throwing out a curtain of blood and gristle.

As I reached the opening, the blocks were halfway up their rise. I threw myself forwards in a Superman dive, landing in Stevie's remains and using them as a lubricant to slide under both of the blocks. I kept my eyes closed until I thought I was through and then skidded to a halt and jumped to my feet. I was clear. As I turned back to look I saw Dobb clear the blocks, along with some guy we didn't know. Cal looked like he was going to make it, using the same technique I had, but the second block dropped down on him when he was only halfway through and as he opened his mouth to scream a torrent of his insides hosed the floor in front of us.

I ran back and grabbed his arms to pull him clear as the blocks rose again. The big ginger bastard came hurtling into him, bumping Cal's remains into the room but causing himself to stop. He looked at me with his one good eye, knowing he was about to die. There was no way he could get out from under there in time. In a final act of defiance – one that would burn itself in my brain until the time came for me to die – he formed a fist with his right hand and, as the blocks came down, roared and threw a punch up to meet them.

It was a pointless act, a futile gesture, but I could tell everything I needed to know about that man by that one simple snapshot of his willingness to go down fighting. And, at that moment, I remembered where I knew him from.

*Crystal Palace, 2013.*

A few more people made their way into this new room and then, suddenly, the blocks came down one last time and stopped. After the echoes had finished bouncing around the walls we were enveloped in a silence so complete that I actually forgot to breathe whilst I listened and waited for something else to happen.

"Congratulation! You success!"

The crazy woman in the pink dress was back, this time on a huge tv screen mounted on a stand in the otherwise empty room. I took a few moments to inspect the soles of my feet. They were throbbing with pain and already starting to swell. Considering I was still alive, I thought that I hadn't gotten off too badly.

Dobb limped over to me, his face red with anger.

"Some cunt's gonna get it for this," he snarled. He looked down at Cal's remains and I followed his gaze. An hour ago we were standing around in the pub, laughing and looking forward to the rest of the night. Now Stevie and Cal were both dead. It seemed incredible but it had happened and the nightmare was still happening. I briefly thought of Stevie's mother and then Cal's ex-girlfriend and daughter. Someone was going to have to explain this, as if anyone would believe it. I forced these thoughts from my mind and looked at Dobb.

"I knew one of the other guys," I told him.

"What do you mean?"

"The big ginger fuck. Manky eye."

"How do you know him?"

"He's dead, Dobb. We met him at Crystal Palace a few years ago. He was part of their crew."

Dobb looked back at me.

"I don't remember. Even so, it's just a coincidence, right?"

"I'm not sure. I don't think so."

"So these cunts knew who we were right from the get-go?" he asked.

"Possibly. I don't know."

In all, six of us made it through the blocks, including myself and Dobb. I took a good look around at the others but didn't recognise any of them. It would have been difficult anyway, considering we were all frightened out of our wits and covered in blood.

"Preparate round two!" screeched the Japanese woman from the tv.

"Fuck, there's more of this?" asked Dobb.

There was a hissing sound and we looked up to see plumes of mist billowing down from the ceiling. Now what? Were they gassing us?

“Find a way out of here,” I told him. “Everyone! Listen to me! Find an exit and shout when you’ve found it!”

Nobody argued. We split up, running in different directions, each of us frantically hammering against the walls and looking for a doorway. All the while, the mist pumped into the room and descended. Soon we were all coughing.

I couldn’t find a way out. Angry, thinking that these were my last seconds on Earth, I starting walking back towards the television set. If I wasn’t getting out of here, I was going to smash that fucking thing to pieces. It would be nothing but a small act of defiance in the scale of things but it would have to be enough.

I didn’t even get halfway. Coughing violently, my vision dimming, I collapsed to my knees and don’t even remember toppling the rest of the way to the floor.

I was out cold.

*Crystal Palace, 2013.*

The train pulled into the station and we poured out of it, excited and half cut with cheap lager. The ride down had been a noisy one and the passengers had all moved to the back end of the train to get out of our way. Couldn’t blame them, really. Still, that hadn’t stopped one or two chopsing off at us and getting a good kicking in return.

These ‘civilians’ couldn’t understand our world and viewed it with fear and contempt. They didn’t understand what it was like to be part of a firm, how alive it made you feel. Normal life was an inconvenience, a mixture of chores and other mundane bullshit necessary to see us through to the next game where we could tool up and let loose and feel that beautiful adrenaline rush as the opposing crew ran towards us.

The Crystal Palace hoolies were called the Dirty 30. There were more than thirty of them, of course, and they were a tough crew. Most were. You didn’t end up getting into this if you were a fucking weakling. You had to have bollocks the size of wrecking balls. Even though I’ve caved quite a few faces in over the years, I have the utmost respect for everyone I’ve maimed.

They were waiting for us at the station, as we’d expected. I turned to see Cal loading up with his knuckle dusters, one on each hand. He’d cracked dozens of skulls with those in the past. Stevie preferred a Stanley knife, he liked to rush in and start slashing. Once or twice we’d had to talk him out of bringing his favourite machete – I mean, there’s got to be *some* restraint – but we all knew that one day he'd hide it on himself and bring it anyway. Dobb generally didn't bother with a weapon – being eighteen stone and boxing since he was a nipper meant he could handle himself very well using only his fists. He loved nothing more than cracking his knuckles against a stranger's nasal passages and rearranging their face before knocking them over and stamping on their head. As for me, I favoured an extendable steel baton, a handy little thing that locked into position at a foot long and extended your hitting range accordingly. With a baton, you could crack somebody's skull whilst they were swinging a blade and cutting nothing but air.

People screamed and dragged their children out of the way as our two firms converged on the platform and went at it. Even though it was an exceptionally violent pastime, I have to say that hooliganism provided me with the only peace I'd ever known. I'm not going to make excuses for my past, horrible though it was – I loved fighting and injuring people simply because I was a nasty cunt, regardless of any historic abuse or psychological trauma. In the middle of a good ruck, everything else faded away to nothing, every single problem, big or small, just disappeared for a while and I reached a kind of Zen state, a safe place where I could focus on nothing but my physicality and the ballet of violence playing out around me. You just don't get those moments of beauty anywhere else. To find true peace, you need to go to the extremes once in a while.

I lashed out at a few people, whipping the baton into their faces. Blood pumped through my veins and it felt like I was waking up after a hundred years of sleep. There was nothing on Earth like smashing people up, feeling them break under the power of the violence you gave out.

It worked both ways, that was the nature of these things. Within moments, I felt a hard crack against the side of my head and saw an explosion of lights before I fell to my knees. I readied myself for a blade or a boot but nothing came and when my vision cleared I saw Dobb standing over me with an arm extended to help me up. On the floor between us was a bloke lying face down, out of it.

"He hit you with a brick," said Dobb, heaving me up.

The side of my head was hot with pain and when I reached up to touch it my hand came away red.

"Thanks mate," I said, grimacing. He'd been there for me more than once, and vice versa. I really do mean it when I say these guys are my brothers. When you're in the trenches and the heat's really on, there's nobody else I'd want watching my back.

I gripped my baton and waded in for some more.

The battle lasted a good ten minutes before the police sirens started and we saw them coming through the station building. Some of the filth had been there for ages but they only come out to play when there's enough of them. Until they have decent numbers, they're happy to stand back and watch. And in that ten minutes, we'd all done enough damage to fill up the local casualty department. Blokes had been thrown off the platform onto the tracks and one had even been hoofed through a plate glass window. I hope somebody had filmed all of this so we could have a good laugh at the footage over a few beers later.

As the police piled out, both firms scattered and ran. Sometimes this gets reported as cowardice but nothing's further from the truth. We run so we can regroup and fight again. The next hotspot would be in the town so we made our way there in dribs and drabs, getting into minor scuffles with similarly displaced Palace goons.

When people read their newspapers the morning after a good ruck, they start up the usual discussions about what scum we are, how we're all mindless yobs. What these people fail to realise is that we're the backbone of society, the workers who keep the wheels turning. We're the mechanics, the cleaners, the chefs and estate agents, factory workers and waiters who keep the country running so all these moaning arseholes can continue to do whatever the fuck it is they do.

They don't realise that hooliganism has been a part of football for over a hundred years and always will be. Mostly young men, blowing off a bit of steam, there's no real harm in it. Civilians rarely get injured so I don't see what their fucking problem is. All these moaners who get on their high horses when we do a bit of fighting would soon change their tune if we ever got invaded. Do they think our army, with its diminished budgets and lack of equipment are going to save them? No, when things get ugly, and the Russians or the Germans are on our streets, it's going to be people like me who bear the brunt of the fighting and take these bastards down. We're the true saviours of Britain, make no mistake about it. And tear-ups on a Saturday afternoon are our way of staying sharp. People should be thanking us.

In the middle of town we met up with the rest of the stragglers and reformed our little army. The Dirty 30 weren't fully ready yet so we put a few shop windows through to keep the boredom level from dropping. As we stood around waiting, little figures hurried out of shop doorways and started pulling down their metal shutters. I saw a newsagent barricading up the front of his shop and briefly wished we'd waited to put the windows through so I could have nipped in and bought a packet of fags.

The two firms stood at each end of the main drag and slowly advanced. A big ginger man seemed to be leading up the opposition. He looked pretty handy, built like a brick shithouse and ready to cave in a few skulls. I moved to the front line of our group. I wanted a crack at that cunt before anyone else tagged him.

We were fifty yards away when some metal canisters landed in the street and started spewing out tear gas. In seconds, we were enveloped by a choking, eye-stinging cloud and we all started coughing and rubbing at our eyes. I heard someone shout as they were hit by some sort of projectile, followed by more shouts as stones and other missiles rained down on us.

"Get back!" somebody shouted. We retreated, stumbling our way through the gas, and were met by a wall of baton wielding filth with riot shields. That would be right. They waited until we were all incapacitated before giving us a good beating. And they beat the shit out of us that day, telling us never to return and packing us on a train home before the match had even started.

It was something of a downbeat end to the trip. When we got back home we had to get our frustration out by swarming a few of the city pubs, tearing it up a bit on our home turf and giving a few of the local lads a decent pasting. So not all bad.

It wasn't a particularly memorable day, not compared to some of our better outings, but one thing I did remember was that big ginger bastard, hoping that one day I'd get a chance to fuck him up.

I never did see him again.

Until now.

I awoke, my head pounding. I'd been laid out on a thin white mattress and stripped naked. As I groaned and rolled over, I saw another five guys laid out in a similar fashion. I sat up and looked around.

We were in a different room than before. Time had obviously passed and I had no idea how long we'd been unconscious. My feet had been bandaged and it looked like we'd all been cleaned up a bit. We must have been out for hours. The room had plaster walls and looked different from the warehouse and I guessed that we'd been transported to a different location. My throat felt dry and sore and my eyes stung but I otherwise didn't feel too bad.

At the end of the bed I saw a packet and opened it to find another pair of overalls. They were coloured in red and white stripes. My colours. I reached over and nudged Dobb in the leg. He stirred and looked at me with slitty eyes.

"What.... where the fuck are we?"

"I don't know. Get dressed and let's see if we can find a way out."

He groaned and slowly stood up, giving me a most unwelcome close up of his big hairy balls and cock. He pumped out a fart.

"For fuck sake!" I said, standing up and moving away a few yards to get dressed.

The other guys started to wake up. They looked around in confusion and rubbed at their eyes.

"What's going on?" asked one, looking at me as though I were somehow responsible.

I shrugged and started examining the walls of the room. There were two doors, both locked. A tv screen was mounted above one of them. I gave one of the doors a good kick and it didn't budge so I took a few steps back and tried again. Still nothing. We were trapped.

The other guys dressed themselves and I noticed they had different colours. One wore overalls with black and white stripes, another claret and blue. I walked over to him.

"Inner City Firm or Villa Youth?" I asked.

"Villa..." he said in a Birmingham accent, eyeing me with suspicion. "How do you know?"

"Your colours," I said. "All of us, we're dressed in our team colours."

"What does it mean?" he asked.

"It means that we weren't chosen at random."

As if on cue, the tv screen flickered into life. The Japanese woman was back.

"Contestants, listen!" she cried, still grinning like a maniac. "You best of best in British! In few moment, you meet best of rest of world. Fight to the death!" She erupted into a fit of giggles. She was replaced by an image of a rack of weapons. "Choose wisely!" she said. "Last man left win prize!"

The screen went dark but music continued to play. Happy, demented music completely at odds with the way we were all feeling. There was a clicking sound and one of the doors slowly opened. Dobb went through first and we all followed. Inside a new room the walls were lined with weapons. Axes, staffs, knives, swords, lances, you name it. There was another tv screen and high up in one corner a camera was watching us.

The Villa Youth guy started to cry.

"I want to go home," he said, his voice choked with emotion. "I can't do this."

"Pull yourself together, mate," said one of the others. "We're representing England now."

I looked at him with a mixture of horror and admiration. He'd simply accepted the situation for what it was. He walked over to the wall and took down an axe. When he looked back at the rest of us he was smiling. He looked insane.

Dobb reached up and took down a sword. He held it up in front of himself and then moved around a little with it to test how it felt. Satisfied, he lunged forward and stuck it straight through the guy with the axe. As the Villa Youth man screamed and covered his face, Dobb hacked up the other two guys as they panicked and reached for weapons. With three bodies on the floor he took a swing and cut deep into the neck of the Villa man, killing him instantly. When he looked up at me there was a glint in his eye.

I'd known Dobb for nearly twenty years but, at that moment, I had no idea whether or not I was going to be next. When he put the tip of the sword down onto the ground I finally exhaled with relief.

"All right?" he asked.

"What the fuck did you do that for?"

"You heard the lady – it's going to be every man for himself where we're going."

"But what about us, Dobb?"

"What about us?"

"What if there comes a time when it's just you and me left?"

"We'll worry about that if it happens. For now, it's going to be us against everyone else. We can work as a team."

"Don't you think these guys could have helped us?"

"I didn't know them. I didn't trust them. Any one of them could have fucked us over at any time. I just happened to get in early, that's all."

"Jesus, mate."

"You know I'm right."

At that moment, I didn't know anything any more. This was the single most insane, terrifying and ridiculous experience of my entire life and would undoubtedly, if I survived, define what I had left.

I'd spent most of my life around violence, either taking it or dishing it out. I thought I was used to it by now, thought I'd seen everything. In the past I'd been bottled, stabbed and even shot at. I'd been left for dead in a shop doorway in Hamburg and thrown over a wall in Tenerife. I'd done some terrible things to other people, hospitalising them, maiming them. But this was another level completely. This was actually killing people. I didn't know if I could handle this.

"You'd better tool up," he said, interrupting my thoughts.

"I'm not doing it, Dobb."

"What do you mean?"

"Like I said." I looked up at the camera and shouted at it. I had no idea if anyone was listening or if they gave a shit about what I said. "Fuck you! Who are you people? Tell me what's going on here or you can all go fuck yourselves! I want to speak to somebody in charge. You can't do this to us! Do you hear me? Is anybody listening?"

We stood there in silence. Dobb was looking at me with a mixture of pity and disgust. I could tell he wanted to speak but he kept his mouth shut. Just as it seemed as though nothing was happening, the door behind us opened and two guys in body armour and helmets stepped into the room. One carried a baseball bat with nails in the end and was adjusting the strap on his helmet as though getting to us had been a rush job. The other guy had a taser in one hand and a long dagger in the other.

The screen flickered into life and a man in a black suit stared into the room.

"Contestants," he said, his voice calm. "You need to continue. If you don't comply within thirty seconds it will be game over for you."

I looked at Dobb. He smiled at me and I knew exactly what he was thinking. He was ready to tear these fuckers apart. I turned to the rack of weapons and took down a set of throwing axes. When I turned back I nodded and Dobb and, without a word passing between us, we attacked the new arrivals.

They weren't ready for us. Unless you're a hooligan yourself, and you've experienced a tear up that can spark off in an instant, there's no way to prepare for the sudden violence that people like Dobb and I are capable of. I don't know where they'd recruited these guys from, maybe they were ex-police or ex-military, but handling yourself in an arrest situation, or even a warzone, wasn't preparation enough for an instantaneous flare up of intense violence in close quarters by ferocious animals like us. And we *were* animals, dirty bastard honey badgers with attitudes from Hell. Violence is like a switch for us, it can be turned on and off quicker than a lightbulb. We can be smiling at you one second and have a blade at your eyeball the next, ready to carve you up before you even get the chance to scream.

The ability for invoking total carnage at the drop of a hat isn't a skill you can put on your CV, but it's a skill all the same. I've seen people run from Dobb just because of the way he looks at them. A quick change of expression is enough. There's something in his eyes that can bore deep into the soul of another person and terrify them beyond measure. I know what it's like to give that look to someone and I know what it's like to receive it. The intensity, the sheer heat and aggression coming off it, it's like looking into a furnace.

I threw one of the axes and it lodged itself in the armour of the guy on the left. It wasn't enough to hurt him but it was enough to shock him for the time I needed to cross the room and hit him with the flat end of an axe head in the side of the knee. His leg collapsed, no doubt with ligament damage, and I kneed him in the ribs and followed him down to the floor. As Dobb put his sword through the other guys neck, I hacked away and broke apart my guy's helmet and started getting through to his face. He was screaming but that didn't last long.

When we were finished, Dobb and I stood up and walked back to the centre of the room.

"Your men are dead," I shouted at the face on the television set.

"So I can see," he said. I thought he'd be angry now but his voice was still calm. If anything, the corners of his mouth had turned up in a tight smile. No doubt the footage of what we'd just done would be used at some point and it was all good for him. "Why don't you tell me what you want," he said.

"I want to get out of this place," I told him.

"You can. Just finish the game."

"And if I don't want to?"

"Then i'll just keep sending more of my men into that room until they manage to kill you."

Dobb looked up at the camera and gave him the finger.

"Who the fuck *are* you?" I asked. "And where are we?"

"I'm Dan Whistler, Head of Operations," he said. "And it doesn't matter where you are."

"Why don't you just tell me anyway?"

"You're in the Ukraine. Does that knowledge make you any happier?"

"No, it doesn't."

"I didn't think it would. Can we get a move on? We're on a tight schedule."

"What is all this?" I asked him. "What are you doing to us?"

"You know what this is. It's a game show."

"So I keep hearing. This isn't like any game show I've ever seen."

"That's because it isn't *any* game show – this is something special and it's taken two years to plan. We're networked up globally and about twelve million people are about to tune in and watch you on the dark web."

"This is a joke, right? Some sort of 'gotcha' type shit?"

"It isn't a joke, Mr Penn."

"How the fuck do you even know my name?"

"We know everything about you. That's why you're here. Are we done?"

"No, we're not. This is illegal. People are dying!"

"Of course they're dying. Nobody would be watching if we gave you pillows to fight with."

"You can't hope to get away with this... Murdering people on live television."

"I'm not murdering anybody. You are. You both seem rather good at it, especially your friend there. We'll sell a few t-shirts with his face on, I'll bet."

I could tell I wasn't getting through to this man. I certainly wasn't going to talk him out of going through with this.

"Just tell me why we're here," I said. "Why us?"

"Because you and your friends are the worst kind of scum society has to offer and normal people have been sick of your antics for decades. All across the world, you gather in gangs and cause havoc, costing millions of pounds to deal with and clear up after you. Governments have tried to shut you down but nothing has worked. This is our solution."

"What, killing us?"

"No. Letting you kill yourselves. You people seem to want to get together and cave each others heads in and your confrontations have been getting increasingly violent. The only logical solution was to get you off the streets and to give you an environment and the weapons to do it properly. And, of course, to film it and put it on a pay-per-view broadcast. Everyone's happy, don't you see? The public aren't bothered by your violence, businesses aren't losing money shutting down while you terrorise the cities, you all get the chance to fight each other to your hearts' content and an audience bored of cinematic violence gets to see some of the real stuff. It's a win-win for everyone involved."

"Except for us," I said. "We're dying here."

"Everyone's got to die sometime," he said.

"The authorities will shut you down if word gets out. Twelve million people won't keep quiet about this. Footage of what you're doing to us will leak."

"Who do you think sanctioned all of this to begin with?" he asked, genuinely surprised that I hadn't realised.

"My own fucking government are involved?" I asked, incredulous.

"Of course. They detest you, Mr Penn. Now, are we done?"

I supposed we were. There wasn't a great deal I could do about any of this except go through with it.

"Just one last thing," I said. "The prize – what is it?"

"Your life," he said before the screen went black for the last time.

I stood there, shoulders slumped, thinking over his words. It was a lot to take in. This said, I could see his point of view. If I wasn't up to my neck in that shit I'd have been first in the queue to watch it.

"Ok, then," I said to Dobb.

"What are you going to choose?" he asked. "Those axes seemed to suit you."

I ran my eyes over the available options and saw something that leapt out at me. I had no idea why but it just felt right. I reached up and pulled a mace down from the rack. A spiked metal ball, attached to a chain and a heavy wooden handle, thumped into the floor.

"Good choice," said Dobb, nodding.

The door opposite clicked open and we walked down a long, brightly lit corridor. The sound of cheering, a chorus of thousands of voices, grew louder as we approached an opening and stepped onto a ramp leading down to a large arena. I took a few seconds to look around and take it all in. There must have been twenty thousand people in the audience. Down in the arena, dozens of other competitors were milling about in small groups.

"Are you ready to fuck some cunts up?" asked Dobb, smiling.

"All day long," I said.

Together, we walked down the ramp knowing that, at best, only one of us would be walking back up it when this was finally all over.

## THE SEAGULL

Brighton Close might once have been a decent place to live. It might once have been quiet, and possibly even clean.

A narrow back street buried in the guts of the city, its single row of terraced houses provided rented accommodation for the university's seemingly most delinquent students and a handful of older residents that couldn't afford to move elsewhere. During term time, every night, young people would shout and scream and laugh, arguing about academic subjects in high-pitched, drunken voices before leaning over the walls and vomiting into the gardens. Sometimes they even rutted on the gravel, or in the bushes.

Early every morning, when the student dregs had finally found their way back to their stinking pits, the few available parking spaces were stolen by workers desperate to avoid the charges levied by the council in their designated city car parks. Despite numerous letters of complaint, the council had refused to put yellow lines on the road. Although a dead end, a pedestrian channel cut to the business district and footfall was heavy during the rush hours. People in suits passed through, people who would never choose to live in the close but were more than happy to use it each morning and evening as a short cut to their offices. They talked loudly on their mobile phones and dropped cigarette butts in the gutter.

And then there were the seagulls. As dawn broke, they would stir and soar into the sky, crying out to each other, a raucous din that broke into sleep and dragged the residents into a disturbed wakefulness. Every morning, Dougie Whipp was woken up by the racket and it had been this way for years.

He'd curse, blinking away the sleep and staring at his bedroom window. Supposed to keep the sound of anything out, that's what Ted fucking Moult had said on the adverts. No wonder he topped himself, probably driven mad by the noise coming through his own windows. What a racket!

It went on right through the day, the cawing and shrieking. Fighting over scraps of food, spreading their enormous wings and threatening each other. They were worse than the bloody students and that was saying something. Everyone in the street had woken up to the contents of their bins spread all over the pavement on a regular basis. The gulls had even learned how to lift the bin lids. They'd fling out bits of rubbish, splitting open bags and gobbling down whatever morsels they could find. Filthy, disgusting creatures.

They sat on walls and the tops of lamp-posts, staring with their evil yellow eyes. They weren't scared of people. They weren't scared of anything. Numerous times Dougie had seen a gull swoop down and steal a sandwich from somebody's hand. Once he'd seen a gull snatch an ice cream from a toddler. The child burst into tears, bawling to his mother at the unfairness of it as though she could somehow make amends. That little episode had kept Dougie chortling for days but, on the whole, the gull business was far from funny.

Once, he'd even seen one take on a rat. A big rat too, one that Dougie had already tried to kill and had lost his nerve when the rat turned on him and hissed, baring a set of gleaming yellow teeth. He'd closed the front door and surrendered the front garden to the beast, letting it hold domain over the cracked concrete and riot of unkempt bushes. But the gull had no such qualms. Over a morsel of sausage roll, the gull and the rat had faced off against each other, hissing and screeching and causing such noise that it had disturbed one of Dougie's afternoon tv shows and had drawn him to the front window in alarm.

He watched as they circled each other, as the gull spread its wings and the rat stood on his haunches hissing and spitting, the air between them fizzing with tension. Why didn't Attenborough ever show this? Fucking marvellous entertainment, thought Dougie. The rat suddenly launched itself at the gull, sausage roll now forgotten, and the gull screeched and pecked at the rodent, puncturing its side with a dagger-like beak. The rat bit down on the gull's neck and dug its claws in, wrapping its body around that of its foe.

And then, as Dougie watched in amazement, the gull lumbered out of the garden onto the street outside, took a few lolloping steps and then, with a few flaps of its great wings, left the ground and took off towards the sky, taking the rat with it. He could imagine the rat's terror as the ground fell away. He watched, entranced, as the weight of the rat threatened to pull the gull back down to earth and the gull flapped its wings to stay airborne. These two creatures, locked in a deadly embrace – the following seconds would spell certain death for one of them, and Dougie knew which one.

As he expected, the rat soon came hurtling down from the sky, hitting the road right outside Dougie's house. There was no great explosion of gore, no rat brains slopping out onto the tarmac, but it was enough of a fall to kill it instantly and the rat didn't move again. Not until the magpies came and ripped it to pieces, rat-at-atting to each other in their horrid little voices and tearing through rat fur to get at the glistening stuff beneath. The gull watched from the top of a nearby lamp-post, its face expressionless. When it had seen enough, it glided down to Dougie's garden and ate the bit of sausage roll that had caused all the carnage in the first place.

Before ambling off, it looked up at Dougie.

That's right. Don't fuck with me or that's what you get.

It made Dougie shudder inwardly. Bloody seagulls. Evil they were, evil. They were noisy, they were messy and they shat everywhere. Pavements, windows, rooftops, car windscreens, people – everything was a target. Filthy white snow, falling from the sky, landing with a splat! Hardening in the sun, staining in the rain, the whole street looking like the aftermath of a dirty paintball party. He could barely remember the time when everything in his world wasn't covered in shit, couldn't recall the days before the gulls moved in and took over.

There used to be starlings and sparrows. Robins, blue tits, wrens and wagtails. Beautiful little things that brought a smile to the face of most people, if not Dougie. They weren't friendly, no bird was, but they were very pleasant to have around, flashes of colour and their little musical trills filling the air. Even if Dougie didn't feel it, he could sense the joy that these little creatures had just by being alive. All gone now. First the pigeons came, thousands of them, stupid and grey and boring but even they were bearable compared to the gulls. Monsters they were, invading and driving everything else out. And what were they doing here anyway? The nearest beach was eighty bloody miles away. This shouldn't be their environment, the inner city, there weren't any fish for them here. They'd even scared the foxes away, and even though Dougie had hated the foxes at least they were interesting to look at and they tried to stay in the shadows, out of view.

No such attempts at stealth for the gulls. They were in your face all the time. Blatant nuisances, obnoxious bastards who seemed to think that humans were the invaders in their world. Dougie hated them. Hated them with a passion, couldn't even spend a day without something they did upsetting him, leaving him simmering in his armchair wishing they were all dead.

The chick had fallen off the roof somehow. Perhaps a strong gust of wind had caught it by surprise and sent it tumbling, or perhaps it was just so young that it simply didn't realise the edge of the roof gave way to a drop and it bumbled around up there until one foot stepped out over the edge and it was too late to turn back. Whatever had happened, the chick had ended up in Dougie's front garden, unharmed but bewildered.

Although a gull chick had wings, they were useless, nowhere near big enough to fly but just about big enough to flap madly and stop a sudden descent turning into a deadly fall. It waddled around, unsure of what had happened, examining its new surroundings. Somebody walked past, on their way deeper into the city, and the chick scrabbled under a bush and hid. It would be a long time before it had the confidence – and the weapons – to carve a place in the world where predators were something to be merely wary of. The sudden appearance of a thing other than its parents was a terrifying event and it stayed under the bush for the better part of an hour, mute and afraid, eyes wide and staring at the empty gateway.

High above, on Dougie's roof, the mother gull called out for her baby, again and again. She looked around the rooftop in disbelief, wondering where the chick had gone. She flew to a nearby lamp-post and scanned the street, calling out for her child and listening for a response that didn't come.

Later that evening, once the last of the city workers had passed on through, and after the students had passed the other way into the city, the close grew quiet and the chick ventured out from under the bush. It was hungry and thirsty. It waddled around, forlornly pecking at stray leaves in the hope of finding food. When nothing was forthcoming, it let out a cry.

Above, on Dougie's roof, the mother gull stirred and flew to a nearby telegraph pole to get a better view of the street. It saw its child and squawked. Mother and child communicated to each other for a few moments and a curtain moved as Dougie shifted it aside to look out of his window.

He saw the chick and looked up to see its mother on the telegraph pole. The sight of the birds, and the sounds they were making, made him angry. He banged the window and the chick scattered out of his garden and onto the pavement, looking around in terror.

The adult gull looked at Dougie in the window with an accusatory stare and flew down to be nearer the chick, out of sight behind the wall. Dougie watched for a few moments, his lips moving in a whispered curse, and then he let the curtain fall back into place and disappeared back into his lounge.

He forgot all about the seagulls until the early hours of the morning when a commotion woke him up and brought him to the upstairs window.

It was like a damned warzone out there. Squawking and screeching, something clattering into the empty wheelie bins and almost knocking them over. Under the yellow light of the old lamp-post, Dougie saw a flash of red fur and then an adult seagull came hurtling out of his garden into the street, screeching and stretching its wings out to make itself bigger. From somewhere unseen came the cries of the baby gull.

He watched as a fox continued with its attempts to get at the chick, which was defended by its desperate mother. Time and time again the fox tried to rush into the garden and was beaten off by the adult gull. Eventually, with a shriek of anger, the fox turned and fled. The gull waddled back into the garden and after a few moments the cries of the baby quietened down so that Dougie could no longer hear them.

He didn't like being disturbed like that. How long was this sort of thing going to go on for? Until the bloody thing had matured enough to fly? He didn't know anything about birds – that could be weeks away, maybe even months. Is that what he had to look forward to, disturbed nights at creatures fought outside his house, screeching and screaming as they tried to tear each others throats out? Maybe he should put some rat poison down and kill them all. With these dark thought swirling around his head, it took him a long time to get back to sleep.

The next morning Dougie was up and out early. First thing every weekend he would walk into town and get a bit of grocery shopping and whatever bits and bobs he needed from various shops. There were a lot less people around this early on a Saturday morning and that was just the way he liked it. He was old enough to remember a time when the city seemed a lot less crowded in general, before the workshy bastards of the world bred like they were out of control and before all the bloody foreigners moved in. After ten in the morning, everyone else would crawl from their pits and head into town and you wouldn't be able to move for all the people milling about like zombies. Dougie hated it, and hated them too. Far better to get in and out before they all turned up.

When he stepped out of his house and closed the front door, he looked down to his left and saw a bundle of grey feathers in a pile beneath one of the bushes. As he bent down for a closer look, the bundle moved and the baby gull stirred and looked up at him in alarm. Little shiny black eyes watched him without blinking as it tried to back further under the bush, out of sight. During its second winter, if it survived that long, the eyes would change colour to the evil yellow that Dougie found so disturbing.

A terrible thought flickered across his mind: stamp on the bastard. Put an end to its miserable little life and have done with it. No more racket, no more being woken up at some ridiculous hour of the morning. A few good stamps would squash the tiny fucker into oblivion.

Something made him glance up. There, sitting on top of a wall, staring at him with a look that made him think it could read his mind, was the mother gull. The sudden realisation that it had been watching him made him shiver. There was intelligence there, he could feel it - it knew enough about Dougie and his world to know that he hated them, hated their offspring. The thought of it made Dougie afraid on some deep, primal level.

"Get out of it," he snarled.

The gull stared back, expressionless. Dougie looked around for something to throw. It was then he noticed the little plastic water bowl. What was that doing here? Obviously some do-gooder knew about the chick in his garden and was doing what they could to help the thing survive. It hadn't rained for a few days and there were no puddles to drink from, so some person had filled up a little dish and had placed it in his garden.

"Dirty interfering bleeder…." he muttered, picking up the dish and hurling it at the gull on the wall. It jumped off and took flight, circling the row of houses and descending back down to sit at the top of the lamp-post. There it sat, watching him.

Angry, Dougie walked out of his garden and made his way towards the shops. He could deal with the chick later, when its mother wasn't around.

When he returned an hour or so later, the mother gull was on his roof, looking down onto the close below. Dougie could see it watching him as he approached his own house. He entered the garden, door key already in his hand, and saw the chick hiding under a bush, also watching him.

"Little shit," he muttered, opening the door and stepping inside.

He unpacked his groceries in the kitchen. A bit of fruit, some biscuits, a new replacement bandage from the pound shop for his elbow, which was never the same since a fall a couple of years ago. Some haemorrhoid suppositories. A packet of cough sweets. Aspirin.

The older he got, the more he noticed that his grocery trips were turning into missions to resupply various medicines. He was slowly disintegrating and falling apart. He was dying. Not long now, he often thought, knowing that each birthday might well be his last. At his age, you never knew if you'd make it through another day, let alone another year. As a young man he was never big, never anything special to look at, but he had always been lean and wiry and as tough as an old boot. Now he really was an old boot, and the strongest thing about him was the intense hatred for all sorts of things the modern world brought, a hate that kept him going. His body was frail, weakening all the time, filling up with aches and pains, signs that time had almost caught up with him and it was simply a matter of waiting until the day came when the world no longer wanted him and he'd just be some bit of rubbish to bury or burn. He hadn't given serious thought to what would happen to him after his death. He had a bit of money in the bank, not much, but enough for some government official to arrange for some sort of disposal and go for a piss-up with the change.

And death had been on his mind a lot lately, as though he somehow knew his demise was imminent. He supposed all old people had the same depressing ideas, the same confrontational thoughts about mortality. He welcomed it, he realised, welcomed the signs that it would soon be time to go. Rather that than end up in a nursing home somewhere, no doubt abused by incompetent staff with his faculties dwindling away until he was nothing more than a dribbling vegetable. People weren't meant to stretch out their twilight years if it meant pissing yourself in comfortable armchairs that were already piss-stained from the people that died in them before you. He knew that old age was very cruel for a lot of people – deafness, blindness, arthritis, pneumonia and dementia. Some unlucky bastards ended up with all those things and a lot more besides. That wasn't for him. A few good ales and a heart attack in his sleep, that's how Dougie wanted to go. The less he knew about his own death the better.

He finished unpacking, made himself a cup of tea and sat in his lounge watching television. This was how he spent most days. He didn't need to go out of the house that often, unless it was to go to the pub, and he'd pretty much seen everything the world had to show him. Anything he hadn't seen by now wasn't worth seeing. He hadn't taken a holiday in over ten years. What was the point? Where was he going to go that he hadn't been before? He'd always hated going abroad, even during his army years – everywhere else was always too bloody hot and foreign food made him ill. He'd been to more countries than most people and he hadn't liked any of them. As for his own country, he'd been all over that too, slept in caravans from Inverness to Whitby, Porthmadog to Penzance, sometimes taking a woman (never the same one) and more often than not finding himself bored and missing his home comforts.

The fact was he loved being at home. He loved his little house and nearly everything outside his front door made him angry and hateful. Especially now, when he was far too old to get any sort of enjoyment out of a new experience, even if something new miraculously caught his interest. He knew what he liked and he liked what he knew. Routine and order made up his days, and even though he did the same things over and over he didn't mind.

So he watched Colombo and Bargain Hunters, Ice Road Truckers and Jeremy Kyle. He watched Countdown and The Chase. And he never missed the news. God, how Dougie loved the news. Every single day, an endless supply of madness and carnage, killing and murder, explosions and racism, genocide and religious intolerance. It was everything he really hated about the world, everything he really hated about his fellow man, all wrapped up in an hour of reports and footage of countries at war, religions causing chaos, politicians telling lies and people fucking each other over. Every day was like filling up the petrol tank, enough material to fuel the fire and keep the hate burning away inside him.

Just before seven, he put on his coat and his cap and left the house. A tiny bundle of feathers burst into life and scrabbled under a bush. It was still there, in his garden. Nothing had killed it yet.

He thought about the gull chick on the walk to the pub, how it would grow into one of the menacing army of thugs that terrorised his part of the city. It might look like a children's toy right now, and there would always be an endless supply of idiot children that wanted to pick it up and cuddle it, but they'd have a right old shock when it shat on them and pecked their eyes out. They wouldn't want to be anywhere near it when it grew talons and the beak was full size. It'd rip their little faces right off.

It wanted killing before it matured.

Those were his thoughts as he stepped into the cool interior of the pub and ordered a pint of ale at the bar. He looked around at the other customers, all of whom he knew. They weren't his friends – he didn't have any friends – but they were companionable enough, in short doses.

The pub was out of the way for most people, out on the edge of town by the ring road. The buildings here were tightly packed, built long before the need to park a car was even a consideration. As a consequence you had to walk and most people didn't bother. The customers were mostly like Dougie, regulars who had been coming for years. Occasionally a group of young people would wander in, order a round of drinks before necking them quickly and wandering back out, never to return. There was a certain stuffiness to the place – old men talking in quiet voices, no music, decrepit furniture and a landlord who served lager drinkers with obvious disgust. They were all snobbish about their real ale and discussions about which micro-breweries were the best would last deep into the evening.

Dougie took a seat at a table on his own, nodding to a few similar men at their own tables. Twenty minutes passed before one of the others put down his newspaper, folding it neatly and laying his half-moon spectacles on top, and looked over at Dougie.

"Alright, then?" he asked.

"Not too bad, Alfie,"

"Watching the football later?"

"No interest in it."

Alfie had been going to the pub even longer than Dougie. He was a widower with a gammy leg who lived up by the train station in one of the few remaining pre-fab houses left in the city. He used to be a welder, or a panel beater, or something like that. Dougie used to know, a long time ago. For what it was worth, Alfie could have been an astronaut, or a big game hunter, or a world champion golfer - it wouldn't have mattered anyway. Whatever he was – whatever they all had been – nobody cared, not even themselves and certainly not the rest of the world. Once you got past a certain age society labelled you as 'old' and lost all interest. War hero, master criminal, business guru, adrenaline junkie, ordinary man of the street – as pensioners, history was redundant. Grey, old, in the way – that was how they were viewed now. Dinosaurs in the twenty-first century, remnants of a dead era.

Alfie nodded and smiled, got up and walked slowly to the bar where he engaged in a conversation with the landlord for a few minutes before returning to the same empty table. He supped from his glass with obvious relish, froth attaching itself to his grey moustache, and looked back at Dougie.

"Heard about Pete Greggs?" he asked.

Dougie sighed inwardly. Too bloody talkative, this lot. Can't a man come for a quiet pint without being bothered by anyone? In an ideal world, Dougie would come to the pub, nod at a few people and then sit by himself for four hours without saying a word. Sometimes, even a fellow drinker saying hello was enough to irritate him and ruin his evening.

Dougie Whipp was not a very nice person, he knew that. He'd never been one for small talk, even as a boy, and he'd grown from a sullen child into a cantankerous old bastard, a miserable old shit who only really laughed when some sort of misfortune befell his fellow man. He'd navigated life on his own terms and he was happy enough with that.

If humans could mind-read they'd have avoided Dougie like the plague. If heads came with a window that meant the inside of Dougie's mind were visible, they'd recoil at the ugly sight of black worms writhing in vomit, of deformed foetuses drowning in merconium. If they only knew what he was really thinking as they exchanged perceived pleasantries with him they would soon stop making any sort of approach and leave the old coot to rot in a corner. But people are essentially good-natured creatures – most of them, anyway – and the other regulars actually seemed to like Dougie and find a certain eccentric charm in his grumpiness. Every customer was difficult, in their own way, lacking the normal social etiquettes and quiet confidence of successful and popular people – the pub acted as a sort of gravity-well for the socially awkward, the ones that never really fitted in.

Dougie was one of them, he had enough sense to know that.

He knew that should some disaster befall him, he wouldn't be one of those old people that are found in their houses six weeks after they died, their absence from the world only registered because of a foul smell seeping under the front door. At the moment, despite being friendless, he knew that someone or other at the pub would at least raise a question if they hadn't seen him for a few days. And although he generally had no time for other people, that small thought did bring a level of comfort to him.

So he kept up the pretence of friendliness, to a degree.

"No, what's up with him? Split up with that Thai bride of his, has he?"

"He'd dead,"

"Dead? Dead how?"

"Hit by a car crossing Gedge Street. Two days ago."

"Bloody hell."

"I know.

"They get the bastard that did it?"
"Young woman, they say. On her mobile phone. Wasn't looking."
Jesus, old Pete was gone. That was the third since Christmas. Year by year his contemporaries were dwindling away. Soon, everyone he knew would be dead, and he be sitting in an empty pub. Then he'd be dead and nobody would remember any of them.
"That's a real shame," said Dougie, shaking his head slowly. Pete Greggs was one of the few people he almost liked. He raised his glass and toasted his memory.
"Funeral's next Friday," said Alfie, sipping his ale and staring off into space.
"I'll be there."
A few years ago he wouldn't have bothered but now it seemed the right thing to do, to make the effort and attend. In a way, the ceremony would be like attending his own, future death, a chance to stand and mourn all the things he'd lost in his own life. It didn't matter who had died, not really. The need to attend a funeral, any funeral, was something he felt deep inside, another tick of the clock that counted down the remaining segments of his own mortality.
Minutes passed in silence and Dougie surprised himself by initiating further conversation.
"Know anything about seagulls?" he asked.
"A little bit. Why do you ask?"
"There's a little one hanging about my garden. Fell out of the nest, I think."
"Oh, aye. What are you going to do with it?"
"No idea. Damn thing is driving me crazy with all the noise."
"Have you phoned the RSPCA? Or should that be the RSPB?"
"I haven't got a phone. Can't bloody afford one, not when the robbing bastards want twenty quid a month before I've even made a call."
"They could have come out, see, taken it away."
"Do they do that?"
"I think so. It's a bird, ain't it? Do you want me to give them a ring now?"
"Can you?"
"Don't see why not. It can't hurt, can it?"
Dougie watched as Alfie dug a small mobile phone out of his pocket and started jabbing at the screen with his gnarly old finger. Eventually, he stopped jabbing and held the phone up to his ear.
"Hello? Yes, I want you to come and pick a bird up for me. Wait a moment."
He held out the phone for Dougie. With a sigh he got up, wandered over and took the phone. Bloody thing. It wasn't right, people walking around with phones in their pockets. He held it up to his ear.

"Hello?"
"You were saying something about a bird?" said the voice on the other end of the line.
"Er, yes. Got one in my garden. Baby gull."
"Do you know where the nest is?"
"On my roof."
"And it fell out you say?"
"That's right."
"Is it injured in any way?"
"No, I don't think so."
"Are any of the parents tending to it, do you know?"
"I think the mother's hanging around, yes."
"Do you know if she's feeding it? Does it have access to fresh water?"
"What's with all the bloody questions? Can you come and pick it up or not?"
The voice paused and Dougie heard a small sigh before it continued.
"I'm afraid there's very little we can do, not unless it's injured or has been completely abandoned by its parents. At the moment it seems to be looked after and we usually leave them if that's the case."
Now it was Dougie's turn to sigh. Bloody RSPCA, or whoever the hell it was he was talking to. Like everyone else, they wanted to do as little as possible, the lazy bastards. He handed the phone back and sat down. He listened as Alfie thanked the voice and hung up.
"So they're not coming out then?" asked Alfie.
"Doesn't look like it."
"So what are you going to do about it?"
Dougie shrugged.
"Haven't got a clue," he said, downing half a pint of ale in a couple of large glugs.

He was a little pissed by the time he left. It was the same every night. He'd be just drunk enough to make the world feel like a slightly better place but not too drunk that he couldn't walk home without falling over. Well, he did fall over a couple of years ago, hurting his elbow quite badly, but that wasn't really the drink's fault, more the council's and their incompetence and inability to fix a broken paving slab that jutted up and caught the tip of his shoe and sent him tumbling. He should have sued the bastards. If he had any regrets in life it was not following that up. Maybe, if it wasn't too late, he could find a payphone give one of these bloody compensation companies a ring. After sitting through thousands of their adverts on daytime television he could remember their telephone numbers off by heart.

The streets were quiet for a Saturday night. A few drunk students milling about, some dole scum. Usually he'd have to keep his eye open for puddles of vomit or rivers of piss running from shop doorways but it seemed fairly clear of obstacles. Maybe it had to do with the talk about football earlier – some match was keeping all the pissheads at home, glugging tins of lager as they stared at the gogglebox from the comfort of their armchairs. He felt safer because the streets were empty. He walked home from the pub most nights and it was rare that he made it home without feeling threatened in some way. Young men, half cut with drink, had no idea how menacing they were to an old gent like Dougie. They were always loud and boisterous, pushing each other and laughing, their physical presence intimidating for a man that knew he could no longer handle himself in a scrape. Those days were long gone. Even twenty years ago he'd have had no reservations about taking two or three on at once – his army training had taught him a few things about hurting people – but not now. Now he was frail and hardly had the strength to fight a cold. He was weak. Vulnerable.

He'd seen countless news reports of pensioners getting duffed-up by youngsters. It was getting more common as the years passed by, or maybe it was just because he was a pensioner himself that he noticed it more. But old people were easy targets and with more people out of work than ever there were more young thugs circling like sharks, looking for an easy way to top up their dole money. Vicious little bastards.

He made it home without incident. He fumbled for his door key and put it into the lock, and as he turned it he heard a soft rustling from under a bush and stooped down for a better look. The nearby lamp-post threw a soft orange glow across his garden and gave him enough light to see a bundle of grey feathers and a pair of glittering black eyes looking back at him from the shadows. The gull chick let out a single, quiet cheep as though questioning Dougie's interest.

Dougie was filled with revulsion. This creature made him feel angry and sick. Why was it still here? Why was it hanging around his garden? It might be quiet now but give it another hour when the foxes started prowling around and it'd be making a hell of a racket and waking him up again. He wished the fucking thing would piss off and take the rest of the gulls with it. He was fed up with its mother hanging around, watching him whenever he left the house to go out.

He looked around. Where was its mother now? He couldn't see it.

He looked back down at the chick. All the times he'd thought about stamping on it came flooding back, putrid oil and dog shit thoughts swilling around the inside of his skull, filling his head until nothing else was in there. The urge was indescribable, and he could feel his veins filling with adrenaline as his body prepared itself for the abominable act of wantonly ending a small, fragile life for no other reason than he hated it.

He lifted his right leg and brought his foot down hard. The chick scattered, narrowly escaping the sole of Dougie's shoe. It flapped and squawked and Dougie grunted with anger, kicking out at the chick in a blind rage. The bush was a riot of leaves and feathers, the street echoed with Dougie's grunts and the baby gull's shrieks of terror. Dougie connected with a hard kick and the bird was silenced, falling out of the bush in a slack bundle of tiny limbs and feathers. He stamped down on it, again and again, the tiny body splitting open and spilling its sticky insides onto the paving slabs. On and on he kept going, an old man gone insane with a lust for killing, only stopping when his body started to fail him, unused to all this exercise.

He stood there, bowed, his hands on his knees, catching his breath. The red mist began to dissipate and he emerged from the fog of violence and looked down at the ruined gull chick, the smear of once-living matter spread out across the slabs, and realised that he'd sunk to an unimaginable low.

Jesus Christ, he thought. What have I done?

He felt sick. Seconds later, his own insides came tumbling out, splattering all over the remains of the dead chick.

He felt it rather than heard it. A disturbance of air right next to his head. When he turned to look, he saw the spread wings of an enraged mother, her claws open and ready to tear his eyes out. He cried out in alarm as the bird slammed into him, pecking and clawing and shrieking like the end of the world had come. He felt scratches on the back of his neck, the painful stab of a beak into the back of his hand. He fell over, rolling in vomit and entrails, crying out and trying to bat the adult gull away with his hands.

The attack was ferocious and the gull seemed determined to kill him. Whenever it saw flesh it lunged forward with its beak and stabbed him. It scratched and clawed at his old suit, trying to get at his face. Dougie managed to stand, no longer drunk, his mind racing. He had to get inside the house. He fumbled for his door key, risking everything as he uncovered his face to search his pockets for the key. Furiously beating wings smacked him around the head and the gull managed to peck at his cheek. Dougie lashed out and sent the beast tumbling to the ground.

He suddenly remembered that his key was already in the door and, before the gull could recover and resume its attack, he turned the key, opened the door and rushed inside, slamming the door behind himself.

He stood there, his back against the door, shell-shocked. The bastard seagull had attacked him! It wasn't supposed to do that – stupid birds didn't attack humans! Did they? He slowly walked into the lounge, turning on the light, leaving a bloody fingerprint on the switch plate. His hand was bleeding from a puncture wound, and he gingerly touched his cheek and felt fresh sticky blood on his face. The fucking thing had done quite a bit of damage.

He stripped off his old suit in the kitchen and left it on the floor by the old twin-tub washing machine. It was covered in sick, blood and baby bird guts and would probably need three washes to come clean again. He sighed, feeling every one of the years he'd lived pressing down like a weight from above. After he had washed his face and examined his wounds in the bathroom mirror he poured himself a glass of rum and sat down. He felt exhausted, as though he'd just run a marathon. It wasn't just the exertion, the stress of being physically attacked – it was guilt as well, the overwhelming feeling that he'd taken things too far.

He had no illusions about himself, he knew he was a horrible bastard and was capable of terrible things. He'd killed people, a long time ago during his army days. He couldn't remember how many, exactly, perhaps a dozen or so but he'd never once had a bad dream about any of them, never once felt any remorse. That was his job, and he'd been good at it. But this was different. This was a defenceless animal. At least those people were trying to kill him when he killed them, there was a fairness about the transaction.

He was surprising himself, feeling this way about a stupid little bird. Hadn't the thing been keeping him awake at night? Wasn't it just a piece of vermin, and wasn't he doing the world a favour by wiping it out? He'd told himself this many times before committing the act, justifying the future killing of the chick in any number of plausible ways, but now that time had passed he wasn't quite as sure of himself.

He swigged down his rum and went to bed. A good sleep would sort him out, he'd be back to his old miserable self in the morning.

But Dougie didn't get much sleep. Well into the early hours, the mother gull grieved for her dead chick with a series of squawks and mournful howls and croaks. Dougie put his head under the pillow in an attempt to block out the noise but it was too loud, too close. From his front garden, the sounds of avian grief seemed to pass through his window as though it wasn't there, right into his bedroom and into his earholes. He tossed and turned, desperate for sleep, the sounds scouring the inside of his skull until he felt like stabbing his ear drums with a bradawl in an attempt to make the noises stop. Finally, with dawn not far off, the sounds died down and he managed to get some sleep.

And then he dreamed. A small grey feathered face with jet black eyes stared at him, growing bigger in his mind until it filled his dream-vision, staring with accusations of murder. Dougie writhed in a pool of sweat, his bed sheets soaking, unable to escape the face of the dead chick, unable to turn away from those black eyes.

He awoke with a cry, sitting bolt upright in his bed, shivering and soaking, freezing and afraid.

He hadn't drawn his curtains. Outside, as the early morning light illuminated the street outside Dougie's house, he could see the lamp post. Sitting on top of it, looking right in through his bedroom window, was the mother gull.

It had been out there as he dreamed.

Watching him.

He slept in a little late, falling into a dreamless sleep for a few more hours. When he finally got out of bed he started the laundry before eating a bowl of cereal in front of the television. Thoughts of the night before kept trying to intrude but he forced them away and tried to concentrate on the tv shows. Jeremy Kyle was doing a programme about young mothers who thought the father of their baby might also have been the father of their boyfriends. Young men in tracksuits flounced onto the stage, acting like they were the stars of the show, giving the audience a smile filled with dirty, crooked teeth before ultimately giving them the finger. Fathers and sons threatened to kill each other and DNA tests revealed the sordid truths about modern life.

Dougie found some light relief in their indignity, marvelling at the stupidity of these people. He used to wonder where they found them but he soon realised that the country was full of them. His own city was overrun with this sort of scum. He hated them all and the hate made him feel good.

In the early afternoon, he ran out of milk. He wasn't due to go out until after seven, for another night at the pub, but couldn't make it that long without at least half a dozen cups of tea. He usually had a carton of UHT in but last time he went shopping he'd decided he couldn't be bothered carrying a litre of milk along with all of the other stuff – it might not sound like much but carrying that extra bit of weight all the way home was draining, and carrier bag handles had a way of tightening into thin bands that cut into his fingers and made his hands sore for days.

It felt fairly warm so he didn't bother grabbing his coat. He opened the front door and stepped outside. He hadn't even reached the street before the seagull came swooping down from a nearby roof and attacked him.

With a series of screeches, it clawed at his head and aimed its beak at his eyes. Dougie screamed, batting it away and turning back for the house. He made it inside with only minor wounds and stood in the hallway breathing heavily. He felt giddy with adrenaline, as though he might faint. He put one hand against the wall and stayed there for a few moments, recovering.

Had that really just happened? He understood the first attack, where he'd stomped a chick to death, but this was a new day. It meant that the mother gull remembered, and not only that – it had waited for him to come back outside. It had remembered the house and had recognised him. It was a premeditated attack.

It wasn't possible. This was a god-damned bird, a flying rat with a brain the size of a pea. They weren't clever enough to harbour motives of revenge, surely? He went into the lounge and looked out of the window. The gull was standing on his garden wall, staring back at him.

Waiting.

He drew the curtains, waited for a few seconds, then peeped out through a crack. The gull settled itself down on the wall, its eyes on Dougie's front door. Jesus Christ, it really was waiting for him. The fucking thing was out there, biding its time.

He retired back to the lounge and sat down in front of the television. He barely even registered what was on, his thoughts completely on the bird outside. So this was a clever one, that much was certain. It wasn't going to let him off easily. He understood that – if the tables were turned, he'd probably be doing exactly the same thing. The question was how long was that bird going to keep this up for? How long before it became bored of waiting, or forgot about him? For the first time in his life, he wished he had the internet so he could look up this kind of thing and see if anybody else had been through it. He didn't even know if seagulls were territorial – did it live nearby or was it always on the move? Did gulls migrate? He had no idea. For all he knew, the gull could have a permanent nest somewhere nearby and could have lived here for years already. Dougie would never have known if he'd ever seen the gull before – they all looked the bloody same.

Terrorised by a seagull! His face cracked a grim smile.

He'd wait the bastard out. Give it a few more hours and the thing would fly off.

The afternoon turned into early evening. Every time he checked, the gull was still out there, seemingly prepared to stay exactly where it was until Dougie ventured back outside. He knew there was no chance of that happening. How could he? The fucking thing would have his eyes out and there was little he'd be able to do to stop it.

The idea of being bullied by a seagull was preposterous. Were he a few years younger, he'd have grabbed it and snapped its neck. But he wasn't quick enough for any of that now. He wasn't strong enough. He knew it and, more importantly, the gull knew it.

He felt defenceless in the face of a vicious predator.

He felt like a baby gull waiting to be kicked to death.

He took a few nips of rum and the longer the gull stayed out there the angrier he became. It was getting closer to seven, the time he usually left the house and walked to the pub. He resented the idea of being stuck inside for the night because he was too frightened to go out. And there was no telling how long this could go on for. Was it possible that the gull would never allow him to leave the house ever again? Was it laying siege, hoping to see him starve to death? Would it only fly away when it could smell death seeping under the front door?

After half a dozen drinks he was in the mood for a fight. Muttering to himself, he grabbed a tin of soup from the kitchen cupboard and opened the front door, ready to throw it at the gull and then retreat inside before it could attack him. He was amazed at the sight that greeted him – the gull was gone. Letting his arm drop to his side, he stepped out and took a good look around. It was true – the gull really had disappeared. He let out a snort of triumph. He'd beaten it. It had realised who was the boss and had fucked off to wherever it came from in the first place.

Even though he was gloating, he wasn't completely stupid – he knew there was still a slim chance that it had merely gotten hungry and had flown of to get a bit of food. Recognising his chance, he stepped back inside, grabbed his keys and coat and left for the pub.

All the way there he kept an eye out for the bird. He scanned the rooftops, looked up at the sky, walking under the continuous vague threat that the gull might come looming into view at any moment. It was a tremendous relief to arrive at the pub unscathed. He ordered a pint and sat down at his favourite table with a sigh. Alfie looked over.

"Brought your own dinner?" he asked, smiling.

"Eh?"

Dougie looked down and saw the tin of soup sticking out of his jacket pocket.

"Just bought it," he lied. "For my supper."

"What happened to you?" asked Alfie, his smile evaporating.

"What do you mean?"

"Your cheek!"

Dougie gingerly touched his cheek and felt a thin scab on his wound.

"It was that bleedin' seagull," he said.

"It did that to you?" said Alfie, his eyes widening. "You should bloody report it!"

"We tried, remember?"

He offered Alfie a rueful smile and looked away, signalling that he didn't want to continue with the conversation. How could he? It would mean admitting what he'd done to the chick. He didn't want anyone else knowing about that, that he had it in him to do what he did.

He looked around the pub lounge. Dave Smart was there, and Bob Tranch. No doubt Skinny Harry would soon join them, as he always did. And Bill Eavis was in, as was Fred and Madge. He felt happy to see them all, for once taking great comfort in their presence. He leaned back and took a large swig of ale.

Madge was looking in fine form tonight. He felt the stirrings of something long forgotten, of urges buried for decades. Twenty years ago he'd asked her to leave Fred and come away with him, to leave all of this behind and take off like a couple of youngsters. He'd gone so far as to enquire about renting a place by the sea and had invested hours of daydreaming into how their new life could be. Holding hands as they walked along the promenade, sitting on a bench to look at the sea as they ate fish and chips. It was all a pipe dream, of course. One night, when they were all in their mid-thirties, Fred had taken ill with a stomach ache and had gone home early, and when Madge had come into the pub to meet up with him – she'd been out with some of her work colleagues and had been a little drunk by this time – she'd found out about Fred and Dougie had offered to walk her home.

It turned out that Madge had a habit of unloading her troubles when she was drunk and for a good part of the walk home she had unburdened herself onto Dougie. Fred had been playing away, she thought (and she'd been right, as Dougie already knew that Fred had been seen out with one of the barmaids from the Crow and Feathers). Not only that, he was mean and tight-fisted and hadn't taken her on a good holiday in years. Dougie had listened, nodding and murmuring in all the right places, and Madge had warmed to him and as they found themselves walking past the Willows recreation grounds she had reached out to give him a hug, a grateful hug for listening to her blather on about this and that and then, because drink was in the air and because there had always been a small amount of chemistry between them – but mostly, he thought in retrospect, because she wanted to get her own back on her unfaithful husband – she had kissed him. They had ended up like a pair of teenagers, rutting on the grass in the darkness.

It had only ever happened that once. Whenever he saw her after that night, she acted as though nothing had happened. And when, after a few more years of hoping that she might leave Fred of her own accord, of waiting for his meaningful glances to be reciprocated without success, Dougie had plucked up the courage and had asked her outright – come away with me.

She'd turned him down. In fact she'd laughed in his face, something it had taken years to forgive her for. But now, with age, he understood. They weren't right for each other, never could be. Walking hand in hand along the fucking promenade? Sitting on a bench watching the sea? What a hoot! Who had he been kidding? He'd have ended up being more tight-fisted than Fred had even been, and would have no doubt continued to play the field whenever he got the chance. She must have known it, and that's why she'd burst out laughing.

He sat there, mulling over his past, wondering why all these thoughts should come bubbling up from the swamp of history. The what-might-have-beens. Why now, after all this time?

As the night progressed, thoughts of the seagull gathered like storm clouds inside his head. He looked up at the window, at the darkness outside. It was out there somewhere, waiting for him. He was going to have to walk home, alone, exposed and at risk of attack. He realised that he was terrified.

By closing time he was drunk. The extra shorts at the start of the night had done him in, had upped his alcohol intake considerably and when he stood he felt the room shift around him.

"You alright there, Dougie?" asked Alfie, pausing before leaving the pub and heading off home.

"All good, all good," he slurred, waving him off.

He made his way to the door, mumbling a good night to the stragglers, avoiding any kind of eye contact with Fred and Madge. He wondered if she'd ever told her husband about that night in the park. By her nature it seemed that she probably had, and it said a lot about Fred that he'd never said a word about any of it.

Dougie stumbled outside. The night was warm, uncomfortably so. He started the walk home, through the throngs of young people, shouting and swearing and just getting warmed up for the rest of their night. He walked past people pissing in shop doorways, stepped around a young woman on her knees on the pavement, throwing her guts up as a friend stood there holding her hair out of the way.

Before long he was away from the lights and the bustle. The streets got narrower and the darkness closed in, punctuated by the odd lonely oasis of dull yellow light thrown out by the occasional lamp-post.

Dougie felt an indescribable urge to get home, to close his front door behind himself and shut the rest of the world out and deny its existence until the morning. He stumbled along, trying to co-ordinate his movements, concentrating hard on placing one foot in front of the other as if the conscious effort would somehow shorten the distance or make him walk any faster. Instead, he found that the concentration made him tired and once or twice he stopped to lean on garden walls to reorient himself and catch his breath.

He hadn't been this drunk in a long time. Although he very much enjoyed being slightly drunk, there was a line that he didn't like to cross.

Even after fifty years of steady drinking, that line had remained more or less the same – four pints of strong ale, five if he'd had a big dinner before venturing out. More than that spelled disaster. He'd suffered a number of nights in his late teens and early twenties where the bedroom span around him so fast that it made him vomit until he dry-heaved and the dizziness kept torturing him until he felt like his brain was melting. Each time he promised himself he would never get that drunk again but it took a lot of practice to keep that composure, to get the balance right. And for decades he'd managed to do just that. The way he felt now, the way he knew that the next few hours were going to be a thoroughly miserable experience. It was like being visited by an old enemy, one that could disappear for half a lifetime but would never be a stranger.

A screech from a nearby rooftop made him look up. He immediately felt a knot of terror forming in his guts. He desperately scanned the row of rooftops and the rest of the street around him. He couldn't see anything but he knew the gull was there. His hand reached down and he pulled the tin of soup from his pocket. It felt heavy and solid, a weapon some might call clunky but it could be deadly in the right circumstances.

He started walking. His legs were betraying him and his feet seemed to have a mind of their own. Not far to go, he kept telling himself, just a few more streets. He forced his way along, a lonely figure stumbling through the darkness, willing himself sober. He heard another cry from somewhere above and then claws scrabbling on roof tiles. The sounds followed him, off to one side, and then he heard a loud shriek that stopped him in his tracks.

The sound of beating wings drew closer. Whup-whup-whup, feathery limbs working against the air. Ahead, a white shape emerged from the darkness. The seagull bore down on him, getting bigger with every flap of its wings. He raised his arm and took aim, throwing the tin at the approaching bird with all his might. Like a professional boxer slipping a punch, the gull banked just enough for the missile to sail past harmlessly, landing with a dull thud in the dark.

The gull shrieked and swooped, hacking up undigested food and vomiting it right at him. Dougie felt it slap into his face, hot and fetid, and the gull clawed at the top of his head before disappearing behind him and climbing back up into the sky.

It was a shock to Dougie's system, enough to get him moving again. Using his hands to wipe the muck from his face, he finished the job with his jacket sleeve and lumbered forward, his focus firmly entrenched on reaching his house. He ignored the screeching from behind, tried to shut out the sound of wings beating against the still air. After fifty yards he was hit in the back by something heavy, staggering forward as the gull ploughed into him. He sprawled onto the pavement, putting his arms out to try and break his fall. His hands hit the slabs and he cried out in pain. He had enough time to roll and hope that nothing was broken before he felt the weight of the gull as it landed on him and started a furious attack.

He was too frightened to scream, flailing his heavy limbs as though drowning in treacle. The bird caught his face with its beak and with a monumental effort Dougie swept it aside and dragged himself to his knees. The bird gathered itself and turned on him, hissing and spitting and spreading its wings wide. It hopped forwards and Dougie managed to stand and lash out with his leg to send the creature crashing into a wall.

This was his chance and he took it, hobbling as quickly as he could. He reached the end of the street and turned right, crossing to the other side and seeing the alley that led into Brighton Close just up ahead. Grunting with the effort, his frail old body feeling as hot as a nuclear reactor and sweat beginning to soak his clothes, he picked up the pace when he heard a terrible shriek from behind and entered the alley as the air was scythed in two behind his back. The gull climbed up into the night sky to circle around and resume its attack. It soared above the rooftops, glittering eyes searching for its target. When it saw the man rushing along the darkened alley below, it cried out and began a sharp descent.

Out of breath, fearing a heart attack at any moment, Dougie stumbled onwards, counting down the doorways until he reached his own. He started to feel as though he was going to make it, certain that all this effort was going to pay off and see him safely indoors before the gull could reach him again.

But he was wrong. With only a few houses left to go, the gull came hurtling out of the sky, crashing into Dougie's back to send him sprawling once more. Frustration, fear and rage united in a howl of despair. The bird hissed and pecked at his legs before hopping around to the side and spearing his forearm with its lethal beak. Dougie cried for help but no words came out, only a desperate, drunken wail that had one or two neighbours look out onto the street before firmly closing their curtains and going back to bed.

Too many drunks had used this particular street before, the neighbours were used to shouts and even the odd scream and rarely paid any attention any more. Curtains briefly parted and then closed. Nobody was coming to help.

He fought with every ounce of strength left in his body, hauling himself up and lashing out with his fists and his feet. He was so pumped with panic and adrenaline that he couldn't even see the gull any more, it was just a white blur of feathers moving around him. Sometimes the beak would get through and tear at his exposed flesh and others he would feel the dull thump as one of his limbs connected with the beast to send it crashing away. Bit by bit he forced his way to his front door and he grabbed his keys and put them into the lock, shuffling forward as the door opened. The gull jumped up onto his back, scrabbling for purchase with its claws on his shoulders, and pecked viciously at the back of his head.

For a moment, Dougie thought that the gull would also force its way into the house and he feared that if it made its way inside there would be no escaping it. That would be the end of him. With a defiant shout, he turned and smashed his back against the wall, briefly crushing the gull with enough force to make it drop back down to the ground. A deft kick sent it rolling into the garden and he seized his chance to fully enter the house and slam the door.

The gull squawked in anger. It slowly waddled into the street and shook its wings, a flurry of loose feathers spiralling off in all directions. It clacked its beak and, satisfied that no serious damage had been done, it walked down the street and disappeared into the darkness.

Inside the house, Dougie examined his wounds in the bathroom. He was covered in cuts and gashes, his grey hair red with blood. The gull had really worked him over. He put the plug in and started filling up the bath. Feeling completely sober, he stripped and eased himself into the water. As the bath filled, the water turned pink around him. He turned off the taps and tried to relax. The encounter had taken more out of him than he thought. Within minutes he was asleep. When he awoke, the bath water was stone cold and bright red.

There was no sign of the gull the next day but he could sense its malevolent presence. Wherever it was, Dougie knew it hadn't gone away. It wouldn't, not until it had finished him off. It wouldn't have gone to all this effort simply to walk away whilst it had him on the ropes.

And that's exactly where he was. Fresh wounds were heaped upon slightly older wounds and his hands and face were scratched and punctured with holes. He felt drained, as though the gull had pecked away more from him than just bits of flesh.

He wondered if he should carry a knife with him from now on. A big kitchen knife, one that he could put straight through the gull if it attacked him again. He felt confident enough that he could end things that way, should another encounter come about. But how would he explain it, if anybody saw it? What would all of the regulars at the pub make of him if it emerged that he was arming himself with a deadly weapon – for the sake of a bird! They wouldn't understand – how could they? He'd be a laughing stock. A grown man, terrorised by a fucking seagull. And in the cold light of day, it did sound ridiculous. Even though he'd almost been killed by the beast a small part of him couldn't help but see things the same way everybody else would. All those people that walked around with nothing to fear.

But they hadn't been attacked, had they? They hadn't been helpless on their backs in the darkness getting stabbed by a dagger-like beak, its owner determined to gouge out their eyes, or their throats. Unless it had happened to you, you'd never understand.

He kept checking the street throughout the day. There was no sign of the gull. Maybe the few licks he'd managed to get in had convinced the bastard that Dougie really wasn't worth messing with. He vaguely remembered giving the thing a good kick. That must have hurt it, must have made it think twice about coming back. Even though Dougie was old, and his strength wasn't what it once was, he knew that he wasn't completely hopeless. Maybe that was why it wasn't showing itself. Maybe it had buggered off, this time for good.

Even so, that evening he did arm himself with a knife. It stuck out of his jacket pocket and he kept his hand tucked in there next to the blade, hoping his arm would shield it from view. Surprisingly, now that he was out of the house again, the knife wasn't giving him much confidence. As he walked to the pub, glancing furtively at rooftops and the sky, he tried to run through scenarios in his head, playing out fights where he emerged the victor, knife dripping with gull blood. But each time, in his mind, he ended up on the ground, the knife clattering away on the paving slabs as he used both arms to cover his face.

As he walked, sounds from the environment made him nervous. He jumped as a distant car backfired, flinched as he passed a doorway and someone coughed within the recess. He heard – or imagined he heard – gull claws scrabbling on roof tiles. From above came shrieks and squawks, each one piercing the failing psychological armour he'd been temporarily granted by possession of the knife.

Sweating, he reached the pub and hid the knife in one of the plant-pots by the entrance. He buried the blade up to the hilt and bent the foliage to cover the handle. Inside, he took off his jacket and ordered an ale.

"Jesus," said the barman, looking at Dougie's face. "Are you alright?"

"I'm fine," snapped Dougie, taking his drink and heading to his usual table. He sat there sipping ale, angry at what the gull was doing to him. He hadn't seen it all day and he was still a mess, drenched in fear and sweat, his pulse racing and his nerves practically shattered. He drank greedily, slaking his thirst. He needed the dull fog of drunkenness around him. He wanted to forget about the gull for a short while, and when he left he wanted to be drunk enough to flip out, to ignore the pain and discomfort the following days would bring if he exerted himself in the violent ways of a younger man.

Let the gull come.

Alfie wandered in, ordering a pint of ale at the bar and walking to his usual table. As he was about to sit down, he glanced over at Dougie and winced. Breaking protocol established over decades, he walked over to Dougie's table and sat down.

"Don't tell me a bloody seagull did that to you," he said, incredulous.

"Aye, it did," said Dougie, slowly shaking his head.

"I've seen some nasty ones in my time but this one's got balls."

Dougie and Alfie took a large swig from their ales and placed their glasses back down onto the table at the same time.

"Do you want to borrow my gun?" asked Alfie.

Dougie looked up, surprised.

"You have a gun?"

"Don't get too excited, it's only an air rifle. I use it for the rats. It's powerful enough to take a seagull out, if you know what you're doing. You ever fired a gun?"

Dougie smiled grimly and nodded.

"I know my way around a gun," he said in a quiet voice.

"Services, eh?" said Alfie. "Thought so. You can always tell."

"You too? I thought you were a welder."

"Navy boy, 'til '68. Invalided out after my foot was crushed. I had to learn a new trade, so I learned to weld. And a lot more besides."

They regarded each other for a quiet moment. Dougie realised that had he made the effort in the previous decades, he might have made a friend out of Alfie. Perhaps, if he survived this nightmare, it wouldn't be too late.

"I'd love to borrow it," he said at last.

Alfie nodded. "I'll phone my boy in a bit," he said. "He can bring it with him and give us both a lift home as well."

They spent the rest of the evening seated at the same table, talking and swapping army stories. For the first time in God knows how many years, Dougie found himself laughing, actually laughing at something another human was telling him. Not laughing at Alfie, the way he sometimes laughed at the endless parade of idiots on the television, but with him. A warmth crept into his old bones. It was the first real connection he'd made with another person in a very long time.

Alfie's son turned up just before closing time, joining them for a quick half before walking with them to one of the back streets where he'd parked in an empty residents bay. It was almost as far as Dougie would have walked if he'd gone the other way and headed for home but he said nothing. He was glad of the company, glad of the security it offered.

And Alfie's son, Chris, seemed unconcerned about the gangs of youths they walked past, showed complete indifference to the lone drunks walking around offering hateful stares if you happened to catch their eye. Chris was a big lad, much bigger than his father, and had probably never worried about being mugged, or attacked by a gang out for a bit of fun. But he would, thought Dougie, one day when he too was old.

They reached the car and he listened as Alfie berated his son for risking a fine.

"Who is going to ticket me at this hour?" said the youngster, shrugging and smiling.

The ride home took a few short minutes. Chris asked where he lived and knew immediately where to go. Dougie looked out of the window, up at the night sky. Searching for the gull, wondering if it was out there looking for him. It was probably on a rooftop, scanning the streets, waiting.

Chris parked up at the start of Brighton Close, fifty yards from Dougie's house so he could use the road entrance to turn around easily. He clambered out and opened Dougie's door for him before opening the boot and pulling out a long black case. Dougie gratefully accepted it and leaned into the car to speak to Alfie.

"Thanks again," he said in a quiet voice.

"You just get that fucker before it gets you," said Alfie. "There's plenty of ammo."

Dougie nodded and looked at his house. It seemed so far away. Suddenly, he was frightened again.

"Do you mind waiting?" he asked Chris. "Until I'm inside?"

"I'll walk with you," he said, taking Dougie's arm.

They walked the fifty yards together, Dougie marvelling at the young man's good manners, wondering if perhaps the world was not lost to the yobs and the idiots after all. Chris wasn't the sort that would end up on the Jeremy Kyle show, bleary-eyed and paranoid through smoking too much dope with some young slut and her mother arguing because he'd made them both pregnant.

"This is me," said Dougie, pointing at his front door.

"Nice to meet you," said Chris, holding out his hand for Dougie to shake. He waited as Dougie walked up the path and opened his door. With a brief wave, he stepped inside and closed the door behind himself. He'd had a good night but it felt wonderful to shut the world out again, to be in the sanctuary of his own home.

He went into the lounge and gently placed the case down onto the coffee table. After pouring himself a shot of rum, he sat down and opened it. The gun was in tip-top condition, as he expected it would be. He took it out and quickly learned his way around it. Alfie had attached a small sight and he held the gun up and looked through it. He snapped open the barrel, loaded a pellet and firmly closed it again. He laid the gun on the table and took some pellets from the case, putting them into his trouser pocket.

That fucking gull was going to get it, he thought. Tonight was going to be its last on Earth.

He finished his drink and quickly brushed his teeth before heading to the bedroom, taking the gun with him and placing it onto the end of his bed. He left the room in darkness and opened the window an inch or two before securing the latch and drawing the curtains almost closed. He stood there, looking out onto the street through the gap. There was no sign of the gull but he knew it would come.

After twenty minutes his legs were aching and he sat on the bed. He was suddenly tired and reasoned that a few minutes leaning back against the headboard with his eyes closed wouldn't do any harm.

When he awoke, the room was freezing cold. A noise made him sit bolt upright, his senses bursting into heightened awareness. Something was trying to get into the room from outside. Through the narrow slit in the curtains he saw a flash of white feathers, illuminated by the lamp-post outside.

It was here! Trying to get into the house! He swung his legs onto the floor, moving like a man half his age, and grabbed the gun. He held it out in front of him and approached the window. He saw the gull's head flick into view, its eyes glittering. As it if knew its chance was slipping away, it resumed its attack on the window, furiously trying to broach the gap and force its way inside.

Something about the way it was so determined to reach him made Dougie stop dead in his tracks, paralysed with fear. The freezing ambience of the room felt tropical compared to the ice swilling around his veins. For a few moments, he wondered if he should flee and abandon the room. At any moment it was going to break through. He could hear the latch rattling as the gull kept pushing backwards and forwards at the frame. It would soon work out that if it hooked its beak through the gap it could undo the latch and the window would swing open.

It reminded him of some magazines he'd read years ago, filled with true crime articles about rape and murder. Grown men creeping around in the darkness, breaking into women's homes, usually through the bedroom window, the women lying terrified in their beds unable to move. That was what they said, the few who survived – too frightened to move, to fight back. That was what it felt like for Dougie.

He willed himself into action, mustering every last ounce of grit to lurch his way to the window and jab the end of the gun barrel into the gull in an attempt to make it fall off the ledge. It had grit of its own, the tenacity to keep going, to risk injury when it knew it was so close to solving the puzzle and getting into the house. Dougie jabbed the beast again and again, and it was knocked off the ledge and resumed its position by hovering, the tips of its wings smashing against the panes in a quick succession of loud beats.

Dougie was so panicked that he had forgotten to pull the trigger and it seemed to happen by accident. There was a PFFFT! sound and a muffled bang, a loud squawk from just outside the window and the gull fell away. He heard it crash onto the wheelie bin in his front garden.

He'd shot the beast! Fear turning to excitement, he opened the curtains and opened the window, leaning out to look for the gull. It was down there, screeching and rolling about in a ball of angry, flapping wings. It shook itself down and looked up at him with a cry of pure hatred.

Long buried memories resurfaced in Dougie. All of the training from his youth kicked in and, with his mind calming, he snapped open the gun, took a pellet from his trouser pocket and reloaded it. He leaned out of the window and pointed the gun at the bird. It cried out again but this time there was something different, this time the sound held a note of fear. It seemed to know that Dougie had the upper hand, that the tables had been turned. Flapping its wings, it waddled out of the garden and started a run to throw itself up into the sky. Dougie tracked it with the barrel and just as it lifted off the ground he pulled the trigger.

The pellet slammed into the gull's neck and brought it crashing back down onto the road. Screeches filled the street, bouncing off the walls. The gull rolled over on itself again and again, hissing and spitting, its feathers turning red as blood leaked from its wounds. With a stony face, Dougie turned away to reload the weapon. In seconds he was pointing the gun at the struggling bird again, tracking it before firing off another shot. There was a loud crack as the bullet hit the left wing and snapped the humerus bone in half. Screaming now, the gull dragged itself down the road, desperately trying to get out of sight. It lurched along, dragging its useless wing behind itself, a trail of blood smearing on the tarmac. Just before it made it out of Dougie's line of sight, he caught it in the back with another pellet. A flurry of feathers launched into the air and lazily circled back down around the broken, bleeding body of the gull. Dougie stayed where he was for a full five minutes, watching it. In all that time, it didn't move.

He'd killed it. The nightmare was finally over.

He sighed heavily and closed the window before drawing the curtains.

Outside, from various high vantage points around the street, a dozen sets of eyes blinked in the darkness, witnesses to the slaughter.

He slept well that night. When he awoke, already in a tremendous mood, he walked over to the window and opened the curtains. Glorious sunshine spilled into the room. He could feel its warmth penetrate his old bones.

His eyes were drawn to the spot in the road where the dead gull should have been. It wasn't there. There was a dark stain and a few feathers but the carcass was gone. He felt a slight shiver but dismissed any fear as premature – a fox must have had it in the night. He'd filled the bastard thing full of pellets, there was no way it could have survived. He'd watched it die. It wasn't possible that it had just played possum until he stopped firing and left it alone.

Was it?

Of course it wasn't. This was a bird, a clever one at that, but no bird was that clever. No, it was dead and gone, and right now some fox was hacking up pellets after swallowing a free bounty of raw gull flesh. He could forget all about it, and write the whole episode off as finished with. Business with the gull was well and truly concluded.

It was a pleasant walk to the pub that night. A real weight had been lifted from his mind and the world was a little brighter for it. Everyone he passed seemed to be in good spirits and he couldn't help but feel glad to be a member of the human race for once. Maybe this business with the gull had been necessary for him, a trauma to get through and be reborn with a shifted perspective. Maybe he could start to enjoy life again, whatever small sliver of it was left for him.

He carried the case with him, determined to buy Alfie's drinks all night to say thank you for lending him the tool to save himself. When he arrived at the pub, Alfie was already seated at his usual table and Dougie walked straight over to put the case down. He held out his hand and a bemused Alfie reached out and shook it.

"You get the bastard?"

"I didn't half. I can't thank you enough, Alfie, but I'm going to start by buying you a fresh pint."

"There's no need for that, you silly sod."

"No, I want to. Another ale, is it?"

Alfie smiled and nodded and Dougie walked over to the bar to order the drinks. Upon returning, he sat down at Alfie's table and looked around the room. In all the years he'd been going there, he'd never seen the room from this viewpoint. It was another change of perspective, he reasoned, another small sign that the world might not be the stale old place he thought it was.

"So come on then," said Alfie. "Tell me all about it."

And Dougie did. He told him how he'd fallen asleep and woke up to find the gull trying to get in through the window, and how he'd jabbed at it with the barrel before firing off a shot and then picking it off as it tried to crawl its way up the road. He told of the relief that the gull was finally dead, how he didn't have to live in fear any more. He opened up about how terrified he'd been, something he thought he'd never really admit to another person but it was easy saying all of this to Alfie. Dougie was certain that he understood.

The night passed quickly and Dougie found he was really enjoying himself. It was good to have a friend, someone to talk to and share stories with. He found himself wishing again that he'd made the effort years ago but the important thing was that he had made the effort now. Maybe he wouldn't stop with just Alfie – there was a whole bunch of people whose faces he knew like the back of his hand, all regulars in the pub, all of whom he knew virtually nothing about. Maybe it was time to open up and get to know them a little bit too.

Come closing time, he was pleasantly inebriated. He wished Alfie a good night and started the walk home. He ignored the drunks and noisy students, stepped right in the piss running out of the shop doorways. It was time to stop worrying about all of that. He was too old to live in fear of anything any more.

He left the hubbub of the city centre and entered the quieter back streets. Darkness closed in around him and the temperature dropped, only a little but enough to notice. He turned up his jacket collar and walked with his head down, and realised his thoughts about refusing to live in fear were a little too optimistic. He looked around at the unlit houses. There was no denying the fear that the darkness brought with it – it was primal and instinctive and would never be dismissed completely.

A cry from above made him stop in his tracks. It was joined by another, some way off, and then a third. Gulls, all around him. The fear returned with a vengeance. It was irrational, he knew that, but it didn't stop him shivering with fright nonetheless. He hunched his shoulders and started walking again, faster this time.

To his right, claws scrabbled on the roof tiles of the adjacent houses. In the black sky above, white shapes circled. They were calling to each other. Communicating. He crossed the road and entered the alley leading to his own street, his shoes clacking on the paving slabs in a steady rhythm as he walked. The light from a lamp-post enveloped him and made everything else darker for a few moments. Usually the street lighting made him feel safe but tonight he felt exposed.

He was panicking over nothing but he couldn't stop the rising tide of terror. Up above, a chorus of shrieks rang out, gulls circling in growing numbers.

When he was a stone's throw from his house, the first wave attacked. Diving from the darkness, screeching white beasts swooped down and splattered Dougie with vomit and shit. Claws scratched at the top of his head and wings beat him around the face. He cried out, flapping his arms to try and ward off the gulls as they drew closer and started to peck.

He couldn't understand what was happening. Why were they attacking him? Far from being over, the nightmare had simply changed gears and had increased in intensity. Now it wasn't just one gull that was trying to kill him but a dozen, maybe even more than that.

Something slammed into his back and he momentarily lost his balance. He could see his house and lurched towards it, determined to get inside. He'd have to ask Alfie to lend him that gun again, and enough pellets to cut down half the bloody seagulls in the city. As this thought flitted across his mind, a second gull hit him in the back, followed by third. He lost his balance and was sent sprawling. As he crawled along the road, calling out for help and trying to reach the pool of light cast off by the lamp-post closest to his house, the horde of gulls descended and attacked him in unison.

He didn't stand a chance. They pecked at his face and ripped holes in the flesh of his hands as he tried to protect himself. A beak cut through his defences and buried itself in his eyeball. When he screamed, a gull latched onto his face and grabbed his tongue with its beak, trying to tear it from his skull.

He rolled from his side onto his back and birds landed on his chest, his belly, his groin. The weight of them held him down and more gulls were joining in all the time. Anybody looking from their window would have seen a melee of feathers and beating wings, with no hint of what might lie beneath the tumult.

Dougie was in agony, puncture wounds accumulating all over his body, and was so terrified that he pissed himself and lay writhing in a pool of urine and blood.

A loud shriek cut through the noise and the gulls ceased their attack. They hopped off Dougie and parted for something approaching from the far end of the street. With gulls lined up on either side, Dougie lifted his head and looked with his one good eye.

A gull was dragging itself towards him. Broken winged, leaking blood from numerous pellet wounds, it crawled slowly closer, its eyes glittering. Dougie moaned but couldn't tear his gaze away. It inched towards him, ruined wing dragging on the road behind itself, a trail of feathers and a smear of blood in its wake. As it drew nearer, the other gulls started chattering excitedly, opening up their wings and hissing at Dougie. They hopped about, squawking and spitting at him, barely able to contain themselves from attacking him again.

Even with the closeness of those terrible claws and beaks right next to his head, he couldn't look away from the approaching gull. It had come for its final revenge, this one last confrontation. It reached his feet and dragged itself up onto his legs. Slowly, painfully, it hauled itself along his body and planted one great claw in his groin as it sought purchase and heaved itself up onto his belly. As Dougie lay there, helpless, a moan of terror rising in his throat, the broken gull reached his chest and stood, its ruined wing draped across Dougie's ribs.

It looked into Dougie's one good eye for a long time.

And then, with a single shriek, it lunged forwards, quickly followed in its attack by the rest of the gulls.

## About the author:

I'm a UK based author with books in a number of genres including horror fiction, micro street art, retro gaming, travelogues and illustrated children's books. I have over 200 four-star and five-star reviews for my books on Amazon. For an independent writer, I feel that's a decent achievement.

My travel books are light-hearted and fun, covering such journeys as a three month road trip around North America, a grand tour of Europe in a VW Campervan and a month long cycling trip through France from Cherbourg to Perpignan. They bring the *'get-up-and-go'* attitude to travel and represent the sort of experiences ordinary people have when doing similar things. I have no production company behind me, no personal assistants to organise meetings or events in advance – I just get in a campervan, or get on a pushbike and go, and then tell you what happens.

My fiction is usually quite dark, often with horror elements. My period fiction (such as *'The Whaler'*, or the *'New Orleans Trilogy'* which was set during the days before, during and after the 2005 Hurricane Katrina disaster) usually involve intense bouts of research to bring in authentic background details.

I've also written children's books, working in collaboration with the late artist Simon Schild.

**steveroachwriter@gmail.com**
**facebook.com/writerroach**

**Other Books by Steve Roach**

**Short Story Collections**
The Hunt and Other Stories
Resonance
Tiny Wonders

**Novellas**
Ruiner
People of the Sun
Conquistadors

**Travel**
Cycles, Tents and Two Young Gents
Mountains, Lochs and Lonely Spots
Step It Up!

**Non Fiction**
Retro Arcade Classics
Small People, Big World

**Illustrated Books For Children**
Crackly Bones
The Terrorer

Printed in Great Britain
by Amazon

f9d56e0d-8d5f-4fb6-a5a4-021b7259f596R02